PRAISE FOR DiANN MILLS

A pulse-pounding blend of romance and suspense, *Canyon of Deceit* has a gripping plot and unforgettable characters with a story that keeps you on the edge of your seat until the very last page.

CARRIE STUART PARKS, award-winning author of *Fallout*

Set against the rugged, dangerous beauty of the Guadalupe Mountains, *Canyon of Deceit* is a riveting tale of high stakes, survival, and trust that I couldn't put down. DiAnn Mills has crafted a page-turning novel. This is romantic suspense at its finest!

ELIZABETH GODDARD, award-winning author of *Storm Warning*

Buckle up, readers! *Canyon of Deceit* is a heart-pounding suspense packed with intrigue on every page. Danger, action, and adrenaline-fueled drama make this a must-read for fans who crave edge-of-your-seat adventure.

NATALIE WALTERS, bestselling, award-winning author of the SNAP Agency series

In *Lethal Standoff*, Diann Mills works magic—weaving suspense and intrigue into a heart-pounding hostage thriller. Hostage negotiator Carrington Reed is a hero with heart who refuses to quit even when it means risking her own life for strangers. Don't miss this high-stakes gambit set in south Texas that will keep you flipping pages to the very end.

ANDREWS & WILSON, bestselling authors of *Dark Fall*

Lethal Standoff combines gripping tension with a captivating mystery, skillfully woven by DiAnn's signature storytelling. She navigates the high-stakes world of hostage rescue, proving once again why she's a master of the genre.

JERRY B. JENKINS, author of the Left Behind series and The Chosen novels

Warning: do not start this book if you intend to put it down anytime soon. This is a roller-coaster ride. A bullet-biter. A heart-thumper. This is DiAnn Mills at her best.

EVA MARIE EVERSON, bestselling author and CEO of Word Weavers International, on *Lethal Standoff*

Lethal Standoff has everything I look for in a great novel! Alongside a heartwarming romance, the plot and themes of this page-turner are pulled from current events and offer a hopeful, triumphant message for readers. Highly recommended.

DEBORAH RANEY, author of the Camfield Legacy series

Well-developed characters, vivid imagery, and thorough research guide this storyline every step of the way. Mills . . . delivers another action-packed novel that offers intrigue and an adventurous ride.

LIBRARY JOURNAL on *Concrete Evidence*

Confident plotting keeps the mysteries coming, and red herrings will have readers guessing the culprit through to the satisfying conclusion. . . . Thrilling.

PUBLISHERS WEEKLY on *Concrete Evidence*

CANYON OF DECEIT

CANYON OF DECEIT

DiANN MILLS

Tyndale House Publishers
Carol Stream, Illinois

Visit Tyndale online at tyndale.com.

Visit DiAnn Mills's website at diannmills.com.

Canyon of Deceit

Cover design by Dean Renninger

Interior design by Cathy Miller

Published in association with The Steve Laube Agency, 24 W. Camelback Road A-635, Phoenix, AZ 85013.

For information about special discounts for bulk purchases, please contact Tyndale House Publishers at csresponse@tyndale.com, or call 1-855-277-9400.

Library of Congress Cataloging-in-Publication Data

A catalog record for this book is available from the Library of Congress.

ISBN 978-1-4964-8515-1 (SC)

Printed in the United States of America

31 30 29 28 27 26 25
7 6 5 4 3 2 1

This book is dedicated to every person who finds it difficult to forgive themselves. You can take this spiritual step with God's help and move beyond the past and embrace the future.

PROLOGUE

HILL COUNTRY, TEXAS
TWENTY YEARS EARLIER

THERESE

I smoothed a tattered quilt beneath a live oak about a mile from our home and laid my guitar atop it. "Are you ready for a concert?" I said to Kate.

My little sister sat on the quilt and lifted her pale face stained with blackberry juice. She'd had her fill of berries on our walk here. "I am. What a fun morning. I love spending time with you, and you picked the perfect picnic spot." She touched her chin. "Remember when we went to the mountains in . . . Colorado?"

"Yes. The best vacation Mom and Dad ever took us on."

Kate nodded, her white-blonde curls brushing her shoulders. "We went before I got sick, when I was three." She squeezed her eyes shut. "Five years ago. Anyway, sometimes I close my eyes and hear the water singing."

"I loved the sound of it rippling over the rocks and rushing down the waterfalls. What else was your favorite?"

Kate tilted her head, and the sunlight glowed on her face. "The deer, elk, and the bighorn sheep." She startled. "Remember the eagle, Therese?"

"Oh yes. We'll ask Mom and Dad to take us back when you're feeling better."

"This time I want to learn how to do the special fishing."

"Fly-fishing. Dad will teach us."

Kate sorted through the remains of the picnic snacks. "Sissy, any more blackberries?"

"You ate them all, Katie-Bug. I wish you'd eaten your egg sandwich. How about a little more? I'll peel off the crust."

Kate shook her head. "No, thanks. Would you sing the Willie Nelson song about the road?"

I laughed and scooted next to her on the quilt. I tucked my guitar in the crook of my arm and pulled the pick from my shorts pocket. Every concert began and ended with "On the Road Again."

"Why do you like that song so much?" I said while tuning the strings.

"'Cause I'm on the road to heaven, silly."

I swallowed several times to rid myself of the acid-tasting fear. God would heal her. He had to. The doctors had made a mistake. "You have a beautiful reason. Mom says we are all on the road to heaven. But I'll get there first 'cause I'm older."

"But you're not sick like me." She patted my knee. "It's okay. Angels tell me I'll love being with Jesus."

"You talk to them?" I held my breath. *Please, heal my sister.*

"Oh yes. At night they stand around my bed and keep watch over me."

"Kate, I'm in the same room, and I don't see them."

She giggled and covered her mouth. "You're not looking good enough."

"Next time, wake me up, so I can see them too."

"Okay." She touched my arm. "Sissy, what do you want to be when you grow up?"

I smiled because she knew the answer. "I'd like to sing and play my guitar."

Kate clapped her hands. "You'd be the best country-western singer in the world."

I dreamed of performing at the Grand Ole Opry. I'd write my own songs, but Grandma said I should do what God said, and He hadn't told me. "We'd sing together—The Palmer Sisters."

Kate drew in a breath. "Ouch. Something bit my leg."

I searched Kate's matchstick-thin leg and found a quickly swelling bump on her ankle. "Looks like a fire ant nibbled on you. Let me make sure no more are crawling on the quilt."

An ant hill rose three feet from our picnic site, and we moved several feet away. I washed the bite with water from the thermos and a clean cloth. "I'll put soda on it once we're home. Do you want to leave?"

"No. I'm fine." Kate curled up on the quilt and closed her eyes. "I'm ready."

I sang the song twice, picturing brighter days ahead for my family. My sister would win this fight.

Kate's eyelids hung at half-mast. *The ant bite?* I stuffed the remains of our picnic into my backpack and hoisted my guitar strap over my shoulder.

"I'll carry you," I whispered. "Go ahead and sleep, and I'll tuck you in when we're home." I picked up Kate and nestled her close to me.

"Would you sing your song about me on the way?"

"Of course." The words and tune had come to me one night when Kate sobbed in pain. Love burned inside me, and I'd much rather God take me and heal her.

"Where are you going, my little girl?
Has your innocence laced the stars?
Are you warm in sugar-sprinkled dreams?
Have you seen the angels from afar?

Where have you wandered, my little girl?
Have you tasted nature's honey?
Are you skipping down a rainbow path?
And singing with daisies in harmony?

Where will you journey, my little girl?
When life's troubles are all you see?
Will you rest secure in childlike faith?
And remember the One who set you free?"

The mile of green rolling countryside to our off-the-grid cabin that my great-grandfather had built took me across the pasture where our temperamental bull, three cows, and two spotted goats grazed. I kept one eye on the bull—Kate had named him Kitty. Cautious of his horn-filled fury, I made it to the gate, then latched it behind me. My shoulders ached. But Kate wouldn't have made it on her own.

In the distance, corn tassels waved in the breeze. Our half-acre garden grew vegetables and every herb and plant our parents plied into home remedies to try to kill Kate's leukemia. My sister's soft snores and rhythmic breathing calmed my worries.

Please God, make her well. I'll do anything You ask.

Once home, I laid sleeping Kate into her bed, cleaned her bug bite, then covered her with a new pink-and-green quilt that Mom had made for her. I pulled the rocking chair close and clung to her cool hand, the bluish color filling me with dread. I blew on it to warm her up.

Mom joined me and kissed Kate's cheek. "You shouldn't have worn her out." She gasped. "Why is hydrogen peroxide and soda here? Did you let her get stung or bitten?"

I gazed into Mom's furious face, and my eyes welled with tears. "A fire ant. I didn't see the hill." I showed her the swollen spot on Kate's ankle, but Kate didn't waken.

"What have you done?" Mom wailed. "Get your dad right now."

I raced to the barn, my tears blinding every step. "Dad! Hurry! It's Kate."

He rushed past me. The smell of animals following in his wake.

He tossed back the blanket and examined her cold feet. "She needs socks. More blankets." His eyes never left her ashen face. "Kate, wake up, honey. I want to see your sky-blue eyes."

Mom and I tugged on Kate's warm socks and piled blankets on

her. She slept on. Mom crawled into bed with her, drew her close, and cradled her like a baby. "Please, Katie-Bug. Mommy's here. Talk to me."

Dad knelt beside the bed. "Sweet girl, wake up."

Mom's high-pitched demands grew shrill.

Kate jerked involuntarily and Mom screamed, "No. Not my baby."

"Have you been giving her turmeric and ginseng? Essential oils?" Dad grabbed Mom's arm. "Did you give her a massage this morning? When's the last time she had water? Are you watching her diet?"

Mom's splotchy face reddened. "I've done it all. It's . . . it's the ant bite. She was fine this morning until Therese took her on a picnic."

I shuddered. Had my stupidity shortened my sister's life?

Dad yanked his phone from his jeans pocket and called 911. "What do you mean over an hour? My daughter has leukemia!" He threw the phone at the door, splintering the wood.

"Therese, get me the thermometer," Mom yelled.

"It's broken." My heart beat so hard, it felt like it would burst out of my chest.

"How?" Dad swung to me. "Don't touch her. This is your fault."

I stepped back. "Daddy—"

"Get out of here. Your mother and I need to take care of Kate."

"Can't I stay? She's my sister."

Dad's jaw tightened, and he pointed to the corner. "Not one word."

Evening shadows drew a shroud over the small bedroom. Kate took one labored breath after another, and I couldn't keep my eyes off her. Why was she congested?

Fifteen minutes passed.

Kate gasped for air. Mom's hoarse cries continued, like a wounded animal caught in a trap.

Dad paced the floor, swiping beneath his eyes, wiping his nose on his flannel shirt. Complaining about the slow ambulance.

Thirty minutes ticked by. No matter how hard I listened for the ambulance, silence met me.

Mom's quivering finger touched Kate's throat for a pulse. "No." She shook Kate's shoulders. "She isn't breathing."

A hollow emptiness trampled on my hope for my sweet sister. My ears rang with death's gasp for air. *Please, Kate. Breathe. I love you. Don't leave me alone.*

Three weeks later, both my parents were dead of natural causes, and a kind lady took me to a foster home. Had I killed my little sister, like they said? Had I killed Mom and Dad?

ONE

NEW CANEY, TEXAS
OCTOBER, THURSDAY, CURRENT DAY

THERESE

The shrill ring of my mobile phone jolted me awake at 2:00 a.m., a haunting prompt that emergencies seldom emerged in daylight. Someone had ventured into the wilderness and needed me to lead a rescue mission. My skills of trekking over precarious terrain to find victims who suffered from physical injuries, dehydration, starvation, or all three, kept me on alert. At times I viewed my life like a *Star Trek* tagline, "Where no man has gone before."

I grabbed the phone off my nightstand. Unidentified caller. "Hello?"

"Ms. Palmer, this is Professor Rurik Ivanov from Houston Leonard University. We met nearly a year ago. You taught a course in wilderness survival as an adjunct professor."

I captured a mental image of the Russian man—gray-blue eyes, stone-gray hair, angular face. "Yes, sir. How can I help you?"

"I apologize for the hour, but I'm in a desperate situation."

The angst in his voice zapped me into guarded mode, especially when I barely knew the man. I snapped on my bedside lamp. "Are you all right?"

"No, ma'am, which is why I'm calling you. Do you remember my wife and daughter?"

"I met them both at a faculty dinner last Christmas. A lovely family."

"My wife was murdered today, and kidnappers have taken my daughter."

I inhaled sharply, and alarm for the professor's family fired hot from the soles of my feet. "Daria? Alina? What happened?"

"A man called me late this afternoon while I prepared to leave for home. He said he'd taken Alina. Then he sent a link to a video showing my wife's execution—"

He stopped abruptly, his final words drumming into my senses. The seconds ticked by, and I waited.

"I watched Daria grab her chest and struggle . . . The blood rushed from her precious body—my dear Daria's life gone forever." He grappled again to control his tear-filled voice. "He said they would release Alina unharmed if I paid three million dollars. They'd call with instructions. When the man hung up, I hurried home thinking it had to be a terrible mistake or someone had used AI to generate the video. On the way, I phoned Daria and the call went to voice mail. I also redialed the man who'd contacted me. The phone rang repeatedly, but the number offered no way to leave a message. I contacted Alina's school and learned Daria had picked her up before noon.

"At home, reality rooted. A lamp and a table in the living room lay in pieces. Daria would have fought hard, but there were no signs of blood. I didn't recognize the place in the video where they killed her. I even checked for geotag information on the clip, but it had been stripped. I later clicked on the link . . . the video had disappeared."

I ached for his loss. "What do the police say?"

Silence answered me, then Rurik finally said, "Contacting them is impossible. The man warned me against telling anyone who works in law enforcement, or I'd never see Alina again." He sobbed into the phone. "Please, give me a moment."

"Take all the time you need."

The professor taught Russian language and literature at Leonard

University and was highly respected and liked among faculty and students. I'd enjoyed our occasional chats, and he'd observed some of my classes. What had he done to upset the wrong people?

"Thank you. I can talk now," he said. "I have no idea where the killers have taken Daria's body or how to find Alina. Neither do I suspect anyone."

I willed my pulse to slow. "Professor, the police are trained in handling confidential matters and how to find who is responsible. They have families and understand what you're going through."

"And endanger my daughter?" Panic throbbed in his ragged voice.

"I'm sorry." My grief over losing Kate many years ago surfaced raw and bleeding. "Are you alone?"

"Yes. At home."

"Are there family or friends who can stay with you?"

"My family is in Russia, and I do not trust anyone."

"You could very well be in danger too."

"My welfare is unimportant."

"Who are these people, and why has your family been victimized?"

"I have no idea. The man refused to identify himself, but he did say 'we.' Maybe he thinks I have money or believes I have done something criminal to my country or to the US."

What was he not telling me? I tossed off my blanket and stood in my bedroom, shivering, not from the cold but the horror of this unfolding story. "Professor Ivanov, I'm confused. Why call me? This is a job for the police or the FBI."

"I cannot risk my daughter's life. You are my only hope to find Alina. You have the skills to get her back."

I ran my fingers through my hair. "I'm a wilderness-survival specialist, nothing more. I'm not equipped to carry out a hostage negotiation without backup, which is another reason you need to involve the authorities." More questions bolted into my mental space like a landslide. "How would I find her?"

"That's where I can help you. Alina has GPS trackers hidden in her shoes. Not even Daria knew about them."

"Why would you track your young daughter?"

"Alina's biological mother died when she was a baby, and I've been consumed with protecting my daughter ever since. I checked my phone app and learned at one thirty this afternoon, Alina was taken to a private landing strip west of Houston. I called there, and a woman who worked in the small office said no one had filed a flight plan. But she made a mistake. The tracker had stopped registering." He coughed and asked me to wait while he got a glass of water.

A connection at Harris County Office of Homeland Security & Emergency Management popped into my consciousness. They had the technology to confirm the date and time a plane took to the skies and where it landed.

"I'm better. I apologize for my lack of control," the professor said. "My app showed tracking again near an abandoned airstrip in a remote area south of Hobbs, New Mexico. The tracking indicated ground-speed movement for two and a half hours to a section on the north side of Guadalupe Mountains National Park called Dog Canyon. That's where the tracking ended, and I've detected nothing since. I assume the kidnappers parked the vehicle and proceeded on foot with Alina. Research shows the area is off-grid. Ms. Palmer, did they remove her shoes? How would they expect her to walk in bare feet?"

My thoughts trailed to the worst possible scenario. Why take Alina to a remote location unless they planned to dispose of her body there? Another argument lay with logic. Why go to the expense of transporting a kidnap victim there when they had the ability to dispose of her body in their backyard? A morbid idea, except true. Whatever the reason, they risked exposure from security cameras until they reached an off-grid area.

"I can't stress enough how the authorities have technology and skills to find Alina. They can unravel valid threats and comprehend the danger of taking your story to the media."

"The man who called me said they'd be watching my every move. I bought a burner phone tonight to call you."

His anguish rippled through me, interfering with my ability to think clearly. "What about the ransom?"

"I can liquidate assets here and in Russia to meet their demands, but the statistics on kidnappers returning my Alina alive are not good. Perhaps they would accept what I can put together now. I'm sorry . . . I wish I had an answer. Why harm an eight-year-old little girl?"

"I have empathy for your grief." Daria's lovely face and the white-blonde-haired little girl refused to leave me alone. "Although I could lead you into Dog Canyon, I have no idea how to pull her out of the clutches of dangerous men. You'd need armed law enforcement and possibly a negotiator."

"That would draw attention. I'll pay you whatever you want."

"Money is not the issue, Professor—"

"Alina means more to me than anything else in this world. What is love but to take ownership of a problem and do all I can to stop those men?"

"What if I fail?" The terror of not finding his daughter alive resurrected an echo from the past that had shaped my career.

"Can you live with yourself if you don't try?"

Unaware, he'd pressed my weakest button. "I'll hear you out. But I don't believe you've given me the whole story, and I need the truth before I risk my life."

"I've . . . I've given you all of it."

"You've stated what you *want* me to know. What have you done or not done in this tragedy that Daria is dead, Alina is missing, and you can't go to the police?"

TWO

NEW CANEY, TEXAS

I paced the floor of my bedroom, battling the war within my soul. Professor Ivanov's tragedies reached into the fiber of the woman I am today. A helpless little girl caught up in a vicious crime? My emotional fiber screamed to say yes to a rescue mission, but reason shouted just as loudly that I didn't have all the information to make a solid decision.

I arranged to meet Professor Ivanov at The Breakfast Brew restaurant at 5:00 a.m. The early hour meant Houston traffic hadn't paralyzed the interstate. The time gave me a few hours to think and pray about his tragic story and how best to respond. I had no idea what to do about his missing daughter. If answers were supposed to come with a morning sun that streaked orange and yellow across the sky, would I soon see through the darkness? How had I been caught in the middle of such an impossible situation?

I weighed the odds of finding Alina alive, and doubt shook my confidence. Maneuvering uncharted trails across rough terrain where others refused to venture or weren't equipped with the wilderness skills didn't frighten me. But something far worse hovered over my psyche.

I'd found the hideous remains of adults who'd succumbed to nature's pitfalls, but never a helpless child.

Kate dictated my life after twenty years. Alina was the same age as Kate when she died. I couldn't save her, and now Alina faced potential death.

Alina suffering under the control of the monster who might have killed her mother caused me to forget all manner of good sense. How had the kidnappers navigated her to Dog Canyon? How had they raised and lowered her over steep inclines and slippery shale rock? With ropes? Carried her?

If I accepted the job, I needed a member of law enforcement whom I trusted . . . Someone wilderness-worthy with negotiation skills and able to expertly use a firearm without hesitation.

A man's name held my attention. Seven months ago in Houston, I'd trained Texas Rangers on wilderness-survival skills through a four-day-long series of hands-on classes. One of the Rangers worked in the Crisis Negotiation Unit—CNU. A man I respected. He had a master's degree in psychology and a reputation as a risk-taker. I needed a trained professional who put others first . . . providing he let me lead and give the orders.

Captain Blane Gardner.

I hesitated to call him. We'd gone out three times, and I enjoyed his company and commitment to the Texas Rangers. Then I invited him to church. He claimed he and God weren't on speaking terms, so I ended the relationship. Although I'd made the right decision, several sleepless nights passed before I could push his pecan-colored eyes, thick red hair, and fit physique out of my heart. My pulse sped at the idea of spending hours alone with him in the wilderness, and the thought of putting myself through the emotional roller coaster again sent my pulse racing, but saving a child's life took priority.

With thirty minutes before I had to leave to meet Professor Ivanov, I pulled up Blane's contact info on my phone. Any other time, I'd have been considerate of the early hour, but not this morning. I pressed in the numbers, and a groggy man answered.

"Blane, this is Therese Palmer."

He yawned. "What time is it? I doubt this is a social call."

"Little after 4:00 a.m." Hearing his voice brought back our dates, hours of conversation, and gazing into his eyes. *Moving on.* "I apologize for the early hour."

"Sounds like you have an emergency. How can I help?"

Encouraged, I braved forward. "I'm looking for someone with your expertise as a Texas Ranger, a negotiator, and a man who can trek through off-grid areas."

"And my name popped up in a search engine?"

"Yes."

"Glad to know I have hero stats. Where would this mission take place?"

"Guadalupe Mountains."

"You're talking a lot of territory. What's the situation?"

"I've been asked to help find a little girl who is being held there for ransom. Timing is critical."

"Who is she?"

"I can't tell you until I'm sure you're willing to take this on." I paused and let my words sink in.

"Let me get this straight. You need a Ranger, which says law enforcement jurisdiction. A kid's been kidnapped, which says possible murder, and I'd better carry plenty of ammo. You need a person trained to talk down volatile people and arrange for her release. And we'd be hiking across dirt and rock. How many other Rangers have you asked?"

"None but you."

He chuckled. "How did I make the lucky cut?"

"Contrary to some of your colleagues last March, you didn't discount my skills just because I'm a woman. Another reason is Rangers are private people, and I need someone I can trust."

"Next time, I'll disguise my appearance. Is the kid family or a friend?"

"Depends on your definition."

"How much is the ransom?"

"I'm not ready to divulge details."

Blane huffed. "Remind me not to try interrogating you. Wait a minute. I did try, and you shut me down."

That I did. "You're a good fit, which is what this mission needs."

He gave a low-throated laugh that I'd almost forgotten. "I won't tease you about our past, unless it serves my purpose."

His dry sense of humor appealed to me, as long as he avoided the topic of "us." I could work with a mission-oriented man who balanced life with a carefree and cheerful attitude. But I must keep my attraction out of it. "Can you meet me this morning at The Breakfast Brew on I-45 near The Woodlands around five thirty?" I counted to ten. I hadn't talked to him in months, and now I was asking him to risk his life. "I understand your apprehension. I assure you this is a legit problem, one that requires secrecy."

"Okay. I'm available to talk. Understand, I must be given every detail, or you'll be lookin' for another negotiator. I don't have a good feeling about this, but I'll hear you out, only because I like you. If I can assist you within my job description, Major Sergio Montoya will also need to approve the plan and the time away from my responsibilities."

"In your shoes, I'd demand the same." At least Blane didn't blow me off. This gave me an opportunity to talk to Professor Ivanov and convince him of bringing in firepower. "Thanks. I appreciate your meeting me."

I texted a friend who worked at the park's Pine Springs Visitor Center near Dog Canyon. She texted back stating I needed a law enforcement official to authorize access to the camera footage and the Guadalupe Mountains covered over eighty-six thousand acres.

My next text went to a friend at Harris County Office of Homeland Security & Emergency Management, who said a pilot who didn't want to be identified and used abandoned airstrips would have turned off his transponder. No one would bother with the flight unless it flew into controlled airspace. If someone looked for the aircraft, they'd find it. There were always ways to uncover the hidden. Except I wanted answers now.

I searched online about Rurik and Daria Ivanov. Nothing problematic jumped out about the couple. Neither did anything surface about Russian organized crime—ROC—other than the usual FBI alerts. Another connection at the FBI could tell me if Rurik and Daria were under the radar or if US/Russia relations had recently escalated.

Professor Ivanov had made an enemy who wanted a lot of money—and had already proven their seriousness.

God, what am I to do?

THREE

BLANE

An adventuresome streak flashed through me as though I considered riding the tail of a lightning bolt. I wanted to accompany Therese Palmer into the harsh, high-desert area of West Texas to find a kidnapped little girl. More so, I craved the excitement and an opportunity to redeem myself to a woman who had attracted me since I'd first set eyes on her. But insight told me to gather all the facts about the little girl's kidnapping first, and that meant listening and observing—my best tools.

During the wilderness-survival training, Therese had jolted all of us Rangers with her maneuvers, martial arts, and survival skills. For four days, she outdid us with one jaw-dropping tactic after another, never condemning our lack of skills or the speed we took to accomplish them. She showed the slower ones how to master a technique and asked those who'd succeeded to help their fellow Rangers. Those of us who were single did our best to impress her, but we all failed. She ignored the compliments and jokes, leaving us feeling stupid.

I must have gotten on her good side. Therese agreed to three dates, and I thought we had the beginnings of something worth the effort, then she told me that spending any more time or money on her was a mistake. Someday I'd ask how I'd offended her. It bothered me. A lot. Like expecting a promotion that never panned out.

An image of her honey-colored hair flowing around her shoulders and her sparkling eyes that weren't quite blue or green held me in emotional chains. No one would ever guess the natural beauty had eaten bugs, wrestled a bear, and swam crocodile-infested waters, or so her reputation claimed—and she could navigate her way out of treacherous switchbacks in the mountains at night. One Ranger dubbed her Davina Crockett.

I showered, contemplating every word Therese had spoken during our early morning call. I dressed, and the sky held on to the blackness with no hint of ever lifting, like the unanswered questions galloping down the bridle path of a rescue mission and spending hours with Therese.

Had I thought through the mission, used logic and reason as to what lay ahead? I wanted to see her, and I wanted to avoid her. I yanked on my boots. With any luck, she'd grown a wart on her nose.

I pressed in her cell number, and she immediately picked up. The hum of road noise indicated she drove to the meetup.

"Yes, Blane. Change your mind?"

"Not at all. I have a truckload of questions, so why don't you start with what's really going on."

"I've learned more. Some of the info I can share."

"Great. Nothing's hit the news cycle about a kidnapping. No Amber Alert has been issued."

"It needs to stay that way. This is a need-to-know rescue operation."

Whoa. "Why me, other than what you mentioned earlier?"

"Still the same. If you have new questions, I *might* have an answer." Her slightly upturned voice told me she'd do her best.

"Why is the mission private?"

"The family isn't American."

"Does the kidnapping have political or international ramifications?"

"Maybe both. Maybe neither. The father says neither, but I have no way to confirm it without a face-to-face. You can read people far better than me."

I'd sort this out after the meeting. "And he's a friend?"

"A colleague."

"What about his wife?"

Silence told me she two-stepped around her answer. "He says the kidnappers murdered her."

I winced. "The man is desperate." I envisioned a man leaning over his wife's body. "I've seen nothing on the wires about a murder either."

"I don't think the police are aware."

Alarms in my head sounded an alert. "Then he's not reporting a crime, which is against the law. Are you sure you aren't climbing the wrong mountain?"

"You aren't obligated to meet with us, and I get it. Like you, I need more details before I make my final decision. Your ability to read others will help me. In answer to your question about his wife, he says her body is missing. I've told you most of what he told me, and I'd prefer he fill you in on the rest. Later, you and I can compare notes and judge if the moral and legal issues are worth the danger."

The hesitancy in her voice troubled me. "Are you having doubts?"

"More like how do I—or we—move forward in recovering a child being held by kidnappers? Are we the best choice, or is someone else better equipped?"

"You and I are *definitely* a small team."

"It appears so."

Curiosity nipped at my heels. Who was this man who'd lost his wife and feared his daughter might meet the same demise? Why the violent crimes against him? Or would his identity explain the secrecy? Did I want to get stuck in a quicksand of crimes?

FOUR

THERESE

Professor Ivanov's slumped shoulders and red-rimmed eyes tugged at my sympathy strings. His slow approach from the restaurant entrance contradicted the image of the confident, energetic professor at Leonard University. I'd walked through the same fire of losing a loved one, and the agony burned physically and mentally. Drawing each breath took courage.

I'd secured a corner booth in the rear that offered visibility of those entering, a habit I'd picked up in college. A roommate had been stalked by an old boyfriend, and she told me how facing the entrance to a restaurant or any public building gave her comfort. The position prepared her for any challenges, and I adopted her wisdom and never regretted it.

Professor Ivanov wore a wrinkled shirt splattered with coffee stains that told me more about him than a thesaurus full of words representing grief, sorrow, and shock. His anguish crept into a part of me that I normally kept locked away.

"Professor, I'm so sorry about your family." I shook his hand.

He moistened his lips, his grip clammy. "Thank you. I appreciate you choosing to discuss this further." He seated himself across the table from me. "Normally I'd be up assembling last-minute plans to greet my students. So much has happened in such a few hours." He inhaled and slowly exhaled. "My wife's death and Alina facing the same merciless fate torments my every moment. They are victims of evil-infested men."

"I agree. You asked me to help you. But I'm not sure how or if it's possible."

A server approached and took our orders for coffee. Professor Ivanov watched her leave and surveyed the small crowd as though one of them had pulled the trigger on Daria or held Alina.

"Do you see someone familiar?" I said.

"Everyone looks like a killer or a kidnapper to me."

"Do you suspect you were followed?"

"I don't think so. I kept my eyes on the rearview mirror." Rurik pulled a small notebook from inside his sports jacket and handed it to me. "I've written what happened in chronological order. Perhaps you'll see something I have missed."

His jerky handwriting conveyed his tormented mental state. My reasoning to help rescue Alina wavered between hot indignation against whoever had abducted the little girl to stone-cold dread if the child had been killed. My reservations said I fell below the skills required.

I read through his notes. Professor Ivanov received the distressing call at 3:00 p.m. yesterday. He attempted to contact Daria, phoned Alina's school, learned his daughter had been picked up earlier at 11:45, and then he returned to an empty home near 4:30 p.m. His notes mirrored his early morning plea to me.

"Have the kidnappers contacted you since we spoke?" I snapped a pic of his notebook and slid it back to him.

"Not yet. I keep thinking there's a reason they chose such a desolate area, and I shudder at the fears plaguing Alina. While the high desert mountains would be difficult for her, the kidnappers are minus conveniences too." He slipped his pad inside his jacket. "My daughter . . . I refuse to believe she's dead."

I wrestled with the same horror. "You must not lose hope. Concentrate on finding Alina alive and well."

He gave me a thin-lipped smile above a quivering chin.

"Professor, this isn't a solo mission. The abductors are dealing with high stakes too. Are you trained in wilderness survival and weaponry?"

"No, Ms. Palmer. I battle with words, not nature or unscrupulous men, and I'm sadly out of shape. I admit I'm powerless to be the rescue-father Alina deserves. She is in excellent physical condition. She's involved with gymnastics three days a week and competes regularly."

I nodded at his pride in her and bit back my disappointment at his inability to help with the search. "Do you see the necessity for at least one trained person to accompany me?"

Rurik paled. "Have you told the police or the FBI?"

"I gave you my word that I wouldn't. But if I'm to accept your request, I will not take this mission on by myself. It's useless even to contemplate the idea. Surely you see the danger and implications for all concerned."

"I do, Ms. Palmer—"

"Therese, please. We're talking about your daughter's life, and the formalities seem cold."

"You're right. I'm Rurik. Who are you recommending? Please, not the FBI."

"I shared the highlights of the situation with a friend who's a Texas Ranger. He has no name or information that would jeopardize Alina."

He scrubbed his hands over his face. "Do you trust him?"

"I've dealt with him on a prior occasion, and his record is impeccable. He's a hostage negotiator and an expert marksman. He refused the mission without more information, so I asked him to join us here at five thirty." I paused. "I can call him and cancel."

Rurik stared at me, but I couldn't read his emotions. "What are you thinking?"

"It's apparent that you need assistance. Are you proficient with a firearm?"

"Yes, but I've never shot anyone."

He lifted a brow. "The crimes involve more than one man. At least two. One to manage Alina and another to pilot the plane. I suspect a third man as a guide."

"Makes sense. Would she have fought her kidnappers?"

"I taught her how to show bravery in all circumstances, and I also taught her to use her brain."

"Then in your opinion, she'd not fight them."

"Right. She isn't a whiner and doesn't cry easily, but I have no idea what her captors have demanded. I want her back safe, to live a child's life, and forget what she's experienced . . . I'm afraid she witnessed my Daria's murder and might not ever recover from the sight." Anger narrowed his eyes. "Nothing is guaranteed. Neither life nor death. Alina's ordeal has the potential to make her strong, invincible . . . The caller said if I went to law enforcement, he'd kill her. Can you assure me that the kidnappers will not learn I reached out for help?"

"I will do my best."

"I see no alternative but to risk talking to the Texas Ranger."

FIVE

BLANE

I spotted Therese sitting at a booth in the rear of the restaurant, her attention intense on the man sitting across from her. She waved at me, and I joined them. A slight-built man with stone-gray hair and narrow shoulders stood with Therese to greet me. Taller than most women, she reached my eye level, and I found that appealing.

"Mornin', Therese."

Her loveliness rivaled the dawn, her athletic body clad in jeans and a green plaid button-down shirt. Yeah, green. My favorite color, representing growth, nurturing, healing.

"Hi, Blane. Thanks for meeting us so early on such short notice." She introduced me to Professor Rurik Ivanov.

I stuck out my hand. "Pleasure to meet you, sir."

A trembling hand met mine, and I grasped it firmly. His gray eyes clouded with grief. US relations with Russia had its rough edges and many secrets. That didn't mean two men couldn't have a civil conversation that focused on a humanitarian need.

"The dire circumstances surrounding our conversation needs strict confidentiality. My daughter's life is at stake." Professor Ivanov spoke with a slight Russian accent.

Therese slid over in the booth, and I sat beside her and faced Professor Ivanov. I wanted to offer the professor friendship and establish a foundation of trust from the beginning. I removed my work Stetson to the corner of the table. Therese had already briefed me on his aversion to law enforcement.

I placed my phone in front of me. "I might need this to take notes. Do you object?"

He eyed me. "No, sir." The professor placed his phone beside him. Was he willing it to ring? Holding on to it like a lifeline? Or . . . wishing he hadn't given me permission to use mine?

"Professor Ivanov, your loss is beyond any words."

"Thank you. You're a Texas Ranger with negotiating skills, right? A captain, I believe?"

I dipped my chin in a nod. "The western dress makes me a little hard to miss." I allowed a moment to settle between us, to study the man for any signs of deceit and how to gain his confidence. "I'm sorry for the loss of your wife and the kidnapping of your daughter. I see the pain in your eyes. Our conversation is about determining if I can be of assistance in rescuing your daughter. That may include the arrest of those responsible. I have some tough but necessary questions. Some will sound insensitive."

"I . . . I understand the importance of your questions and the accuracy of my answers."

"Whenever a life is at risk, stakes are high. Have you reported your wife or daughter missing to the police?"

"No. I must obey the kidnappers. Anything else endangers my daughter. Against my better judgment, I am talking to you." Ivanov choked back a sob. "I'm sorry. This is a risk, but I must do more than pay a ransom."

"No need to hide your grief from us. Local and federal agencies have the manpower and knowledge to bring justice to an otherwise unpredictable outcome. It's in your best interest to contact them with what's happened to your family." I kept my voice low. "I am required to report crimes, and it's against the law to conceal illegal activities."

I let silence sink into my words. "Sir, I want to offer you the same credible advice that I'd share with a friend. I have no proof of a crime being committed and haven't contacted my superior at this point."

"Are you insinuating this is a hoax?"

"No, sir. The opposite. I'm alerting you that the police will discover your wife and child are missing, and they will demand answers. Far better you explain the circumstances now than after they are notified of violent crimes. Anything you tell me is important to making arrests and finding your daughter. You've shared what happened with Therese, but I'd like to hear it in your words."

A bead of sweat formed on Ivanov's upper lip. "Please promise me the information will be shared with only those who can keep the crimes private."

"You have my word. If the situation changes, I will contact you immediately."

"This all makes it difficult to think sensibly or trust anyone, but I will do my best. I'm a professor at Leonard University. Yesterday afternoon . . ." He gripped his white knuckles on the table and stated what Therese had told me. "I haven't heard anything since. The helplessness . . . anger . . . and sorrow are unexplainable."

"I'd expect no less from a husband and father who is grieving. When your daughter is safe, I encourage you to seek counseling for you and Alina. In the meantime, confiding in someone you trust will help ease the stress. This isn't a load to carry alone. I want to do everything possible to locate and return your daughter, even if it means informing others who are better equipped, and I step back."

"I have no one I can trust within my circle of friends. Daria and I were very close. We told each other everything, and now she's gone."

"Did the man who called you have an accent?"

"No. Unless he hid it well."

"Have other Russians living in Houston experienced the same trauma?"

"I've not heard anything. If it's the same man, he'd have warned them not to talk."

"How long have you lived in the US?"

"Five years in Houston. Why does that matter?" His high-pitched tone demonstrated he walked close to a breakdown.

"Everything is important concerning your daughter."

Therese touched Ivanov's arm. "I'm praying for you and Alina."

His gaze bore into her eyes. "I'm not a man of faith, but I value your prayers."

"Professor Ivanov," I said, "do you have a suspect or suspects? Were you threatened in Russia or since you've moved to the US?"

"Nothing. I am a peaceful man."

"And you haven't spoken to anyone at the Russian embassy?"

"What if one of them is involved?"

A strange response. "Have you upset anyone in Russia? Has—?"

"I am loyal to my country. Check my background. It is spotless." He leaned back against the cushioned seat.

Did he fear his own country had turned against him? Why? "Professor, I'm not the enemy. Those are the ones who've committed these crimes against your family."

A slight twitch beneath his right eye caught my attention. I'd nearly missed the unconscious hint of holding back information.

"If the kidnappers learn I talk to the police or FBI, my daughter faces death. What if the kidnappers have connections in those places?"

I added gentleness to my tone. "Our goal is to help you bring Alina home safely, and we want to proceed in an effective and efficient manner. I trust law enforcement, but I also understand your reluctance to do the same. No one can promise you the best outcome, but we can do everything possible."

"One minute my thoughts are racing, and the next fear imprisons me. I assume you've negotiated in life-and-death situations."

"Many times, but experience doesn't make the job easier."

"Are you trained like the FBI or others in federal law enforcement?"

I peered into his eyes. Not the first time someone took a Texas Ranger for a slow-witted cowboy. "We are all trained to do our jobs." I rose from the booth. "Do you need someone else?"

The professor motioned for me to sit. "Please, I am fine. I must be sure of every step."

I took my original spot. "Do you have a photo of Alina and a description of what she was last wearing?"

He scrolled through his phone and shared an image of a white-blonde-haired little girl with a sweet smile. "Yesterday morning she was wearing her school uniform—a blue plaid jumper, navy-blue shirt, and dark-blue tennis shoes."

"She is a pretty little girl," I said. "My guess is you haven't slept or eaten since the ordeal began."

"Would you if your wife had been murdered and your daughter kidnapped? Every part of me is in panic mode—willing the phone to ring, waiting to wake up from this horror, longing to hear my wife's voice and Alina's laughter." He took a glimpse of his daughter and covered his phone with his hand on the table beside him.

"Let me order you something to eat. You need your strength until this ordeal is over."

"Your kindness is much appreciated, but I'm nauseous."

"You're scared. I would be too. Professor, you should take care of yourself for your daughter's sake."

He held up a finger. "Maybe later. Please, call me Rurik."

"I'm Blane." I positioned my fingers on my phone's keyboard. "Can we move on?"

"Go ahead. Daria is not Alina's mother. My first wife died when Alina was seven months old."

"The three of you were a happy family?"

"What does our relationship have to do with the kidnapping?" He held up his palm. "Ignore me. I'm Alina's primary caregiver, so our family isn't typical, but we've never had problems."

Wouldn't Daria have been the only mother Alina had ever known? "This is a hard one, but I must ask. If your wife didn't share in the parenting, would you want her out of the picture?"

Rurik's pale blue eyes widened. "I loved my wife. We were unable to have children, and at times she resented Alina. She asked me to take over parenting. Daria also wanted Alina in private care or in school when I wasn't at home."

Why hold back love for a child? "But she picked her up the day of the abduction."

Rurik inhaled deeply. "Although she's authorized, she hadn't done so before. I assume the kidnappers coerced her."

"I plan to check the security cameras at the school. The video could give us the abductor's identity. Is your wife's vehicle at home?"

"No. Neither have I reported it stolen." Rurik snuffled back a sob, and Therese handed him a napkin.

"If you're up to it, I have questions about Alina." Rurik nodded, and I moved ahead. "You mentioned this earlier. Am I correct in assuming Alina is independent?"

"I raised her to observe and think prior to speaking, keep her eyes open, listen to what others are saying, and devise ways to take care of herself."

"You're a good father. How does Alina charge the tracker in her shoes?"

He licked his lower lip. "Wireless charging. She puts them on a special shoe pad at night. Each pair of shoes is placed on a color-coded spot. I told her the shoes go there so her feet don't run out of energy the next day."

I smiled. "Great idea. How long does the charge last?"

"Up to thirty days. I've always been afraid something might happen to her, so I insisted she place them on the pad in her closet nightly." He hesitated. "Always a game, and she gladly played along."

"What else?"

"She wears a gold ballerina necklace linked to her shoes via Bluetooth. I told her never to take it off. Ever. She believes it gives her special powers."

"Your wife didn't question the shoes or the necklace?"

"I kept the trackers from her." He glanced beyond me and back. "Daria claimed I was overprotective. No point in upsetting her."

Rurik just said he and his wife told each other everything. Unusual family arrangement, and Daria missed the nurturing gene, unless the little girl was badly behaved. "Have you told us everything?"

"I believe so."

"If Therese and I take on your request, we must have all the information, no matter how unimportant it may seem to you. My boss, Major Sergio Montoya, must give his permission for the mission, and he will insist on being updated. If we require backup or a life flight, he's the one who would arrange it."

"I understand. You have protocol to follow."

Good. "What did you do in Russia?"

"I taught Russian and economics at Lomonosov Moscow State University. Then I was contacted by Leonard University. A smooth transition for all of us."

"What will you do when the authorities find your wife's body?" I sent compassion into every word.

"I'll say she wanted a few days away to do shopping."

"Was this a common occurrence?" I said.

"Yes, and I'd tell the police I didn't report her missing because I had no reason. I have no idea what I'd say about Alina's whereabouts."

My phone alerted me to a recent incident. "One more thing. You filed a police report a month ago regarding a prowler. No arrests were made. Do you think the two crimes are connected?"

"I'd forgotten about the trespasser. My backyard entrance is locked, and I have a motion detector. The lights flipped on, and a man dressed in black and wearing a stocking mask stood in the backyard. He quickly scaled the fence and fled. Daria screamed, became violently ill."

I folded my hands on the table, matching his posture. "Rurik, tell us what's really going on. You're skirting the truth."

SIX

A negotiator's sharpest tool in dealing with high stakes was often silence.

Rurik's ghostly features stared back at me. "I'm terrified about telling you this, but if it helps find Alina . . ."

"Truth is always the key to unlock fear and doubt," I said. "I can't emphasize that enough. Every detail has the potential to help rescue your daughter."

"And find out who killed my Daria."

"True. Therese and I are listening. Take your time."

The professor conducted a few of the inhale-exhale procedures I used to calm myself during hostage negotiations. He'd been trained or counseled by someone.

"Two nights ago, Daria and I were at a dinner hosted by Russian friends. We do this to speak our native language and feel like we're closer to home. During the evening, I had a headache and excused myself to get fresh air. I left Daria to sip kvass and chat with friends.

"Outside I set my vodka on a poolside table and walked around the pool and landscaped garden into a wooded area. My headache lessened and I lingered there a few minutes. I'm not as social as Daria, and I needed time alone to reenergize. The low voice of a man engaged in a phone conversation caused me to step away. But my ears perked at the mention of Edik Baranov, a Russian colonel general who recently fled my country."

Rurik's gaze swung from me to Therese and back again. "The one-sided conversation was disconcerting."

"I'm familiar with Baranov," I said. "Your government claims he stole military secrets, and he's saddled with a death warrant. About two weeks ago, the media reported he'd escaped Russia with his wife and young son. Media has spent cycles trying to figure out where he's gone."

Rurik stared at his folded hands. "Since then, he's been declared one of Russia's most wanted men. But what shocked me was I recognized the voice of the man speaking."

"Who?" I said.

"I'm hesitant to give his name . . . But it is Jurg Falin. He said they were using a network of people to learn if Baranov was in the US or en route here. They have a plan to take him and his family out. Jurg has either declared allegiance to the ROC—Russian organized crime—or he's simply a patriot who craves accolades from our homeland. Jurg has never indicated discontent with the US or stated anything radical to cause me concern. I slipped into the shadows and made my way back inside to the party. I struggled with what I'd heard and if I should act. The US has been good to me, and many of its citizens are friends. Our governments often don't see eye to eye, and my friends share varying opinions. But I didn't want to be responsible for innocent people's deaths."

"Do you believe Baranov is innocent?"

Rurik stiffened. "How would I know? He had access to government and top military secrets, which makes his charges of treason valid. But his wife and son have not broken any laws to deserve death."

"You and Jurg must be friends."

"Yes, since we were boys in Russia. Close as brothers."

"Sometimes people surprise and shock us," I said. "Did he indicate who he was talking to?"

"No."

"Is Jurg Falin the kidnapper who called you?"

"That is ridiculous. I would have recognized his voice." Rurik lifted his chin. "If I had a name, I'd give it to you."

"I'm sure you would. Continue." I leaned in.

"Once we arrived home and the babysitter had left—"

"Who is the babysitter?"

"One of my students from the university."

"I'd like her name for a background check."

Rurik pulled a small notebook from his jacket and wrote a name and phone number. He ripped the page and handed me the paper.

"Thanks. Go on."

"I relayed to Daria about what I'd heard from Jurg. I wanted to contact the FBI, but she panicked. She feared for my life and asked me to wait until the next day after I finished my classes at the university. She'd then go with me to ensure our family would receive US protection. She was extremely upset and insisted I not leave her or Alina that night. Neither did she want me to call the FBI for fear our phone might be monitored."

I held up my finger to get his attention. "Why would your phone be bugged?"

"I have no idea, except Jurg has been to our home on several occasions. In my opinion, Daria made a valid argument, not that I'd ever participated in Russian or American affairs. One more day wouldn't matter, so I agreed." Rurik's gaze darted behind him at the restaurant gradually filling with customers.

"Do you recognize anyone?" I said.

"No. Just observing. If I'd followed my instincts the night I heard Jurg's conversation, none of this would have happened. I blame myself . . ."

"Sir, we must assume your overhearing an assassination plot and the following day your wife and daughter are missing are linked. Have you spoken to Jurg Falin?"

Rurik glanced at his fists. "He isn't responding to calls or texts."

"Is this normal for him?"

"If he's busy."

I turned to Therese. "Any more questions?"

"Not right now." She swiped beneath her eyes.

I handed Rurik my business card. "Call me day or night. I need to talk to my boss and Therese before making a decision."

He glared, then softened. "I need an answer soon. Please, I'm begging you to help me save what's left of my family."

From the core of my gut, I wanted to say yes but not without investigating more of Rurik's story and digging deeper into his background. "Give me a few hours."

"All right. I'm going to the bank from here and wait until they open. I'll withdraw money from my account."

"How much is needed?"

"Three million dollars."

"On a professor's salary, that's a hunk of money."

Rurik shrugged. "Some here. Some overseas."

"I advise against it. The kidnappers will take what you give them and ask for more."

"If Alina were your daughter, what would you do?"

"I'd feel the same. You're suffering and the kidnappers know you'll do anything for her safe return."

"What are you suggesting? That I wait on their next call?"

"Put yourself in the kidnappers' shoes. What is their goal? Why are they desperate for your money? Why kill your wife and take your daughter to an off-grid location? Who are your enemies? Do your political views offend your government? Where does Edik Baranov fit in their scheme?" I paused when he inhaled sharply. "Panic solves nothing. Only a clear mind and logic will help us rectify the situation."

"I admit, it's hard to focus."

"A word of caution here. Once the authorities discover your wife and daughter are missing, they will be at your front door. You didn't inform them of what has happened, which will make you a person of interest in one, possibly two, murders."

He glared, then shook his head. "You're right. It will look like I covered up atrocious crimes. But I'd rather be arrested for crimes I didn't commit than have Alina killed. Those men have taken Daria's body where no one will find her." He rubbed his temples. "I've imagined several vile ways they might destroy her body, like a chemical vat, the ocean. The waiting is dreadful."

Therese touched the top of Rurik's fisted hand. Her silent support increased my admiration for her.

Rurik's cell phone sounded, and he pulled his device closer. "The number is blocked."

"Answer it in case it's the kidnapper," I said. "Don't give the caller your location or reveal who you're with."

He held the phone to his ear. "Yes, this is Rurik." He stared at me, and from his stiffened features, I'd made a correct assumption. "I'm working on getting the money. Where is Daria's body?" Rurik's features froze. "Yes, sir. Can I talk to Alina?"

Rurik laid his phone on the table and clicked a link to play a video of a dirty-faced, frightened little girl against a black background. She wore her navy-blue school uniform. "Please, Daddy, I want to come home. I'm scared. The man said you have something he needs."

The video stopped.

Rurik grabbed his phone and attempted to replay the video of Alina. "Like yesterday, the video is gone." His voice cracked, and he handed me his device.

I confirmed the link to the video as invalid and returned his phone. "What were the man's demands?"

"He'd give me a number to wire the three million dollars tomorrow. If I failed or went to the police, I'd receive a video of him killing Alina, like he'd done with Daria. After I wire the money, he will tell me where to find my wife's body and Alina will be returned to me."

"Did you recognize the voice?"

"The same man as yesterday." Rurik stood from the booth and stuffed his phone in his jacket pocket.

"What did Alina mean by you having something they need?"

"Money—"

"Sir." Our server garnered Rurik's attention. "Are you Professor Ivanov?"

"Yes. Why?"

The young woman handed him an envelope. "A man entered the restaurant and asked me to give this to you."

Rurik opened the envelope, and a lock of white-blonde hair fell onto his palm. He enclosed it in his fist and openly sobbed.

"What did the man look like?" I said to the server.

"Average height. Wore an Astros baseball cap, and from the bulge in the back of it, he had a man-bun. Khaki pants and a light-blue shirt. Said delivering the envelope was important, then he left."

My gaze flew to the front entrance, and I hurried past customers and on to the parking lot. With no one in sight and rush hour traffic, I had no way of identifying a vehicle. I jogged to the rear of the building with the same empty results.

Rurik and Therese met me outside. They hadn't seen anyone either, but the security cams would have captured the man's image.

Rurik held up the envelope. "This is my daughter's hair."

Rurik left Therese and me alone to sort through what had been said—and what hadn't. The restaurant manager verified my ID and allowed us to view the security-cam footage—a guy in his early thirties.

"Do you recognize him?" I said to Therese.

"No one I've ever seen."

I sent the footage to Sergio with a note that the man was a person of interest in a crime. We returned to the restaurant booth and ordered more coffee.

"Do you believe Rurik told us everything?" she said. "I probed him more and so did you. Each time, he shared another aspect of the crimes."

"He's not been entirely forthright. Fear has a way of crippling our senses and causing us to look at the world irrationally. Whoever is behind the crimes followed him here. The person who called Rurik might not have been the one who delivered the envelope. The timing's a bit off but not impossible."

"Have you heard and seen enough to consider a search for Alina?"

"I'm heading to the Ranger office. As soon as I have an ID from the footage, I'll update you." I kept my voice barely above a whisper. "I must share with the major what I've learned. He might refuse my participation, claiming this is a Federal case."

"I've been thinking the whole time Rurik talked, and I can't abandon a child." The resolve in her eyes left no doubt.

"If you've invested empathy for Rurik and his family, you are one strong woman, and your intentions are honorable. But sympathy could lead you to make a rash or poor decision. Both are good traits. Empathy in understanding Rurik's loss and grief is what we both need, but not sympathy unless sharing an experience helps us find Alina."

"What do you mean?"

"Just think about it, okay?"

Her shoulders lifted and didn't budge. "I'm leaving today to find Alina. With or without you."

"All right. I respect your stand." We stood, and I walked her to her car, a high-end SUV. I groaned. Her tires had been slashed. Doubtful she had more than one spare. "I'll call AAA."

She frowned. "Better check your truck first."

I'd been left the same calling card. "This just makes me mad." I cursed. "If the coward thinks he can slice my tires and run me off, he's messed with the wrong man."

"And the wrong woman."

SEVEN

Major Sergio Montoya and I had dodged trouble, partied more times than we remembered, and became Texas Rangers together, resulting in a solid friendship. But that didn't mean he approved of everything I attempted to do. Sitting across from his desk, I stared into his earth-colored eyes.

"Rusty, this undertaking could get you killed. Two years ago, you were assigned to a protection detail involving a former cartel member who'd given state evidence."

My risk-taking personality had opened dangerous doors in the past. I bit back a smirk and listened to make sure he didn't leave anything out.

"We needed more direction to stop a rumored plan to assassinate the governor, and the informant feared for himself and his family." Sergio squinted. "You chose to dress in the man's clothes during the drive to Austin and took two bullets."

I grinned to talk him down from a refusal. "I've been in hostile situations plenty of times. I enjoy those broncs."

"Some, like what I just mentioned, showed idiocy. This time you're asking permission for a solo mission—to leave a team of trained Rangers behind." He jutted his chin, and a stare down ensued between two stubborn men.

"I'd like the opportunity to investigate what Ivanov claims."

"I have no doubts . . . I will say you've always managed to accomplish where others failed. That said, I trust your ability to negotiate the impossible."

"Thanks—"

"I'm not finished. You and I agree the crimes against Rurik Ivanov's family are related to what he overheard regarding Edik Baranov."

"Are he and his family in the US?"

"Not to my knowledge. Baranov has a pack of blood-hungry wolves after him. His uncle is Russia's prime minister, so that's another reason why the Russians want him dead. His uncle went public condemning his nephew's traitorous actions. That doesn't mean the Baranovs aren't here." He peered at the wall behind me, not looking but processing information. "Let's find out everything we can about Ivanov, Baranov, and Falin." He typed into his laptop. "I'll let you know what I find if possible. Depends on the security level."

"Thanks, Sergio."

"Not so fast. I have questions. What have you researched?"

I shared Therese's and my conversation after Rurik left the restaurant. I concluded with the slashed tires. Once ended, I air-dropped him a photo of Alina Ivanov with the description of what she had worn to school. I'd never held anything back from Sergio and had no intentions of starting now.

I let the info sink in and moved ahead. "Sending a drone won't work with its limited charge, mountain ranges, and seven-mile span of control. I'm assuming the pilot who flew out of the Houston area and landed near Hobbs turned the transponder off. I'd appreciate it if you'd confirm any tracking of an aircraft, although with the transponder disabled, I doubt it can be identified. I ran a background on Alina's babysitter, and her dad's the university's president. Crossing her off my list. I researched Rurik Ivanov and Jurg Falin, but nothing surfaced that triggered any alarms. Except—"

"Except what?" Sergio said.

"I found nothing about how his wife died, but it's not lining up. His family life is off, and he's married to a possibly dysfunctional woman."

"The trackers on his daughter are a bit over the top." Sergio took notes.

"He claims to have the ransom. Since when do college professors rake in that kind of money?"

"They don't—normally."

"Is there a link between Ivanov and Baranov other than what we know?"

Sergio huffed. "I'll do what I can to find answers. Ivanov failed to keep his daughter safe. Our job is to find out who, what, and why. Ever hear what you fear most will happen?"

"Comes back to bite you hard in the rear."

Sergio typed into his laptop and made the request to obtain the security-cam footage at Alina's school. He added the video footage to all the entrances into the Guadalupe Mountains National Park with an emphasis on the visitor's center at Pine Springs and Dog Canyon from yesterday late afternoon to today. I stared out the window of Sergio's office, my past conversation with Rurik repeating his claims and pleas.

"We have an ID on the man who delivered the envelope this morning," Sergio said. "Nick Peterson. No record. Physical therapist at a private hospital in The Woodlands. I'll have him picked up for questioning."

"I'd like to talk to him."

"Sure. I'll post Alina's photo on the worldwide missing child database. The father won't approve, and the Russian embassy might not appreciate it either. But it's our job to report missing kids."

"Rurik will view that as a betrayal of confidence. Can you hold off for forty-eight hours?"

Sergio squinted. "Why is this so important to you?"

Greedy men victimizing innocents always spiked my anger. "Goes back to what you and I already discussed. Where is Daria's body? Why take the little girl to such a remote area? Why not lock Alina in a closet or bind and gag her somewhere? And how does Baranov's escape fit into this?" Working alongside Therese pulled me in but not like the unanswered questions.

"The who holds the key to the why. The worst-case scenario of discovering a murdered little girl is a real possibility. Be prepared."

I thanked him. "Finding an adult's body is difficult enough."

"Right. Rusty, if I had more answers, I'd feel more confident about your heading into the Guadalupe Mountains. Once I receive security-cam confirmation and we talk to Nick Peterson, I'll decide if your requests are valid."

"Finding the wife's body would provide some validation to Rurik's story. Nothing's hit the radar about Russian activities other than the search for Baranov. I checked IAH and Hobby Airports, and no one under the name of Alina Ivanov has left the area. But her kidnappers wouldn't use her name anyway, and they'd disguise her looks. The possibilities keep me rethinking facts and making suppositions on what could be happening."

Sergio again typed into his laptop. "I'm checking security cameras at both airports for Alina and Jurg Falin. If he's behind the crimes, he's not sticking around." He finished and studied me. "Do you think Ivanov contrived a story about a murdered wife, a kidnapped child, and refused to contact authorities or the Russian embassy due to a motive linked to Baranov?"

"It's entered my headspace. I viewed the video with his little girl. Wouldn't surprise me if someone used AI to frighten Rurik or to convince us of its validity for either abduction." I drew in a breath. "Unless Rurik's been trained, his emotional tells convinced me of his grief. I've been reading people a long time, and dread washed all over him. His wife was killed, and his daughter's life is in danger because of what?"

Sergio tapped his fingers on the desk. "You suspect a bigger scheme than what you've been told?"

"I'm not checking it off my list. Rurik can shove reasons about being the loving parent all day long, but something's missing. Makes me suspect he killed his wife and daughter, and this is his way of burying his own mess. And he could be grieving his actions." I shook my head.

Sergio leaned back in his chair. "If that's the case, why not fly home to Mother Russia and avoid arrest here? The holes don't line up with the pegs."

"I'm right there with you, and it won't leave me alone."

"And you want to head out to the most treacherous mountain range in Texas?"

"Yes."

"One positive is Palmer is the best survival expert out there. If anyone can track down the child, it's her. She's demonstrated a wild streak of her own." He stared at me. "You have the skills to make this another positive. But it's a huge risk."

"Trouble can happen anywhere. We're talking about an innocent child caught up in a situation out of her control. Are you giving me permission to trek out to secure the little girl's release?"

Sergio exhaled his frustration either with me or with the status of the crimes. "I have a feeling this will come back to haunt me. I'll arrange a flight for both of you tonight to Hobbs. You can stay at a hotel in New Mexico and start fresh in the morning. I'll have a vehicle for you at the airport. In the meantime, I'll do a little digging."

"A four-wheel drive sounds good."

He raised a brow. "No promises." He glared at me. "If anything happens to you, my mother will disown me. She'd trade me for you any day."

We laughed, and the tension between us disappeared. "And she'd feed me well." I stared into his face. "Odd, but I believe I'm supposed to do this. Thanks."

"Don't thank me too soon. I'm heading to the FBI with Ivanov's story. A crime's been committed, and how it's handled might have a negative impact on our relations with Russia. We'll question Jurg Falin, see where he fits with this. If the FBI has intel that pulls you out of this mission, or they send their agents with you and Therese Palmer, trust me I'm behind them. In the meantime, I want around-the-clock updates." He lifted his chin. "Don't make me contact my mother's priest for a wake."

Sergio's favorite line when he suspected where my maverick streak might lead me. My biggest concern rested with what we might find. A child had been caught up in the ploy of ruthless men, and if anyone got out of the Guadalupe Mountains alive, that person must be Alina Ivanov.

EIGHT

THERESE

Rurik called me twice before I had the go-ahead from Blane that we'd leave tonight for the Guadalupe Mountains. Shortly after lunch, I met Blane at the Texas Ranger office on West Road in Houston. He introduced me to Major Sergio Montoya who shared his reservations about our mission. He cut our conversation short due to a meeting at the FBI field office about the case.

"Who else are you telling?" I said to Major Montoya. "Rurik expressed his desire for this to be kept confidential."

"The FBI is fully equipped to keep the matter secret. They understand the life of a child is in jeopardy."

"He specifically asked *not* to contact the FBI." I hesitated. "But I trust your judgment. Do I need to alert Rurik?"

"What if he's behind the crimes? Ms. Palmer, you and Blane map out all your plans, but don't be surprised if the FBI insists on joining you or shuts this down. We might have jurisdiction in Texas, but international jurisdiction is another ball game. Oh, and don't forget to stop in at the Pine Springs Visitor Center so they're aware of your plans to enter Dog Canyon. I'll alert them to your approximate arrival. They will verify your IDs."

I shut down my thoughts to keep from telling him that once I was determined to do something, it took God to change it—not the Texas Rangers, FBI, or ROC.

"Another thing," Major Montoya said. "Jurg Falin hasn't shown up at the accounting office where he works for two days. Neither has he reported in. He has a condo, but the security cams indicate he hasn't been there since the night Rurik Ivanov overheard the phone conversation. I've issued a BOLO."

"Do you have a photo of him?" I said.

Blane shared his phone screen with me—bald, dark-blue eyes, thin lips, rectangular face.

"What about Nick Peterson?"

"He'll be here around three thirty today." Major Montoya nodded at Blane. "I'll be back to listen in on the Peterson interview. Rusty, text me if anything comes up."

The nickname fit Blane's hair color. The two men must go back a long way.

Major Montoya's phone rang. He frowned and held up his palm. "Thank you, sir. I appreciate the call." He pocketed his phone and peered at Blane, then me. "That was Houston's FBI special agent in charge. I have confidential info about Edik Baranov. What I'm about to say stays right here. Baranov not only stole military secrets, but he also hacked into the Russians' security system and stole intel regarding a critical strategic move by their military. He's made a deal for US asylum for him and his family. The Baranovs are making their way to safety. The date or the means is classified. Just keep your eyes and ears open."

Blane and I talked behind his closed office door. Adrenaline flowed between us like a high school football team an hour before the big game. We both gulped strong, black coffee like our bodies needed to keep up with the task before us.

"How long have you known Major Montoya?" I said.

Blane grinned. "Since college days. His mother calls me *mi hijo*. Great family."

My son. Now I understood why Blane insisted on seeking permission from Major Montoya—personal and professional reasons. "Did he give you the nickname Rusty?"

"That came from his dad who called me the Spanish version—*Oxidado*. Believe me, I'm not sure how this gringo snuck his way into a close-knit Mexican family. I think they pitied the kid who struggled to stay out of trouble and academically stay in college. Sergio and his dad tutored me in math all four years."

"I love math," I said. "It's the only discipline that shows order in the world."

"My go-to is anything related to human behavior . . . and guns."

I laughed. "And you have the credentials for both."

His gaze swept around his office. "What should we get settled to leave tonight?"

"I'll meet you at the airport. I need to pack and tie up a few projects."

"Me too. One call is to make arrangements at the kennel."

My longing to own a dog nibbled at my curiosity. "What kind?"

"A bit of shepherd, collie, and rottweiler."

"Name?"

He laughed. "You've shown more interest in me in the last sixty seconds than during our three dates." He grinned. "Don't worry. Not going there. In answer to your question, his name is Scully. If you're nice to me, I'll let you meet him one day." Blane yanked his phone from his pocket and showed me Scully's pic.

"He's beautiful. Look at those huge brown eyes. In the future, I plan to have a dog or two." The seriousness of what lay ahead blinded me with resolve, and I shook off the daydreaming. "Will Major Montoya keep you informed about his conversation with the FBI?"

"I made the request, and I'm sure he'll honor it unless the FBI puts a lid on it. The complications bother me more than the remote location."

"Don't underestimate the location, Blane. It's off-grid and hard to get to."

I scrolled through my phone for a map of Dog Canyon with its trails and landmarks. "Here's a glimpse of the area where we're going. It's in the northern part of the Guadalupe Mountains National Park. The contour lines indicate the elevation."

"Would you send me the link?"

I agreed and met his thanks. "Google Earth will give you the topography. I'll give you a hard copy tonight. The terrain, according to the elevation, is a mix of forests, some grassland, and the cactus-type vegetation of the high desert. The area we're heading to will be a strenuous hike and rugged." I pointed to the map on my phone. "Initially, I have off-trail places to check. If we're lucky, we'll find the kidnappers or evidence of where they're camped."

"And you have no doubts about what's ahead?" Blane said. "The more we learn, the more dangerous this looks."

"Are you thinking Alina is dead?"

"I'm concerned about what we might find."

"I've experienced tragedies." If I refused an attempt to rescue Alina, I'd lose a piece of myself. I needed to save her when I failed with Kate. And if I backed out, an old wound would open its mouth and devour me. "I gave my word, and I will not let Rurik down."

"I had to make sure. These guys play Russian roulette for kicks."

"I have five hundred thousand dollars cash from Rurik to barter with while he's putting together the rest of the ransom. The money's in my backpack, a little extra weight." I breathed in and out to clear my head. "Although the caller told Rurik he'd contact him with instructions where to direct deposit all the money, Rurik insisted I take it."

"And what if they demand more than the original amount?"

"What choice do I have? He said the cash would show his sincerity."

"Hear me out," Blane said. "We bring part of the ransom and ID whoever is behind this, what's to stop them from putting bullets in our heads?" His tone lowered. "You and I will do whatever it takes to bring the little girl home. I hope your loaded backpack doesn't backfire on us."

I blinked. "I—"

"You can't control their trigger fingers."

Those words of wisdom popped up in some form whenever I faced a dangerous mission, but they'd never stopped me from battling nature, and they wouldn't stop me from kidnappers. "I can try."

Blane gave me a tight-lipped smile, my guess to reassure me. I wanted to burst with the rage inside me for Alina, but anger solved nothing, and unfairness had existed since the beginning of time.

"Do you have a few minutes to give me an idea of what else to expect on the trail?" he said.

"Sure, and I'll fill you in more on the flight to Hobbs. I've hiked the Guadalupe Mountains many times, and I can assure you the kidnappers aren't camped on the trail. They've diverted to where they believe no one can find them. I have a few ideas where those spots might be, but searching without being spotted will be a challenge. No doubt they have someone glued to binoculars."

"I expect them to be packing high-powered firearms right along with those binoculars," he said. "Desperate people take desperate measures. I'm thinking at least two men, possibly three, and I'm trying to be positive, Therese. We must be prepared for anything to go wrong. You and I have walked into snake pits of trouble before. We can pack and plan, but two things we can't take lightly—one is greedy men who believe money trumps everything. I've seen enough of those types to understand their depravity. Alina's life is nothing more than collateral damage to them. The second is in your department—the vagaries of nature."

"Nature can be a predator too. Loose rock, a gust of wind, mountain lion, black bear, or an unsuspecting snake can be deadly." Blane had a lean and muscular body for his average height, which would be to his advantage. "Do you have experience hiking in the high desert?"

"Hiking, yes. But not high desert. I'm not a pro, so hiker terms are foreign to me. Just an FYI, I aced a wilderness-survival course taught by a seasoned professional."

I bit back a laugh. "Your lighthearted attitude will help over the next few days."

"I'll try to hold in the reins and keep it under control during our hike."

I needed survival tools to keep my attraction to Blane at arm's length. His calm, brown eyes reminded me of a walk through the woods. Oh, and his thick red hair and scruffy beard added to his rugged appeal. *Back to business, Therese.*

"Do you have medical issues like asthma, diabetes, high blood pressure, or a condition requiring medication?"

"Nope. I'm healthy. What about Alina?"

"Rurik says she's in excellent health. He's given me a change of clothes for her, a jacket, and gloves." I pointed to the phone map. "Our flight takes us to Hobbs, New Mexico. Can't get to Dog Canyon from the Texas side. It's about a four-hour-total drive time north to Carlsbad, then on to the Pine Springs Visitor Center, and Dog Canyon Campground. The temperatures will be chilly at night and windier the higher we climb."

"Are you saying, we'll share a sleeping bag to stay warm?"

I lifted my shoulders and narrowed my gaze. "Not on your life."

Blane grinned. "Prepare yourself, we'll need to sleep in shifts. I don't want a two-legged killer creeping into our campsite."

NINE

Blane's bulging backpack was propped against a corner of his office. A good brand and design to distribute the weight, and it contained a hydration bladder.

"What have you packed?" I said.

He pulled a piece of paper from his pocket. "I have the survival list you gave in class. And I've stuck to the base weight you recommended of around eighteen pounds. I've read the Guadalupe backpacking guidelines. It states there are no water sources except what we can carry from the Dog Canyon Ranger Station. They recommend a gallon of water a day per person. Sounds like we need a couple of mules and more hydration packs."

"Mules require water too. The best way to carry water is to store it in different places on us." I pointed to his backpack. "It's not my intention to insult you, but can I see what you've packed?"

"Go for it." He handed me his bag. "I've read all the suggestions, and I'd welcome your opinion. You want to start by searching me first?"

I rolled my eyes. "Just what you're carrying on your shoulders. You're responsible for yourself."

He laughed. His innuendos were funny, but why encourage him? I couldn't help myself, and this might be a huge mistake.

We scooted our nearly empty coffee mugs aside, and I unloaded his backpack on the table. True to his word, he'd packed everything we needed.

I held up the empty leather backpack. "You did a good job. Even packages of GORP." He'd need granola, oats, raisins, and peanuts for energy. "I prefer scattering my supplies over my body in case I lose something."

"I'd rather have my supplies in one place. Outside pockets make it easy to access water bottles. I wouldn't need to remove the backpack to grab a drink."

I sorted through his survival items. "I have an Iridium solar package kit to charge our satellite phones, and you have extra batteries. First aid kit is good. I have extra mule tape. Rope is a must. Also swap your shoelaces for lightweight rope."

"All right. You're the expert. I've taken a Wilderness First Aid course, and I'm a certified paramedic."

I smirked. "I read that from your file, Mr. Ranger."

He grinned, coaxing a smile from me. "I believe hiking a mile takes about thirty minutes plus another thirty minutes per one thousand feet elevation change. But we're conducting our own SAR mission. My estimation is four or five days in and out of Dog Canyon. What do you think?"

"Two factors play into the duration of our trip—how quickly we find Alina and how rough the trail."

"And if the kidnappers chase us out of there with buckshot in our rears."

"Persuasion is *your* expertise." I tipped my lips up in a half smile. "Maneuvering a child down off those steep trails will take longer." I shook my head. "How did the kidnappers manage to transport her to their destination? Rhetorical, I know. There's a helicopter pad at the Dog Canyon Park Center, but the kidnappers wouldn't risk detection or security cams. The other issue is the twelve to sixteen miles over some of those areas. Our guys will trek off-trail."

"Have you ever done a search and rescue for a child?"

"Not in an area like Dog Canyon. I've helped bring injured adults over rough terrain. We can do it. Granted, it's a challenge but not an impossibility. And although her small size is to our advantage, it may take both of us to manage her around some of the nasty switchbacks," I said. "Rurik said Alina enjoyed gymnastics and competed in contests. I believe her flexibility works to her favor. I'm a decent shot, and I'd not hesitate to save your life or Alina's."

He nodded. "Glad I'm in safe hands." His light tone shifted to a serious one. "Are you prepared for the worst outcome?"

I understood his repeated warnings, and yet voicing the possibility cut to the core of my soul. His gaze lingered on me, and I imagined his mental gears turning. "I'm not giving up on finding Alina alive. I admit some possibilities have caused a few anxious moments, like if she's crying and the kidnappers have lost patience. Rurik said she's independent. But she's got to be scared, and a panicked little girl might react in ways that might get her hurt."

Exhaustion pelted me, and we hadn't even started the hike. "I'm not using my head, Blane. A SAR team on foot often takes hours or longer to locate victims. And a helicopter needs a place to land, which is possible only if the pilot is aware of the coordinates. If not, the pilot would hover and extend a rescue harness."

"I have experience with SAR teams. Everyone does their best." Blane bounced a compass in his hand. "Do you speak Russian?" I shook my head and he continued. "Me either."

I handed him a few items to place back into his bag. "We pray no barriers to stop us."

"You've mentioned prayer twice. So you're Christian?"

"Yes, I am."

He snapped his fingers. "Your faith is why you turned down any more dates with me. I told you about my . . . problem with God."

"You're right. Faith is important to me."

"But whatever it's worth, you can add me to your prayer list. My friends who are believers will thank you. Especially Major Montoya and his family."

I had more than one job cut out for me.

His phone sounded, and he read a text. "From Sergio. He's at the

FBI office and confirmed neither Daria, Alina, nor Jurg Falin have left the country from any airport in Texas or the US. Neither have any unidentified bodies been reported. The private plane that landed at the abandoned airstrip in Hobbs is registered in Mexico." Blane rubbed his chin. "High likelihood of a cartel piloting one of their planes to aid the Russians."

The image of a man who could be guiding the kidnappers dug its heels into my thoughts. No, couldn't be him. He played for bigger stakes. "Have Major Montoya and the FBI made this conclusion?"

"Just my perception. The FBI requested the guest list from the Russian dinner party and will investigate every one of them."

My pursuit of the helpless had always been my choice, and I'd long ago accepted my wilderness-survival ventures could turn on me at any time. Russians working with a Mexican cartel. Blane's record said he spoke fluent Spanish if we met up with more than Russians. A chill rippled through me, a get-prayed-up foreboding for what lay ahead and a sense that something might go terribly wrong.

TEN

BLANE

Therese excused herself to pack for the trip, and I stared out my office window as though the busy street had the answers about whether to trust God or live life my way. Therese's faith explained why she'd walked away from a possible relationship between us months ago. My straw-thin hold on God got me into trouble once, and I refused to bridle that horse again. No lies. No phony faith. No manipulation. No good woman losing her life because of my selfishness. Only regret.

God had put two single women in my path who claimed He took top billing in their lives. I wrestled with my feelings for Therese, Wendy's death, and where I stood with the God-thing. Rather wrestle a bear. Sergio said I had a mule streak when it came to God, and one day I'd see the truth—if it wasn't too late.

Shaking off my emotions branded with rejection, I turned my attention to the mission. I had extra time before Sergio arrived for Nick Peterson's interview, and I dug deeper into Jurg Falin's background. He'd arrived in Houston to work at an accounting firm almost five years ago, not long after Rurik Ivanov and his family arrived. Nothing in his background raised a red flag. Outstanding work record. Well-liked. Single. Paid his bills.

My office phone buzzed. Nick Peterson had arrived and waited with Sergio. I closed my laptop and hurried to his office.

Peterson sat across from Sergio, fidgeting. Wild-colored hair in purple and orange hung to his shoulders. This morning the security cams showed his hair in a man-bun and under a baseball cap. His teeth held more spaces than my grandmother's picket fence, but he practiced the value of a timely appointment. Unless he complied immediately out of fear.

I kept my gaze on Peterson, who refused to meet Sergio's eyes. I bit my lip to hide a grin.

"Mr. Peterson," Sergio said, "your image was videoed this morning at 6:17 at the drive-through window of The Breakfast Brew restaurant on I-45 North. You were seen talking to a man through your passenger window who gave you an envelope."

Peterson inhaled, choked, and coughed for several seconds. "Yes, sir. I was waiting in line when this guy tapped on my window. I powered it down to hear him out. He said he'd just received an emergency call from his wife and would I make sure Professor Ivanov inside the restaurant received an envelope. He stuck out a white, legal-size envelope with Professor Ivanov's name typed on it. All I had to do was give it to the person at the food-delivery window."

"And you agreed, no questions asked?"

"Not at first. Told him I needed to get to work. He received a text and said his son had fallen, and his wife had called an ambulance. I'm a good guy and took the envelope."

"Weren't you concerned about the contents?"

"No. Wasn't fat like it had a bomb inside."

Sergio ran his fingers through his jet-black hair. "Then what happened?"

"The man dashed across the parking lot and behind the restaurant out of sight. At the drive-through window, I asked the kid to deliver the envelope. He refused. Left me no choice but to park my car and deliver it myself. I gave it to a server." He blew out a huff. "Later someone from your office called me at work, and here I am."

Sergio gave me a chin lift to take over.

"Mr. Peterson, we appreciate your coming in to help us identify a possible criminal. We respect good citizens. Can you describe the man who gave you the envelope?"

"Not really."

"Why is that?"

Peterson's gaze darted from me to Sergio. "I'd been smoking to calm my nerves. Takes the edge off at work. Stress rattles me."

"I understand. Our jobs are often demanding. What were you smoking?"

"Uh, medical marijuana."

Wonderful. "Can you describe the man? The sound of his voice? Anything will help."

"Medium build. Black hoodie pulled down over his eyes. Mustache and trimmed beard."

A lot of info for a man who claimed he didn't notice much. "What about his age?"

"I'd say early to late thirties."

"Nationality or accent?"

Peterson shook his head. "Nothing unusual there."

"Had you ever met or seen the man?"

"I've told you everything. I didn't see his car or anyone with him."

I scrolled through my phone for a pic of Jurg Falin. "Do you recognize this man?"

Peterson peered into the screen. "No." He hesitated.

"Got a memory flash? I get it, buddy. When we're upset or in panic mode, we have problems firing straight." I used my best tone to show I held no grudges, only caring.

"Uh. He gave me a hundred-dollar bill and said not to tell anyone."

"Do you have the money with you?"

"I spent it at lunch."

"Must have been an expensive restaurant. Where did you go?"

"I said I spent it at lunch."

I guessed what the hundred dollars had bought and questioned the validity of Peterson's statement.

ELEVEN

As the clock hit 7:41 p.m., Therese and I hurried to board our flight from Houston to Hobbs, New Mexico—just two hours in the air, but more than enough time for everything to go wrong. We'd gain an hour as we crossed over to Mountain Time, which would make the early morning start a bit easier. We stuffed our backpacks into an overhead bin and fastened our seat belts. The early day's activities had taken a chunk out of my normal energy level, but I'd rest after we returned Alina to her father.

Within minutes, we were in the air and connected to Wi-Fi. The closeness to Therese sent my emotions into areas that needed to be padlocked. Safe to admit I hadn't gotten over her, and spending the next few days with her made me want a relationship more than ever.

"What can you tell me about your interview with Nick Peterson?" Therese lowered her tray to prop up her iPad.

I shared the details.

"You believed him?"

I shrugged. "Maybe. Peterson and the security cams can't ID him, but Sergio warned Peterson to take precautions. The ROC isn't a team of Boy Scouts."

"Do you have the clearance to receive updates?"

"Sergio will do his best."

Therese didn't frown, but she didn't smile either. "All I've put into my brain about the ROC is they are Russian bad guys, and I haven't had time to search online. What can you tell me?"

"It's not just one organization but several who may or may not be from Russia. Often the members are Eastern European and use the ROC name as a fear factor. Many launder money in the US for Russians who are apprehensive their government will confiscate their funds, using whatever methods necessary. Other groups accomplish criminal activities through various businesses. They are connected but work under a loose structure. They're like any other organized crime—they use modern technology and control through internal and external violence around the world."

She nodded. "Where does Edik Baranov fit?"

I snorted. "With the Russian government's charges against him, he made a smart move to get his family out of Dodge. My opinion? If Falin and his ROC boys kill Baranov, the Russians will declare them heroes."

She tilted her head as though working through all I'd said. "Not sure I trust Rurik."

I laid my Stetson on my lap. "He says his daughter means everything to him, but what about his loyalty to Russia? We don't have the full picture, and until we do, we ride this storm out."

"Incredibly complex. I need to do a better job of keeping up with world affairs other than a daily scan of the headlines."

"I understand." Reality nudged me. "One thing keeps picking at me—the ROC got wind of what Rurik overheard from Falin at the dinner party. So why didn't they take out the whole family and leave the bodies as an example?"

She shivered, her oval face clouded with concern.

We were on the same page in many areas. "Where does the ransom fit? Unless it's a ploy to keep us in the dark? Which makes me wonder if the real issue is not the money but the ROC wanting him to do something, or they'll kill his daughter like they did his wife."

She stared at her phone. "I'm sorry for thinking the worst about Rurik, like I should apologize. He shook most of the time we talked to him today, and you were amazing in your conversation. So much caring about what he'd gone through."

"He visibly grieved the loss of his wife and missing daughter. That's why I'm here."

"Me too. A little girl in trouble needs all I can do to help."

If an innocent child was involved in a political tug-of-war, no one had better leave me alone with the kidnappers. No matter who was responsible.

"We're quite the rescue team," I said. "I'd give my right arm for the names of those kidnappers."

"Maybe I've heard of them. I'll keep thinking." She tossed me a weary smile. "You look exhausted. And I'm operating on fumes."

A look at her drawn features and a few fine lines around her eyes confirmed they'd endured the same grueling type of day. "We'll get a good night's sleep and search tomorrow. Leaving at five a.m. stretches my beauty sleep, but I'm looking forward to a Guadalupe Mountain sunrise."

She massaged her neck muscles. "Part of the road there is free range, so we'll also need to keep our eyes open for cattle and deer."

I nodded. "Cattle I can manage from the time I spent working on my uncle's ranch. Negotiating with potential terrorists is a game of wits, and I thrive on the challenge."

"Well, a challenge you will get," she said. "Dog Canyon's labyrinthine structure disorients many hikers. People can wander around dehydrated, suffer with the warm temps during the day and the freezing temps at night, until they find help or die."

"Like you, I've given all I had to a situation only to find a victim dead," I said.

She swallowed hard. "Those incidents haunt me for months. Where did you receive your training before becoming a Ranger?"

"Total of ten years with Houston Police Department and the Texas Department of Safety. I was attracted to the Rangers' versatility, and not once have I regretted my decision. I went from riding broncs and stopping bad guys to negotiating with them."

"How long have you been with them?" she said.

"Six years in January."

"You've accomplished a lot. I read your personnel report during the time I taught the survival class."

"Did you think I was hot?" I bit back a chuckle at her look of surprise.

"I examined every Ranger's background." She fought to hide a hint of a smile.

"I'll bet mine was the most impressive."

She laughed. "Oh, of course. I'd forgotten about your humility and incredible charm."

"Therese, we need sleep."

TWELVE

THERESE

At 5:00 a.m., I waved at Blane in the hotel lobby, his mass of rusty-red hair wet from the shower. And hosting a cowboy grin minus his Texas Ranger gear.

"You look rested," I said.

"You mean I'm not wearing saddlebags under my eyes?"

"I call them pits, but your description works."

He'd opted for hiking pants, a brand with sun protection and water-resistant. A long-sleeved shirt with the same qualities, hiking boots, a puffer jacket with a hood tossed over his arm, and a backpack. A wide-brimmed sun hat sat angled on his head, giving him a seasoned hiker flair. I sorta missed the Stetson. His five-pointed-star badge must be in his zippered pants pocket. A Ranger never went anywhere without it. He'd listened in class those months ago, and together we looked like pro hikers.

We filled paper cups with the hotel's freshly brewed coffee.

"I have a favor to ask," he said in his best Texan drawl. "Would you drive since you're familiar with the area?"

"Sure."

He tossed me the keys, and we set out on US Highway 180 to find Alina and scale whatever obstacles the kidnappers placed in our way.

If the sun had been up, we'd have taken the extra time to stop at the abandoned airstrip south of Hobbs to scan the area.

"I'm sure the wind has blown dust and dirt across most of the tracks of a private aircraft, vehicle tire tracks, or footprints," Blane said. "Sergio told me the FBI are on their way to the landing strip this morning."

"Their own agenda?"

"He said the FBI questioned and requestioned Rurik. A search team was assigned to his home, office, and car. I'm glad they and the Rangers are investigating this with technology that you and I can't carry in our backpacks."

"How—?" I swerved the Jeep to miss a male deer leaping across the road.

Blane whistled. "He has a huge set of racks. Anyway, you were about to say something."

I righted the vehicle. "How did Rurik handle the FBI?"

"Not well, but we expected his protest."

"Is the FBI hands-off with what we're doing?"

"Depends on how long it takes us and what we find. Whatever they uncover on their end could influence our path forward."

"What have you learned about Jurg Falin?"

"Nothing more. He might be with Alina." Blane gulped his coffee. Silence fell between us for a moment. "Why do you risk your life on dangerous ventures?"

Memories haunted me of my little sister, but I'd keep that to myself. "A deep conviction to help others survive physical challenges."

"Sounds more like you belong in the medical field."

"Hmm." I stared at the road ahead. "Above rescue and teaching survival skills, I consider myself a guide for a person to achieve greater things, to instill confidence, inspire, encourage, and find a relationship with God."

"That's admirable, Therese."

I tossed a sideways glance his way. Sarcasm?

"I'm serious. You're bigger than life. In the little time I've spent with you, I've seen you demonstrate inner strength. You're fearless."

I slid a grin at him. "Am I living up to the Davina Crockett legend?"

"You got wind of that?"

"Yep. And I haven't wrestled any bears. Yet."

"Where did the story come from?"

"I taught a private group wilderness-survival skills. One of the sessions focused on staying alive by eating bugs. So I proved it to them. Never swam in crocodile-infested waters, but I once dove into a Florida swamp to save a drowning woman who'd fallen out of a boat." I shrugged. "Between the alligator and the water moccasin, I got a bit too close to their open mouths for my comfort."

"Wow. I'm impressed."

"Just needed to set the story straight. Seriously, I try to build my clients' self-esteem through physical activity." I paused. "Thanks for risking your life and reputation to find Alina."

"I'm ready to bring a little girl home, like you are."

"This mutual-admiration moment might shatter with what's ahead."

"Neither of us want a partner who doesn't contribute their thoughts and expertise. Together, we'll tackle the job and face the trials."

Blane's professional preparedness had my attention. I'd read about his background, and I had seen his leadership in action, but I didn't know he had expertise about hiking over rugged terrain.

"Excitement is racing through me, just like you said last night," Blane said. "We can't get there fast enough."

"Would you like for me to speed things up?"

He huffed. "We're already flying faster than sound. What's the one thing you can tell me about the high desert other than staying hydrated?"

I focused on the gray highway. "I'd say get used to scorpions and centipedes. They aren't your friends—neither are they good sleeping companions."

"Thanks for the tip. If we're looking at only two men, then one is the kidnapper and the other is a guide who's skilled in survival techniques, a specialist like you."

I'd encountered few evil people in my line of work, mostly those struggling to survive against incredible odds.

He talked on. "Another question is, who flew the plane? Is the person one of the men holding Alina, or are there three men like Rurik speculated?" Blane blew out his exasperation. "Sergio and the FBI suspect a cartel member. What a mess of unanswered questions."

My heart thudded against my chest, and my ears sounded warning alarms. "Blane, what have I been thinking? We're looking at a man who understands surviving in the high desert and has no value for human life. I've thought of little but who that person could be. One who can pilot a plane with strong connections to the cartel. That's him."

He swung to me like I'd spoken an alien language. "You have a name for someone who has those characteristics?"

I swallowed hard, fear creeping up my throat. "I've had two dealings with a man fitting that description. Nasty. Cruel. He uses different aliases and disguises, making it easy to escape the authorities all over the southwest. He's wanted for murders and a suspect in other violent crimes. He runs guns for a cartel, steals whatever he needs and whatever else brings him money."

Blane grabbed his phone. "Name?"

"His signature calling card is a peregrine falcon feather." Scaling a cliff was easier than sorting through names. "Rumors are he chose the bird of prey because of its hunting skills and incredible speed." His image confronted my sanity. "He has a nasty scar down the right side of his face. I swore I'd never forget Chan—"

"Are you talking about Tom Chandler? His criminal activities are usually associated with the cartel. He's like a chameleon and deadlier than a lit fuse." He snapped his fingers. "He flies his own plane in and out of Mexico and South America. Why would he take on a kidnapping unless the ROC have more at stake than the conversation Rurik overheard?"

"Chandler has the skills to pull this off." I grabbed my coffee from the cupholder and finished it. I'd hoped, no prayed, I'd never see Chandler again except a photo of him cuffed in police custody. "He's memorized every rock and bush of the Guadalupe Mountains."

"If Chandler flew the kidnappers here, he wasn't involved in the murder or kidnapping, or he'd have left a feather." Blane pressed in numbers on his phone. "I'm texting Rurik to find out."

How could one demonic man be involved in this?

Blane's phone sounded with a text. "He says, no, and asked why." Again Blane typed into his phone. "I told him we had a possible suspect but nothing concrete."

I stuck a loose strand from my ponytail behind my ear. "If it's Chandler, they paid him well."

"He's a piece of work—arrogant. Would double-cross his own mother." Blane's worry lines deepened around his eyes. "Chandler doesn't release hostages."

I shivered. "Makes me sick."

"What were your dealings with him?"

Not exactly a fond memory. "Happened about four years ago. A man had gotten lost while hiking Mount Whitney in California. His hiking partners called for help, and I led a search team. We found him unconscious off an icy trail. He'd encountered Chandler, who'd stolen his backpack and shot him in the leg. Left him to bleed out.

"While some of the men tended to his injuries and prepared to carry the hiker to safety, I led two armed men to hunt for Chandler. At the time I had no idea what he looked like, only had the wounded hiker's description." I gripped the steering wheel of the Jeep. "I'll never forget those beady, near-black eyes, fitting for a peregrine. We heard gunfire and backtracked to find he'd ambushed those we'd left behind. A man ordered Chandler to drop his weapon. He whirled around and fired at him. I kicked the gun out of his hand. Took him down. He bested me, retrieved his gun, and got away. I have a scar on my left arm where I survived a bullet. I had a knife in my boot, and . . . I gave him the scar on his face." I couldn't stop my body from shuddering. "Anyway, the hiker and two other men didn't make it."

"I've heard tales, and none of them give me any reassurance. I understand he likes to taunt his prey, then tells them exactly what he will do to them. He despises women."

I gripped the steering wheel and hoped Blane didn't notice my terror. "I had my hair up and wore a full-face hat in the cold."

"Probably what kept you alive. I'm sorry. If he's with Alina and the kidnapper, we'll need our guns more than negotiating skills."

"There's more. Later in the news, my name came out. I'm sure he's not forgotten me." I sent a silent prayer to the One who routinely out-negotiated the devil.

He used his phone and greeted Major Montoya. Blane relayed that Tom Chandler might be involved in Alina's abduction. "Would you check out Chandler's latest whereabouts and get back to me?" Blane waited while Major Montoya talked. "Right. I'd be interested in learning if the city's security cams link him with Rurik Ivanov, Jurg Falin, or any Russians who might have had a hand in this." He waited again. "Yes, and a link between the cartel and Russians might open this up more. Check security cams in Texas and New Mexico around these mountains."

Blane listened to his major. "Did the security cams around Alina's school grounds give us anything? Any cams that traced Daria's route home or passengers? What about security cams from the homes around the Ivanovs'?" He gazed at me, no doubt repeating what Major Montoya had said for my benefit. I wished I'd heard the major's words firsthand.

Blane laid his phone on the Jeep's console. "Nothing at this point."

"Why did Daria pick up Alina from school when she obviously didn't spend time with her? And how did her decision affect her murder and Alina's kidnapping?"

"You and I are experts at asking questions without answers. Those will come just like rain when we need it most."

"Thanks for the vote of confidence. You do know high altitude affects memory."

"But not a seasoned wilderness-survival expert like you."

"Hey, Jack."

Blane's deep-throated laugh tickled the soles of my feet. I hadn't met a man in a long time who tugged at my emotions like Blane Gardner.

"Another tidbit is the FBI is giving us twenty-four hours to locate Alina. Or they're sending in their own sniper and rescue team."

"No surprise there. But we have a head start."

"Sergio said most info about Edik Baranov was above my pay grade, a matter the FBI's handling. But one thing he could tell me." He paused. "Ready for this, partner? Rurik Ivanov and Edik Baranov are first cousins."

I startled. "Rurik acted like Edik was a stranger."

"Might have been intentional."

THIRTEEN

BLANE

Even when approaching danger, I always admired a sunrise streaking across the horizon. The sun had begun its ascent in blended, chalklike pastels of yellow, orange, and light purple—a landscape that paled in every art galley's replication. I let the beauty relax me when my phone rang. Sergio's name lit up the screen, breaking the silence of the long drive toward the looming Guadalupe Mountains.

"Yes, sir." I mouthed *Major Montoya* in Therese's direction. "Is it okay if Therese listens to this?" He agreed, and I laid the phone on the console. I pressed the speaker button.

"Thank you," she said to Sergio.

"No problem. Our buddy Rurik gets deeper and deeper into this mess. Were you aware of his relationship to Baranov?"

"No clue," Therese said. "His secrets are . . . frustrating. Since he and Baranov are cousins, is the prime minister also related to Rurik?"

"Rurik's on the other side of the family. We've confirmed Tom Chandler and one other man are somewhere in the Dog Canyon region. Yesterday evening, Chandler drove into Dog Canyon in a white Dodge pickup, extended cab. The security cam videoed enough of his face for the FBI to run facial recognition. One other unidentified person was with him. Could be Jurg Falin. And if Alina sat in the rear seat, the camera didn't pick her up. The truck belongs to a man from Carlsbad who reported it stolen two days ago. The owner's clean."

"Has Rurik wired funds to anyone?" Therese said.

"Yes, from his Houston bank account. The FBI is running down his overseas accounts. Another thing, Rusty. The FBI has prepared a SAR team and will soon be en route, expediting their earlier estimated arrival."

I licked my lips. "Can you buy us any time?"

"No. Already went that route. Other things are brewing. Things I can't relay to you, but it's deeper than you and I discussed."

Compassion washed over me for Therese. "A part of me says we can use all the manpower available. But if Chandler sees a team of heavy guns, he'll kill Alina. He or another man will make good on Rurik never seeing Alina again."

"You are hours ahead of the FBI to negotiate with the kidnappers, and you have the best guide out there. You two have your own big guns."

"We'll do our best." I glanced at Therese, but she kept her attention on the road.

"Keep me posted. This is critical," Sergio said.

I slipped my phone back into my jeans pocket. Reservations about seeing this through successfully bit into my ego.

"Do we approach this any differently?" she said.

"Hold on to your thought. First, I need to find everything out there about Chandler. Figure out how his reasoning affects his actions."

"Good idea. I won't speak until you're ready to talk."

I tossed her a smile, and the one she gave me lifted my spirits higher than the mountains ahead of us. I logged into a secured site and typed in my authorization creds.

Chandler's background history met my scrutiny, and I read every word. His life experiences shaped the man who had victimized so many people.

"Chandler didn't have much of a chance from the moment he

was born. Genetically, his father, now deceased, was a psychopath. His drug-addicted mother abandoned him at the age of three, and his maternal grandmother took him in. She was the only positive influence in his life. According to an interview the grandmother gave Social Services, his mother beat him, leaving horrible scars. She also neglected to feed him. At age four he started speaking, but the signs of abuse were there. He wet the bed late into childhood, started fires for fun, truant in school, and cruel to animals. She encouraged him to study and urged him to play sports, but he refused to do the schoolwork or comply with the rules. We're looking at a means to understand him. Put our feet into his shoes and find his weaknesses."

Therese squeezed the steering wheel. "His past is horrendous, but none of it justifies his horrific choices."

"Chandler was under the care of a psychiatrist off and on from age six through fourteen. Then he rejected the sessions. By age sixteen, he'd been sentenced twice to juvenile state-supported rehabs. A psychiatrist who treated him in his early teen years claimed Chandler needed medication for his violence, but the kid refused. By the time he turned eighteen, there were countless warrants for his arrest. The crimes ranged from theft, drunk and disorderly, assault with a deadly weapon, person of interest in murders, and several miscellaneous atrocities committed against those who fell prey to his endless displays of torture. His IQ is 137."

Therese exhaled a heavy sigh. "He made the choices of a predator, but the problem already existed. Choosing a peregrine feather fits the bird's traits."

"People with antisocial personality disorder are usually highly intelligent and manipulative." This was the man Therese and I faced? The lines across her forehead showed me Chandler terrified her. "Do you want to abandon our pursuit?"

"No." She set her jaw. "I made my decision in Houston. Any other info?"

"When Chandler was twenty-two, his grandmother died in a car accident. He blamed the police officer, stating the officer failed to call 911 in time. His grief sent him on a rampage—he robbed a liquor store and killed a clerk. When the police looked for him, he killed two officers."

"Deadly decisions. Any other relationships that offer insight?" she said.

"No family—male or female—mentioned. Prefers high-end living in areas of the world decent people avoid. No-questions-asked and anything-goes clubs appeal to his lust. No permanent address, except authorities have their eye on an area outside of Mexico City. Authorities are searching for overseas accounts. Nothing connects him to the ROC, and he apparently operates independently for the right price."

Nothing jumped out to offer in exchange for Alina or a way to lure him into a trap—but money.

"Blane, why an area where food and water mean life, and money means nothing?"

"He could have something valuable hidden in Dog Canyon." I shrugged. "The question is, what and why?"

"How does what you've learned affect negotiations?"

"I'm thinking. His grandmother was his only lifeline. From his past, it looks like my negotiation skills will be useless. The only way to stop him is with a gun pointed at his chest. But I have to try."

FOURTEEN

THERESE

I drove through Carlsbad, taking in the autumn sunrise over the high desert—a radiant scene that felt like a praise song spreading inspiration across the sky. The farther I drove, the sight gave way to a clear blue canopy, a perfect shade like Kate and Alina's eyes. Maple and oak trees welcomed us, weighted with their display of shimmering gold, orange, and scarlet. Their vibrancy was a sharp contrast to the rock that lay in higher elevations.

The terrain gave way to cactus, rocky pastureland, open-range cattle—animals that wore colors of black, brown, burnt orange, and some were speckled. Three mule deer froze in place and gave us a brief nod before scampering into a shield of color. We were the intruders. They were home. A part of the wilderness that I valued and revered.

My mind clicked like a photographer's lens, sealing incredible views into my life's album. The Jeep climbed higher, and the forest gave way to loose rocks, creosote, occasional sage, pinyon pine, sierra juniper, prickly pear, and my favorite soap tree yucca that led up to layers of multishaded gray peaks, many of them rounded like bulging muscles.

Not a cloud in the sky, although a storm chased a frightened little girl.

I drove the Jeep around horseshoe curves confronting more of the same rugged high desert landscape. Caves and shadows drew my attention as potential hideouts, and we'd encounter more once the hiking began.

At the Dog Canyon Visitor's Center, the ranger station and home were deserted. A sign alerted park visitors of the Indian Meadow Nature Trail at the base of the mountains. Across from the sign, campers had space to set up tents or dry camping, but none were there. We stopped to fill our water bottles and drank plenty of water while examining the desolate surroundings—"camel-up," as the park rangers said.

The dry air met my nostrils, a familiar and welcoming scent. The air and sixty-degree temps served as a reminder that the higher we climbed, the gustier the winds. Temps dropped at night, but we were prepared.

I drove slowly past the horse corral that doubled as a helicopter pad—fitting with the number of horses grazing around the fenced area. I continued until I found a lone spot off a small clearing near the hiker trailhead and cut the engine. Totally desolate. No signs of life anywhere.

"What did Chandler do with the Dodge pickup?" Blane said. "If the second person in the truck drove it out of the park, we'd have the security footage."

Thinking like a criminal was way out of my norm. "Did he hide the truck somewhere in the area?"

"If so, it can't be far." Blane tossed me a serious look. "Let the Feds figure out the where and how."

"I agree. I told Rurik I'd call him when we left the Jeep and headed out on foot." We stepped out of the vehicle, and I used my satellite phone to inform the professor of our arrival.

"You will call me the moment you find her, right?" His weak voice showed his lack of sleep and emotional status.

"Yes. Blane and I received new information. Why didn't you tell us that Edik Baranov is your cousin?"

"It's too complicated."

"Really? Every crime that's been committed or planned is wrapped around your cousin. Oh yes, it's complicated, especially when I have no reason to believe you're not one of the bad guys. Did you pay the ransom when you were advised against it?"

"I paid the three million plus what I've already given you."

Fury sparked in me. "And where do we find Alina since the kidnappers have their demands?"

"I don't know!"

How could I stay angry when I'd have done anything to heal Kate? Blane must have sensed my warring emotions and asked to speak to Rurik. I handed him my phone.

"Sir, Therese and I are upset at your unwillingness to provide needed info. But we are committed to finding Alina. The FBI is a part of the case due to varied implications. I encourage you to cooperate in every way possible. Has anything else happened that we need to be aware of?" Blane's gaze flew to me. "Have you alerted the FBI about the third call?"

My patience with one-sided conversations had met its limit, and my patience with Rurik plunged into a canyon.

"Only you can make the decision. Therese and I are supporting Alina . . . We'll keep in touch." He glanced at me. "I'll tell her of your apology. Take care of yourself. You have our cell and satellite phone numbers." Blane returned my device.

"What's going on?" I drew in a quick breath. Spouting off at Blane solved nothing.

"The man who previously contacted Rurik phoned about three this morning. He questioned why the FBI had stuck their nose into the ROC and Rurik's private business. I suspect the ROC spotted the Feds snooping around his house and the university."

I groaned. "What did Rurik tell him?"

"That he'd been mistaken."

"Doubtful the caller believed him."

"Right. The caller repeated that seeing Alina again was up to Rurik. The money meant nothing when he'd gone to the FBI. The FBI put a tracer on Rurik's cell phone."

"Are the Feds aware of the burner phone he used to call me?"

"What do you think?"

I tapped my fingers on the steering wheel. "I'd love to hear about an arrest anytime now. Why didn't Rurik tell one of us about the call early this morning?"

"He has Mule Syndrome. No one's going to tell him what to do," Blane said. "We can't trust him, but our mission is Alina. I suspect law enforcement is two steps behind whoever is responsible. We have no time to lose."

"We're a team. I have experience with nature's challenges, but you have insight into negotiations and behavior."

"No stress whatsoever." He narrowed his gaze. "Let's go find Alina."

"Exactly." I tossed Blane the keys. "You can keep these until we drive out of here with Alina."

He opened the Jeep's door. "I'll zipper them in my backpack."

We shrugged on our gear and positioned our water bottles—Blane had finally seen the wisdom of scattering supplies if it only meant the water.

"I'd like to cover a lot of ground before making camp tonight," I said.

He stared up at the rocky terrain littered with loose limestone. "You lead out on the off-trails, and I'll keep up. I'd appreciate it if along the way, you'd show me how to read any signs or evidence."

"My pleasure. I won't even charge for the tutorial."

With his familiar chuckle, we followed a narrow, rocky path into the secluded area. At the base of the trail, we removed trekking poles from our backpacks. I peered up at the cloudless blue, then bowed my head. We needed divine guidance, direction, safety, and help finding Alina. And staying alive.

"Are you praying?" Blane said softly.

I lifted my head. "I asked for safety and wisdom."

"We need both. Glad one of us is on speaking terms with God."

What's preventing you? I stopped myself from speaking aloud. *Please show Blane Your power and love, Lord.*

While we maintained a strong pace, parched earth, loose gravel, and sharp rock became the norm. A sudden slip or heavy burst of wind could send one of us over the edge and to our death below. But I'd rather struggle with the familiarity of nature than the likes of Tom Chandler.

I gazed at the towering peaks holding up the sky and breathed in the crisp, earthy smell—purity and a blend of freshness. "I love the mountains."

"You're not afraid?"

"Depends on how you define fear. For me exploring new territory and revisiting special places is a type of respect, a mix of love and fear." I swung another look at the sky. "Like how I feel about God."

He scowled. "Must everything have a God-response?"

"Most of the time."

"Am I going to hear about God the whole time we're together?"

I wanted to stand bold in my faith but not chase him away from seeking a personal relationship with Him. "I'd rather show you faith in action."

"Hmm. Okay. Deal. Ever have any doubts?"

"Sometimes."

"I assumed you never backed off from your faith."

"If a Christian ever tells you his or her faith never wavers, he's lying."

"Come to think of it, Sergio has mentioned his faith giving him a kick in the rear when life goes south."

We hiked higher, and the wind blew a brisk chill. Desolation spread in all directions, but I valued the sights and sounds. Indications of a past summer fire caught my attention with charred black bark and the stubbled remains of trees. In the heat of summer, the wind rubbing the dry grasses together often caused a spark that burned acres of wood and shrub, causing damage to all things growing and wildlife. But nature needed fires to regrow plants, which provided wildlife's food and increased the water supply.

"Have you explored the caves?" he said. "Just thinking about places for Chandler to hide."

"The Apache nation revere them as sacred."

"Meaning we can't check them out?"

"I respect all Native Americans and avoiding the caves is an unwritten agreement. But if I think Alina's in a cave, I'm heading in."

A few minutes later, he pointed to a spindly soap tree yucca, which flourished in abundance. "Soap tree?"

"Right. Originally used by Native Americans to make soap. They took the fibers from the leaves to weave mats, baskets, and sandals. It can even be fed to cattle during a drought."

"Thanks. I'm getting educated," he said. "Uh, tell me if we come across any scat whose owners might not want me trespassing. What little scat I know is cat and bear."

I laughed. "Sure thing."

He pointed out different shrubs, and I had difficulty believing he didn't have names for all of them. His ranch-life experience must not have been in the high desert. So I gave him the info—creosote, honey mesquite, sierra juniper, straw-colored broom snakeweed, side oats grama, wild rue, silverleaf nightshade with its poisonous berries, and alligator juniper, named for its bark's resemblance to alligator skin. His questions kept me busy and my mind off the dangers ahead. Made the hiking easier, and we had miles to go before finding any traces of Chandler.

"Are your parents living?" Blane said. "The conversations on our three dates weren't about your family."

He'd not let me forget how I'd damaged his pride. "No."

"Siblings?"

The question slapped me hard. "A sister, but she died a long time ago. I have a cousin who is a trusted friend."

"Is that person a wilderness gal like you?"

I grinned while I shook my head. "She's into piano, plays at a small church west of San Antonio."

"Looks to me like nature is part of your family too. Good times and not so good, but you still love them."

"Well said. And yes, my respect for nature mirrors my love of family. Thank goodness rocks and trees don't talk."

"Imagine the stories they'd use to blackmail us."

I stopped and pointed to a bull elk making his procession through the underbrush. His kingly stance gave him a regal look, and his rack served as his crown. "If I were alone, I'd be snapping pics."

"Something we have in common. I'd be taking photos to paint later."

I faced him. "Really? What medium?"

"Oil."

We continued to hike. "How did you develop an interest in painting?"

"Ah, she probes deeper." A few seconds passed. "I see my painting, specifically of landscapes and animals, as an expression of a longing in my soul. A means of putting emotions into words."

This new insight into Blane stirred up the attraction I'd fought to suppress. Not at all what I'd expected. "Do you sell your work?"

"At times. Why do you take pics?"

I struggled with transparency, then braved forward. "Photography is not my sweet spot. It merely serves to jog my memory about places I've visited and treasured. The wild is a worshipful experience, and I want to capture a snippet of God's creativity."

"If you pick out a favorite photo, I'd be glad to paint it." His sincerity infused every word.

"We can come back another time," I said. "Right now, our lives are bombarded by evil men."

"We'll have to steal away, then. In my world, every day is filled with bad guys."

FIFTEEN

Six miles into Dog Canyon, and Blane and I hiked at a steady pace. The smell of the high desert filled my nostrils, and the distinct tapping of a woodpecker made me smile. Normally, I'd be listening and whistling back to the various birds, the magnificent, blue and black Steller's jay with its rather harsh five quick *shook, shook, shook, shook, shook*. Sometimes the bird had a harsher call, and at times it mimicked a red-tailed hawk. A male rusty-sided spotted towhee with its chorus of high-pitched trills offered his song.

A chorus of others serenaded us, but I kept my attention on any indication of humans trekking the same path. In my world, I enjoyed the beauty unfolding around us, yet my troubled emotions for Alina stopped any appreciation today.

We veered off the trail, then backtracked. I wanted to believe we were getting closer, but enthusiasm no longer powered my steps. Nothing pointed to Chandler's trail. Every moment weighed against a little girl's life. Of course not. Why should it? We were waging a war of wits.

I concentrated on Tom Chandler's habits and characteristics. He would have headed to the most desolate area in Dog Canyon. He'd hike in obscure places and push whoever was with him. I wouldn't be surprised if he'd strapped Alina to his back. He'd move from one rock to another. How would Blane handle the rough terrain? What if one of us got sick? Or hurt? What if Alina had gotten sick or hurt and been abandoned to die?

Chandler paralyzed my confidence, more like a huge boulder of angst casting doubt on my abilities to track him. He'd repeatedly evaded law enforcement. Tales were told of him chasing away mountain cats and eating a rattler raw. With a reputation like that and my own near-death experience with him, the sound of his name terrorized me.

The more notions attacking me, the more frightening the outcome. Those fears originated from the evil one, not God, and I prayed hard for wisdom and insight into what lay ahead. Preparedness ranked as a priority, and there I'd stay—and do my best to stay on mission.

Shaking my head to rid myself of the unwelcome thoughts, I turned to view Blane over my shoulder. "Talk to me."

"What do you want to hear? I can't sing."

"I thought all cowboys sang."

"I'm a Ranger and we don't all have music encoded in our DNA."

"What do you see as your life purpose?"

"Is this a trick question?" Blane said. "Or is conversation a means to ease the stress?"

"Knowing each other better strengthens trust."

"I agree one hundred percent. No argument there. My life purpose is unfolding. I have career goals to teach other Rangers negotiation skills. I believe training and prep helps build confidence in trials."

"Outstanding. Where does your risk factor come from?"

"That *is* in my DNA. I come from a family of law enforcement—my dad, uncle, two brothers, and my mom retired from Houston PD."

"Competitive, tough. Family get-togethers must be interesting."

"My mom is the only exception. She's quiet, likes to cook, garden, and paint. Hard to think of her working violent crimes."

"Do they ever relax, other than your mom?"

"Sure. We're just regular people who regard the law and keep people safe. Your turn. What's your life purpose?"

"You're looking at it. Showing others how to survive in the wilderness and rescuing those who have allowed nature to gain the upper hand."

"Dreams of a family one day?"

"Maybe. Depends if the right man comes along."

"I'm working on it."

I gave him my best glare. "We are polar opposites."

"But opposites attract and make the best long-term partners."

I shook my head. "We'll talk about it this time next year."

"It's on the calendar."

We hiked on. The diversion worked . . . at least for the present. I set my dread of Chandler aside, and we explored an area a quarter mile wide. Not a thing caught Blane's or my attention, and he had good instincts.

Had I lost all thought of logic in thinking we'd find Alina today?

I bent to the ground to examine three-inch-wide animal tracks.

"What did you find?" Blane said.

"Mountain lion tracks." He joined me and I showed him the distinctive markings. "I'm sure you've seen these before, but this is one large cat. See the three lobes at the bottom of the pad and the teardrop-shaped toes? Fortunately, these cats avoid humans unless they feel threatened."

"I came across one near Lubbock. I yelled, and the cat took off—" His satellite phone sounded, and he answered.

The call lasted a few minutes, and Blane's responses were comprised of mostly "yes," "how long?" and "thank you." He stuffed his phone back into a zippered pants pocket, and I eyed him about the caller. "Sergio?"

"Yep. It's not good, Therese."

My pulse sped. Rurik? Alina? "I'm ready."

"The sheriff's department found the remains of a woman west of Houston in a burned car that was identified as Daria's—what was left of it. At this point, the body hasn't been identified, but it makes sense it's her. The victim had a bullet hole in the chest, a 9mm. Badly burned, and her teeth had been pulled, which means confirming the

ID will take a while. The body's condition buys the killers time to accomplish their plan."

I shivered. "Poor Rurik. Not sure how he's holding on to his sanity. You encouraged him to ask a friend to help him through this, and he claimed not to need anyone." I glanced out into the wild.

"He has a sister in St. Petersburg. Parents are deceased. The Russian community in Houston or colleagues would offer support too. But he doesn't trust anyone."

"He trusts us to find Alina." So many times I'd asked why evil and injustice exist. But if I had the answers, God wouldn't be God.

"That was before deputies found his wife's car and a body." Blane leaned on one leg and nodded. "He'll agree to whatever the ROC demands."

I grimaced. "I don't see how a ransom of three million dollars is worth the crimes stacking up against the bad guys. It seems low. Unless it's additional payoff or more dollars in the pot to pay expenses."

"There's more motivating their activities than money. And speculating scares the—"

"We're both nervous." I covered my mouth as though saying more might release unspeakable crimes. "Normally my patience level is good, but not today."

"Negotiations take self-restraint to read people. Here's my take. Find out what's driving Chandler and the ROC, learn about their past, read and interpret their body language, trust your instincts, and be ourselves. We're not alone in this. I'm having a tough time proceeding without a clear picture, with only speculation . . . Are we walking into a trap?" He held up his hand. "We talked about this on the way here. Doesn't mean I've given it a rest."

The compassion in his tone failed to soothe me. "Alina's life hangs in the balance."

Blane let out a long sigh. "Years ago, my mother said children were to be protected at all costs. They are our future, our world's treasure and hope in humanity."

"Wise woman." But I hadn't protected Kate . . .

"I'll introduce you after Alina is found."

"Thanks." I'd wanted an older woman as a friend and mentor for years. Preferably one who shared my faith, and perhaps Blane's mother shared those traits. My mother had been too occupied with caring for Kate during her illness to help me through my rough times, but I missed Mom after all these years—or the relationship we could have shared.

I peeked at my watch. "We've been hiking for seven hours. I'd like to search another thirty minutes or so before we set up camp."

Time. Alina's biggest predator. Our biggest enemy. The FBI were on schedule to arrive in the morning, and a delay meant Alina's captors might hike out of the park.

"Therese?"

I kept walking.

"Therese, you can't ignore reality. Bringing a child into these mountains is an easy way to dispose of her."

I fought a nasty churning in the pit of me. "You're right. The odds are against finding Alina alive, except I refuse to give up hope."

"Where has that gotten you? I'm not criticizing but trying to find out what drives you to attempt the impossible."

His gentle tone wrapped me in a safe cocoon. "Hope is a reason to live when the world erupts into madness."

SIXTEEN

BLANE

We'd hiked miles today over off-trail terrain and often doubled back to recheck obscure signs, but nothing surfaced. If Chandler had trekked this way, he'd left no visible trace. The view displayed nature's paintbrush in unexpected ways. Shades of brown and gray swirled into deep rose stood as a stark contrast to a cloudless blue sky.

We pitched tents and made camp. Cold gusty winds blew around and through us, much like my attitude. My sixth sense had never failed me, and it warned me we were being watched. Who was obvious. But how and where from? I slipped behind one of the trees and reconned our surroundings. Nothing looked off, but foreboding pressed down hard. My teen years on the rodeo circuit were useless, but my wilderness-survival class gave me a little insight.

Therese eyed me warily. Did she feel the same sensation? "You feel the uneasiness?"

"Yep. Keep your eyes open."

"I have. Creepy."

"Make sure your gun is within easy reach."

She patted the side of her backpack. "I'm good. Ready to help build a fire?"

She'd explained the process months ago during our Ranger

training, and I hadn't practiced other than barbecuing. Fortunately, my recall was good. I dug a hole according to her instructions using a small trowel from my backpack, and we laid stones around it. We gathered dried grass, kindling, and a few pieces of dried wood. She arranged them, and as I watched her at work, she stoked my admiration. Not sure why I let myself continue to fall for a woman who had this God-thing going.

She bent to the pit with her fire starter and fanned a fledgling spark into a flame. Shielding it with her hand, she blew lightly, nursing it with patience and skill. She added dry tinder just like I'd been taught as a Boy Scout back in the day. She roughed up finger-size kindling and carefully placed it on the fire. Dried wood came next, forming the fire into a triangle. Her skill impressed me as . . . intrinsic.

"Glad we have permission to build this," I said.

"Right. We're cold, and I much prefer nature's cookstove. I'll build it low—"

"Chandler's already on to us."

Her gaze darted to me. "You still feel him breathing down our necks?"

"Yep. My SIG always stays within inches of my fingers. I'll take the first watch tonight." No one ever lived to say they saw Chandler coming, but I wouldn't state it.

"Doubtful our vigilance will do any good." She blinked, and fear met me from those blue-green depths. She had good reason to dread any signs of the part animal, part man. If fright motivated a person to be careful, then I supported it.

The sun slipped into the western sky around six o'clock, and we settled in around the fire. The freeze-dried chicken Alfredo soothed the emptiness in my stomach. I pulled out my paper topographical map to study where we were headed in the morning and compared it to the map on my satellite phone. The contour lines represented points at the same elevation. The closer the lines in elevation, the steeper the climb.

Therese moved closer to me. "Tomorrow we'll encounter a few challenges. Expect slopes of small loose rock, called scree. Those can be slippery. We'll use ropes when necessary. Do you remember the knots from class?"

"How about a review for this old schoolboy?"

She pulled a rope from her gear and moved into instructor mode. "I'll show you the three basic loops and a couple variations of the hitch knot, which I'm guessing you already know." Therese chose a nearby pine tree and demonstrated the knot we'd used on the ranch.

"Thanks. What else?"

"I'd sure like to find Alina tomorrow."

I infused caution into my words. "We can't stumble onto them or we're dead. We've got to figure out their exact location and surprise them." I touched her hand. "With two armed kidnappers, we both must be ready to defend the other and protect Alina."

She lifted her chin. "I'm your partner, and I won't fail you."

"Pulling the trigger on a killer is likely a given in our mission." In the low firelight, her features paled slightly. According to rumors, she'd encountered dangerous situations before. But this one had *personal* branded on it. Maybe one day she'd tell me. "I'll follow your lead on the trail, and I need you to follow mine when we meet up with Chandler."

"Yes, I agree."

"A code word or phrase that indicates trouble?" She nodded, and I continued. "Do you have one?"

She tapped her chin. "Scree." I gave her a thumbs-up, and she heated water.

We stayed in our own thoughts until she stirred instant coffee into two mugs of hot water. "I assume you're thinking through negotiations," she said.

"I am. But a fat lot of good it will do talking to a man who prefers to wield violence to words." I took a long drink of the hot, bitter brew. "We called this fence-coffee on the ranch. The only thing available when riding fence. Tastes like it was brewed over a pile of manure."

"Ouch. That hurt." She finished hers and grimaced. "It is bad. What were you thinking while drinking my bad coffee?"

"Chandler's grandmother is his weak link, unless he's blaming her for dying and abandoning him. He faced theft and murder charges to attend her funeral by disguising himself. No one suspected him until he broke down at the graveside service. I'll use the grandmother angle to test out his reaction. With no family, friends, or pets, it's difficult to determine his vulnerability." I lifted a brow to lighten the moment. "But my cowgirl partner's got my back."

A faint smile met my gaze. "Have you considered his favorite places to visit? He obviously likes the high desert mountains," she said. "He's been spotted in the Alps, the Andes, the Himalayas, and the Rocky Mountains."

"You've kept tabs on him."

"Blane, my dad told me the best way to overcome an enemy is to walk every step of his journey."

"Sounds like some of the lessons my dad taught me. Chandler's motivated by M&M," I said. "Mountains and money."

"Not a sweet mix."

"Is it possible to live weeks at a time up here in a well-hidden place?"

She nodded. "Skills and supplies are the key, and Chandler would find access to both."

Myriad stars burst onto the scene like lightning bugs on a summer night. "Who tells the first ghost story?"

"Mine are all true." She added kindling to the fire. "Tell me why you and God aren't on speaking terms."

"Why don't we start our first night on the trail with deep stuff?"

She waved at me to begin. "Texas Rangers have the best stories."

"All right, partner." I held up a finger. "I'll tell my ghost story tonight, then you tell yours tomorrow night."

"Maybe. Might not be as good as yours. You came from a family of police officers, and Major Montoya's family adopted you. Anything else shaping the man today?"

"It's dark."

"Most of our stories are."

"You believe in God and have the faith thing going. Whatever your past, I'm sure you've rationalized it."

"Not really," she said. "But we're talking about you. As you've said to me more than once, I'm listening."

"If I share what I've done, any chance of us taking our relationship up a notch is gone. We already have our faith differences, so I guess we're already headed down a dead-end street."

"Rusty, is it okay to call you by your nickname? I'm your friend, not a legalistic judge. We trust each other, and that means the past stays right there. Maybe I can offer insight."

Long seconds ticked by. Could I tell Therese what I'd done?

"All right. First, the way you say Rusty sounds good. I'll tell you my disgusting story, but you've been warned." I stared into the low flames. "Back in my freshman college days, before meeting Sergio, I dated a girl. Wendy was smart. Gorgeous. Funny. And a Christian. I rode the fence with God. Even went to church with her a few times to make her happy and hinted about making a commitment. I faked any righteous responses around her. One night we went to a party, and a group of guys decided to bring out a Ouija board. Wendy wanted nothing to do with it. Called it a devil's board and asked me to take her home. I refused. Made fun of her. Yep, I'd been drinking. One of the guys said he'd take me home later, so I tossed her my truck keys. As she left, I said, 'May the curse be with you.' Everyone thought it was hilarious. I . . ."

"I'm listening," she said. "Who else have you shared this story with?"

"You're the lucky one. Sergio and my parents have heard bits and pieces."

"Keep going."

She didn't give up. "On the way home, Wendy lost control of my truck and ran it off a bridge. She lay in a coma over two weeks, and I never left her side. The doctors convinced her parents to remove life support. I begged God to save her, bartered with Him, but she died. I decided God had taken seriously my parting words to Wendy, and I wanted no part of Him."

"You blame God for her death." Therese poured compassion into her tone, like I would do in her shoes. "And yourself."

"Yes." I stoked the fire. "I vowed to help people not become victims. It's been my mantra ever since."

"Tragedies don't define us unless we give them permission."

How many times had I used similar verbiage to others?

"Oh, Blane. Don't torture yourself. Wendy made the decision to leave the party. Your words and actions had nothing to do with the accident."

SEVENTEEN

Day two into the hike, and I'd wished a thousand times that I'd done more prep-training. Missions like this required physical endurance, certainly more than a few hours over terrain designed for sightseeing and photography. Not testing rock footholds. Every time I stuck my foot on hard ground and walked a path less than two feet wide, I envisioned a mountain cat pouncing on me, sending me into the gray depths below. My legs and back protested every step.

Some Ranger-cowboy I'd turned out to be. My wild streak shifted to constant self-talk to stay hydrated and alert for who was watching our every move.

The wind blew steadily around thirty miles per hour, sending a chill through my jacket. The gusts would increase as we climbed, and the temps would drop ten degrees from the trailhead. I'd endure the bitter cold and keep my mouth shut. My lack of expertise in hiking steep inclines slowed us down. Every moment decreased the likelihood of finding Alina Ivanov alive.

On the edge of a rock cropping, Therese stopped and lifted her binoculars in a northern direction. I joined her and she pointed to rock formations. I adjusted my binoculars.

"See the narrow trail winding around the cave and on to the top of that peak?" she said. "Zoom in and you'll see trampled brush indicating the kidnappers' route."

I focused on the area. "I'm there."

"Follow the trail up and to the left."

I focused on the steep terrain. "Loose stones have fallen over the brush, like someone slipped."

"My thoughts. Chandler can lead them anywhere, but their ability in navigating the trail is another matter."

"Unless he wants us to follow him." I continued to pan the area. Movement near a northeastern ridge caught my attention. The backs of two adults and a child between them. "There you are."

"You see them?" Therese peered in the same direction. "They've moved off the trail. I'd say a good two hours or more from here."

Meaning my inability to keep pace was a disadvantage. I pulled out my satellite phone and connected to Sergio. I checked my coordinates and the proximity of the kidnappers. The FBI team had set out at 11:00 a.m. yesterday, camped last night, and hiked about four hours behind us.

"Do you want a helo with backup and medical help?" Sergio said.

"Wait until we're closer. I want to pin down their location first. Then bring in the big guns. No point alerting the kidnappers and deal with how they might retaliate."

"Why not allow the FBI to help?"

"Not an option. Waiting takes time."

"Rusty, keep me informed. I can get a helo in the Dog Canyon area with short notice. We can figure out what to do from there."

"We're covering a lot of area." No point telling him about rescue teams spending hours and even days tracking lost hikers. Therese could verify the stats in a heartbeat, and we had our phones and flares. "How's Rurik holding up?"

"FBI twenty-four seven protection. He objected at first but agreed after they relayed the dangers. Not sure about his mental state. Nothing showed up on his cell phone records." His pause told me of his apprehension. "You're looking at two desperate men who'd think nothing of using Alina as a shield."

I'd thought about the same thing—and other barbaric actions.

We picked up our pace, and in two hours we hiked to where we'd spotted the kidnappers with Alina, but no sign of them. I studied the trail, although Therese's skill set was more advanced than mine would ever be. I veered off and detected the toe print of a tennis shoe leading uphill over rocks and dead shrub.

Therese followed the single shoe print. She stood on a narrow rock overlooking the steep terrain and peered through her binoculars. The grim look on her face told it all. The wind whipped her hair back, whispering a gust could blow her away.

"The wind is picking up," I said.

She kept the binoculars glued to her eyes. "I'm fine."

"Have they disappeared?"

"Appears so. The shoe print angles off the trail. I'm not sure why. Probably Chandler destroyed them. The climb is strenuous for an adult."

The view displayed nature, raw and beautiful. "What's on the other side of those mountains?"

"More of the same."

An icy burst swept by me like a bad omen. "Spotting them in the open was no accident. There's a reason they allowed us to see them." Suspicion clamored in my head. "We're walking into a trap."

Therese surveyed the area. "If we take the western trail, it leads to a clearing lined on two sides with boulders. Not big, but if they're waiting to ambush us, that's where they'd hide. We'd be easy targets."

"So, we'll outsmart them. How can we get behind the clearing?"

"It's a hard—"

A burst of wind knocked Therese off-balance, and I caught her—or she'd have toppled headfirst into a canyon. A shot rang out and a bullet bounced off a rock not a foot from her. I rolled her back from where we'd been standing and sheltered her body while rifle fire exploded around us.

The bullets stopped. "Are you hurt?" My blood pressure soared for the woman beneath me.

"I'm good. They expected us to walk right into their line of fire."

I rolled off Therese, taking in every inch of her. Droplets of blood stained her lower-right pant leg. "You're hurt."

"It's nothing, really. The bullet grazed me." She inspected the wound like she'd done with footprints and broken twigs.

"You're lucky the bullet didn't do more damage."

"I've hurt myself more stumbling and falling."

I crawled to the upper rock where we'd stood and searched the area with my binoculars.

"Blane, you'll get yourself shot."

"I'm staying down. Somewhere they're watching what we'll do next, and our best chances to survive are to take the unpredictable route."

"Any movement?" she said.

"No. The rifle fire came from the north. Chandler's a crack shot, and yet we're still alive." The wind had saved her . . .

"You and I know exactly why I'm alive."

I refused to say God, although I had no belief in coincidences. "Chandler is playing games with us, which follows his MO. My question is why? What's the goal here? Waiting on confirmation that Rurik's wired the ransom, then hightailing it out of here?" I shook my head. "That's crazy. He'd have received notice within moments of the transfer." I searched the northern rocks where I wanted to be.

She pointed to a golden eagle soaring above us. "Like many Native Americans, I believe the bird symbolizes majesty, power, truth, wisdom, and honor."

"I could use a few answers."

"Me too." She'd already ripped open an antiseptic pad, cleansed the minor wound, and placed a Band-Aid on her leg.

"Can you walk on that?"

"Sure. Do we move east and attempt to approach them from behind? The hike is grueling there."

"Sounds like the best trail to take. With your wounded leg, Chandler will expect us to head straight to where he or they fired the shots."

"One more time you're right," she said. "He'll find ways to inflict pain until he's looking at us through his rifle scope again."

"Therese, listen to me." I captured her gaze. "Head back to the trailhead, and I'll go on alone. The FBI will find you. I have supplies, my weapon, a compass, and sat phone. No need to put yourself through this. Once I have zeroed in on Alina's location, I'll call for backup."

"Impossible." She sucked in a breath and added weight to her leg. "I'm ready. Finding Alina is more important than running from a jerk who fired on us."

I scowled at her. "Rest a few minutes. Might give you a change of mind."

"Not going to happen. I'm afraid of Chandler and whoever else is out there, but God's with me." She offered a fragile smile.

"He shot you. He's dangerous. Has no value for human life. Think of your loved ones who would mourn your death. Do you want them to experience such heartache?"

"My distant cousins understand my personality and so do my friends. They are familiar with how I live."

"There's a difference between courage and acting foolishly."

"Then I'll take the former."

I gave up convincing her for now. She had the tracking skills, and I had the gun power. We needed each other.

Chandler, what motivates you? He had so many charges against him in the US and other parts of the world that he might be planning to slip into seclusion. How did the ROC's scheme to assassinate Edik Baranov and assist in kidnapping Alina entice Chandler? In planning an assassination, murdering Daria Ivanov, and kidnapping Alina, where did all the players fit?

The answers weren't available to me, but I determined to work all the harder. I came here to rescue a little girl, and I had no intention of leaving empty-handed or any of us leaving in a body bag. The clichéd phrase "This isn't my first rodeo" blew through me like the wind. But this time I rode an unbeatable bronc.

I called Sergio and apprised him of the shooting. "Can you check to see if any of those on our list have crossed paths in areas other than Houston?"

"I'll see what I can find out. A helo with armed Rangers is headed to Dog Canyon. The FBI is also working with intel in Moscow. I'll check in as soon as I have anything."

I slid my phone into my zippered pocket and sensed Therese frowning. "What's bothering you?"

"Reality. Fear is dancing through me to the tune of how to make it out of here alive with Alina. I haven't lost my optimism." She swallowed hard. "Chandler's proven his actions are more like a rabid animal, and that's not good for any of us."

We both had our analogies of Chandler. I needed to pay attention to how Therese handled fear. Stress was normal, and even a good thing for self-preservation. Except headaches and other physical symptoms paved the way for mistakes. She'd read those in others, but did she have the discernment to see the same in herself?

I adjusted my backpack for the trek ahead. "Those odds were laid out right from the start. Are you hiking back to the trailhead?"

She lifted her chin. "I'm being honest with my partner."

I expelled a frustrated sigh. "You're not alone, and while we're talking truth, the best way to outsmart him, or them, is to put ourselves in their shoes. That's my number one rule of negotiation."

"I understand. Tell me more."

"The game of cat and mouse doesn't work when the mouse understands the cat's instincts. I've spent our hiking hours putting my feet into his boots. The only way to square off with Chandler is on even ground."

"Theoretically, you make sense," she said. "But how are we to implement it?"

I directed my attention east. "Just like the choice we made to find Alina in these mountains. Get behind them and beat Chandler and the elements at their own game."

EIGHTEEN

Alina and her two captors had vanished from our eyes. But not from my vow to free a little girl. I failed to understand myself. Me, the negotiator. Me, with all my education in behavior. Me, who'd risked my life countless times in the line of duty. Me, who hadn't figured out if I'd agreed to this mission to save an innocent child or convince a woman I was worth the effort of a relationship. Or both. The part of me who believed man was born good, and evil came from experiencing the world now questioned if Therese had discovered what I lacked. Faith in God.

We all searched for something, and at times a sadness escaped her eyes. I stumbled over those brief moments when something attacked her, as though she wrestled with God. Then she'd blink and the sadness vanished. I'd keep listening and observing—the only way I'd ever understand her.

Demons stalked us all, burying their claws deep into our emotions until we unlocked our chains and escaped, banishing them from our lives. One day I'd discover the source of my real search, then I'd not only escape but chain the demon to what held me.

My mental wanderings worked as a diversion until danger of the mission grabbed a strangling hold. Time slipped like the loose scree beneath my feet. One priority remained.

We hiked our way east, and like Therese had said, the trail—what there was of it—gave me fresh appreciation for the definition of perilous. Sliding rock and unexpected drop-offs caused me to think facing a shooter might be easier. At least I had the skills to balance the odds with my fists or with a gun in my hand.

The good part of the trek was watching Therese's lithe body scale rocks while her honey-colored ponytail swung with each step. She made climbing true beauty and art. My ability to paint people often missed the details of showing character and personality, but I'd be willing to spend time capturing hers on canvas.

We set up camp like the previous night under the shelter of a hanging rock. Hunger curled in my belly, growled, and spurted like a voice of desperation. I never imagined a can of tuna, crackers, and an apple had so much flavor. And it rivaled Thanksgiving dinner after existing on government-issued rations. We ate without conversation, each of us undoubtedly engrossed in our own solutions and figuring out what lay ahead. Plus, I was too tired to make the effort to speak.

"If we were nocturnal, we'd travel at night," Therese finally said. "Catch Chandler and whoever is with him off guard and be finished with this."

I swallowed a gulp of water. "Plan B is a little more to my liking. We're hiking beyond where we saw them. Is there a trail to approach their rear in the least unsuspecting way?"

She pondered my question. "Yes. It's a hard climb."

I leaned in closer and let the fire warm my face. "We can do it. If we found them tomorrow and waited until dusk, is it possible to snatch Alina at night?"

"Nothing is off-limits. Just takes more ingenuity to accomplish."

"We'd need to stay hidden until backup arrived. A place where visibility is zero percent. My concern is once Chandler learns he's been duped, he'll be on our tails. No way the team would arrive in time." I held up a finger. "We have a helo full of Rangers waiting at the Dog Canyon Visitor's Center. They can be ready at a moment's notice."

She eyed me like I'd lost my brains at the trailhead. "Have you been watching too many movies?"

I purposely widened my eyes. "Aren't we the type that movies are made from? We agreed this was *Mission Impossible*."

"You're not Tom Cruise."

I startled. "Are you kidding? We have danger, adventure, and you're the hot heroine who has all the skills."

"Ah, most of his women get killed."

"We'll be successful 'cause I wrote this script."

She gave me a high five. "Best news I've heard all day. Tomorrow will be the day of reckoning."

"Ready to move?"

"What?"

"Let's build a bigger fire, then move to where we can watch our campsite. Take turns sleeping. If Chandler chooses to attack, we'll see him."

"All right. Good call. Cat and mouse, right?" she said.

Grabbing our backpacks and gear, we made our way to a secluded area several feet from the fire where we were protected from the cold wind. I took the first watch.

"I'm ready to hear your life story," I said.

She shook her head. "Not tonight. Maybe tomorrow."

Therese's silence told me she'd dipped to the worst possible scenario. Mine too. Neither humor nor logic covered how our mission impossible would stretch our skills . . . and possibly, Therese's faith.

I wished I was armed with the ammo of faith instead of the sliver of doubt inching through me.

—

I woke in the stillness of early morning, but in the east varying shades of yellow, orange, and purple streaked across the sky. The desire to paint this magnificence filled me. Another time.

I recalled our time in Dog Canyon, and I explored past missions, some with devastating results. I'd call Sergio this morning and request the FBI team behind us to pick up their pace. The argument to stay ahead of the Feds for Alina's sake made sense. But we were running out of time, and the kidnappers might lose patience. They had their money, why not release her? Or dispose of her? I was ready to negotiate that child's release, so why the holdup?

Would Rurik lie to Sergio and the Feds? Was he aware the FBI had placed a tracer on his phone? Unless Rurik had another phone he used to call the kidnappers, like the burner he purchased to contact Therese. The grieving husband and father possibly played a devious role between the kidnappers, the ROC, and those on the side of the law. His tells *were* convincing, and those emotions always yanked me back to where Rurik had fallen prey to ruthless men. I'd pursue the obscurity of Rurik's role once Therese and I freed Alina.

How much did he know about Edik Baranov's escape plans? How close were they as cousins?

Therese tossed off her covering. She had the early morning watch, and sleep crusted her eyes. That meant she'd fallen asleep during her watch, but we were both alive.

"Good morning," I said.

"Maybe. My instincts tell me today will challenge us like nothing we've ever experienced."

"We've faced problems in our line of work and succeeded. We will again."

"Some worse than others," she said.

"You sound pessimistic. When you taught the survival course, you claimed the problems of life make us stronger, better people. Have you changed your position?"

"No. My priority is Alina's rescue. Nothing else matters. And while I'd gladly give my life for her or you, fear rises like the sun and binds me to take precautions." She held up a gloved hand. "I'm sorry. Let me drink my coffee, and I'll get my bearings."

I reached into my backpack, pulled out two granola bars, and tossed one her way. "Should you check in with Rurik? I'll do the same with Sergio."

"Good idea." She pulled her backpack into her lap and unzipped where she kept her satellite phone. She lifted it out as though the device was gold and patted in and around her as though missing something. "Where's my gun?" She lifted her blanket and searched all around. "Where is it?" Her voice rose.

"How can I help?"

She rummaged through her camp gear. "Do you see my gun? It's missing."

I startled. She had organization down to a miniature tack box. "Where did you have it during your watch?"

"Beside me or in my hand. I . . . I did doze off."

I lifted my blanket where I kept my SIG close. I expected my lifeline to be there. I searched around me, certain I'd unconsciously moved it.

Where was my firearm?

An alarm sounded in my brain and jolted every nerve on high alert. Were we surrounded? A bullet away from death? How could I be so stupid not to detect someone stealing my gun?

"Blane." Therese's whisper held an eerie chill. "I'm so sorry. This is my fault."

She held a peregrine falcon feather.

NINETEEN

ALINA

I wakened from the shot the bad man had given me in a new place. I was covered by a thick blanket and in a cave. Blinking several times, my eyes cleared. Outside a ray of sunshine filtered in, showing lots of stuff inside, like people lived here. I made out canned food and cases of water stored on stone shelves. How did they get all the food and water here? One shelf had clothes on it, and another held different kinds of guns. Beside it sat boxes labeled *ammo*. Had the two men stolen other kids and brought them here too? I couldn't tell how many days had passed 'cause the medicine made me sleep, but if I added right, this was my third day away from home.

Voices grew louder at the opening of the cave where the two men talked. I squeezed my eyes shut and didn't move. I must listen to every word. One of them had been to our house, and his name was Mr. Falin. He's mean but the other man was meaner. The meaner man had lines on one side of his face, but not the lines I'd seen on old people. Scary lines, and he hadn't smiled once. He had told me to sit here on the hard ground and not move. I obeyed. My hands and feet were tied together.

My whole body shook. I wanted to wake up. *This can't be real.*

"How long until we get out of this hole?" Mr. Falin said.

The two men argued a lot and used inappropriate language.

"How badly do you want my box of chips?"

"That's not what I asked."

"I have my own agenda to handle before the exchange. Those two behind us need to be eliminated."

"Then why the—didn't you kill them last night?"

The meaner man cursed. "I gave you a good price for everything you demanded. I told you this would be handled my way."

"All I'm asking is why the delay? My people are ready to complete the transaction," Mr. Falin said.

"It's a game. The two trailing us aren't a threat without their guns. Besides, the woman is a worthy opponent."

"A worthy opponent? How?"

"She's a wilderness-survival expert, and she outsmarted me once, but it won't happen again. I owe her a slow death. Let me just say I have set her up."

"But we have a deal. You were paid for Alina, and I'm ready to complete the rest of it."

The mean man clicked something in his hand. I'd seen his gun. They both had them.

"Hold on, Chandler. No reason to get upset. Your timing. Your way."

The meaner man—Mr. Chandler—laughed. "What about the kid?"

"She's collateral until Rurik completes my terms."

"Then what? Do you think I'm going to carry her down these mountains?"

"I can manage."

"Idiot. She can identify both of us. We either kill her or sell her. Pretty little thing would bring a good price. Wire the eight million to my account, or we don't have a deal."

I understood what the man named Chandler meant. He'd kill me 'cause I might tell my daddy what they looked like. Daddy hadn't gotten rid of me. The men had kidnapped me, and he paid them.

My daddy loved me, but it sounded like money wouldn't set me free. They wanted something else.

I promised myself to be obedient and not make the men mad. Two people searched for me, and I bet they could get me home. I'd find a way to run away. Daddy had taught me how to follow the stars if I got lost.

My fingers touched on the cave wall and I scraped my finger. The sting gave me an idea. I rubbed the rope around my wrists against it like a knife. I'd cut through the rope and free my hands. Daddy would be proud of me. It didn't take long for my shoulders to ache. I stopped. Rested. Then kept trying. The ropes were so tight, and wiggling my feet didn't help with the knot tying them. I'd not give up.

Mr. Chandler stomped into the cave and snatched my school backpack. "Listen up."

TWENTY

THERESE

I'd never been violated. Nothing had ever stalked me with such fear . . . The urge to vomit engulfed me, as though Chandler's filthy hands were all over me.

"He watched us while we slept," I said through a quivering voice. I wanted to scream, hear my voice echo off the rock formations.

"Therese." Blane spoke my name in a soft whisper. "Lift your chin and take a deep breath."

I shivered with fiery rage. "I don't want to calm down. I want to kill Chandler with my bare hands."

"He had the opportunity to do the same to us while we slept. It's his game, but he hasn't won. Look at me. Please."

I gazed into Blane's calm face and warm eyes. He laid his hands on my shoulders. "Breathe in and out with me."

"I . . . can't."

"I believe in you, Therese. You're smart and courageous." His gentleness lulled me to listen. "Inhale with me."

I followed his lead.

"Exhale with me."

I did.

"This time inhale your resolve to free Alina."

His bidding was easier.

"Exhale your terror and doubt."

That was harder, but I complied. A deep part of me longed for more of Blane's strength. I leaned into his strong arms, and he pulled me close. There I took refuge from my emotions.

My fear for Alina.

My suspicion that Rurik had not told us everything. Even lied for selfish reasons.

My foolishness for falling asleep and not hearing Chandler steal our guns.

My sin of not thanking God for saving us. The worry and doubt.

My past laced with sadness and abandonment.

My anger at God for taking my sweet sister, Mom, and Dad.

My longing to stay in Blane's arms where safety nested.

I cared for him, but he had *forbidden* stamped on his very being. His comfort touched me tenderly. His soft voice and perfect words were part of him. Did he have any idea what his nearness meant to me?

Releasing my personal sentiments about life's unfairness didn't discount my responsibility. I had a job to do.

I lifted my head from his chest, wet with my tears. "Thank you. I'm sorry my idiocy and meltdown slowed us."

"Never apologize for being human." He brushed the wetness from my cheeks with his thumb, and in his brown eyes I saw what I'd wanted all my life, love that didn't make demands. Cared about me.

God, why have You made my life so hard, and now I care for a man who doesn't believe he needs You.

Embarrassment and humiliation spread through my body like a fever. I'd not cried that hard and long since my family's passing. Normally I pumped control into my emotions, but Chandler's thievery had attacked me blind.

"We hadn't fooled Chandler by rerouting our direction," Blane said. "He won this round."

I gazed out across the gray-brown rock and vegetation, allowing my attention to rest on a pine tree, the only indication of green. Something in me clicked, as though God was giving me a reality check. "Since he's trailing us, is it possible the kidnapper and Alina are in another location, and Chandler is working solo?"

Blane startled. "Sounds crazy, but the same thing just darted in my head."

I smiled. "I'd tell you where it came from, but that would be preaching."

He angled his head and nodded. "You might be right and onto more truth than the absurdity of our thoughts—no matter where they come from. If Chandler tucked the kidnapper and Alina in a hidden place and then followed us, his actions are typical of his behavior. The game is in his playbook. He waits to strike the victim unaware and gains satisfaction in seizing control."

"From what you've learned, what drives him other than what we discussed?"

Blane pressed his lips together. "His young critical years were met with neglect, abuse, and abandonment. I believe his grandmother worked hard to make up for what he'd missed, but the hurt and pain wouldn't allow him to choose the right path or move past his unmet needs. In my opinion, he's searching to soothe his pain by inflicting suffering on others."

I stood on shaky legs and paced. The scrape on my leg stung. "He's dangerous. A highly intelligent killer who has nothing to lose."

"I agree. His actions border on suicide. Life is hell for him, and death may look like a reward."

"How sad a soul is lost who sees no path forward." I paused. "I have no idea who said that. But it fits."

"We need a strategy and firepower. I recommend we wait for backup. We're defenseless without weapons."

Blane spoke wisdom, but I couldn't bring myself to agree. "The longer we wait to find Alina, the more her chances of survival decrease."

"How do you propose we free her? Defend ourselves? Do you have a bow and arrow in your backpack? Some magic flash of lightning to call up from your God?" He stopped abruptly. "I'm sorry. This isn't a time to argue."

I'd failed Kate, but giving up on Alina meant another little girl's death. Injustice surged in me, hot and irrational, like moments ago when I swam upstream in a river of emotion. "I promised Rurik—"

"To do your best to free his daughter. Your best doesn't mean to fight against incredible odds and sacrifice your life."

"You don't understand. I've failed."

Blane frowned. "By allowing backup to help us?"

"Just say it. Forget the negotiation trash. Say it!"

"Why is it so important to rescue Alina on your own?"

His in-control and quiet mannerisms were meant to calm me, so I'd return to some type of a civilized human. But my rage burned hotter. "Didn't you hear me? One more time I've failed."

The lines around his eyes softened. "That's not true. You haven't failed anyone but your own high expectations. And those aren't realistic. You are the survival expert, the guide, the one who can hike these mountains blindfolded." He took a step closer. "You have nothing to prove to anyone."

His words hit too close to the truth. I drew back to slap him, but he grabbed my wrist. "Therese, I'm not the enemy. Never have been."

"Let go of me." I trembled. When had I ever experienced such anger?

"Breathe in and out."

My emotions were off the charts and impossible to rein in. *Lord, help me.* Shame washed over me as though I'd bathed in mud.

"Inhale with me." Blane released my wrist. "I'll help you."

Who was I, and why had I let fear rule me? I certainly hadn't handled this morning well. I conceded to Blane's bidding, and my rage lessened. We breathed together again. "Blane. I'm sorry. I'm the one who is supposed to show you how being a Christian makes a difference."

"You could have pushed me over these rocks."

I blinked back wetness and gave him a weak smile. "That's little consolation."

"Think about all you've been through. Since Rurik called you at 2:00 a.m. on Thursday, you've raced to find Alina. Daria's remains were discovered burned. You've been shot. Rurik's withheld information. Chandler's stolen our weapons. We've met repeated defeating moments. Anyone else would have given up long ago, but not you, Therese Palmer. You are overflowing with despair and bravery."

I valued his gift of empathy, but he'd forgotten one important factor. "This hasn't been a me-experience but a we-experience. You've walked with me every step of the way. I appreciate you, and I'm sorry for the trouble I've caused this morning."

"It's okay. Be on the lookout. My finer moments will come riding in like a herd of mustangs. Might send you to the hills." He held his satellite phone in his left hand. "I'm calling Sergio and requesting all the backup available ASAP."

"I . . . suppose you're right. I'm better." I gulped. "So humiliated."

"No need. We're good. My guess is today triggered something from the past." He started to say more but touched my arm instead and stared into my eyes. "When this is over, we can talk if you like. Or I can recommend a professional counselor."

I met his gaze. No hint of condemnation. "Thank you. I'll think about it." I pointed to his phone. "I'll look for a spot to land a helo."

While he made the call, I crawled low to the top of the ridge, favoring my wounded leg, and used my binoculars to explore the elevation around us. The steep, rocky slopes promised more of the same terrain with less vegetation and trees. I scanned the vast area, although if I stood, Chandler would have an easy time eliminating me.

I whirled around at Blane. "There isn't a safe spot to land here. Chandler would pick them off like swatting flies on a picnic table full of food. We need to find a location higher up with less exposure. And I know where."

TWENTY-ONE

BLANE

The FBI team trekked toward the location where Therese and I planned a meetup, an area where the Rangers could land a helo and be less likely to encounter hostile rifle fire. Still a possibility, but Therese and I had our binoculars to keep a lookout and warn them. With the combined armed men, we'd find Alina and take down Chandler and his sidekick.

One of the FBI agents was a sniper and paramedic. Smart combo in case of a firefight, and Alina might need medical attention from exposure and whatever Chandler and the kidnapper might have inflicted. Until then, Therese and I hiked an off-trail path.

Her emotions earlier in the day demonstrated what I'd suspected—a deeper hurt drove her to risk her life for others. No surprise I recognized the same trait in me. We both carried boulders in our backpacks, refusing to give them up as though they were buds instead of enemies.

What were the chances of two people being thrown together in the middle of nowhere and struggling with painful issues from their pasts—one a Christian and the other angry with how God managed humans?

Guess I wanted to believe in something, but not the God I'd experienced. I'd explored other religions, and all were a bunch of rituals. The list of dos and don'ts along with the expectations that a person's good deeds must outweigh the bad ones caused me to shove all of them into the same outhouse. None of it made sense. No logical answers to why some people boasted extraordinary lives while others endured one tragedy after another.

Therese pointed to an incline ahead but gave me no eye contact. "There's our approach. This climb is more than a boot path. It's a slog. I'll go first. Better I clear the way."

"What are my instructions?" I grinned to ease the tension frosting between us since earlier in the day.

She ignored me. "The loose rocks are not to be taken lightly. So be extra careful. I'll ensure solid footing every step of the way." She indicated a few cracks in the upward terrain.

"What's to keep you from falling?"

"I'll do a free climb until I can anchor my rope. Besides it's not far, and I have my partner to catch me."

"Always." I started to say my arms were open, but I held back to listen to every word.

"I'll climb to the top and assure everything is safe. Once I anchor the rope, I'll drop it to you. Use a hitch knot to secure it around your waist. Take it slow and you'll be a rock star." She nodded at jagged rock within inches of our feet. "Watch your balance. Note it's straight down."

Making a mistake came with a price tag—our lives. What if she slipped? I took another quick peek down at the death plunge.

Get your head in the game, Gardner.

I studied where she planned to scale and added a shot of bravado. "All right. It looks fairly simple. I'll memorize every step you take and watch your rear all the way up."

"Keep talking, and I'll throw rocks at you."

I adjusted my backpack and stared at the mass of sure death below us. "I'll behave. Are you praying for us?"

"After what you just said? You're a mess, but yes, I'm praying."

Good, but I'd not admit it. "If I make the climb in one piece, I want to take you to dinner. You choose the place."

"I'll find the perfect spot once we're back in Houston."

"Deal."

I inwardly winced with my fear of falling. But I'd not admit it. I was a Texas Ranger—the best of the best. *Diablos Tejanos*—Texan Devils. "One Riot, One Ranger."

"What does that mean?"

"I'm the best you've got."

"How reassuring." Therese studied the twisted vine and rock above us and anchored her hiking boot in a secure hold. Stones broke free around her, but she stayed firm. "See what I mean? The incline is not the biggest problem. It's the loose rock. Test your footage even where I find it safe. I'll give more instructions once I'm on higher ground. Slow and easy is the key."

I held my breath with her every upward motion. As before, her body melded with the rough terrain, graceful, a work of art. I feared and admired this mystery woman. Never had I encountered such skill and courage.

She'd panic at the thud of my heart against my chest. I'd advised other Rangers that healthy respect of danger wasn't a bad trait. Experience had taught me the sensation helped us choose our steps wisely and built our self-esteem in a healthy way. I needed to take my own advice.

Therese's third and fourth footings met with success. This trail deserved a blue ribbon as the worst I'd encountered. Chandler had outsmarted us once, but he'd soon have his hands full with armed FBI agents and Rangers. My headspace stayed in think-mode, while she took each slow step with assurance.

Sundown would come early, and no one wanted to be caught hiking at night. A reality check said the team behind us might not make it to us until the morning. Better in one piece and late than dead and unable to help Alina.

Therese reached the midway point to a plateau about twenty-five feet up. A burst of wind blew me off-balance. Stones, sand, and debris pelted my face and irritated my eyes.

I took a step backward.

My right foot slipped.

My left foot failed to anchor me, as though I steadied myself on rolling marbles. I clawed my hands and fingers into whatever I could grab while sharp edges of rock scraped into my face and hands. I twisted my body to roll the descent and protect myself, but I lost control and bounced like a rag doll.

A surreal mix of truth and wrenching panic surrounded me as I plummeted. If not so stubborn, I'd call out to God for help.

Therese's frantic shouts drowned in my ears.

I'm going to die.

I dropped hard against rock, and my lower left arm cracked. My head seared with a heavy throb. Overwhelming darkness claimed my battered body.

TWENTY-TWO

THERESE

Blane had vanished below the rock overhang, and a surge of hot and cold blew against me. Had he hurtled to his death?

"Blane? Blane?" My call to him was met with eerie echoes.

Please, God, he's got to be all right. Give him strength to survive.

I climbed down to the trailhead where we first talked about the strenuous hike. Once my foot slipped on the loose stones. I breathed in and out. Like he'd asked of me, like I'd asked of others who'd fallen prey to the inability to control their surroundings. But my concern was for Blane.

I dropped to my knees and leaned over to study where he lay sprawled out, his left face on a narrow ledge. A mass of rust-colored hair caught my attention, then blood. I inhaled sharply at the awkward position of his left arm. How had he managed to stop himself on that rock slab? Had to be God's mercy.

"Blane, I'm right above you. Can you hear me?"

Nothing.

I repeated my question. No response.

Reacting emotionally solved nothing. I unsnapped my pants pocket to retrieve my phone. "Don't try to move. I'm calling the SAR and Rangers." Not sure if my words were to reassure him or me. My phone in hand, a horror-filled click and hiss alerted me to a rattler. How? Normally they were active early in the morning and at dusk. I dared not move.

From the corner of my eye, a black-tailed rattler coiled three feet to the right of where my fingers wrapped around my phone. Deadly. Ready to strike.

Slowly releasing my phone, I eased my knife from inside my right hiking boot and aimed it at the snake's head. It opened its mouth to strike. I jerked while sinking the knife deep into the rattler's head and knocked into my phone, sending it slapping against rock to the bottom of the canyon.

As I held my breath, the snake ceased to move. The deadly creature's venomous days were over. I yanked my knife out of its head and kicked the snake to its ancestors.

I fought the urge to cry. *You idiot!* How could I arrange a meetup with the FBI and Rangers without my phone?

Guilt assaulted me, messing with my thoughts. Blane's fall and the pain he endured couldn't be eased until I rescued him. I managed a prayer. I clung to the promise of His strength when I was weak. I'd climb down to Blane, treat his injuries, and pull him up. I'd use his phone to call Major Montoya.

I wrapped my hand around the rope in my backpack and secured it to a sturdy boulder. A familiar maneuver, so why did I shake like a leaf? I tied a bowline knot around the huge rock and another around my waist, then rappelled down the approximately twenty-five feet to where Blane lay. Barely a foot of space existed between his body and the ledge leading to a canyon fall.

His left forearm twisted at an angle midway below his elbow, but thankfully the bone didn't protrude through the skin. I'd straightened and set broken bones in the past, and I'd do it again. But blood stained the rock where his face had hit.

"Blane." No answer. "Blane, I'm right here beside you."

Terror dropped to my toes. His unconscious state indicated far too many issues. Feeling his pulse, a steady beat vibrated through my fingertips. Aware of the precious few inches of rock between me and death, I thanked God for His provision.

Where was Blane's backpack? Did I even want to know?

A faint moan escaped him.

"Blane, this is Therese."

His pecan-colored eyes flickered open, and he eyed me strangely. "Where am I?"

Head injury. "We are in the Guadalupe Mountains. Don't move. You're on a narrow ledge."

"Why? Who are you?"

Reality coiled like the rattler. "We are in search of a little girl and her kidnappers. I'm Therese. You fell."

"What?"

His confusion confirmed a concussion, but how bad was it? "Where do you hurt?"

"My . . . arm's broken."

"I can set it. Any other injuries?"

"My . . . head." He attempted to lift his head and smacked it back down on the rock. "What's your name again?"

"Therese." Blood mingled with rust-colored hair seized my concern, but I'd not alarm him. "Save your strength. You're confused from the fall. It takes time for your head to clear."

"Is it just you and me?"

"Yes." *And God.* "Hush. We've both been challenged, but we're survivors. Listen to me. Do not move. Again, you are on a narrow ledge. I need you to stay calm." I considered Blane's broken arm, concussion, and possible internal injuries. My paramedic skills were woefully inadequate for the medical care he needed.

He attempted to lift his head again and uttered a string of cursing that I never appreciated but expected. "Sorry," he whispered. "I think my head's clearing."

"Stay with me. Promise me."

"Yes." Faint. Scary.

"I'm going to tie a rope around your middle, then I'm climbing back up. Once I'm there, I'll pull you to safety."

"That'll . . . be hard. Toss me . . . rope. I'll do my . . . part."

"Your part is to hush and pay attention. I'm experienced in rescue. Your head and arm will hurt like a bear."

"I have my own words . . . to describe it." He gasped.

"Yes, I heard them, rather colorful."

"I'm remembering a few things."

"Good. But don't push it. Do me a favor and stay lucid. I need to position your body so I can get you off this ledge."

"Did you call the rescue team?"

"They're expecting us at another site. Hours from here."

"Leave me. Go meet them."

"Not happening. We're partners."

"Okay." The faint sound told me talking had stolen his strength.

If only I could take away what he'd endured. "No need to say another word." I continued to encourage him while easing the rope under and around his waist twice. Blood trickled from the corners of his mouth. "Think about something fun, a favorite vacation."

"Like kissing you?"

I sighed. "I suppose if that works."

"You're . . . crazy. Leave me here."

"Listen to me. Together, we've got this. And I need your help. I must turn you onto your back. That will make pulling you up easier. Also, I want you to hold on to the rope with your right hand. Don't let go."

"My backpack's . . . gone," Blane burst out. "How did I lose it?"

Earlier he'd placed his phone in the zippered pocket of his pants. "We'll be fine."

"Not sure . . . how."

"Hush." My guess was the jagged rocks cut through the shoulder straps, but now wasn't the time to analyze how his backpack lay at the bottom of the canyon. With my phone.

I bent on the rock and rolled him inward to the incline. He screamed with the pressure of his body on his left arm. I rolled him onto his back. "Blane, I had no choice."

"Not the first time . . . I've broken a bone."

I pulled a sling from my backpack and slipped it over his head and cradled his arm. The excruciating agony on his face while he remained silent tore through me. I secured his glove and wrapped the rope around his right wrist. I stood to make the climb. "I'll tell you when I'm at the top and ready to hoist you up. Don't let go of the rope until we are safe. We'll manage your climb together."

He gripped the rope. "Okay."

"I'm sorry." I choked on the words. This wasn't like me—I'm levelheaded during emergencies. "Stay alert."

I hated to leave him. A wrong move on his part or mine, and we'd tumble to our deaths.

Grabbing the rope, I made it up to the trailhead where we'd started. I lay on my belly and alerted Blane that his time had come. "You can do this."

Blane's slow ascent started. He used his legs to raise himself until his broken arm hit against a mass of rock and debris. He shouted like a madman, echoing across the canyon. Chandler now could have no doubts as to our location.

My arms and shoulder muscles burned, making every upward inch a struggle and yet a victory. I paused, my body needing a moment's reprieve. Blane had helped me gain control of my emotions earlier, and I wanted to reciprocate. I practiced "Blane's inhale and exhale" technique. The strain and stress—worry for a good man—sent my head throbbing.

I needed supernatural strength, the kind only God provided. Determination grasped me like a vise, and I continued to pull Blane closer to me. With muscles screaming in protest, I heaved and prayed until I touched the fingers of his right hand and gripped them.

"Just a little more." I panted. "Push up with your legs so I can roll you onto the edge."

He finally sprawled out on the rock, and I gingerly tugged him away from the edge.

None of his pockets contained a phone.

What little intellect I had left must first assess his injuries—the source of blood oozing from his head needed stitches, the deepening blue-and-purple swelling around his left cheek and eye, and the task of setting, then splinting his arm. *God, help me.*

TWENTY-THREE

Those who affect us emotionally are always the ones we long to protect from suffering. Blane experienced a horrendous fall. My fault. I'd recruited him. I'd put aside my opposition to his lack of faith and coaxed him to join me. I'd done my best to give him solid safety instructions. Had I used his attraction to benefit my agenda?

"I'd give anything to be in your place," I said.

"No, you don't want any part of it. I'm miserable. Hurting. Mean. Cursing. And . . . a little late to use our code word for danger."

"Oh, yeah, scree. You are one strong man, and my hero."

He huffed. "The altitude has made you delirious."

"Blane, we will get through this." I visually explored around us. The wind blew like a vicious attack, and the narrow trail offered no shelter. I placed his hand in mine. "This cold makes it hard to breathe. First order of business—and I will do all I can to make it less painful—I'm going to put my blanket under your head, and I need you to hold it in place with your right hand. This will reduce the pressure on your head. Then I'll drag you down the trail by your feet to a rock cropping that offers protection from the weather. Once there, I'll tend to your head and set your arm. What do you say?"

He closed his eyes. "You're the expert."

"None of this has *easy* tagged on it."

"I might cuss a streak."

"I've heard them before." I kissed his forehead. Not sure why. Except he battled with a lot of pain. Who was I fooling? I cared about Blane far more than I should.

I carefully removed my backpack and carried it to the rock cropping that would serve as my ER room, a good fifty feet from where Blane lay. Once back at his side, I positioned the blanket under his head, placed my hands under his feet, and slowly maneuvered his body down the incline. Unfortunately, his left side with the twisted arm took the brunt of the move.

He closed his eyes.

"Stay with me. Please."

He clenched his jaw. "Hurry."

I told myself the slow descent had to be less strenuous on both of us than the hoist up the cliff. A hawk soared above in an incredibly blue sky. "You're missing a cloudless sky that would make a beautiful painting."

He whispered something unintelligible through tightly closed eyes, and I responded as though I understood. "Yes, you can take me to dinner when we're back in Houston. But I'm buying. Open your eyes so I can see you."

He obliged. "How much farther?"

"We're under overhanging rock where I'll make camp."

I positioned him under the rock cropping away from the wind, heat of day, and cold of night. I lifted my blanket from beneath his head and covered him. I shrugged off my jacket and used it as his pillow. I'd give him first aid, then build a fire. God understood my doubts, and He'd help me.

The flesh beneath his ripped and bloody clothes held my attention. The question of internal injuries bothered me—only a doctor could handle bleeding or damaged organs. I offered him a sip of water, and he thanked me.

Easing onto his back, he licked his bleeding lip. "If I need stitches . . . do it after . . . my arm's set."

"Okay. I'm sure every bit of your body hurts, but what I'm about to do will be worse."

He inhaled and stifled a groan. "I'll pacify myself that a beautiful woman is taking . . . care of me."

"Thank you for your vote of confidence."

A faint smile formed on his lips. "I will make it down these mountains, right beside you and Alina."

"We will." Turning to his arm and its awkward angle, I braved forward. "You told me you didn't have any health issues, was that the truth?"

"Yes. Please, get this done. At this moment, patience is not my virtue."

"I understand."

"Steak. I want a steak dinner."

I brushed my hand across his forehead and kissed it, dirt and all. His eyes were dilated. "Hush. You need your strength. Two steaks."

I used my pocketknife to cut away the jacket sleeve. Lots of blue and purple bruising. I breathed relief the bone didn't stick out through the skin. A three-inch gash above his elbow required stitches. Blane didn't need infection setting in and all those complications.

While I cleaned his arm and head with antiseptic pads, I shared about his injuries and what I planned to do. "Are you numb below or above your break?"

"I wish," he said through a pain-laden grimace.

I cautiously touched below and above the broken bone. He uttered a string of curses, then apologized. "You're doing what's best, but it hurts like—"

"It will be over soon. Please take another sip of water. Just a sip."

He lifted his head from the blanket pillow for the water bottle, but the lines etching into his features told me he was having a rough time. "Have you called Sergio?"

I wish. "We don't have a phone."

His gaze met mine. "It's not in your backpack?"

"My phone went over the edge during a skirmish with a rattler."

"You're not bitten?"

"No. I'm fine. I'll explain later. First, your arm needs realignment. This isn't setting the bone but to improve the circulation. I'm going to pull on it below the fracture. I've been trained in this and have set bones for others." He nodded his understanding, and I continued. "This. Will. Hurt."

"Figured it can't be much worse. My vote is to pass out."

"Might be easier if you did, except I need you awake with your head injury."

"Beats turning into the Hulk." He attempted a smile. "A kiss on my lips would make me feel better. Not my forehead."

I gave him a quick warning while I eyed the best way to straighten his arm. "I've seen the Hulk plenty of times, and kissing wasn't part of the script." I moved my hands down below the broken bone and examined the area. "One, two, three."

I pulled.

Blane shouted.

I tuned out his agony and finished aligning the bone. Resting back on my haunches, I studied him. Huge drops of sweat beaded the sides of his face.

"It's in place, Blane." I brushed a light kiss on his lips.

"That was better than a sucker and a balloon."

I sensed myself blushing like a schoolgirl. Yep, I definitely had the attraction thing going. I hid my realization and pulled out flexible aluminum splints and tape from my backpack. I grabbed my extra shirt.

"You have everything in there to bind it?" he said.

"This shirt will help pad the splints."

"Forget the padding. You'll need the shirt. Alina might need it on a cold night."

"Dirty and stinking might chase away Alina's kidnappers." I ignored him and tore my shirt into padding around his arm. I finished the splinting, not too tight to allow for swelling, all the while thanking God that Blane wasn't dead at the bottom of a canyon.

"How much daylight is left?" he said.

"Maybe thirty minutes."

"First thing in the morning, you've got to meet up with the team and find Alina. I'll be fine."

"Another topic to discuss later." I sterilized a needle and threaded it. "Keep talking to me while I sew you up. I need to place a few stitches in your head. Nasty concussion you have there. Do you feel nauseous?"

"No. Vision's blurred."

"To be expected." I ensured each stitch was precise with swift but careful movements. "What's your favorite boyhood memory?"

"Tenth birthday. My dad got me a horse."

"Aw. What a great gift. You rode as a boy?" I kept my eyes fixed on closing the nasty cut. *Please, no infection.*

"Yep. Competed in high school rodeo events."

"You were a real cowboy. That wasn't on your Ranger application. Did you collect all the trophies?"

"I did all right."

"Your humility tells me you were good. I bet the girls were all over you." I stitched up the open gashes, then applied an antibiotic gel and bandages. "Do your best to keep this clean. So a horse for your birthday. What's the date?"

"In two days."

I inhaled sharply. "I'm so sorry. This will go down in history as your worst birthday ever."

He closed his eyes. "Maybe my best. You kissed me." He slurred. "Back to my original statement before you distracted . . . me." He paused, and again the concussion symptoms showed through his speech. "Leave at first light. Find the team and bring Alina back."

I hated abandoning him or Alina. Choosing between two wrongs meant facing the consequences. The whirling sound of a helicopter grasped my attention. I rushed to my feet and stared up at the steadily darkening sky in the direction of the aircraft. Waving my hands wildly, I attempted to get its attention.

"Here! We're here." I repeated like a crazy woman. Those inside the aircraft didn't hear me, but I wanted to believe they knew exactly where we were. The pilot flew on to where the meetup was to take place—hours from where Blane and I camped. I returned to Blane and slumped beside him.

"Therese, I'm a big boy. You have a huge responsibility, and it's not about me. Alina deserves a chance at life. She's frightened and in danger." He struggled for breath. I touched his lips, but he shook his head. "She needs you and the team to yank her out of Chandler's clutches. And we have no idea about the kidnappers' ultimate plan. Do whatever it takes to get her back to Rurik. I'm glad it's my backpack at the bottom of a canyon. Yours has part of the ransom money."

He made sense. What else could I do? "What if Chandler shows up while I'm gone?"

"I'll tell him where he can put his feather."

TWENTY-FOUR

BLANE

In the bitter wind, Therese dug a hole like we'd done together on previous nights. She had a fire going as darkness wrapped around us and added another plunge of cold temps.

I sunk my teeth into my lower lip to manage the continuous throb in my arm and head. Therese had done a quick and good job of setting it, although I wanted to cry like a baby. Instead, I'd let out a string of curses that would cause Sergio's mother to wring her hands and give me a lecture on bad language.

"How do you plan to find the SAR team?" I struggled into a semi-upright position to reduce the pressure on my head.

"I'll start out at sunrise, but I'll leave you two military rations. Probably something you haven't eaten, but it's filling and nutritious."

"Oh, I have, and I'll eat the chocolate too, or I'll be constipated for a month." I pondered the danger she'd be in. "I prefer you keep the military rations. You or Alina might need them."

"I figured you'd refuse the food, so I'm going to prepare you a roasted feast."

"Rib eye?" We both laughed. I pointed to more tinder and kindling that she'd brought to our campsite earlier. "Are you planning on using those?"

"Just you wait and see. I'll create you a meal fit for a hero." She studied me in the flickering firelight. "I'm not sure how long I'll be gone, and this way you'll have food and water to last a few days. I know you're a trained paramedic, but please stay hydrated. If food makes you nauseous, leave it alone."

"I'll do my best to follow orders."

"A word of warning here, you have a nasty concussion. Do your best to stay awake. Stay warm. Oh, one more thing—if you sense rescuers are nearby, use my whistle. I'm placing it beside you."

"No way. And bring Chandler into the campsite to gloat?"

"As you and I have talked, he already knows where we are."

Talking hurt my whole body. "Grade-one concussion."

"More like grade two. You had temporary amnesia, and I've detected slurred speech."

I'd concede but not outwardly. The fall had done a number on my head.

Therese dug a second pit for the cooking fire. She added stones atop the flames and let it burn down. "I'm going to find an agave, cut off the prickly leaves, dig up the heart of it, and bring it back to roast. It's loaded with complex sugars and lots of calories. You'll have the distinct experience of a desert artichoke. The problem is the plant needs to cook eighteen to twenty-four hours for humans to digest." She adjusted her headlamp.

"Be careful," I said. "Hey."

She stared at me in the flickering light. How could one woman light up the night like she did?

"I will never forget how you saved my life, and the survival skills you've taught me. We have our differences, but I'm drawn to you like no other woman in my life."

Her gaze lingered. "You're speaking through your pain. But thank you, and I . . . wish things were different too."

"Those words will keep me warm."

She grabbed her machete and flashlight. "You'll be fine while I go hunting?"

"Sure. What are you hunting in the dark?"

"Food. The agave."

"You were serious. Be careful. Holler 'scree' if you need me."

Over an hour later, her hunting expedition and the length of time she'd been gone caused too many anxious scenarios to morph in my head. I warmed my hands and kept my attention affixed to where she'd trekked into the wild.

The combo of incessant pain and anxiety threatened to erupt into full-blown, red-visioned rage. My backpack lay at the foot of a pile of rock. It contained an extra shirt, water, and a blanket as well as several much-needed supplies. I added my cell and satellite phones to those essentials. And the keys to the Jeep parked near the Dog Canyon entrance. I swallowed hard to control my anger at what erupted around me. I stressed about Therese and poor Alina who might not have survived her captors.

Chandler might view this as a perfect opportunity to walk into the campsite. I picked up a rock. Fat lot of good this would do me peering down a rifle barrel. A typical David-and-Goliath scenario with the odds in his favor. I squeezed my eyes shut to wait until Therese returned. Maybe if I concentrated long enough, the head and arm pain might take a dive. They didn't. If this was what Therese's prayers had caused for God to get my attention, I'd rather she didn't consult Him.

Several minutes later she entered our campsite carrying the root of an agave, a rather bald agave, on her shoulder.

"Did you find the biggest one out there?"

"The bigger ones have the most sugar."

The stones had grown hot in her absence. She positioned the root atop the stones and used prickly pear leaves to cover it, which was supposed to keep the agave from drying out. Over the prickly palms she placed dead bark, then piled dirt over it.

"This will be your dinner tomorrow night," she said. "While I'm gone, go easy on the food and ration the water until I return. The agave is a bonus. I wish you had a weapon."

"I have a knife in my right boot."

"So do I."

"Then we can single-handedly take out a bear, mountain lion, or the worst kind—two-legged beasts."

"Ah, don't forget snakes. I haven't told you how I lost my phone." She proceeded to give me the short version of the rattler that slithered to coil himself beside her while she wrestled with how to get me to safety.

Having her back helped my attitude. "Thanks to you again for saving my life and ensuring I will again ride broncs with a good arm to keep me balanced."

"You've thanked me enough. We're chiseled from the same stone, Blane. You'd have done even more for me."

"If one of us had to go through the fall, I'm glad it was me."

Therese poked at the fire and hummed a tune. Where had I heard it before?

"What are you humming?" I said.

She tilted her head, with the regal air of a mountain queen. Her honey-blonde hair whipped back in the wind and her cheeks a rosy tint in the orange-yellow firelight demonstrated Therese didn't need a throne. Her demeanor spoke of stately beauty.

"It's 'Just as I Am.'"

"I recognized the hymn from my grandma's church."

"Oh, your grandma took you to church?"

"Yep. But it takes more than recalling a hymn," I said.

"You're so right. It takes an abiding faith in Jesus Christ."

"You don't mince words."

"Not when it comes to what I believe."

An acid bubble crept up my throat. "Where is your God now?"

"With us. No doubt."

"Is He cold? Arm broke? Without a phone? I can't see God or a supreme being in this."

"Blane, relying on God when life experiences challenge our every breath is hard. I agree this all seems unfair, and I'm angry too, but I know God is here. He is with us."

"Isn't life about learning from what is happening around us and processing that with our experiences?"

"Processing with truth that God is in control. He's sovereign and needs to be our first priority."

"Faith in God doesn't fit in my life. Looks like a crutch." I waved my hand. "Ignore me. I'm hurting and angry. Texas Rangers are supposed to be tough and problem solvers. They don't get their guns stolen, break their arm, get the sense knocked out of them, or lose phones and backpacks."

"Are Texas Rangers superhuman?" she said.

"Let me say not *this* superhuman."

"Remember my phone is taking up space at the bottom of the canyon too. That's the way we learn, Blane. Do you think I've never lost a backpack?" A quick dip of her head showed me I wasn't the only one who often learned the hard way.

She eased down beside me and examined my arm.

"Yes, it hurts, but I'll be fine. Therese, I hate seeing you trek out of here alone in the morning. What if you run into Chandler before the SAR team? Have you ever conducted negotiations?"

"Mostly reassuring whoever's lost or hurting that they will be okay." She poked at the fire. "Holding hands kind of thing, encouraging the victim to breathe and keep their eyes on me. I lack solid instruction other than caring and basic first aid."

I longed to chase away the brain fog to communicate what I did best. Weariness pulled me like a magnet into the world of sleep. But that proved dangerous. "You've dealt with Chandler, and he's cocky and manipulative. But who is with him? My money's on Jurg Falin. Though I guarantee you Chandler is calling the shots. Listen to what both men have to say, but more importantly, listen to what Chandler isn't saying." I swallowed hard against the incessant ringing in my ears and drilling in my head.

"Is talking too difficult?" she said.

"I'm . . . fine." I paused a moment more. "Normally I'd say whoever you're talking to is right and agree with them. In this case, concentrate on Chandler. How can you help him? Look inside the man. Keep your tone of voice low and conversational. The goal is for the right solution to be his idea. He must be convinced you sincerely hear and respect his every word. There are some things you can't promise—demands for weapons, money, or a sure escape. Blame the Rangers, FBI, local law enforcement, Russians. Whomever."

"Makes sense. I'm hoping he and whoever he's with want out of these mountains as soon as possible, which says the extra five hundred thousand may entice them to give up Alina." Therese hesitated. "But I have my doubts."

No point denying Chandler's unpredictable behavior. Thinking about Therese and Alina facing death added kindling to my guilt and fueled the furnace of my fall. "Have you ever used a knife to kill a man?"

"No. But I will do whatever is necessary." She patted the dirt on the roasting agave. "Told you before, I'd kill anyone to protect you or Alina."

We drank a little water, and Therese shared her blanket. I fought to stay awake. "I've ruined this mission."

"No, you haven't. We aren't the only ones trying to find Alina. But you are suffering, and I have pain pills. Please take one so you can sleep."

"Someone else might need it more than me."

"There's no reason to suffer when this will alleviate some of the pain. Pride, ego, and losing all manner of strength will stop us from getting out of here." She stared at me through the firelight. "It's not what we lose that defines our character—it's what we learn. You're a strong man, and I think you'll be surprised how this experience will transform you into a more formidable Ranger. You'll be teaching wilderness survival."

I cracked a smile through the pain. "You can leave me a few ibuprofens."

"We call them Vitamin I. I've stacked extra wood so you can stay warm."

"That is a feat considering the scarcity of it," I said. "I have no intention of letting the fire go out. Already set my internal alarm to check throughout the night."

"Perfect. And I'll be shaking you awake throughout the night.

Once I join up with the FBI team, help will be on its way to get you to a hospital."

"No, thanks. I'm staying right here until Alina is away from those animals. You need every available man on that team."

Our conversation ended, and soon Therese's even breathing indicated she slept. Or she wanted me to believe it.

I struggled not to move, although each breath brought a surge of agony. Staring up at the star-studded sky, the flickering sight of such uncontested beauty brought peacefulness that existed outside of my normal world. The dangers behind the unknown ahead butted against manning-up to the situation. Therese thought she'd failed, but I'd been the one to fall.

Fate had dealt us an ugly hand with a coiled rattler, a body slide, no phones or weapons, and limited supplies. Still Therese clung to her faith in a God who provided. So far, He'd done a lousy job of keeping us safe and helping us find an abducted little girl. God and I weren't on speaking terms, but He might listen to Therese.

TWENTY-FIVE

THERESE

Darkness cast its eerie cloak around us, and I kept the fire stoked. Blane did his best to keep an eye on it and not complain about his injuries. But his voice and ragged breathing showed how the pain pounded into every part of him.

Tom Chandler shattered my confidence, causing my knees to weaken. I'd rather wrestle a mountain lion with a taste for blood than what Chandler's evil thoughts conjured up. Death and destruction accompanied him like an old friend. Too many tales darted in and out of my day and night terrors, and whether true or not, those things made me shiver.

Alina, please do your best to appease your kidnappers.

I prayed for Alina, Rurik, Blane, the FBI team, the Texas Rangers, and myself. God had a plan, and I refused to lose faith.

"I'm not asleep," Blane said above the stillness.

I'd rather we pursued silence until sleep overcame us. "Doubtful you will without a pain pill, but I understand your reluctance. Your whole body endured a horrible beating. My worry—"

"Enduring it builds my character."

I smiled in the shadows. *Poor man.* "Do you want me to send up a flare for the rescue team?"

"Are you crazy? That's like your whistle. Increase the chances Chandler and his sidekick step into *our* campsite carrying *our* guns aimed at *our* heads?"

I laughed. "We've been blindsided, robbed, and nearly killed, but you still find a way to make me forget about it all."

"I aim to please. I haven't heard your ghost story."

Sleep evaded me, so his idea would keep me off the mission. The fire crackled, and sparks shot up as though competing with the stars' intensity. "I can't tonight. Finish what happened with Wendy."

"You're a tough one." He drew in a painful breath. "Not much to tell. I stayed at the party. Irresponsible. Drunk. She'd have been safe if I had acted like the man she deserved. Doesn't matter our values were on opposite ends of the spectrum. I made a poor choice, and God punished her. And me. I should have handled the situation better."

"God doesn't work in ways to deliberately hurt us."

"I disagree with you. Others have played the convincing game from my mother to Sergio and his family. Not going there." He bit back a moan.

I wanted to take away his pain—all of it. "You don't need to tell me any more."

"I need to, and I've come this far. If you were the one with the haunting story, I'd be encouraging you to continue. Tell you how much better you'd feel and not to keep a padlock on your past."

"I'm not you, Blane. But I'm thinking hard about it."

"Do men always spill their guts around you?"

"Only those with concussions who break their arm."

"And have their gun stolen and lose their backpack and phone?"

"How did you guess?"

He chuckled, then quickly sobered. "I'm going to try to sleep."

I lay awake thinking about Blane. We'd both suffered loss. We risked our lives for others with some skewed sense of redemption for ourselves, and neither of us had allowed God to heal us. Here we were stranded in the high desert to rescue a helpless child, looking more like two failures.

Tonight, with the pressures of the undertaking bearing down on my shoulders and the obstacles stalking us, I saw how easily a person might walk away from God. I nearly did when Kate and then Mom and Dad had died. But my grandmother's words of God's love never let me go. Even if I couldn't bring myself to tell the story . . . and how rescuing Alina seemed like I was rescuing Kate.

TWENTY-SIX

ALINA

Daddy had taught me about guns, how to clean, load, fire, and be very careful with what he called handguns and rifles. He told me guns were like people and to respect them. Guns in the wrong hands could hurt and kill others, and he said never point a gun at anyone unless I wanted to face the consequences of shooting them. I didn't understand the big word *consequences*, but Daddy said it was like me doing something bad on purpose, knowing I'd be punished.

He also told me not to tell anyone that he'd taught me these things, not even Daria. Why? He kept his guns in a secret place in our house, and he and Daria each had a key to unlock it.

I missed Daddy so much.

The sun hadn't come up, but I watched the two men who'd kidnapped me. Mr. Chandler, the man who used lots of bad words, gave the orders. I was more afraid of him than Mr. Falin, who'd been nice to me back home in Houston. Each laid guns at the cave's opening and packed water into their backpacks.

They must be planning to hurt someone. Maybe the people who were looking for me . . . or my daddy.

Mr. Falin bent and studied me. "You haven't been much trouble," he said in Russian, and I looked into his dark-blue eyes. "Rurik taught you well. If there was a way to spare you, I would, but too much is at stake. Rurik allowed this to happen by being a coward. Your father is *glupyy*."

My daddy wasn't stupid, but I said nothing, only listened. What did the men really want? Maybe I could get my hands untied while they were gone, then I could run away.

"Can I ask you something?" I said in Russian.

He frowned. "*Da*. Keep your voice down."

Mr. Chandler strung a wire across the cave's opening.

"What has my daddy done to make you mad?"

He huffed. "It's what he hasn't done."

"If he does this thing, will you let me go?" I believed he'd take me home, but I wanted him to say it.

"Maybe."

"Have you asked him?"

"He refused in the past, but he didn't anticipate we'd snatch you."

"Have you done something to Daria?"

"She's dead."

I choked back throw-up. One of them had killed Daria?

He pulled a bandana from around his head. "Open your mouth."

I did as he asked, and he placed the dirty bandana in it and tied it around my head. The dirt taste and sweaty smell rolled around in my tummy. I tried to spit it out, and he laughed. "Can't have you screaming and ruining our plans. The irony is if someone enters the cave, they'll trip, setting off an explosion and blowing you and them to pieces."

Mr. Chandler walked into the cave and stood over me like a shadowy giant. He tossed me my backpack. "Untie her. I have an idea." He glared at me. "Do exactly as I say."

TWENTY-SEVEN

THERESE

I left Blane with half of my water, food, antibiotic gel, Vitamin I, and bandages. If I was lucky, I'd find a trickle of water not far from the meetup location with the FBI team and the Rangers. One of the disadvantages of hiking a rescue mission came with negative think time. A pleasure hike promised a worshipful experience but not this morning. My imagination steered toward the worst of the worst.

Did the team believe Blane and I were in a dangerous situation—or worse? Without our phones, no one had means to contact us.

I hiked four hours to the agreed-upon FBI rendezvous only to find it void of anyone. Signs of six agents caught my scrutiny. They'd spent the night and headed in a westerly direction. The impressions of the helicopter's rails indicated the aircraft had dropped off the team, then flew back, possibly to the Dog Canyon Visitor's Center for further instructions. Would the team's search be divided between finding us and Alina?

For the next thirty minutes, I followed the team in a westerly direction toward a section where Chandler was certain to avoid with more open territory. The visibility showed everything for miles, and Chandler slithered like a snake, hiding under rocks and striking when his pursuers least expected it. I hadn't heard rifle fire in that direction, but his skills with a knife had caused good men to lose their lives. Rumors said he'd cut the heart out of his victims and eat it.

Don't go there.

I shook off my terror and concentrated on His peace to take control.

I scanned the rough terrain east to west through binoculars. A faint puff of smoke rose north of me. Part of the team or Chandler's camp? Or a means to throw off pursuers? The last thing Chandler would permit is a fire. But the telltale signs meant humans who might have seen or heard something. I took shelter behind rocks and brush and ventured toward the smoke.

I picked up the trail, about a day old, of two adults and one child and followed faint footprints moving northerly. At times I lost the tracks where the high winds had scattered them. I'd move ahead and check out the westerly indications of life later.

Nearing a rock elevation, I crawled to the top, leaving fall foliage behind me. The terrain before me brought only more of the same barren rock. In the distance, an elk herd moved south toward more vegetation. I searched the area again to catch sight of the three, but if Tom Chandler guided them, he'd stay hidden. Blane had called this a game of cat and mouse. But I was finished playing the role of a rodent. I preferred face-to-face woven with skill.

I took a sip of water, and Blane entered my thoughts. He had provisions to last a few days and a knife. We'd shared serious talks, and I attributed those to the uncertainty of a dangerous mission. Different personalities chose different paths of conversations on rescue missions. Some people, mostly men, chose not to speak. Some were so tired that all they wanted was to fill their bellies and sleep. Some used humor to lighten the seriousness of their circumstances. And a few, like Blane, chose to engage in personal topics. He'd honored me with his story about the girl from college. His experience gave me a better understanding of his behavior and the drive to help and lead others. A trusted friend.

God was using a man struggling in his faith to accomplish good. I longed for Blane to embrace Jesus, but first he needed to want a relationship with Him. My grandmother told me everyone had an empty spot inside him that only the Lord could fill. The man was starting to hold a fragile piece of my heart. Yet it dared not go anywhere.

How many times must I tell myself those words?

Through the binoculars, about fifty yards from me, blue plaid fabric made a stark contrast to the earth colors. Heat rose to my face, and I held my breath. Alina's school uniform—held down by a rock. Beside the uniform sat a pair of dark-blue tennis shoes. The kidnappers wanted me to find her clothing. Through my binoculars, I explored every direction. Only emptiness. What did Alina wear now? Did the little girl lay dead or hurt in the brush and rock cropping nearby? Or were the men hiding until I approached? If Alina was dead, Rurik stepped dangerously close to a mental breakdown, the kind from which some people never recovered.

I'd survive. I always did. Just like Blane and the ghosts stalking him . . . Alina physically looked like my sister, Kate—white-blonde hair, blue eyes. Two little girls facing death through dire circumstances beyond their control.

I pulled out a knife from my boot and scouted a route to Alina's clothes without too much exposure. Blane said the only reason the kidnappers would have brought Alina here was to dispose of her body, and he might have been right. Although the truth scraped at my longing to find her safe, I needed God to prepare me for what the future held. I feared the closer I crept to the uniform, the closer I'd come to her body.

Crouching low, I made my way to Alina's school clothes. The wind rustled the brown vegetation, but I saw no visible signs of life. With dread tracking every step, I studied the little girl's jumper, T-shirt, shoes, socks, and a headband . . . Droplets of blood splattered the jumper skirt and onto the tennis shoes.

A peregrine falcon feather was anchored beneath the dirt-laden shoes.

I slumped to the ground, overcome with sobs in a tsunami of grief not experienced since Kate's death. Images of my sister on her last day mingled with my blurred vision. I wrestled to rein in my emotions, but my futile efforts increased the intensity. Alina hadn't contracted a deadly disease. She'd been kidnapped to prove a point by ruthless men. Chandler and the kidnapper probably watched my display of grief, enjoying my loss of control. What they failed to perceive was how the unscrupulous crime strengthened my resolve for justice.

I struggled to my feet and turned in every direction. "You coward! You miserable animal!" I raised my voice and my fist. "I'll find you. You will pay for what you've done to Alina."

Haunting silence echoed around me, mocking my tattered cries. I rolled up the school uniform and stuffed it into my backpack. Every rock and bush were sealed to memory. Disturbing a crime scene struck me as wrong, but by the time anyone arrived, the wind would have blown away the evidence.

I pursued the compass of logic. The kidnappers had two options—leave the Guadalupe Mountains with charges of kidnapping and murder on their tail or resort to cave mode until we pulled back, allowing them to escape. Both scenarios labeled them as wanted men. Both scenarios put them in hiding. Rurik had paid the ransom, and they might have escaped to Russia or another third-world country.

Why leave Alina's clothes and not her body? I hoped she still lived, and I clung to her survival. If she was alive, what unpredictable spot held her? The tracker in her shoes and necklace had led us to these mountains, and unless she wore a second pair of shoes with trackers, our search was futile. Had Chandler been surprised that we pursued him into Dog Canyon? Many areas around me contained the seclusion he craved. Had he hiked in with supplies? A helicopter could bring him whatever he needed.

I crept back to higher ground. From the sun's slow descent, I barely had time to get back to where the FBI team had camped the previous night, which left Blane alone. I lifted my face to a gray sky and met a sharp wind that stung my cheeks. *God, show me the right direction.*

Think like Chandler . . . Put yourself in his shoes.

Cunning, evil, game player.

Speculation took control of my thoughts. *Help me focus*. What if the clothes were planted to throw me and the rescue team off the real trail? What if they had a change of clothes for Alina? What if they'd discovered the tracker in her shoes?

What attracted Chandler to Dog Canyon? Why bring a helpless child over a perilous trail? Something in this locale called to him . . . but what?

Concentrate.

Pulling out the paper map from my shirt pocket, I smoothed it with my hands. A destination rose in my memory, and I refolded the map. Yes, I'd been there.

TWENTY-EIGHT

Rifle fire split the afternoon air, jarring me into alert mode. Then another crack. Given the terrain and the wind, the shot had originated from the west. The sound hadn't come from Blane's direction, and I breathed out my relief. Had the rescue team found Chandler?

My knife had *pointless* inscribed on the blade.

No more rifle fire sounded. Only wind and high desert quietness greeted me. I'd come this far to check out a secluded site, and I'd not leave until I was sure Chandler hadn't taken Alina there.

I followed a trail toward a deserted cave I'd stumbled onto about three years ago. Behind thick brush and rock, it offered protection from the elements. The way wasn't noted on any trail guides, and none of my park ranger friends talked about it, especially with the unspoken agreement with the Apache nation to keep the caves sacred and unmarked. If Chandler and other men were in the cave, Alina would have found it difficult to climb the steep slope.

Who was I fooling? I doubted she lived. Still, I'd given my word to Rurik, and I'd find her and bring her home—no matter the condition of her body.

I hiked to higher ground and studied the area behind me where I'd left Blane. In about an hour, I'd be down and across the canyon floor, then up to the cave's entrance. If my idea didn't pan out, I'd hurry back to Blane even in the dark. As much as I wanted to investigate the smoke seen earlier in the west, I wouldn't risk Blane spending too much time alone, especially in his physical condition. He'd done his best to cover the excruciating pain, and I fretted about internal injuries.

Once I made it to the cave, I'd send up a flare. Should have done so early this morning, but like Blane had pointed out, we risked alerting Chandler to our latest position and without a gun . . . Most likely he watched every move we made. That theory struck terror as much as finding Alina dead. Or both she and Blane dead.

Something poked me in the small of my back. I whirled around to the grizzled Chandler scowling at me under the brim of a tattered hat. He'd grown a beard that matched his wiry and graying hair. He glared at me through dark, beady eyes over a hooked nose.

Horror washed over me . . . the monster in my nightmares. With the rifle braced against his shoulder and aimed at me, the skull tattoos on his sleeveless upper arm grinned like demons. He resembled a bull from my girlhood days.

A shorter second man, whom I recognized as Jurg Falin, stood with him. He had a rectangular face, dark-blue eyes, bald head, and a rounded body—more like a harmless neighbor than a killer.

"Look who we have here, Falin." Chandler smirked. "Miss Survival Expert."

I tamped down my fear and lifted my chin, trying to recall every word of my crash course in negotiation. "Hello, Tom, how are you this beautiful day?"

"Much better now that you're at the other end of my rifle barrel." His glare stayed fixed on me.

"How can I help you?" *Keep yourself calm.*

"You already have. Made my day."

"Maybe you can help me." I smiled. "I'm looking for Alina Ivanov."

"Really? I saw you found her clothes."

"Thanks. Was that intentional?"

"What do you think?" Chandler's dark eyes hardened. "Worked, didn't it?"

Act like you care about him. "I'm trying to find Alina. What can I do to ensure she's reunited with her father?"

"Not a thing."

"Is she alive?"

"She's headed in the same direction you are."

He planned to kill us. "I understand. She's just a child. Is there something else going on here? How can I convince you to release her?"

"Only money. Lots of it."

"How much do you need? I have five hundred thousand in my backpack, and Rurik paid the ransom. Looks like you have a bonus."

He yanked the pack off my shoulders. "Ivanov gave you this?"

"Yes, he desperately wants his daughter returned."

"It's not enough money. My trouble is worth more than this."

"If you want more, I can call him."

"How? You don't have a phone."

Jerk. "Let me use yours and arrange a drop-off or—"

"Shut up. If he wanted his daughter back, why didn't he follow through with Falin's demands?"

"I'll talk to him again. What can I do to convince you to let Alina go?"

"Not a thing." He sneered and stuck his rifle barrel under my chin.

"Why this remote area? I assumed you'd operate from a Mexican resort."

"I admit to having friends where it counts."

"Tom, are you working with the cartels and the ROC?"

"Both pay the bills."

"If you're afraid, I will do what I can for your protection."

He scoffed at me. "I'm sure you heard the rifle fire. Let me set you at ease. The Texas Ranger? He has two holes in his chest. What's left of him."

Nausea swept over me, and I tossed Blane's advice about pretending to be Chandler's friend. Those tactics spit into the wind. "The rifle fire didn't come from where I left him."

"You made a stupid mistake, and I thought you were better trained."

"Takes a big man to shoot an unarmed, wounded one."

He took aim. "Care to join him?"

Calm down. "Looks to me like you haven't given me much of a choice. Have you been carrying a grudge since we first met?"

"Time to even the score." He snorted. "I told Falin you're a worthy opponent. Gives me a lot of satisfaction to have you look down the barrel of my rifle."

I'd taken a gamble by calling him out. I waited to see if he pulled the trigger, or if I'd bought some time.

"I've planned about how you'd pay," he said. "Sure would be easy to blow your head off, but not my plan." He pointed the barrel in the direction of the hidden cave. I wanted Alina to be there alive and unharmed.

"One more thing," I said. "I saw smoke west of here."

"Not me. A couple of hikers. But they are no longer a problem with their throats cut." He laughed an evil, low-throated sound and spun me around to poke his rifle barrel in my back. "Walk and don't try a thing."

I made my way several feet and searched my survival skills on how I'd escape him. Then Chandler took the lead. I walked between him and Falin across a stretch of canyon floor to a strenuous climb extending up to brush and the rock-hidden cave. I'd been right about their location. Dead right.

Falin grunted and groaned with every step. He had no hiking skills, body strength, or endurance. Doubtful Chandler planned to keep him alive much longer.

Bringing Alina here made little sense and was too elaborate for a basic kidnapping. What had Blane and I missed? The one drawback of me giving Falin a shove backward was the odds of Chandler sending me right down those rocks with Falin.

Chandler's boasting that he'd killed Blane clawed at my unspoken feelings . . . as if I'd fired the shots. He'd lied about Blane to defeat me, but Chandler had no idea about my God's power.

Poor Alina. What hideous ordeals tortured her? I'd learned from my own experiences that the loss of innocence stalked a person—like a hungry predator. Often healing came at the price of mental pain that became physical, and the two formed an emotional dependence that filled the victim with lies and doubts about themselves. They believed they couldn't survive without the familiar hurt. I should know . . . it had walked with me for twenty years.

My faith offered a glimmer of light—rescue might happen. I longed to pray, but only three words repeated. *God, help us.*

TWENTY-NINE

BLANE

I'd been on stakeouts, waited out bad guys, been a moving target, and hit by bullets, but nothing compared to each slow minute with the tormenting sledgehammer pounding in my arm and a dizzying throb in my head. I'd gotten to the point of being willing to welcome Chandler into my camp. Or offering to share a military ration with a bear, including the chocolate bar.

I added another log to the fire and admired the sparks of red and yellow. At dusk the dirt-covered mound containing the agave would be ready to eat. Hunger weakened me, and my head thumped. Taking a sip of water, I gauged Therese might be back tomorrow. I missed her, my gorgeous wilderness-survival expert.

The crack of rifle fire jolted me straight up. Then another. The origin confused me, or was my fever-stricken body messing with my head? *Therese, are you okay?* I gasped. Was the rescue team in a firefight? I wanted a repeat of rifle fire to confirm someone had taken out Chandler.

Like always, in moments with idle time on my hands, my thoughts veered back to Wendy. My mother said forgiving myself was more about me than Wendy's inability to keep my truck on the road. I'd be the first to offer that advice to someone else, but deep down I deserved the condemnation. My fault. I'd cursed her. And God's fault. He allowed the accident to happen.

Blane, you've held on to this for too long.

Startled, I swung to find the origin of the voice. No one but me in the outcropping of rocks. The horror of fever and infection in my arm seized me, convincing me I'd heard a man's voice in my delirium. Was God lecturing me? How could someone I didn't believe in talk to me?

Please, shelter Therese and Alina from harm.

Who was I talking to? Surely not God? Where had the high altitude and my battered body taken my mind?

Perspiration dripped down the sides of my face, and I shivered. I examined what I could see around the makeshift splint. Sure enough, the stitched area above my elbow where Therese had sewn me up flamed hot, red, and swollen. I changed the bandage and applied antibiotic ointment.

Closing my eyes, I drifted into the in-between world of semiconsciousness. Falling asleep between throbs of pain only to waken with my head and arm in a burst of agony.

Therese, are you okay? Have you found the rescue team and Alina?

I craved to hear her voice like a miracle drug. Being alone with her these past few days had ignited old emotions and deepened the longing for a relationship. My attraction spurred me to leave behind a better legacy in death than the one I'd created.

I lay flat under the rock and pulled the blanket over me. Hold on. This was Therese's blanket. Somewhere out there she'd suffer without a covering to keep her warm. Why hadn't I paid attention instead of allowing my fall to control every move?

I slid my knife from my front pants pocket and groaned through the movement to sit. My arm hurt like someone held a match to it, but I had a job to do. I stumbled to the dwindling stack of wood and tossed one on the small fire. Soon a semblance of heat warmed me.

A few feet to the left lay dried brush and pieces of kindling. Biting back the dizziness, I made my way over rocks and gathered more kindling and wood, what I could find. One of the pieces would sharpen into a weapon. I glanced about for a narrow limb to use as a crutch and keep my balance. Took me the better part of two hours to find one. More than once, I stopped to endure the damage done to my body. When this ordeal hit the closed file, I'd invest in ibuprofen stock.

Glancing at the sky, I calculated about three hours left of daylight. Time to check out the valley for a friendly park ranger. My body fought each step, and I vowed to clamp the cuffs on Chandler.

Leaning against a waist-high rock, I gave my body a rest and stared out over the landscape. Leaving the items at the bottom of a canyon in my backpack rubbed against my training—a phone at the top of my list. The rescue team carried those essentials, including binoculars. I waved my crutch in the air. "Help." My voice echoed around me.

Only silence met my frantic call.

My concerns swept back to Therese. I wanted her safe with the rescue team, but what if Chandler had her? I shook and fell to my knees until my head cleared. My response had nothing to do with the wind but my helpless body that couldn't protect Therese. Chandler's reputation for torturing made my skin crawl. If he hurt her or Alina, he'd taste the smoking end of my gun.

I limped back to the mound of dirt that buried the agave and used my trowel to dig into the hole. I slid to my knees with the blinding pain in my head, piercing my resolve to man up. Using my knife, I cut into the agave and poked a piece into my mouth. The sticky, sweet substance had a squash-like flavor. I ate my fill, washed it down with rationed water, and covered the agave back up. Therese had said it contained lots of calories and nutrients for the body. Great remedy if it healed the infection in my arm and eliminated the pain.

Loneliness shadowed me and my concern for others. I should be carrying a gun and tracking down a vicious criminal. Instead, I faced a long night and too much anxiety for even a healthy man. I added dried vegetation and kindling to the fire, creating smoke to rise into a star-flecked sky. Using my blanket, I sent a *help* message through a series of three smoke signals. Therese would have instructed me to build three triangle fires, but that was impossible.

Every twenty minutes I sent another message until I totaled five messages. In the morning, I'd attempt to carry brush and kindling to the higher elevation, make a fire, and repeat the smoke routine. I'd like nothing better than for a park ranger to investigate who'd broken the rules to build a fire.

God, if You're real, keep those in danger safe.

THIRTY

THERESE

The dark climb to the hidden cave shoved dread into my bones. No satisfaction filled me for being right about Chandler's location. Blane dead? It couldn't be true. My knees nearly gave way. I'd heard the rifle fire, no denying it. Had the dear man sacrificed his life for Alina and justice?

Please, let Alina be alive.

Falin removed the brush concealing the cave's entrance and a trip wire. He stepped aside for Chandler and me to enter. A flashlight showed a small figure leaning against the left cave wall.

"Alina," I whispered.

Chandler snorted. "Hey, kid, I brought someone to keep you company." He pushed me toward her. "Get over there by the kid."

I stumbled beside her onto the hard ground. "Alina, are you okay?"

She nodded and attempted to talk with a filthy rag in her mouth. A tear trailed down her cheek. I brushed it away with my finger and drew her close. Sobs racked her little body.

"My name is Therese," I whispered. "I don't know if you remember me from the Christmas party at the college. Your daddy loves you so much. Many good people are looking for you."

Chandler whirled to face me. "Shut up, or we can end this now."

He yanked Alina away from me and tied my hands and feet. But not my mouth. "Cause me any trouble, and the kid watches while I peel back every inch of your skin. Your choice. I want to hear you scream." He pulled his phone from his pocket and disappeared into the night.

I bent close to her. "I'm praying for God to rescue us."

Alina closed her eyes and leaned her head against the cave wall. Had she given up on rescue? Had they hurt her? Fury burned hot in my soul. No child should experience the greed of controlling men.

THIRTY-ONE

BLANE

I lay in excruciating pain that kept me awake and thinking. My ruminating resembled racing mustangs, and the infection in my arm had spread. I touched the blood-red and swollen bandage, where the stitches had popped, and heat radiated through to my fingertips. Yep, my arm needed medical treatment. Oh, yeah, today was my birthday. I might not make it through the first day of my thirty-fourth year with both arms . . . or my life.

My thoughts dwelled on scenarios of what might be happening where I had no control. I'd given Therese a tutorial to help her negotiate with Chandler and his sidekick. I'd always believed good overcame evil. With that animal, I doubted my convictions.

The fever caused my teeth to chatter. I stoked the fire and stared into the low flames. Wendy's face came into view . . . I sat on the beach at night with a crackling fire and Wendy by my side. The gorgeous, dark-haired beauty had become a challenge to me. I proclaimed my love and begged we give ourselves to each other. If she loved me, she'd show her feelings. She said God reserved sex for marriage. And the conversation came up repeatedly.

A lifelong commitment never occurred to me, so I lied and

promised her whatever she wanted to hear at the time. What a shallow and immature kid. No surprise I despised myself now.

To her credit, she never broke her resolve. Why she put up with me was a mystery. Maybe she saw something in me worth holding on to. What did she see worth dying for?

Therese had pointed out that Wendy made the decision to drive my truck. But I handed her my keys with final words that would send me straight to hell. Since then, I blamed God and myself, mostly myself. A bit ironic to blame someone I didn't believe in. Or did I?

I wanted a perfect deity to be in control, but I sure didn't measure up to a good man. I'd seen so much violence from those who wore greed and selfishness like scout badges. I'd fallen over that cliff too, hit the rocks of shame and self-loathing. The accusing demon chased me, always nipping at my heels.

I love and forgive you, Blane. Forgive yourself.

I shivered, and the hairs on my neck tingled. The voice again, the One who had spoken to me moments before. Clear. Audible. Real. Searing heat radiated from my head. Fever. Delirium. No voices. Probably dying.

Forgive yourself, Blane.

I bolted and grabbed my broken arm, throbbing with the quick move. "Who are you?" I whispered.

But the One who'd spoken my name wasn't a mystery. The voice was the One I refused to accept as sovereign. Had God shown up to walk with me into the hereafter, one with more misery than I'd ever known? My grandmother had urged me to turn my life over to Jesus. Instead my spiritual life flattened at zero.

Sharp pain sent lightning through my body. If I recognized God's voice, then heaven and hell had to be real places. Maybe my disbelief in God stemmed more from my anger at why this world was so prone to blackness, and why He did nothing about it. He created this mess and allowed good people to suffer. I groaned with the anger.

My body protested each breath, and I questioned surviving until morning. My fever had spiked, and chills shuddered through me. Guess God would escort me to Satan's doors. I deserved it.

I studied the stars, picking out the constellations. Normally I'd sense immense isolation and sadness in staring at the vastness above me. Odd, I didn't feel alone. I must surely be dying.

My thoughts turned to Therese . . . Her honey-blonde hair and blue-green eyes, the oval face of an angel. A woman of strong faith and a friend of humility. Even with Wendy I hadn't thought of having a lasting relationship. And here I was, dying under the stars with a ton of regret and wishing I had a huge do-over. A life with Therese, building a home, having kids, growing older with gray hair, wisdom lines, and memories. Not happening but what a dream.

She would tell me to put the past where it belonged if only for a couple of hours until I drew my last breath. I never imagined I'd reach out for salvation, but the pull—no, desperate need—had tugged at me since I'd said yes to finding Alina.

Here I am, God. I forgive myself for Wendy's death. While I'm at it, please forgive me for blaming You. I've got a wagonload of sins, so I'm confessing and believing You are here. I have no idea if I'll live one more hour or day or more, but I'm Yours. Thank You for Jesus . . .

The sound of muffled voices roused me from a world where pain burned like a furnace in my body. In the darkness I saw no one. Had I died? If so, how was I supposed to handle life from now on? Should I feel anything? Were the voices demons or angels?

"Blane," a voice said. A man, I think.

I struggled to respond, but verbal and physical paralysis seized me. My body clung to the ground as though invisible strength held me tightly.

"Get his vitals. Start an IV," the voice said.

I must be alive. Someone poked and prodded. I moaned.

"Blane, if you can hear me, I'm Dave with the FBI rescue team. We saw your signal for help."

I attempted to raise my hand and wiggle a finger.

"Good. You can hear me. Looks like you've broken your arm. I'm assuming Therese Palmer set it. We haven't heard from or seen her. Chandler's out there somewhere with Jurg Falin and Alina Ivanov. We—"

"Temp 104. BP 160/120," another man said.

"Call the park ranger at the Dog Canyon Station. We need a helo pickup in the morning to get our guy to the hospital. The ranger there said a helo could land in a canyon about three hours from here. I have the location coordinates. We'll call at daybreak once we're on our way," Dave said. "Blane, sure wish you were able to talk. We've got an IV sending meds that will make you feel better and start the healing process. Help you sleep too. Hang in there, buddy. You're gonna be okay."

Someone covered me with a blanket while warmth flowed through my body. Had he said Jurg Falin was with Chandler?

"I'm calling Major Montoya," Dave said. "He wanted to be notified as soon as we found you."

I wanted to thank him and ask him to give Sergio a message. To tell him I was fine, and God and I were in good shape. Guess I'd tell him later. God had spared me, but for what purpose or why?

"Therese." Her name came out in a hush.

A hand rested on my arm. "We'll find her," Dave said. "And the little Ivanov girl. Which way did Therese go?"

"To . . . find . . . you. Alina."

"The meetup location."

I tried to nod, humiliated that I was helpless to those who had the manpower and weaponry to keep Therese safe. In my own pitiful, fever-infested state, I confessed my growing feelings. She'd be thrilled I'd found God. Even if facing death had shaken my senses. And the voice.

"Major Montoya, this is FBI Agent Dave Tanner. We found Blane Gardner shortly after 1:00 a.m. He's alone. Dehydrated. Concussion. Broken arm with infection. Ms. Palmer set it, but she's not here. Transporting him in the morning by helo to Covenant Health Hospital in Hobbs." Silence. "Part of the team will head out then to pick up her trail. No sign of Chandler." Silence again. "Yes, sir. Be glad to." Dave placed his satellite phone to my ear.

"Blane, this is Sergio. You scared us, bro, and I'll give you a butt chewin' real soon. The FBI team have orders to find Therese and Alina. And to arrest Chandler, Falin, and whoever else might be with them. I've learned more info about Russian involvement in locating Edik Baranov and the details leading up to the murder of Daria Ivanov plus the kidnapping. Will fill you in later. Right now, let these good men take care of you. I'm catching the next flight to Hobbs."

"Th . . . anks." What info had Sergio uncovered? I hated not having the latest intel. I squeezed my eyes shut and willed the pain to subside. Questions pelted me with no answers. Nothing new. I shoved aside the old habit of control and asked God to keep Therese, Alina, and the rescue team safe. What a switch. Anxiety clung to me like wet dirt, but I grasped the reality that I wasn't alone. So new to this faith thing. Who'd ever imagine Blane Gardner would become a Christian?

Sleep called my name, and I despised the way my body refused to work. Therese's welfare chained me. *Please keep her safe.* Chandler never left a vendetta alone, and neither did he let someone assume power.

"At the crack of sunrise, we're going to lift you up and carry you down this trail. I won't lie to you," Dave said. "This won't be easy and it's gonna hurt."

THIRTY-TWO

The meds dripping into my body numbed the pain and allowed me a couple hours of sleep. I woke with the stirring of men and readied myself for the three-hour ride to meet the helo. I counted six armed, buffed agents. The cavalry had arrived. The same helo from the previous day would bring four Rangers to assist the FBI team, and then transport me to the hospital in Hobbs.

I despised not working alongside the others. Another time. Another mission. Therese had shown me the power of trust, and I clung to it with both hands like the rope she'd used to pull me up from the rock ledge.

Dave knelt beside me. "We're about to head down to meet the helo. I've given you meds to relax you, but—"

"The jarring will be painful."

Dave exhaled. "Excruciating if one of the men slip."

"Thanks," I said. "Your team saved my life. I'll never forget it."

He smiled and checked the straps on the stretcher. "You're welcome, but you were the one who had the foresight to signal for help. By this afternoon, you'll be in a clean bed with medical personnel taking care of you."

"I'd stay right here if it meant finding Therese and the little girl quicker."

He patted my right shoulder. "I'm on your side, buddy. You called out Therese's name in your sleep. God too. We're on the same team."

"I'm new to faith," I said.

"My dad showed me how to live a godly life." He held his breath. "My wife died in a car accident four months ago. It's just me and our six-month-old daughter. Life's hard, but He's always there."

"I'm sorry for your loss." What if I lost Therese?

"Yeah. Me too. You'll get through this, just don't let go."

More confirmation of God's presence. "You'll get word to me when Therese and Alina are safe?"

"Count on it."

Two men lifted me from the ground onto the stretcher. Despite their attempt to be gentle, my body protested every move. If the men balancing me tumbled downhill, I'd bounce like a burrito. Later I'd laugh about the idea, but not now.

"Hey, man, we've got you," the agent said on my right. "I'd planned to take my father-in-law fly-fishing this morning. Another day . . . then I can tell him all about carrying you down off this mountain."

"Listen up," Dave said to the men. "Keep your eyes peeled for Chandler and Falin. We're perfect targets out in the open. As soon as we load Blane into the helo and replenish our water, we'll split up to find Alina Ivanov and Therese Palmer."

The slow hike down brought good and dread at the same time. We men were so fickle, especially those of us who wanted to look like heroes when we're crumbling on the inside. One minute I held my breath and in the next, I blew out the agony.

The fisherman on my right must have sensed my pain tolerance waning, and he started telling me his fishing stories. I listened hard. Nothing to do but swallow my moans and close my eyes.

I claimed I had my mental footing, then fell, battering and bruising my body. But in the struggle, I learned the value of trusting God. How strange I'd changed my way of viewing life in a matter of a fall that nearly killed me.

Someday I'd return here and paint the magnificence of these stone citadels.

THIRTY-THREE

THERESE

Leaning back against the cave wall, I'd slept little. Weariness fought my goal of gathering strength to escape Chandler and Falin. From a glimpse of light coming from the cave's entrance, I imagined sunrise creeping over the canyon in an array of pastels that I'd grown to love. God had this, and He'd see Alina and me through the danger.

The sweet little girl lay in my lap. She'd softly sobbed during the night, dampening my hiking pants with her tears. I must devise a plan to escape. Although she had a tiny body, carrying her up and down steep inclines would challenge our speed to get away. I banked on her agility from gymnastics as an asset.

I stared at the gold chain on her neck. The ballerina necklace containing the tracking device. A lot of good it did off-grid.

At the sound of Chandler and Falin arguing outside the cave in muffled voices, I memorized my surroundings. I'd heard rumors of Chandler hiding in the Guadalupe Mountains for weeks at a time, and this hidden warehouse provided the perfect undetected compound. How had he hauled food, water, clothing, an assortment of guns, ammo, and a few explosives stacked against a stone wall? Chandler had his own arsenal in a firefight—probably planned to go down in history with other criminals who'd lost their lives and gained infamy.

The park used security cams and scrutinized those who entered and exited the park. Had Chandler paid rangers to keep quiet? As much as the revulsion raged in me, the ranger Blane and I spoke to at the park entrance had an impeccable reputation. I trusted the woman and kicked the thought into the next state. The supplies must have been transported in by helicopter at night.

What did Chandler have of interest here to the ROC? Why else would Jurg Falin be here?

I prayed God showed me a way to free Alina from this madman—and get word to those who'd stop Chandler and Falin. Good would triumph . . . I refused to lose faith.

My attention rested on Alina. She didn't smell of urine or feces, which meant she'd been given bathroom privileges. Or wasn't dehydrated. I doubted Chandler stooped to render the little girl relief, which meant Falin had the job. I had the skills to take him out but not Chandler.

Alina stirred through the gag. Adrenaline flowed through me in a cool rush.

She slowly sat, and I smiled at her. "I need you to obey me," I whispered. "If I tell you to run. Go. If I tell you to fall flat on the ground. Do it. I need you to obey so we can survive."

She nodded.

Falin raised his voice outside the cave, and I turned to listen. "A helicopter is en route. Scheduled to arrive in a few hours."

"The money's not in my account."

"You have three million and the cash in the backpack," Falin said. "You'll get the other eight when we have the chips."

"Not my problem. Our deal was eight mil in my account before your helo landed."

"You're dealing with the Russian government, and they insist upon seeing the goods first. You haven't shown me the activation chips for the matchup to our laser weaponry. The locked box you claim contains those pieces is labeled *ammo*. If you're not willing for me to check the serial numbers, that implies a double cross. And my people will cut you to pieces."

Chandler grabbed a box from a shelf. He inserted a key, flipped it open, and pulled out a piece of paper. "Check them now."

Falin scrolled through his satellite phone and compared the paper with whatever was listed on his screen. The man looked defenseless, like he was checking his banking statement. "These numbers work. Where are the chips?"

Chandler swore. "Locked up." He pointed to a small metal lockbox. "No money means your laser weapons are useless. I made a deal, and I plan to keep my end. If the money's not in my account in the next thirty minutes, the deal's off. I'll blow up your helo and everyone in it. Then the kid and the woman are mine."

"You don't need either of them."

"You have my terms. Take it or leave it."

Falin eyed him. "I'll find out about the holdup."

"I'm going to scout the area. You'd better have good news when I get back." Chandler stomped off.

Falin yanked his phone from his pocket. He shouted at someone in Russian. Laser technology was foreign to me, but I understood advanced weaponry. Doubtful Chandler kept Falin alive unless the ROC or Russian government had conducted business with him in the past, and it proved lucrative. Then again, someone else could easily replace Falin. I had no answers, only speculation.

A helicopter was en route into the canyon to pick up pieces for laser weaponry. How could the pilot conceal its arrival? Could the aircraft's rotor blades be equipped with stealth technology? With Feds and park rangers on alert, any sound would draw their attention. Hope rippled through me like sunshine. Always hope.

Falin stepped into the cave. He picked up a bottle of water and uncapped it. He removed Alina's gag, tilted the bottle, and she drank eagerly.

"Need to go?" he said, his voice softening.

"Yes, please."

"Please, me too," I said.

He frowned. "One at a time." He sneered at me. "You can wait until Chandler returns."

"Why?"

"As Chandler said, you're a worthy opponent. You'd try to escape."

"You're holding the gun. Are you afraid if you shoot me and deny Chandler the privilege that he'd kill you?"

"Maybe."

"You don't look like a coward."

Falin swore. "One of you at a time."

We had a chance to escape.

Falin released the ropes binding Alina and led her outside. In a few minutes they returned. He secured the ropes around the little girl's wrists and ankles, then untied only my ankles. He stepped back, his gun aimed at me.

"Stand up and walk to the entrance. Any move or word that bothers me, and I shoot. Trust me, I won't kill you, but you'll wish I had."

As I stepped outside and around the wall of rock into the blinding sunlight, I blinked. "Which way?"

"To your right is a boulder. Behind it."

I obeyed, hoping he'd give me privacy. Through my peripheral vision, I scanned the area for the best escape route across the canyon floor to the safety of rocks in the distance. We'd have to make good time, and I had no idea the moment Chandler might return. Or where he'd gone.

One way in and one way out. *Think, Therese.*

Falin untied my wrists. "Make it fast."

I swung back to him, and he raised his gun. "I'll hurry."

"I have no patience, and time's running out."

I tended to business and joined him. "What did you mean that time's running out?"

"We're leaving this hole as soon as our transport arrives. Turn around so I can tie your hands."

He planned to take me and Alina? Chandler wouldn't allow it unless the ROC agreed to pay more money. I whirled and kicked

Falin in the groin, sending him flat on his back. Grabbing his gun, I shoved the barrel into his face.

"Your turn." I yanked the rope from his hands. He nailed me with his fist to my shoulder and used his right leg to send me sprawling. Pain ignited in my shoulder, but I kept my hold on the gun. If I fired, Chandler wouldn't waste any time getting here.

I shoved control into my body and aimed at his face again. "What's it going to be?"

He slowly nodded.

"On your belly." He complied with a few Russian words whose meaning I guessed. I kneed him in the back while I bound his hands. His pocket held a knife, one I'd need. I yanked it from him. "Get up and back to the cave. Not one word."

Inside the cave. I tied his ankles and freed Alina. She said nothing. Grabbing water bottles and my backpack, minus five hundred thousand dollars, I stuffed in energy bars from a shelf and grabbed my own gun.

"We must hurry," I said. "Remember what I told you."

"Yes, ma'am."

I held her hand, and we rushed out to freedom. I scrambled down the sharp incline first. Alina started her descent and slid into my arms. I bent low and we ran together.

I heard the crack of a rifle, and a bullet zinged past my shoulder.

"Stop."

Chandler.

"One more step, and the kid's dead."

We stopped. His low voice grated against my ears. I turned slowly and stared at the monster.

"Toss the gun and the backpack in front of you."

I obeyed. Alina whimpered, and I squeezed her hand.

He nodded back in the direction of the cave, our prison.

THIRTY-FOUR

Chandler ranted the entire time he untied the knots that imprisoned Falin inside the cave. "You are one stupid Russian. I leave you alone one hour, and you jeopardize our deal. And where's my money?"

One curse word followed another. The grim set of Falin's jaw showed the seething anger. His neck and face reddened. He said nothing . . . No need. Chandler had pushed Falin to the brink of uncontrollable rage, and Chandler *always* had control.

Falin approached me. He smacked me across the cheek and sent me flying backward. He kicked me in the kidney, the sides of my abdomen screaming out in torment. I'd underestimated his murderous streak.

Chandler chuckled. "The Russian has a temper."

"Maybe." Falin's tone bordered on venomous.

Falin snatched his backpack from Chandler and pulled out a .357 Magnum. He examined it in his hand. "There are a few things in this life I refuse to walk away from." He lifted his chin and eyed Chandler. "Palmer here used wit to get the best of me. I underestimated her, but I admire her moxie."

"Me too. But don't deny me the pleasure of killing her. Put the gun away or you'll upset me. Not smart. We need to talk money."

"I hear you. But no one calls me stupid and gets away with it."

This wasn't going to end well. I held my breath and motioned for Alina to join me.

I hid her face against me.

She shuddered and stifled her sobs.

Falin raised his weapon and pulled the trigger at Chandler's face. "I killed him too." The blast echoed around the cave. Pieces of blood-covered flesh and brains splattered everywhere. He examined the gun in his hand. "Those hollow points are messier than I remember." He peered at me through a treacherous glint.

"You are not stupid," I said. "I see a brilliant man with a brilliant plan."

"Trying to keep yourself alive?"

"Specifically, Alina."

His phone rang and he responded. "I'm on it. I have what we need."

A faint whirl of helicopter blades met my ears.

With his gun trained on me, Falin swung my backpack and Chandler's over his shoulder. He fired into the locked metal box and lifted the lid to expose the contents. "Ah, my chips." He pointed to the cave's entrance. "Outside." He frowned. "That's not the Airbus. What's going on?"

I'd find an opportunity to take him down and prayed for a means to escape.

THIRTY-FIVE

BLANE

I drifted in and out of consciousness, partly from the meds and partly from my body's condition. Time existed in another dimension, foreign . . . In my weakened and angst-filled condition, the whirl of rotor blades sounded, sparking optimism and the rhythm of a flowing stream. I must be delirious.

"Right on time," Dave said.

I wanted to jump off the stretcher and two-step to that aircraft of mercy. Yes, fever would make a man think of weird things.

The hard, level ground produced fewer jolts, and the helo awaiting us in the distance renewed my longing to live. I opened my eyes to the landscape. On either side of me, men carried assault rifles, their attention focused on anything moving. I'd done my share of the same, and I fought being on the victim's side. If only they'd give me a gun so—

Another set of whirling blades descended over us, a private helicopter, an Airbus, sometimes used as an air ambulance. Good. Help came in pairs. While in the air, the Airbus's door opened, and a chain gun emerged. Behind the weapon, a sniper opened fire on us.

The lead man of the FBI SAR fell.

I raised my head enough to see a man bleeding out from the back of his skull. Dave rushed to his aid while the rest of the team bent low. The four remaining men aimed at the armed helo.

"Help me get the injured to the helo," Dave shouted.

Rangers inside the rescue helo poured out and pumped fire into the Airbus. I craved a gun, mentally etching Chandler's name on one bullet and Falin's on another.

Rangers rushed to assist the agents. The agent fell who held up the left side of my stretcher. A Ranger grabbed it, a man I recognized. My head fought to stay coherent while everyone else ran to safety. I struggled to unfasten the bindings. Not another man would be hurt due to my actions.

Agents and Rangers pulled back, leaving the rescue helo empty.

An explosion roared behind us, destroying the rescue helo in a mass of flames and flying metal debris. The blast sent us to the ground. Through the fiery haze, the Airbus landed on a narrow slice of the canyon floor. In the distance, Jurg Falin pushed Therese and Alina toward the aircraft. Three shooters poured from the attack helo and sprayed us with bullets.

THERESE

Falin tossed me into the back of the tanklike helo with Alina. I held the little girl next to me, shielding her from the violence exploding around us. I never imagined Falin would pull the trigger on Chandler. The monster lay dead, but what about the man who'd killed him? What new monster held me hostage? I'd forgotten Falin had most likely undergone espionage training in Russia. If Blane had been given the opportunity, he'd have read Falin's tells.

I closed my eyes and prayed for Blane and the others. Without water, food, and medical care, he'd die. Without rescue, Alina and I confronted death. Without law enforcement's assistance, Edik Baranov and his family faced assassination. With the potential of laser weaponry that Falin had confiscated, more would die.

God is sovereign.

Falin's men loaded the weapons and ammo from the cave. They spoke in Russian. Alina lifted her head, obviously listening. She'd translate if needed, especially if they were talking about their plans for us.

Alina stiffened, and her eyes widened. She clung to me. What had they said?

"Don't be afraid," I whispered.

Her eyes moistened. "Not good. There isn't room here for everyone."

I squeezed her shoulder. We were meaningless to Falin unless he had a purpose in taking Alina. He'd gotten his supplies, meaning I was extra baggage.

I am going to die.

"Be brave. If we are separated, stay strong."

"I will." Alina nodded. "I promise."

The men approached the helicopter door. My pulse sped, and I failed to cease the trembling in my body.

"Palmer, get up," Falin said.

I pried Alina's hands from me. She grieved in silence and uttered not a word. Such a brave girl.

"Get out," Falin said.

At least he planned to shoot me outside so Alina wouldn't view one more death. I struggled to my feet and walked to the opening.

"To show I'm not a ruthless killer, you will live, providing you find a way out of here with the dead and wounded." He tossed me my backpack.

"Please don't hurt her."

"Maybe."

I hated his pet word or rather his ominous tone when he spoke it.

He shoved me out of the aircraft, and I stumbled and fell face-first, compounding the ache and nausea from the bruising to my kidneys. I stood on shaky feet and limped toward the burning helicopter and the men beyond. I'd tend to their injuries. Search for anything salvageable and figure this out.

The armed Airbus filled with men quietly whispered its ascent into the sky.

A thunder-like roar sounded in the distance. Falin must have detonated the cave containing Chandler's body.

THIRTY-SIX

BLANE

Everywhere I looked, men lay sprawled out on the ground. Bloody masses. Dark groans met my ears. I rolled off the stretcher and wrapped my hand around a wounded man's rifle—the pain in my head and arm were constant reminders of those who'd sacrificed to rescue me.

Through the blinding smoke, I squinted at the Airbus. The sound dissipated over the clear sky. I pulled out the IV in my left arm and held it against me to stop the bleeding. Rolling near a Ranger who failed to move, I stared again into the smoke. Glancing to see who remained standing, I fought the rage igniting inside me.

"Who's okay?" I said.

"I'm hit. Not bad," a man said. "This is Agent Tanner."

Dave. "How bad? This is Blane."

"Shoulder. Through and through. I called for backup when the second helo opened fire."

"I'll crawl to you," I said.

"I'm here with him," another man said. "Call out if you can hear me."

Four other men responded they were injured but nothing serious. The ones who didn't respond had my concern.

"Men," Dave said. "Help is on its way. Those shooters spoke Russian. Had to be the ROC. Look around you to see if it's possible to help another man."

A fierce surge of fury coursed through my veins. *Why God? Why?*

THERESE

Relief and confusion assaulted me in Falin's release. Why? Who was he? I shook my head. Agony from the men around me scraped against my ears. Would any of them hear laughter again or feel joy?

"Therese?"

I inhaled sharply. Held it and refused to exhale until I made certain the voice came from the bravest Texas Ranger known to man.

I swung in every direction until I saw a familiar figure kneeling beside another man. Blane was alive! I rushed to see the man behind the voice. I hurried to Blane who'd forever be my hero and knelt beside him. He'd used a piece of the shirt from his splint to bandage a man's shoulder wound. Around me lay others, some not moving.

"Are you shot?" My eyes roved his body for signs of a new wound.

"No. Not sure how I missed a bullet." He nodded at the man between us. "This is FBI Agent Dave Tanner, a paramedic who saved my life."

Nothing else needed to be said. A debt owed and a debt of gratitude. "Agent Tanner, are there specific instructions before I tend these men?"

"Just do what you can for them. Help is on its way. While wondering if I'd live, I figured it was time to retire from the FBI. My little girl deserves a daddy who isn't risking his life at every turn." He frowned at me. "You have a nasty black eye."

I attempted a smile. "It will heal."

"What about Alina?" Blane said.

Burning anger chased the relief. "Jurg Falin nabbed her with a box of something from the cave. He killed Chandler. Any evidence was destroyed in the explosion." I stood. "These men need me until help arrives."

"Take my backpack." Agent Tanner drew in a sharp breath. "First aid supplies inside. I think one man is gone." He nodded at a man who had received a shot to his head.

Would the bloodshed ever end?

I grabbed Agent Tanner's backpack. Where did I start? I'd disinfect and apply bandages to these men's injuries until paramedics arrived.

In the distance, another whirl of helicopter blades lifted my spirits. With Falin and the ROC gone, the helicopter had a place to land.

THIRTY-SEVEN

ALINA

The people who tried to rescue me were all hurt or dead except Therese . . . and she had no water or food. How sad. On the awful day the big trouble started, Daria had picked me up from school for the first time. On the way to her car, I'd asked her why, and she didn't answer.

"Is Daddy okay?"

"Yes. He's busy and I offered to pick you up." She took my hand, and she'd never even hugged me before. Something sweet and warm flowed through me. "Want to make cookies when we get home?" Daria said.

"Oh yes, thank you." Why had she changed? We'd never made cookies. But I didn't want to ask and spoil our time together. What if we were going to be like a real mom and daughter, like my friends at school? Nothing would replace my real mommy, but I wanted life at home to be better when Daddy wasn't there.

If I'd refused to go with her, Daria would be alive and the others too. We might even be friends. I kept going over what had happened in the cave. Therese hid my eyes from Mr. Falin shooting Mr. Chandler, but my T-shirt had blood down the front of it. I'm glad I listened to her.

Where was Mr. Falin taking me? I wanted to ask, but he might hurt me. In the cave, I trusted he might take me back to Daddy, until he shot the really bad man. Trusting Mr. Falin wasn't smart. Daddy warned me about some people being nice until they got what they wanted. He said I should make people prove they were nice, and that took time. Mr. Falin used to come to our house and have dinner or drinks with Daria and Daddy. They sent me to my room as soon as I finished eating. I never heard what they talked about.

Mr. Falin's voice jolted me back to now. He spoke in Russian to someone on his phone, but he didn't use headphones. I'd been in a helicopter with Daddy and Daria, but it wasn't like this . . . much smaller and loud.

I listened to every word. "They're dead or bleeding out. I have the kid." He paused again. "Right. Ivanov either follows through or I'll kill the kid in front of him. Then blow a hole through his cowardly heart." He brought the phone away from his ear and put it in his pants pocket.

I shook all over. What did Mr. Falin want Daddy to do? It must be something horrible. My daddy would never do anything bad . . . even to save me.

Mr. Falin turned to me and said in Russian, "Alina, if you want to live, you've got to do everything I tell you. Understand?"

"Yes, sir." I'd not show fear and touched my necklace.

"What is that?" he said.

"A ballerina necklace my daddy gave me."

He turned the ballerina over in his hand. "You better bank on your dad keeping his word or you won't live much longer."

I swallowed hard and carefully put my question together. "Mr. Falin, where are you taking me?"

"Does it matter?"

"I suppose not, sir. I'm curious."

He chuckled and almost sounded nice. "I like you Alina, always have. Except I have a job to do. Let me say we're going to a place where you've never been."

"Will my daddy be there too?"

"Maybe."

I hated the way he said "maybe." Nothing good ever came from it.

THIRTY-EIGHT

BLANE

Thanks to FBI Agent Dave Tanner's call for help, two helos landed with FBI agents, Rangers, and two paramedics. One aircraft was designated to carry the injured and the other to investigate the bombed cave, including the remains of Chandler's body. Therese and I waited inside the medic helo, me flat on my back and she seated beside me.

The paramedics and pilots administered medical care and stabilized the wounded before carrying them to the helo. The man who'd carried my stretcher down the mountain and talked to me about fly-fishing had taken a bullet to his leg. The lead man didn't make it, and his death rocked me with grief and regret. Paramedics had closed his eyes and covered his face.

The briefing would come once we landed in Hobbs. The lines around Therese's eyes and her ashen face hinted at her ordeal. Although I shoved away the thought of either of those men abusing her, she shouldn't bottle up the trauma.

I grasped her hand. "What happened when you left in search of the rescue team?"

Her shoulders lifted and fell. "Hard to sort out, but I will try. I hiked to the meeting spot, but I'd missed them. From the rail tracks, a helicopter had delivered the team, then left. I hiked toward a cave I remembered, and on the way found Alina's clothes and a peregrine falcon feather . . ." She swiped beneath her eye. "I continued and Chandler and Falin stopped me. Chandler said he'd killed you."

"I'm sorry. Are you able to go on?"

She told me about the conversation with Chandler and the hike to the cave where he and Falin held Alina.

"What about Alina?"

"Captive but not abused. Incredibly brave, and I think that's why she's still alive." She covered her mouth and held back a sob. "That little girl has more courage than most adults. Rurik taught her well. I pray her immediate future holds more than the present." She stiffened. "Falin is a strange and dangerous man."

"God's got Alina," I said.

She swung her blue-green gaze my way. "What did you say?"

"I had an eventful day, spent a lot of time trying to move and add more kindling to the fire. Once night fell, I found the strength to send smoke signals for help. I was convinced death knocked on my door. The pain and infection had me in and out of consciousness, delirious." I drew in a sharp breath. "God called out to me. To forgive myself. Whether I was afraid of dying and going to hell or finally realizing a need for salvation—I have no clue. But here I am alive and a believer."

She leaned over me, her blonde hair tickling my whiskered chin, and kissed me. Long and hard. "I am so happy. With all that's gone wrong, this is very right."

"Thanks. I feel good about my decision. Sad it took a series of tragedies for God to grab my attention. I have lots to learn, and my reputation speaks for my stubbornness." I attempted to laugh through the agony in my body. "Sergio and his family will have a celebration."

"You've given me so much more anticipation in finding Alina alive," she said.

"A future for us too?"

She blinked. "I think so."

"When the dust settles and father and daughter are reunited, I'd like to have a fourth date. Start over on the right foot."

"We'll need to take a relationship slow."

"I look forward to lots of conversation and just being with you." I raised her hand to my lips and kissed it. "We are a good team."

"We've both survived a sure death."

I smiled at the most beautiful woman alive, inside and out. I was one lucky man in more ways than one. "Thanks, partner."

"I should tell you what little I overheard in the cave. Falin requested Rurik to do something, but Rurik refused. It's wrapped around the critical activation chips Chandler sold Falin. A chip to operate laser weaponry. I wish I had more to report."

"Sergio will be at the hospital. My first question is to find out what's developed since we last talked."

"This horror makes me feel responsible," Therese said.

"Like if we'd done our jobs, these men wouldn't be dead and wounded?"

"Yes," she whispered.

"We're walking the same guilt road, and we're wrestling with crimes not of our doing. Bad guys behave like bad guys. No mercy. No regard for life. Only greed and selfish motives. You've done nothing to bear the blame of it."

"I promised Rurik I'd find Alina."

"You did, and you will report she is alive. Those words will comfort him until she's returned to him."

"I'm the one who claims to have faith and trust while Alina and Rurik are suffering."

I squeezed her hand. "No need to apologize for being human."

"You're wise, Blane."

"Not really, but I've spent years negotiating and studying human behavior."

"I think God's been chasing you a long time."

I nodded. "Certainly a birthday I'll never forget. I wish I'd listened before falling off a cliff. Some of the bloodshed today might have been prevented." I wanted to continue the investigation. Would I be ordered off the case or assigned to a boring desk job? But my negotiator self and trigger finger worked just fine.

Many scenarios about the ROC and Rurik chased my thoughts like a huge boulder rolling down a mountain on my heels. My worst suspicion stayed affixed intact . . . Had Rurik double-crossed us at the expense of murdering his wife and jeopardizing his daughter's life? The high stakes of blackmail caused people to sink to incredible depths.

The helicopter lifted into the air. I'd never forget the courageous men around me—their sacrifice and the incredible loss.

—

At Covenant Health Hospital in Hobbs, emergency personnel awaited us. Triage started treatment, and those much worse than me had priority. I lay on a gurney in the ER hallway with Therese seated beside me.

"You need to rest," I said.

"I am, right here in this chair."

"With any luck, we'll be briefed while we wait."

She stared up at me through sleep-laden eyes. "Luck? I suppose the time might go by faster."

As if on cue, a broad-shouldered figure strolled down the hallway, his Stetson cocked in his familiar Texas Ranger style and carrying a pair of jeans and a shirt. "Rusty, I recall warning you this mission might get you killed."

I grinned and swung my gaze to Sergio. Not a large man but incredibly muscular. He wore his uniform like he'd stepped out of the tailor's storefront. "I've been in dangerous situations many times."

"And one more time you avoided death by the skin of your teeth."

"Glad you came," I said. "Wouldn't be much of a party without you."

Sergio blew out his frustration—for my sake. "I bought jeans and a super-large shirt to fit over your cast."

"You do have my back. Thanks. Mine are a little dirty and ripped."

He laughed and placed the clothes on my gurney. "Ms. Palmer, how are you holding up?"

"I'm all right, sir. Tired and full of questions."

"You and Rusty are two of a kind."

In more ways than one, but I'd reserve the conversation for later. "Try convincing her to rest."

"I doubt if any of us will until Alina Ivanov is returned, and we have those responsible in custody," Sergio said.

"Chandler's dead and Falin got away with Alina. The ROC can now activate laser weapons in their possession." I spit out the words like spoiled food.

"Yep, Rusty, I got the news. The only good thing Falin accomplished was ridding the world of a ruthless killer."

"Replaced by another." Therese's dry tone told me her emotions hadn't changed since Dog Canyon.

"Therese and I haven't heard any news. Has Rurik offered more information? Any updates on the ROC? Daria Ivanov's murder? Edik Baranov? We're ready."

Sergio crossed his arms over his chest. "Park rangers found the bodies of two hikers in the western corridor of Dog Canyon, throats cut."

Therese drew in a sob. "Chandler admitted to their murders. I feel sick about the many dead and wounded."

"I feel the same," I said. "No respect for human life continues to play out."

She took a few moments to stabilize herself. "Prior to running into Chandler and Falin, I saw smoke in that direction. At the time, I wrestled with investigating it, but other issues held my attention."

I drew in a ragged breath. "The rental Jeep? The keys are in my backpack at the bottom of a canyon. Chandler stole our handguns."

"We got the Jeep. Lack of keys never stopped a good Ranger. Don't think twice about phones or guns. They can be replaced."

But not the lives of those who'd suffered and died. "You said last Friday that things had come to your attention."

Sergio lifted his chin. "This investigation is like juggling chain saws."

THIRTY-NINE

THERESE

My stomach had been threatening to unload for hours, and hearing Major Montoya refer to the investigation like juggling chain saws made me want to run to the ladies' room. Not sure the acid rising in my throat came from the horrendous crimes or the ache from Falin's kidney punch. Lack of food, my war-torn body, and attempting to replenish my body's water supply made me envy an ostrich with its head in the sand.

I glanced at Blane. Part of my turmoil came in his declaration of faith. I didn't want this to be a deathbed conversion.

"We want to hear everything you've learned," I said to Major Montoya.

He held up a finger. "Some info is confidential." He stepped closer. "Jurg Falin has a larger role in the ROC than we originally believed."

"In Houston or deeper?" Blane said.

"Overall. One of the top kingpins. Ruthless. Highly intelligent. For him to negotiate the deal with Chandler says Falin was either ready to eliminate him or concerned the ROC might be cheated."

"Or both," I said.

Major Montoya nodded and turned away as though he wrestled

with info. "Intel shows he had an ongoing affair with Daria Ivanov in Russia and here once Rurik and Daria moved to Houston."

I shuddered. "Used her to get to Rurik, then killed her?"

"Apparently. She must have outlived her value. Like Chandler. At this point we have no evidence of Rurik's involvement in the ROC here or in Russia. What we do know is Rurik has ties to Falin—a warped friendship. We're awaiting confirmation on what looks like Daria's remains."

"Not sure why Falin didn't pull the trigger on me." I shook my head. "When I feel better, I'll try to make sense of it."

Blane gasped and apologized. I despised the pain he endured. "Rurik is caught in the middle of two powerful men. One betrays him, kills his wife, and kidnaps his daughter. The other betrays Russia and is on the run."

"And what does he know about both of them?" Major Montoya leaned on one leg. "Or is he on neither side?"

Had Rurik lied to us? "How is Rurik holding up?"

"Quiet. Depressed. Not eating or talking. Holed up at his home. The FBI agents working his protective duty monitor his calls. Around two o'clock this morning, someone tossed a rock through his living room window. Falin must have made demands, or Rurik would be dead. Problem is, he won't confess to what the ROC wants from him."

"Work with them to find Edik Baranov," Blane said. "Seems too simple."

"What skill or info does the ROC need from Rurik?" Major Montoya paced the area. "Falin's mission is to eliminate Baranov and his wife and son, and he has the big guns to make it happen. Intel indicates the Russian government has pressured Falin to follow through with the assassinations. If he doesn't, they will demote him."

Blane cast his gaze behind the major, clearly in think-mode. "I understand you can't tell us if he's in Houston, but it sure sounds like he's there."

Major Montoya maintained a stoic profile, which told me more than if he'd staunchly denied Baranov's location.

Blane nodded. "Or he hasn't arrived."

"I'm not FBI."

The major held a high office in the Texas Rangers. He had the whole story, and he was keeping it confidential. I expected no less.

"What else can you tell us?" Blane said.

"Rurik's deceased wife, Alina's mother, was Jurg Falin's half sister."

"Blood, money, and politics," Blane said.

His words sunk in. "Could be why Alina is alive."

Major Montoya nodded. "Apparently, Falin and his half sister were close, and he was with her when she died."

"He's still a killer," I said. "While the blood connection might be his hesitancy to kill Alina, I don't doubt he'd do it."

"Especially with the high stakes and Russian pressure." Blane studied me. "Laser weapons are useless without the activation chips."

I inhaled sharply to manage the pain in my back and side. Drat Falin and his kidney punch. "Why not sell everything needed at the same time?"

"Multiple reasons," Major Montoya said. "Per the manufacturer, the modular design of the laser-system components increases its security and versatility while serialized pairing chips are to prevent unauthorized use. Plus a seller or distributor of the technology wouldn't want to accept the risk of storing all the required components in one place. Seems to me the ROC have been double-crossed and thought they had a complete package. Once they determined pieces were missing to make the laser weapons function, they had to make different connections."

Blane dragged his tongue across his lips. "If there was anything of value in the cave, it's gone."

"And Alina?" I said. "Do you have any updates on her whereabouts? The last time I saw her, she was wearing the ballerina necklace."

"A text on the way here said the FBI followed up on a report of a private helo landing in a field near Baytown. By the time they arrived on scene, the site had been vacated. Agents snapped a few pics of the aircraft's contrail marks and the vehicle's tire tracks, but nothing caught their attention. Rangers and FBI are investigating the area."

"I want to believe he's keeping her alive as a bargaining tool." I peered into Blane's face, but nothing readable crossed his features.

The major's phone buzzed with a text, and he snatched it from his pants pocket. He read the message and huffed. "A Ranger found Alina's necklace near tire marks of a directional tire tread pattern, which indicates a vehicle has good road-holding capabilities. The chain on the necklace had been broken as though yanked off. Once the investigators are finished with it, I'll make sure I return the necklace to Rurik."

"She's somewhere in the Houston area . . ." I said. "According to Alina, Falin and Chandler argued about killing or selling her. The problem is, she can testify that Falin, her uncle, placed her in a dangerous position."

"Ms. Palmer, it will be a miracle if the little girl survives." Major Montoya's sober expression said more than his words. "Remember, you can identify him too."

Rising nausea and fury tore through me. "I'm not worried about me, but I refuse to believe she's lost until her body is recovered."

"We need to be prepared."

I nodded but didn't comment. Reality often hit hard.

"Therese, you're extremely pale," Blane said. "The hospital's doing their best, but—"

"I'll be all right." I stood on wobbly legs and Major Montoya steadied me. The man appeared to be made of bricks. "The ER will get to me soon enough. But I'm a bit nauseous."

"I'll walk you to the ladies' room." Major Montoya wrapped his arm around my waist, and together we moved down the hall to where I'd find relief. "I'm staying outside the door. Alert me if I should get a nurse."

I thanked him. Inside, I locked the door. Within seconds, my body emptied of what had made me sick. A few minutes later, I inwardly fumed. *Rats.* Blood in my urine.

"I'm okay," I said through the closed door. I washed my face covered with dirt and dried blood. A nasty purple bruise on my cheek and a near-black eye gave me ghoulish color. Not a way to make friends.

Stiffening my shoulders, I unlocked the bathroom door and smiled at Blane's boss. "I'll live."

"I had no doubts. Were you kidney punched?"

"How did you guess?"

"Years of experience. Let's get you back to a chair."

"Keep my injury to yourself. Blane will worry about me."

"He cares about you more than a friend. Hasn't dated anyone since you showed him the door."

"Our relationship has changed. He'll tell you, I'm sure."

The major chuckled. I hooked my arm in his and hobbled back to Blane. An hour later, doctors met with him, treated his infection, and casted his arm. The concussion required the most attention, especially when he vomited during the examination. I wanted to leave the hospital and fly home, but Blane and Major Montoya insisted I see a doctor, so we waited another hour. We received antibiotic prescriptions and pain meds, the latter I didn't plan to take.

The major arranged a flight home to Houston for later in the day. "I'm accompanying you. Wouldn't want you to frighten the passengers. I'll contact Rurik with the latest."

"Thanks," I said. "Home sounds good."

"We look like Bonnie and Clyde after the final shoot-out," Blane said. "I don't care though. Sorta like the beat-up look."

I glared at him. "Speak for yourself. Makeup won't cover this face."

"You're gorgeous just as you are."

"Your concussion is talking." I could sleep in the trunk of a car. As it happened, I slept on Blane's shoulder from the time we boarded an afternoon flight until Major Montoya nudged us awake. What about Alina? Had the poor child been able to rest? Once we landed, I must talk to Rurik . . .

FORTY

BLANE

I slept the entire flight from Hobbs, New Mexico, back to Houston Hobby Airport. Therese's head on my shoulder, as though she trusted me, confirmed the future. I'd wanted her willingness to pursue a relationship months ago, but not at the expense of her faith and other mental scars she denied.

Late afternoon had sent the sun moving slowly westward by the time Sergio drove us to the Ranger office. Therese and I wanted the official briefing done and behind us, no matter how badly our bodies protested. Separately we told Sergio what happened from the time we landed at Hobbs on Thursday night. He recorded every word. Therese's briefing lasted longer with what she'd experienced—Chandler, Falin, the abduction, and Chandler's death.

Sergio pulled us aside and issued a few orders. Neither Therese nor I argued. We needed to regroup. He handed us new phones and even with our cloudy focus, we activated them. My firearm had gone up in smoke in the cave. He reached in his back waistband and handed me a new SIG. "Try to keep this one."

"I'll do my best."

"I have two Rangers and two cars to escort you home. You both need to stay behind closed doors for the next three days. That means no stepping outside until Saturday morning. Do not attempt to work together or solo to find Alina Ivanov. Put me on speed dial. If Rurik talks to you, I want every word relayed to me. If anyone contacts you who is remotely connected to this case, call ASAP. If I see either of you before the weekend, I'll put you in cuffs."

"You sure know how to ruin a good time," I said.

Sergio set his jaw. "Don't pull a stunt like this again. I plan on us growing old playing poker together."

"Not my intention to come that close to the hereafter again. This one made a believer out of me. Literally." I searched his face for a reaction. Curiosity brimmed from his dark eyes. "I'll tell you about it later, but you can tell your mother that her prayers finally stuck."

Sergio grinned. "I'll do it. She'll be planning a party and will want to hear the whole story."

Just as I figured. "Feed me, and I'll be there."

"Did I pick up some romantic vibe between you and Therese?"

"I'm right here," she said. "Half asleep but my ears work just fine."

I laughed. "I think we might be headed in the right direction. Had to face death to admit it. But we're talking."

"Both of you have *that* look."

"Which is?" I said.

"Puppy dog eyes and a bit of sparkle."

"Please," she said, her blue-green eyes narrowing. "I haven't sparkled in years."

"You've spent too much time with your girls," I said.

"Your time's coming, brother. Don't go against my orders and stay low. Have you seen the bruises on your left side? Your body's gotta heal, and then we'll arrest a few nasty Russians."

Therese and I lingered by our assigned cars, me with a cast and head bandage and she with a body that Falin had used for a punching bag and a face-first fall.

"No more peregrine falcon feathers," I said. "Hey, trivia here. Russia's national bird is an eagle."

Therese chuckled. "News to me. Strange since the two countries have different ideals."

"Russia's coat of arms is a two-headed golden eagle. Not sure why that popped into my head. Except to show what we're up against." I hesitated, convinced I was rambling. "I need sleep."

"I'm right there with you. Text me later," she said. "I want to make sure you're all right."

I blew out my frustration. "You're the one. With a little rest we can talk about Rurik and the steps forward."

"I want to call him tonight," she said. "Conference you in?"

"Yep. We keep learning new things he's neglected to tell us. If he and Falin were at one time brothers-in-law, what else is he hiding?"

"I doubt Alina knows he's her uncle. She referred to him as sir or Mr. Falin."

"Does seem odd . . . as though the two men weren't as close as Rurik claimed."

"I need to think about why Rurik kept the info from her." She paused. "Why was Falin with his sister when she died instead of Rurik? And we can't neglect Falin and Daria's affair."

"Should we record the call to Rurik?"

Loyalty to Therese's friend and crossing the lines of professionalism warred in my sleep-deprived body. "I'd like Sergio be kept aware of every detail."

She drew in a ragged breath. Without a doubt, Therese valued Alina's welfare over logic. "I'm having problems thinking clearly. But at some point, I want to process Jurg Falin, the type of man who'd kill his family and friends."

"The kind of ideology that has no room for sentiment or human values."

THERESE

The Ranger and I talked little on my ride home, falling into the stereotypical quiet cowboy-Texas Ranger image. An unfamiliar black SUV, parked across the street from my brick one-story, caught my attention . . . Neighbors must have company. I slipped back into exhaustion mode, and I ignored the vehicle.

Gunfire broke out the moment we turned into my driveway. Bullets flew through the rear window and cracked the windshield. I ducked down into the backseat, and Wes did the same from the driver's side. He lowered the windows and returned fire to whoever attacked us. Falin had taken my handgun, or I'd be firing back too. I needed a firearm, and I refused to sit there and have some shooter fill me with holes.

Wes phoned for backup while skepticism zipped through me of help not arriving in time. What about neighbors getting hurt or kids?

"Do you have another gun?" I said.

He popped open the glove box and handed me a SIG. "You made the wrong people mad."

"Jurg Falin left us all for dead in Dog Canyon and confiscated our weapons." Bullets continued to whiz by. "Except an FBI agent got a call through for help." I squeezed off two shots from the rear driver's side window into the parked car.

"We need to get out of here." His calm voice told me he'd been in previous firefights. "Open your door as a shield, and I'll provide cover while you escape to the rear of your house. Then cover me and I'll join you."

A firestorm of bullets continued, stopping me from pulling my new phone from my pants pocket, although Wes had gotten through on his phone. I opened the rear passenger door. The possibility of the shooters aiming at my feet nudged me but getting to safety motivated me more.

He wasted no time exiting the car on his side and raining bullets at the shooters. "Are you okay?"

"Yes. You?"

"I'm good." His strained voice told me he'd been shot.

FORTY-ONE

BLANE

On my ride home, I managed a little conversation with the driver. But I dozed on the passenger side of the car. Adrenaline had been my creditor, and now it called for overdue payment.

"Hey, any effort at making sense is worthless," I said to stay awake.

"Then don't. Hate to ruin a negotiator's reputation."

"Thanks." I laughed but everything hurt.

"Want help getting inside your house?"

"I'm good to go."

"Right. Major Montoya told me to unlock your door. Being a considerate guy, I'm asking first. You and Therese Palmer look like the other guys won that round."

My eyes fluttered shut. "Depends. One of them is dead. We'll catch up on sleep and be back on track."

His phone rang, and he snatched it up. A few words in, and his jaw tightened. "Yes, sir. We're on our way." He made a sharp right into a parking lot and turned around.

Alarm ignited with worry. "What's going on?"

"Active fire at Ms. Palmer's home. The major suspects we're headed into an ambush too."

"Is she all right?"

"No idea. Police and Rangers are en route to the scene. Shooters opened fire the moment the car pulled into her driveway."

"I'm done with this. We're within ten minutes of her house. Those guys have made the wrong man mad." I rattled off Therese's address. "My shooting arm is itching to pull a trigger."

THERESE

"Have you been shot?" I said to my driver.

"Yes, get inside your house. I'm good to cover you." His weakened voice told me how badly he'd been wounded.

"I won't leave you to fight them alone. Where is backup?"

"On its way. Please, get inside."

"What if—?"

Gunfire whizzed past us. I peered around the car door. Two men approached, firing with each step. I aimed at the man nearest me and squeezed the trigger, sending a bullet into his chest. He jerked back and fell. Blood trickled down the front of a black T-shirt.

The other shooter kept coming and firing.

"I'm hit again," the Ranger said.

The shooter fired, and I rushed to help Wes. Blood seeped from his side and chest. In the distance, the sound of sirens gave me a twinge of hope. A car squealed to a stop. Car doors slammed. Were they police? Rangers? Or backup to assist the men bent on killing us?

The shooter moved closer. I raised my gun to stop him. My magazine was empty. I grabbed Wes's gun, but my senses screamed I'd run out of time.

Car doors slammed. The shooter spun away, giving me a moment to dive at his legs. I caught him off-balance, but he righted himself. Law enforcement would neutralize him, but that didn't help the blood escaping the Ranger's wounds.

Gunfire pierced the afternoon air.

The shooter startled and fell over me.

Footsteps tapped on the driveway, and I swung around to make sure another shooter didn't have me in his sights. A Ranger pulled the first shooter off me. Blane's driver.

"This man needs an ambulance. He's been shot at least twice."

The man bent to the injured Ranger and touched his neck for a pulse while calling 911. "Hang on. Help is on the way." He shot me a glance. "He's alive. Faint pulse."

"What can I do?"

He added pressure to the gaping hole in the man's side. "Pray."

"On it." I rolled away from them, sensing the man had more experience about ER care than I did. Had he taken Blane home? "Thank you for saving my life."

"It wasn't my shot."

"Therese!"

A familiar voice warmed me to my bones. Making slow strides up the driveway was my hero. "Blane."

FORTY-TWO

BLANE

I'd experienced two other times in my life when I sensed caring and compassion in the way a woman spoke my name, Wendy and my mother. It struck me that my maturity and newfound faith caused the lyrical sound from Therese to imply more—a hint of love and thankfulness. God had been in control of my firearm, not me. He'd saved her, not me.

Sobering and real.

Police officers and Rangers worked the crowd, some quickly managing the gathering people and others hurrying to our aid. Two ambulances entered the scene with paramedics racing up the driveway, gear in tow.

"Are you okay?" I said to Therese.

"Yes. Shaking a bit though. Blane, I shot and killed a man. I mean, he would have killed me, but I feel awful."

"I understand. It never gets any easier." I moved aside to let the paramedics give the wounded Ranger attention and to check on Therese. She assured them she wasn't hurt and joined me.

Leaning against the Ranger's bullet-ridden car, I gave her a slight smile. "God controlled that shot, not me."

She took my hand. "We need the same control to save my driver. Shot three times. So much blood."

"I'm sorry you've witnessed all this violence."

"There's a reason we've endured it, even if we never learn why." She glanced at the street and stiffened. "Do those people think this is a show?"

"They're curious. If the victims were friends or family, their reactions might be different."

Exhaustion plowed into her delicate features. "True. They have no idea what has happened over the past few days."

We walked to the rear of her house. "I need to phone Sergio."

"Should I step away?"

"Not at all." I called Sergio and gave him the details.

"Can't even get you two home in one piece. Hold on, Rusty, got a call from the FBI coming in."

I waited and stared at the aftermath of innocent people gawking at the bloodbath. Curiosity had a way of shoving people into the way of trained professionals, and I understood Therese's indignation. I was right there with her—and not the first time. Did they have any idea how quickly someone's life could be snuffed out? I wanted them to voluntarily go back to their homes. Love on their families and be thankful no one else was hurt.

Sergio clicked back on the line. "Two FBI agents will escort you and Therese to an extended-stay hotel. They are assigned protective detail. Therese is not to enter her house without the FBI clearing it first. One more thing, the guests at the Russian dinner party cleared."

"Got it." I secured her attention. "She's standing beside me. Her safety is a priority." I repeated what Sergio ordered and she nodded. "Anything else you can tell me?"

"Not yet. Have the shooters been identified?" Sergio said.

"I'll confirm names and text you."

Therese raised a finger before I ended the call. "Falin couldn't have ordered the hit. He had the opportunity to kill me in Dog Canyon and spared me."

"I heard what she said," Sergio said. "His boss must have sent the shooters, which means we could also be dealing with rivalry within the ROC. Get back to me with any IDs."

I pocketed my phone and approached the paramedics loading one shooter's body onto a gurney, the man I'd shot. "I'm a Texas Ranger." I displayed my ID. "I want to check the deceased men for identification."

A female paramedic pointed to the crowd. "A police officer asked for their wallets."

A fraud. "That's tampering with evidence. Illegal."

"Which is why he didn't get them. I asked him to wait while I verified his ID with another officer. Odd, he didn't stick around."

I didn't find it odd, rather a smart tactic. "Can you identify him?"

"Yes, sir."

I requested a Ranger handle the report while I accessed the bodies. I pulled wallets from each man's pocket and examined their IDs. Both Russian.

I texted Sergio the two men's info and the incident with the paramedic. He immediately responded.

No surprise the ROC have their men out. The two deceased are on our watch lists. Both suspected ROC members and wanted for questioning.

I assume a task force has been initiated with the FBI, Rangers, and HPD?

Yes. The same day you and Therese landed at Hobbs.

I shared the texts with Therese. We kept our silence . . . too consumed with the tragedies and few answers.

Two men walked up the driveway and handed me their creds—both FBI. I validated each one. "The rest of our team is on its way. We're to clear this home before the owner enters," one man said and directed his attention to Therese. "Are you Therese Palmer?"

"Yes, sir. My ID is in the car parked in the driveway."

The second agent offered to retrieve it and thanked us for our patience.

"We've been briefed on the crime activity here," the first agent said and stuck out his hand. "Agent Blackburn. Sorry this happened to you. We're dealing with a determined bunch, and it looks like the two of you have contracts on your lives." His relational demeanor told me he was a good, seasoned man. A lot had to be said for the wisdom of salt and pepper.

"I have no idea who or what is inside," Therese said.

"Do you suspect a bomb?"

"Nothing would surprise me."

He pulled a phone from inside his sports jacket. "I'll request a bomb squad."

Therese and I waited in the FBI's SUV, bone-tired and filled with unanswered questions—our mode of operation. Darkness created a cover of mystery increasing my frustration. A bomb squad searched her house before they'd allow the FBI agents inside. We all waited for our turn. Law enforcement officials moved the crowd back and encouraged them to return to their homes, but news media and bomb techs arrived, creating more curiosity for the crowd who failed to leave. Exhaustion flowed through my body, but tomorrow I'd sleep. We'd both sleep.

"Let's call Rurik," Therese said. "Give him our new phone numbers. The FBI agents protecting him have no reason to refuse us. Why don't you make the call?"

I agreed and she pressed in Rurik's cell phone number. Placing the phone on speaker, I addressed the FBI agent with my credentials. Once verified we were put through to him.

"This is Blane and Therese. We're back in Houston. We have new cell phones. I'm texting those numbers to you."

"Thanks." Rurik's voice held more pain than the last time we spoke. "I've been watching the news about an exchange of gunfire at Therese's home. What's going on?"

The agents were listening, and I relayed enough that the media would confirm. I continued with the happenings over the past few days in our attempt to rescue Alina and omitted the contents in the cave. "We're not giving up, Rurik. The Texas Rangers, FBI, and HPD have formed a task force to find Alina and end the crimes."

"What about the trackers in her shoes and necklace?"

"Alina's shoes were found in Dog Canyon, and Rangers found her necklace near Baytown. Major Montoya has it."

"Major Montoya will keep the necklace safe? It's special to Alina. And me."

"He's already assured us. He has daughters and understands those things."

"Thank you. I never told anyone about the trackers, but Jurg is smart. Therese, you were with Alina." His fragile voice echoed his angst. "How was she?"

Therese moistened her lips. "They had not harmed her. She wore new tennis shoes, jeans, and a T-shirt. Jurg Falin protected her from Chandler. Your daughter is the bravest little girl I've ever seen. She neither pouted nor whined, showing respect to her captors and complying with their requests. You have taught her well."

Rurik broke into sobs. "Jurg was once my brother-in-law, a half brother to Alina's mother. But he has my daughter, and we have no location."

Therese's eyes welled, and she mouthed for me to continue the conversation.

"Why didn't you tell us about the family connection?" I said.

"I . . . I didn't think it made a difference or was important."

I wanted to ask Rurik why we wouldn't think the family connection vital to the case, but I risked angering him. If he shut down, we might not get back in his good graces. "We could have used the information in our negotiations, and for sure we'll use it in future dialogue."

"How would Jurg's relationship with my daughter affect her return? His priorities are the ROC's intent to assassinate Edik Baranov, and Jurg will put his own life on the line to ensure their agenda. My daughter means nothing to him."

"What have you not told us? We need all the details to return Alina to you safely." I let silence set the stage. Was Rurik aware Falin and Daria had been having an affair?

Therese opened her mouth to speak, but I shook my head and took her hand, a little awkward with the cast.

"We aren't talking about political opinions or a country's sovereignty. We're talking about my daughter's life!" Rurik swore. "A face-to-face with no one else around."

FORTY-THREE

THERESE

Nearing 10:00 p.m., the FBI bomb tech found explosives attached to the front and rear doors of my home and a secondary bomb inside the rear door. The killers planned my demise no matter where I entered. I understood the code of criminals to take down anyone representing law and order, and Blane fell into the category. But why me? Was it my testimony that identified them as kidnapping Alina and the laser chips? But that proved meaningless once Falin killed Chandler, and Falin blew up the cave.

The answer must originate with what Falin believed Rurik had told me or what I might have seen in the cave. Whatever the expectation, Falin viewed losing men, murder charges, and kidnapping worth the risk to seal his plans. I shuddered at the bloodshed of terrorist activity on US soil.

Blane's soft snores caught my attention. He'd leaned back in the seat and finally found a reprieve from the intense pain—or his exhaustion outweighed the agony in his body. I'd wake him on the hour. I'd drifted off and on since we'd been escorted to the FBI vehicle, but I continued to jolt awake. My own bed sounded heavenly, but the closest I'd get would be tossing a few pieces of clothing atop it while packing my backpack for the extended-stay hotel.

In the shadows, Blane's hand wrapped around mine, resting between us. Was I selfish to call our longing to pursue a relationship a blessing amid the violent crimes? His newfound faith testified to answered prayer—after Alina's rescue, after the killers were stopped, after the answers to why I'd been targeted, then Blane. But I had to be sure his faith lasted in the days ahead. I needed to see his hope in Jesus, not just hear it. I must guard my heart above all things. And pray.

A tap on the window captured my attention—Major Montoya. I touched Blane's shoulder, and he immediately popped awake and opened the passenger door on his side.

"Rusty, you've been to the dark side of purgatory and back," Major Montoya said. "Both of you."

Blane attempted to scoot out of the car, but the major stopped him. "Stay put. I don't want to see you fall. Might break your other arm."

"Very funny."

"No, it's not. I fell out of a tree as a kid and broke my leg in two places. Even the memory hurts."

"Appreciate your empathy." Blane attempted a laugh, but it fell flat. "You didn't need to come out tonight."

"Right. And answer to my mother? You are her favorite, and the dear saint texts me hourly about your condition."

Blane shook his head. "Love that woman."

"That goes both ways," the major said. "The house has been cleared so Therese can pick up items for the next few days. The team needs ten more minutes."

"Thanks," I said. "I'll hurry. Blane needs to pack too."

"Nope. I got you covered," the major said. "I've been to his place and have a to-go bag in my truck."

Blane nodded. "You're better than a brother."

"You'd have done the same to help me. Already have. Hey, I heard about the conversation you two had with Rurik. Your lives are a tad on the worthless side. The task force has dug deeper into what's going on with the ROC, and it looks like the crimes are mounting with the contract out on Edik Baranov and whatever Rurik is hiding about the laser chips in the cave."

"Two separate issues?" Blane said.

"Depends if Rurik knew about the cave. Keep it to yourself."

"We'll do our best."

"I agree both of you have a rapport with him. Tread lightly. Until we understand the scope of the ROC's operation, trust comes with a price. I'll arrange a video interview for tomorrow late morning. That's the closest he's getting to a face-to-face. Does the time work?"

"Sure," Blane said. "We're open to talk again tonight."

"Not on my watch. Neither of you have the brain power to fight your way out of a wet paper bag."

"You might be right," Blane said. "Is Baranov and his family safe?"

Major Montoya held up his hand. "It's confidential for security reasons."

"I'm aware of my limitations. But I already have my answer. Speculating here, but if Baranov is making his way to the US, then his arrival must look like his own idea without the aid of our government."

"No comment."

Blane had made an accurate conclusion.

"Another speculation is whose side Rurik is on," Blane said. "Or maybe he's playing both."

The major had the stoic thing down to a science.

"Or maybe you and the suits are working both assumptions until the truth sails in." Blane blew out frustration. "I saw your twitch."

Major Montoya frowned. "Nothing's easy. If it were, we'd be in another line of work."

His words hung in the air, sobering. We'd lost friends, friends absent from our lives forever, and how many more would shed blood and give their all?

"I'm in this for the long haul," Blane said.

"Count me in," I said. "Sir, do you have any idea where Falin has taken Alina?"

"No, and neither has anyone contacted Rurik."

I ventured further. "Has forensics identified the woman's body as Daria Ivanov?"

"No, but we have no reason not to believe it's her. No one's reported a missing woman. Daria's neighbors haven't heard from her either."

Blane sighed, and it wasn't from pain. "Providing Rurik didn't have a hand in her murder, confirmation of Daria's body would give him closure. Burying her remains also allows the healing to begin. Outwardly, his emotions are spent, and I suspect a breakdown. Finding Alina's body would push him over the edge." He paused. "Unless his emotions are fear of being charged with two murders."

I had my own opinion about Rurik. "I think you're wrong to suspect him. He's a good man. I mean, how many losses can one man handle?"

Blane studied me. "If he's innocent, he needs strength to accept the tragedy and move on with his life."

"If?" I said.

"I want to believe he's a victim. But if he's as guilty as Jurg Falin with blood on his hands, Rurik deserves whatever a judge and jury toss his way."

"He might have already chosen his country over his family," Major Montoya said. "Time will tell, and remorse doesn't bring lives back from the dead."

How well I comprehended the grim reality of remorse. I inhaled a retort. Rurik hadn't killed Daria. I was sure of it.

Major Montoya checked his watch. "Therese, you can enter your home. I suggest expediting your packing. The hotel has laundry facilities since we have no idea how long you'll be there. You two are to stay put. I'll keep you updated."

I released Blane's hand and grasped the door handle on my side.

"One more thing," the major said. "It's obvious you two are together. I'm glad, really glad, but be careful. Emotions can cause mistakes. Deadly ones."

FORTY-FOUR

BLANE

At 12:15 a.m., I lowered my beat-up body onto a bed in a hotel, located on the southeast part of Houston, not far from Pasadena. Why there? I had no clue, but I'd take a bed and figure it out once I slept. The two agents assigned to protect Therese and me took turns sleeping on the couch. Therese had a room on the opposite side of the hallway, and I detested how she must feel physically and emotionally. Sergio had warned us about our newfound relationship. Hard to hide anything from a friend who stuck closer than a brother.

How many times had I cautioned Rangers to leave their emotions for their families and loved ones separate from their jobs? A worse situation occurred when two Rangers were dating and involved in a dangerous mission. Apprehension for Therese over the past few days had consumed me, and I'm sure it wasn't about to go away with the snap of my fingers. But . . . God had her safely in His hands. Alina too. Such an odd observation from me. Didn't stop me from worrying, but I had to put my newfound faith in action.

I'd swallowed a pain pill despite my resolve to stay coherent and sensed the meds relieving the agony and moving me toward sleep. Tomorrow we'd talk to Rurik. Tomorrow we'd investigate the destination of the chips. Tomorrow we'd work on Alina's location. Tomorrow I'd be one more day closer to finding answers. All tomorrow.

Last night the hotel could have burned to the ground, and I'd have slept on and wakened in a pile of ashes. I blamed the pain meds. Normally my eyes snapped open when the house creaked, pipes shifted, or the AC kicked on. This morning light flooded the room, and I found it impossible to pry open my eyes. This man was getting old.

"Hey, sleepyhead."

The sweet voice rivaled the gates of paradise. I opened my eyes. Therese sat in an upholstered chair scrolling through her phone. I liked the way she swept her honey-colored hair back in a ponytail, making her seem younger than her thirty-three years. No makeup but a smile guaranteed to melt granite. A red plaid shirt, jeans, and tennis shoes showed me she dressed to relax today. I moistened my lips, dry like the high desert.

"How long have you been here?"

"Not sure." She held up a mug of coffee. "I brought this in for you and drank it while you slept. But there's more."

"Great. I need a whole pot."

She pushed herself up from the chair, but I motioned for her to sit. "I'll get it. Talk to me, and I'll inhale the caffeinated air."

"You must be feeling better. How's the head and arm?"

"Ready to wrestle a mountain cat." I moved and a bolt of pain leveled my eyes shut. "Training starts tomorrow."

She giggled, and I'd not heard the sound from her before. There were a whole lot of things about Therese Palmer I wanted to learn. "Any new developments?"

"None. You'd hear updates first." She examined the coffee mug as though she'd never seen it. "I'm eager to talk to Rurik."

"We need to insist on an in-person interview. I appreciate the FBI protection, except a phone or video-chat online solution defeats the purpose of drawing out the truth."

"What will the agents do if we walk away?"

I lifted a brow. "Might not welcome us back to their hotel." I let reality settle. "I don't blame you if you want to bow out. I'd feel better if you did. No one looks forward to a death sentence."

"I think we already crossed that bridge."

"Therese, you can stay right here until arrests are made."

"Why would I cower and hide? I gave Rurik my word to find Alina—"

"You did and were nearly killed."

Her face reddened. "I held his little girl. I witnessed her bravery when most adults would be basket cases. I'm not giving up or hiding until she is rescued." She rose from the chair and set the empty coffee mug on a small veneer dresser. "Doesn't matter what Rurik has done. Alina deserves a chance to live her life."

"All right," I said barely above a whisper. "I assumed you were in this for the long haul, but I had to be sure you were aware of the risks. By refusing protection, Falin and his thugs will be on to us real quick."

"I understand, and I also understand Major Montoya's warning about our emotions potentially causing a deadly mistake."

"What does his caution mean to you?"

She eased back onto the chair, her features drawn. "If I'm worried you're in trouble or the other way around and I react out of emotion, then we jeopardize the mission and both of us might end up dead."

"Exactly. The job comes first. Period. No heroics." Could I heed my own instructions?

"Okay." She inhaled deeply. "It was easier hauling you up steep rock."

I widened my eyes. "Maybe for you."

"All right, Ranger Gardner, what's the plan?"

"I'll contact Sergio to arrange a rental vehicle. We want to avoid any tails. I'll figure out how to get it here and talk down his objections. Adding we're in this together will look like we ganged up against him." He hesitated. "Guess that's true. I'll call Rurik and arrange a time to meet. In my estimation, the sooner the better."

"You'll handle the conversation?"

"Sounds like a plan unless he's more comfortable with you."

Her shoulders relaxed. "Good. I'm not trained in gentle persuasion or reading the innuendos of body language beyond the basics."

"He's been trained well."

Therese rubbed the back of her neck. "Not sure what I'll do if I find out he was involved in Daria's death, and Alina is nothing but a pawn. His first wife died of cancer, right?"

"Yes, natural causes. But the ruling on paper might not be accurate. We trust no one without credible evidence."

"I'm putting the negotiations out of my mind for now."

"Good idea," I said. "Be prepared but not trigger-happy."

"I got it. How about I whip up some bacon and eggs while you talk to Major Montoya and get dressed."

"Perfect . . . and a whole lot of coffee."

She walked to the door, then faced me. "What are our chances, and I mean with all those involved, of rescuing Alina?"

"I won't speculate. The maelstrom keeps building. The stakes are high, and I doubt any of those on the bad guy's side care about an innocent child's life."

Therese left me alone to think the case had morphed into an intricate series of crimes that leapfrogged to the next. I rode the fence on where the suspects fit in the plan to assassinate Edik Baranov, Daria's murder, Alina's kidnapping, Chandler, and the laser chips. But Rurik's name linked through each crime, but how? Maybe he had more of a connection to Russia's prime minister than originally thought.

I called Sergio. Our heated argument about Therese and I meeting Rurik in person went on far too long, but my stubbornness won out. Would my persistence pave the way for truth?

FORTY-FIVE

Right on time, a Ranger delivered the gray rental car, the color a blend of black and white, life and death. I had my new SIG, and Therese had a firearm in her handbag. The agents at Rurik's home might confiscate them, but I wanted a weapon within easy reach going and coming.

Therese drove the thirty minutes to our destination, obviously absorbed in her thoughts. My headache roared like a lion, and I needed to clear it before talking to Rurik. "Do you want to head back to the hotel?" I said. "This has potential to be dangerous."

She shook her head and offered a smile. Wasn't a real one, but I wouldn't comment. "I think facing a firefight might be safer than your driving." She slid me a sideways glare.

"Not true, but I don't want you hurt."

"Every hour that passes means one more hour Falin has Alina," she said. "Questions pelt me like someone throwing stones. How do you read people with accuracy?"

"Like I said before, it takes practice. Listen to what they don't say, do say, choice of words, their body language, and follow your gut."

"Sounds difficult."

"The key word is caring. Whoever you're talking to must be persuaded into believing you care what happens to them. Pure empathy.

And we can't be fake. In this instance, we're unsure about Rurik's stand. We don't want anyone to die or be treated like manure. But let the courts deliberate Rurik's fate, not me or you taking things into our hands."

"I'll be scribbling notes," she said. "I spent time last night reading online articles about body language. I'll be an expert in about ten years."

"You'll be fine." My arm and head did their twinge of pain thing, and I sucked in a breath.

"Take three ibuprofens." She held up a bottle of water from the console. "The meds are in your pocket."

At the next stoplight, I obeyed. The last thing I needed was my bruised brain distracting me from the job ahead. "Rurik could have been using the burner phone to negotiate his daughter's release."

"That's what I'm thinking too . . . Do the agents know he has a burner?"

"Good question. Doubt he'd offer the info."

"That's where I'd fail as a negotiator. I'd want to punch him."

I placed my hand on her arm. "His truth or lies hit the bottom rung of our mission. If you see or hear something that shocks you, ignore it. Relay sympathy and concern. Put yourself in his shoes and pretend Alina is your daughter. How desperate would you be? Would you do anything illegal to save her? Are you ready to give up your own life for your child? Push aside all the frustration with Rurik. Our job is to rescue Alina."

She swiped a tear rolling down her cheek. "I have no problem putting myself in his shoes. I won't disappoint you."

"You are one courageous woman, and your faith—our faith—tells us God won't abandon us. My mother told me those same things, but I never believed them. Seems like the advice from my mother and grandmother finally took root. I'm too mule stubborn. But we're a team, partner."

FORTY-SIX

THERESE

Blane phoned the agents at Rurik's home of our arrival soon, and I drove into an open garage. The moment we were inside, the door closed. Neatly arranged shelving and modest gardening tools were displayed in precise organization. Sort of creepy. An FBI agent entered the garage from the house and introduced himself—he stood over six and a half feet tall.

"Sir, we have a new development," the agent said. "We found a burner phone that Rurik has been using to converse only with Jurg Falin. Since confiscating it, no calls have come in. We have orders for Rurik to take any incoming calls."

Lies and more lies. I exchanged furious glances with Blane.

"We deal with it as negotiators," he said.

The agent escorted us through the kitchen and down a hall to Rurik's office where we met his partner, who sported dark, curly hair and a mustache. The office had a traditional style and was again neat and clean. The blinds and drapes were closed. Would the faint light filtering in be enough for Blane to read him? The agent flipped on a lamp, and the two left us alone.

Rurik's gray pallor indicated a man who'd given up. Had he put on this facade for us? I wished my fears about his deceit were unfounded.

Blane and I sat across from Rurik in brown leather chairs with a small round table between us. A cup of coffee perched on a saucer, the cream forming a skin-like layer on top.

"Rurik, I have no idea what you're going through." Blane's tone resembled my dad's when he wanted me to feel important. I treasured those memories in a special place in my heart.

"I'm grateful you and Therese risked your lives to find Alina." Rurik scrubbed his hand over his face, as though he physically wiped away his emotions.

"We've all walked through danger in this search," Blane said. "Unresolved issues and continuous threats have taken their toll on you since we last met. You asked us to meet you in person, and we left FBI protection to accomplish this."

"The FBI agents here discovered a burner phone, not the one I used to call Therese." Rurik avoided looking at me. "I've been in contact with Jurg since the first video showing Daria's execution. He . . . he was the one who made all the calls. I've never doubted he killed her."

I fought the urge to punch him, scream. But common sense told me to calm down, relax. But his unreliable character set my face aflame. Why hadn't he shared about the phones from the start? The Rangers or FBI could have monitored and traced the calls. I bit my tongue and listened like Blane had instructed.

"Why did you keep this secret?" Blane said. "Help me understand why you put Alina's life in jeopardy. Are you aware Therese and I were nearly killed?"

Rurik's lips trembled. "Jurg told me if I relinquished the phone, he'd kill Alina."

"Have you spoken to her?"

Rurik shook his head.

"What was his reason?"

"Jurg wanted me to keep him informed of what law enforcement were doing in connection to Alina's disappearance and Daria's death."

"I assume you did as he asked?"

Rurik nodded. "I passed on everything."

"Such as?"

"I overheard the agents talking late one night when they thought I was sleeping." He stared at the ground. "I . . . I told Jurg about the helicopter bringing agents and Rangers into Dog Canyon."

I gripped my fist. He'd initiated the death and wounding of good men! *Lord, help me not to strangle him.* "Do you want pics of what those good men looked like after Falin's men sprayed them with bullets? Your eight-year-old daughter saw the blood, the wounded. One man died. They were trying to rescue Alina. Is that the behavior of a good father?"

Blane rested his hand on my arm, and I swallowed hard. "I'm sorry," I said. "Your actions are difficult for me to understand."

Rurik's faced darkened. "It's difficult for me too."

"You begged Therese to find and return Alina, then you set her up to be killed with the rest of us." Blane lowered his voice. "Murder in the name of love? How can we ever trust you?"

"I fail to trust myself," he said through tear-filled eyes. "And Jurg still has Alina."

"What was Jurg's response to the info you gave him?" Blane said.

"The ROC needed a missing chip for their weapons, and they weren't concerned about Alina."

My anger rose again. "Who is the target for those weapons? It only takes three bullets to bring down a man, his wife, and child."

Rurik glared at me. "Edik is an enemy of Russia. Once the Baranovs are eliminated, then he'll return Alina."

"So all the cost and planning to purchase the chips needed to ensure those weapons were operable involved one family?" Blane said. "What else does Falin want you to do?"

Rurik stared at Blane. "Do what you want. Nothing matters but her."

"Rurik, I'd feel the same way," Blane said. "What is your next assignment?"

"It's a long story."

"Therese and I have plenty of time. What's going on?" Blane waited while silence exploded in the room.

"I'm sorry I withheld the truth." He moistened his lips. "My excuse is I love my daughter. She's all I have left."

"The tragedies you've experienced would send most men over the edge. We want to help, we really do. Please, tell us what we need to do our job."

"Five years ago, Jurg invited me to join the ROC. I didn't know he was already deeply involved." Rurik huffed. "I refused due to my objection of violent takeovers or anything resembling it. Neither would I endanger the lives of my wife and daughter. He said he respected my position as a friend, but I'd go down with the Americans. I didn't tell Daria. Her emotions have always been fragile. Over the years, he repeated the same invitation. Each time I worked hard to convince him otherwise . . . He promised a lot of money and prestige when my family returned to Russia. I always declined. He asked me again about six months ago. My answer was the same."

"Did you think he'd respect your family connection and resign from the organization?"

"An illusion on my part. In my first wife's honor, I didn't tell anyone. That's why I told you he was a friend from Russia, which was the truth. He'd been more than a friend to me, even if we disagreed about politics." Rurik shrugged. "Had he sent the prowler that night to . . . to persuade me? Later I asked and he denied it. He also said his sister loved Russia, and if I ever loved her, I would agree to his demands."

"Were you trained in espionage in Russia?"

Not even a twitch on Rurik's face. "I refuse to answer."

"You just did," Blane said. "I want to hear the rest of your story."

"I overheard more from Jurg the night of the dinner than I originally claimed."

Silence. I wanted him to get on with it while impatience surged through my veins. Rurik should be thrilled I wasn't the one questioning him.

"I'll compose myself." Rurik lifted his chin. "I will tell you everything. Your government might have already discovered this, but that doesn't matter. I need to be honest with you and Therese."

My head pounded. How could one man not see the evil going on around him?

Rurik cleared his throat. "I value the United States, the culture, and its people. Not perfect, if any place on earth held such a distinction, but it's a welcome change from the oppressive Russian regime. Beyond any country, my number one priority has always been my family. With Daria's death and Alina caught in the middle of politics and power, I admit I'm a fool, and I am prepared to face the punishment your government issues."

Had Rurik set up more innocent people to die?

"This is the rest of the conversation I overheard. Edik Baranov is on a cargo ship scheduled to enter the Houston Ship Channel in fifteen days." He held his breath. "Edik is my cousin. At one time, the three of us were close. Edik chose the army. I chose education, and Jurg chose accounting. We were young, idealistic. Ready to take on the world. Jurg opposed Edik's uncle, who is Russia's prime minister, who encouraged him to move up the ranks of the army. Jurg claimed Edik lacked the ability to lead, but I think he was envious.

"Jurg broke away from the three of us. I maintained contact with both men. The assassination is critical, but it masked securing a laser chip needed for a recent arms purchase to advance the ROC in Houston. Jurg wanted both missions to occur at the same time."

"Sounds like Jurg is motivated by rivalry and greed," Blane said.

Rurik nodded. "Assassinating Edik was Jurg's opportunity to make a name for himself and the Houston ROC. The killing would occur when Edik and his family left the ship. Jurg believed Russia would call them heroes for devising and implementing the plan."

I calculated seven days remained until Baranov and his family entered the ship channel. How had all this chaos happened in just over one week?

Blane snatched his phone. "I need to alert Major Montoya." He stepped into the hallway.

I wanted to give Rurik a generous piece of my worst thoughts, but once I got started, I might murder him.

"I'm sorry," he said.

I waited in silence.

Blane returned. "I spoke to Major Montoya and told the agents they should talk to their superiors about an update."

Rurik sighed. "I offer full cooperation. My fear is by informing you, my daughter will pay the supreme price."

"What's changed?" I said, breaking my silence.

"My deceit has cost lives and Alina is still missing." He rushed to his feet and paced.

Blane pointed to the chair. "Rurik, sit down and finish."

Blane maintained control while my fingernails dug into my palms.

Rurik seated himself. "I assure both of you, from this moment on, I will be honest."

"I'm counting on your word being your integrity," Blane said.

I wanted to scream that Rurik had no concept of the truth.

"You can. I promise." Rurik squared off with Blane. "Promise me you won't give up on finding Alina."

"You have my word."

"What is your next assignment?" Blane repeated an earlier question.

"Falin hasn't said."

I refused to hold back my ire any longer. "You lied about your use of firearms."

"Yes. But I'm finished with the ROC." He captured my attention. "Dear lady, through all of this you've never let me down. Only you and Blane are trustworthy. I beg of you . . . if anything happens to me, please take my Alina. There's no one in Russia who would care for her properly. I've drawn up my will and given it to the agents here to ensure an American attorney delivers it to the Russian embassy. It's a legal document."

My eyes widened. "You'd like me to take Alina in the event of your death?"

He shook his head. "I want you to adopt her as your daughter, love and cherish her as I have. Be her mother. My attorney will be in contact. No matter what happens, I'm on a hit list."

A chill raced from my head to my toes. What dare I say? My own mother ignored me after Kate's death . . . and I'd suffered ever since. I didn't have a good role model, but if God ordained it, I'd find a way to embrace motherhood. "All right. I already love Alina. If anything happens to you, I will raise her as my own."

Blane gave my hand a gentle squeeze. He supported me like no one had ever done. Still, doubt of my ability to be a mother wrapped me tightly.

Another question burned in me. "What does Falin believe we know?"

"Your presence in Dog Canyon confused him, and he hasn't learned how you found him and Chandler. I didn't tell him about the trackers in Alina's shoes or the necklace."

"Does he think we have inside information from one of his cohorts?"

"Right. He asked me if I'd given you Chandler's location. Giving him a name tempted me, but if that person had an alibi, Alina's life would mean nothing. Jurg doesn't take any risks. If he believes you have something valuable, he'll want what you learned and who told you. And he has the means to extract it. You need protection twenty-four seven. They are professional killers."

"Then why try to kill me?" I said.

"The order didn't come from Jurg."

"Then who?" I kept my tone low.

"I don't know."

FORTY-SEVEN

BLANE

Rurik had made heroic gestures, but that didn't make him a hero. He'd also successfully frightened Therese—and me for her. The men who'd bled and died placed my caution on high alert. Who else had Ivanov talked to on the burner phone, and what was said? If not for my commitment to Alina, I'd walk away. Hard to sift through the truth from a man who'd been trained to conceal it. When this ended, Rurik might spend the rest of his life in prison.

I pulled out my phone to record the remaining conversation. "I need details about every call you've made on the burner supposedly only to talk to Jurg." I pointed to my phone. "This will be recorded and sent to the Rangers and the FBI."

Rurik slowly nodded. "There weren't many. Not sure I remember them all."

I kept my demeanor in check. "I think you have excellent recall."

I suspected he formed his words . . . carefully. "I already told you, the original call about Daria's murder came from Jurg. I was afraid to tell you. I have no idea of the other person's identity that night in the garden. Jurg told me he'd been eliminated. The day of Daria's death and Alina's kidnapping, I returned home to find the burner phone on the kitchen counter. Attached to it was a note instructing me to answer if it rang, not to use it for anything, not to tell anyone about the phone or Alina would be killed. I complied with all the demands."

"Did you recognize the handwriting?"

"Typed."

"The first call from Jurg happened while you were at the university. He phoned you late that afternoon again."

Rurik nodded. "He restated the note's contents and asked if I had followed instructions. I said yes and asked what I must do to ensure Alina's safe return. He said she was with him, and if I wanted to see her again, I must join the ROC."

"Which you did."

Rurik tightened his jaw. "I didn't have a choice with my wife dead and my daughter's life in jeopardy."

"I agree you were blackmailed with your most prized possession."

"Thank you." He exhaled heavily. "I wasn't sure you'd understand."

I didn't fully comprehend or agree, especially when too many lives had been sacrificed. "Have you ever been an active member of any terrorist activities initiated by the Russian government other than what you just confessed?"

"No, sir. My political views don't coincide with terrorism."

"What were Jurg Falin's demands besides keeping him informed of what the FBI, Rangers, and police were doing?"

Rurik rubbed his forehead. "To book a flight through Istanbul and on to Moscow on the evening of Edik Baranov's arrival to the port."

"Which is a week from today." He agreed, and I continued. "What name did you use to book the flight?"

"Isaak Mishin."

"False ID?"

"Yes. The passport would be provided sometime later."

"What else?" I said.

"To write out in my own handwriting and sign my name to a document confirming I supported the ROC and was a part of the organization prior to leaving Russia five years ago. In the event of my death, all my assets in Russia were to go to the ROC under the management of Jurg Falin. I complied and mailed it to an address in Russia that Jurg provided."

"Did you make a copy of the document?"

"Jurg forbade it. Neither did I write down the address in Russia."

"You have the means to conceal a copy of the documents," I said.

"And risk my daughter's life?"

If Rurik was telling the truth, Falin had covered his tracks and nailed Rurik for anything the US might uncover. "Who were you to contact in Moscow?"

"I have no idea. I assumed Jurg would tell me at his convenience."

"What were the contents of the calls since then?"

"Nothing specific. Jurg thanked me. Told me Alina was alive. Said my usefulness hadn't expired and to be prepared for other duties. He also instructed me to attend an ROC meeting, but the agents arrived. He expressed his concern about the FBI staying here, but I told him I was a person of interest in Daria's and Alina's missing status. He called me a liar and asked who told the FBI my family were missing. I said Alina's school had contacted the authorities when she was absent, and no one returned their calls to the home. I told him the FBI agents assigned to me were in place until they found my family."

"Did he ask about your job at the university?"

"Yes, and I said I'd taken a personal leave, which I have."

"Do you think he believed you?"

"I have no idea. According to the agents here, no one has called since they found my phone early this morning."

"Why not contact the school about Alina's absence?"

"Jurg instructed me not to talk to school officials."

I deliberated the reasoning of not letting the school believe a problem existed . . . But if Rurik was set up to take the fall for Daria's murder, possibly Alina's too, and Edik Baranov's assassination, his lack of communication with the school added more evidence to his guilt. "Why has Falin leveled the guilt your direction?"

"I don't know."

I toyed with telling him about Daria and Falin's affair. "Let's go back to the document mailed to Moscow. Who was the recipient?"

Rurik paused, obviously not wanting to respond.

"Who was the recipient?"

"First deputy prime minister of Finance, Economy and National Projects."

"Looks like you're a member of the ROC, guilty of falsifying documents to leave the US, and involved in criminal activities to support the ROC."

"No need to say how it looks, but I'm innocent."

"Rurik, if your case reached a US court, there's enough evidence to convict you of spying, terrorism, and murder. The sentence ranges from prison to death."

"I'm a dead man whether I face your justice system or Russia's."

I leaned in. "Not if you leave the US on next Wednesday's flight."

Rurik shifted uncomfortably. "I won't leave this country without my daughter."

Ah, new info. "Is Alina scheduled on the flight to Moscow?" Rurik nodded, and I continued. "What name is her ticket under?"

"Larisa Mishin."

"In the event of your inability to care for Alina here or in Russia, who has custody?"

"No one. My sister in Russia is in poor health, and neither does she have an interest. That's why I asked Therese to adopt her. My sister claimed I betrayed her by leaving Russia to teach in Houston. She needed financial help. However, I have sent money to her while living here."

"On a professor's salary?"

"My wife had inherited her family's wealth."

"What about Falin?"

"The other side of the family."

"In the event of your death, the money transfers to Alina?"

"Yes. It is a reason for my demise."

"Would Falin have the role of Alina's legal guardian?"

Rurik clenched his jaw. "Yes. Another reason I placed Therese as her guardian and future adoptive parent. I regret the loss of life and the suffering, but I don't regret anything I've done to keep her alive."

Therese touched her mouth. Alina had no quality of life without a rescue. Neither did a future with Rurik nor Jurg Falin hold much optimism.

FORTY-EIGHT

THERESE

Blane and I left Rurik's home the same way we entered—through the garage. I backed out the rental through pouring rain, splashing against the windshield faster than the wipers swished it away. The weather matched my mood. The more we learned, the more it rained disillusion.

I pulled into a Starbucks drive-through. "I need coffee and truth."

"Yes, to both. I have the location in Baytown where Rangers found Alina's necklace. An FBI team swept the place and found nothing."

"But you want to see for yourself. No coincidence Alina's necklace was found in the vicinity of the next scheduled crime." I ordered our coffees, and we drove to the east side of Houston to Baytown . . . and the ship channel.

Blane sent the interview recording with Rurik to Major Montoya. We talked about the conversations and our analysis. Mostly I listened since Blane had the expertise.

Blane finished and I jumped in with my opinion. "I don't trust him. Neither do you."

"Good call. Sergio said Rurik's key words were 'I don't regret anything I've done to keep her alive.' Rurik has either done or plans to follow through on more of Falin's demands. We need to be one step ahead of both men." Blane held up a finger. "I'm asking Sergio for confirmation of the things Rurik claims he's done."

A suspicion climbed into my brain and perched itself front and center. I drove while my reasoning spun like the ballerina on Alina's necklace. Blane texted Major Montoya, and I braved forward. "What if Rurik has more burner phones? What if he and Falin made provision if this very thing happened?"

Blane lifted his chin. "One of the agents assigned to Rurik's protective detail raised the same question. He went a step further and questioned if the one burner we found was a setup."

"Ouch. I assume the FBI plans to sweep the house?"

"They already have and found no other phones or anything incriminating. I trust Rurik about as far as I can throw him with my broken arm. If he has burner phones stashed away, he's stored them where they can't be found, as though we've wasted our time since we agreed to help find Alina."

I allowed the possibility to settle a little more. "Just like we left the safe house, can Rurik do the same?"

"As long as he's not under arrest, he's free to go anywhere. His refusing protection doesn't stop anyone from tailing him, no matter who they are."

I shivered. "All those concerned seem to operate much the same way." Reality jumped onto my mental perch. "The game goes on until Alina is found, and Edik Baranov and his family are safe."

"Or they are all dead."

I grimaced, but he spoke the truth. How did I get in the middle of a kidnapping and murder case? I taught others how to survive in the wilderness and lead others to rescue those who'd met an adversary in the wilderness. My wheelhouse didn't include killers and terrorists. Although Rurik had lied from the beginning, I'd given my word to find an innocent child. Alina's sweet face refused to leave me. None of this was her fault. Like Kate's struggle with leukemia.

"Do you get the impression Rurik has an answer prepared for every question?" I said.

"Many times. He's a highly intelligent man with the perfect answers to every question. He reads us like I read him, which tells me he's been trained in every area of espionage."

"The question is, whose side claims his loyalty?"

Blane studied the passenger-side rear mirror. "We're being followed. I suspected it at Starbucks. A dark-green Toyota pickup. Driver and one passenger."

"The roads are flooding in this rain, and we're being shadowed. What's next?"

"I texted Sergio. In the meantime, increase your speed."

I glanced in the rearview mirror and held my breath. The truck raced toward us. I pressed my foot on the gas. Wove in and out of a line of traffic, then glanced again in the mirror. The truck stayed on us. "Plan B?" I attempted to stay calm, but my fingers gripped the steering wheel. "Race car driving isn't in my blood."

"You're doing fine, Therese. A prayer sounds good right about now."

"You stole my line." *God, we need help.*

"Someone was either watching the safe house or one of us has a tracking device."

"On a rental car?" I said. "Impossible."

Blane tapped his finger on his jean-clad thigh. "Think back to the cave. Do you recall a pinch or a sting?"

What was he talking about? His question irritated me. "I'm trying to stay ahead of a truck that might have armed shooters in it. Concentrating on what Falin might have done in the cave will need to come later."

"Thanks for putting me in my place. I'd like nothing better than to be driving, but I do have a good shooting arm."

Despite the circumstances, I grinned. "And that shooting arm saved my life."

The truck rode my bumper.

Panic seared through my veins. As often as I told God I was ready to die and be with Him . . . facing the unknown path frightened me.

The road cleared, giving me room to accelerate. The truck did the same behind me in obvious pursuit. I focused on the road. *God has this. God has this.*

Blane pressed the auto-window button on his side and raised his SIG. "The guy on the passenger side has a handgun."

The roar of the truck's engine burst in my ears. I shoved the urge to scream back down my throat. The truck jammed into my bumper. Then harder.

I jerked and fought to keep the car on the road. A bullet whizzed by my left shoulder. I pressed the gas pedal to the floorboard. Chaos surrounded me.

Blane whirled and fired. I heard two shots. Had the shooter in the truck fired again?

The truck bumped me again. I had no idea how fast we were going, when I couldn't take my eyes off the road. Didn't matter. I intended for us to survive.

A loud crack like a massive vibration rocked the car and pulled it sharply to the right. A bullet had hit the right rear tire, causing it to thud against the pavement.

"Ease off the gas. Don't brake." Blane's loud voice still had the calm tone I'd come to respect. "Hold on tight. You can do this."

But that's where his calm voice fell flat against the truck slamming into the rear of the car again. The world outside the car blurred.

Bullets whistled past my head into the windshield. The car veered more to the right, skidding on the wet pavement, then hitting loose stones on the shoulder. Jolting. Bouncing. An unseen enemy picked up the car and flipped it three times.

My screams echoed around me as the car danced on the verge of devastation.

FORTY-NINE

BLANE

I never lost consciousness in the car's harrowing triple flip. A miracle. Instincts told me I'd fallen off another cliff. We'd landed upside down, then the car rocked and righted us. Rain doused the vehicle. I smelled gas. Releasing my seat belt, I pressed on the start button ending the engine's steady hum.

Therese.

I swung her way. The left side of her face had sunk into the inflated airbag, her blue-green eyes closed. She whispered my name. Sweet lady. A trickle of blood flowed from her temple. "I'll get you out of here."

The odor of gas increased.

Therese lifted her head. "Where . . . where are the shooters?"

I looked behind us. "Long gone. They probably think we're dead." The gas smell permeated the air. "We need to get out of the car."

She blinked.

"Unfasten your seat belt."

She looked at me as though unable to comprehend my words. I stretched over her limp body to unfasten her seat belt. Wouldn't budge. In my jeans pocket I carried a pocketknife. Had it for years. I struggled to retrieve it from the pocket with my broken arm. Finally yanking it free, I cut the seat belt binding her.

I attempted to open her door. Jammed. I shifted to open mine. Jammed. My open window gave me access to the door from the outside. It refused to budge. I squeezed with my good arm, and awkwardly jerked.

I drew my SIG from below my seat and used the grip to pound the door lock. The door released, and I blew out relief.

The gas stench rose.

Another glance at Therese showed her eyes were closed. I pulled her from under the deflated airbag and tugged her toward me. My casted arm slowed every move while time ticked, and I feared a spark would ignite the gas fumes, detonating us into the hereafter.

"Therese, wake up." She failed to respond. I maneuvered her body over the console, adding more bruises to her body from my vigorous rescue attempt.

I backed out of the car and ignored the rain. I grasped beneath her arms to pull her out, then slid backward in the mud with her atop my chest. Now wasn't the time to panic but to put distance between us and the car.

Car doors slammed, and two teenage boys in torn jeans towered above me. "We're here to help," one said.

"Thanks. Guys, this car is going to explode. We need to get clear ASAP."

"Let's do it," the same teen said, a lanky youth sporting cactus-green hair.

One of them, an Asian young man, lifted Therese off me and carried her to safety, and the other, a muscular Latino boy, wrapped one arm around my waist and assisted me down the road's shoulder. We limped several feet until the fiery explosion behind us sent us flying into a water-laden ditch.

I spit out muddy water, my hearing muffled. The three of us crawled to the top of the ditch with the other teen carrying Therese. *Please, let her be all right.*

"Anyone hurt?" I managed.

"We're good," the teen said who cradled Therese. "The lady is unconscious."

The wails of an emergency vehicle screamed to a halt.

"Thank you," I said and thanked God. "We'd be dead if not for your bravery."

"No problem," the Latino teen said near me. "We were just driving by. Glad to help. You must have had a blowout and the car flipped."

"Something like that. Did you happen to see a pickup tailing us?"

"No, sir," the other kid said. "Not a thing in sight."

"What are your names?" I didn't ever want to forget these teens.

The Latino kid pointed to himself. "I'm Gabriel and this is Michael."

Go figure. Angels in ripped jeans and lettuce-hair.

FIFTY

A paramedic inserted an IV into Therese's battered but conscious body. The ordeal in Dog Canyon and the injuries from the car flip compounded the bruising. I held her hand firmly in the noisy ambulance ride to Pasadena. The sound of sirens split the air coupled with the fainter beeps of equipment attached to her. Whistling from the vehicle's speed around the doors punched me hard, like a phantom trying to get inside and take her from me.

Not happening. I should call Sergio, and I would once Therese was stable.

The cut along Therese's hairline had ceased bleeding, indicating no need for stitches. Relief swelled in me unless an ER doctor ran tests and discovered otherwise. She'd need tests to diagnose the extent of her concussion.

I'd prayed more in the last hour than my whole thirty-four years.

The two teens, Gabriel and Michael, drove away as soon as a police officer took their statements. I looked forward to telling Therese about our "angels."

My head pounded, either from the accident or stress. How had the shooters been alerted to us? Before the pickup arrived on scene, Therese and I had discussed the possibility of a tracker.

"Sir," I said to the paramedic. "Not sure if you heard me talking to the officers. We were targeted by two men."

"Yes, you were lucky any way I look at it."

"Yes," Therese whispered. "Everywhere I go . . . someone wants me. Dead."

"Or us," I said.

—

At the hospital ER, while the doctor examined Therese, I phoned Sergio. My words sounded like a repeating chorus to a bad song.

"Oh, I heard the news and grabbed my blood pressure meds," he said.

"Let me help you with this. You're about to drag me over the coals and I deserve it. First, let me give you the details . . ."

Sergio listened without a single interruption until I finished. "A tracking device would explain how Falin is on to your every move. The question is, where and how?"

"I'll talk to her when she's coherent."

"Have you learned anything from this?" he said.

"Never underestimate an enemy."

He swore in Spanish. "How about staying put where it's safe?"

I preferred silence as my response. Sergio and I had covered a lot of territory over the years—physical, mental, and spiritual. We'd seen each other through complicated missions, and we'd do it again. I stared at Therese's backpack and suspicion anchored a hold. "Sergio, can you hold on a minute? I want to check out Therese's backpack."

"Are you thinking a transponder?"

"Yep." I laid the phone on the chair beside me and searched the dirty and worn bag. My fingers touched on a round object inside a zippered pocket. The pocket was empty but inside the lining, the circular item stayed intact. The lining opened with a gentle tug, and I pulled out a round tracker. I snatched up the phone and told Sergio what I'd located.

"Hold on to it until I get there, and we figure out how to catch Falin at his own game."

The doctor who'd been treating Therese stepped into the ER waiting room. I caught his attention and said my good-byes to Sergio.

"How is she?" I said.

"Mr. Gardner, Ms. Palmer has given me permission to give you details about her condition. She has a mild concussion and several bruises. I noted on her chart a recent injury to her kidney, and she told me the antibiotic she was prescribed—"

"What kind of kidney injury?"

"A nasty punch. I recommended a follow-up with a specialist."

Falin or Chandler must have hit her. "Thanks. Is she up to visitors?"

"Give me about ten minutes to write up orders. I want to keep her a couple of hours, monitor her condition before I release her."

I thanked him again and watched him disappear behind the ER doors.

Was Rurik aware of the tracking? No doubt he'd held back more info than Therese and I imagined. I wanted to send a fist into his face. Several of them.

I waited eleven minutes, smiled at the white-haired woman at the reception desk, and trekked back to where Therese lay in ER. She had her eyes glued to the curtain opening as though she anticipated seeing me. Right. I was a bit full of myself.

"Glad you're here," she said. "Did you escape unscathed?"

"Unscathed?" I raised my brows like a comic character. "I broke my arm on our last adventure. Survived on Vitamin I and a good woman. The question is, how are you, Miz Kidney Punch Who Forgot to Tell Me?"

Therese laughed. "We've lost it, totally. Probably left them in the rental, but I don't remember what it looks like." She slurred her words. "All this incredible, death-defying, kidnapping, murder, espionage, and Russian mob stuff has—"

"Therese, what pharmaceuticals are you on?"

She shrugged. "The doctor said it would relax me."

I crossed my arms over my chest. I hadn't had this much fun in days. "If that's the case, would you marry me?"

Her blue-green eyes widened. "I'm loopy, not crazy. But maybe."

"Can I kiss you?"

"If and when I'm ready, I'll send you an invitation."

"I like you better this way. Can the doctor prescribe your relaxing juice in a pill?"

"I don't take meds unless it's on a much-needed basis." She lifted her chin, but her eyes slid to half-mast.

"I rest my case." I dragged a chair closer to her bedside. "Nothing left to talk about but the jerks who tried to kill us." I wanted to tell her about Gabriel and Michael, but I'd wait until she was coherent to share our teen heroes. Instead, I shared what I'd found in her backpack.

She bit her lower lip. "Where is it?"

I patted my jeans pocket. "Got it right here. Now Falin is tracking me, not you."

"We're always together."

I smirked. "Not always."

She fumed. "Why haven't you destroyed it? Or are you giving me the pleasure?"

"Sergio needs to make the decision."

Her eyes curtained shut. Chances are this conversation would never enter her head again, and I'd keep her drugged persona to myself for just the right occasion.

Within the hour, the ER curtain opened, and Sergio towered over me, all five-foot-ten-inches of him, broad shoulders, and meaty biceps.

I exhaled. "Hey."

The lines across his forehead looked like railroad tracks. He asked how Therese was doing and held out his hand. "Transponder?"

"In my pocket."

"How long have we been friends?"

"Long enough to determine who always wins, and it usually isn't me." I reached inside my pocket.

"From the looks of you, might not hurt to listen. I determined a few things on the way here," Sergio said. "You won't like it."

"Not unless we're calling the shots together. Literally."

"The FBI needs intel on everything we've uncovered. No secrets," he said. "Every problem has a solution, and it usually involves teamwork. This isn't a game of cattle rustling from the old west chronicles. We're looking at more deaths to follow if it's not stopped."

I eyed my old friend. "No argument with me. We're in this together. I do have a request, though. Let's ensure the Texas Rangers get the credit for preventing a foreign assassination on US soil, solving murders, and rescuing a kidnapped child. In the meantime, we use the tracker to sniff out the ROC."

"You're the negotiator."

"I have something to say," Therese whispered. "I might be under the influence, but I'm all in. I've played the victim long enough."

FIFTY-ONE

THERESE

I opened my sleepy eyes the following morning in an unrecognizable bedroom with a vague recollection of how I'd gotten there. Snippets of the truck tailing us, the firefight, and the car flipping zipped between reality and a shadow. I vaguely recalled a teen boy and the hospital. Wilderness-survival training failed to cover race car driving or dodging bullets.

I turned my head and winced at the sledgehammer beating into my temples. Ah, a concussion. *Thank You that I'm alive.*

"Sounds like you need a painkiller." Blane's voice made me smile.

"We've switched roles."

"On a regular basis. How's the head?"

Pay attention to him. But my sleep-filled eyes fluttered. "I'm not moving if that answers your question. Where are we?"

"Different address, another extended-stay hotel. Same agents guarding us as last night."

Oh yes, the agents. I scrambled through my fog. "What's the rental car look like?"

"Totaled."

"Like my head."

"Have you noticed we use humor to mask how awful we feel?"

"Sounds better than crying." I swallowed liquid emotion before it streamed down my face. "Are you okay?"

"No new problems. In case you need a dose of optimism, our survival story is a bit miraculous."

I could easily fall in love with this man. "Tell . . . tell me what happened. I . . . I simply have no recollection."

"Do you want a pain pill first?"

"Not until I hear every detail."

"All right. We talked to Rurik and drove to where Alina's necklace had been found. I picked up a truck tailing us . . . And we were taken to this safe house."

"God's sure got His hand on us. The two boys—Gabriel and Michael—do you have last names?" I said.

"No. They left the scene once the sheriff's department had their statements. I'll find out."

"Good. I want to express my thanks too. I'm . . . ready for that pain pill. Sleeping sounds better than enduring how I feel."

Blane popped the lid to a bottle, and I lifted my head. A lightning bolt seared me.

"Let me help." He cradled the back of my head with his hand.

I willingly chased down the pain med with water, then I remembered. "Who has the tracker?"

"Long story."

My marshmallow mind needed a poke of reason. "You didn't destroy it?"

"Sergio and I discussed using the transponder to draw out Falin. Currently it's in a separate hotel with Rangers inside and a surveillance team outside."

"Is the FBI aware?"

"I assume so. But I'm not sure what they've learned or their position at this point."

Talking hurt. My face must have taken more of a beating than I thought. "Do you have a mirror?"

"You're beautiful."

"I wear black and blue well. Guess I'll find out soon enough if

I'm ready to enter a beauty contest. Anything else? The sleep meds are gaining traction."

Blane chuckled. "You were talkative at the hospital. Rather entertaining."

"What did I say?"

"I'm saving it for my future benefit."

Had I told him he was hot or something crazy I'd never say? "Blackmail is against the law."

"I'll be cautious."

Alina entered my concerns. "Is Falin holding Alina near the ship channel? Is he considering her release?"

"I wish, but other explanations are more likely, such as that the location is easier to manage the assassination's logistics. The waterway provides an escape route either by boat or a helicopter landing." He planted a kiss on my forehead. "Rurik is still holding out on us."

I closed my eyes. "Getting the truth out of him is like scraping plaque off dirty teeth."

"Great simile. My guess is Falin believes we have details about the assassination attempt and got the info from Rurik."

"Why is Rurik alive? Why not toss a bomb into his house?"

"He must be worth more alive than dead. Whatever happens surrounding Baranov and his family's arrival next Wednesday, you can bet Rurik plays a critical role."

"Like he might be the one in charge?"

"Nothing is out of the question at this point."

I startled. "Are you saying Alina's kidnapping might be a ruse?" I dragged my tongue over cracked lips. "Of course you are."

"You need your rest."

"Please wake me in two hours. I want to talk about what we're doing next." My thick tongue barely got the words out.

"Maybe."

I hated that word. Falin used it with deadly implications. But I was too tired, hurting too much to protest.

FIFTY-TWO

BLANE

Back at my hotel room, I logged in to a computer and accessed secure updates. The unbearable waiting made me cranky, and my personality insisted on having answers or control of situations. Enter God, but eliminating old habits teetered on the impossible side. During a negotiation case, I viewed waiting on answers as a challenge, part of the process of my job, but this was different. Too many lives were at stake for me to do nothing.

Secure sites told me nothing new. Neither the Texas Rangers nor the FBI were talking about escorting Edik Baranov and his family off the cargo ship—and the US stayed mute about the defection. Hackers would have a field day going public with a covert operation.

I wanted in on it . . . like Therese had said yesterday in the ambulance.

Six days to stop an assassination.

Six days to trap Falin and the ROC.

Six days to draw the truth out of Rurik.

Six days to find Alina alive.

I phoned Sergio. "What are the next steps in recovering Alina?"

"Out of your hands, Rusty."

"I'm in this with both hands and feet. My one-arm fighting ability is limited, but my brain power works like the latest technology. Who's checking security cams around the ship channel?"

"We're on it. Don't tell me how to do my job."

Remorse hit me hard. "My apologies. I'm edgy and want this ended. I need something to do. I assume techs are checking credit cards and all the obvious. Any action with the tracker?"

He blew out his exasperation. "What do you think? Have you learned about any arrests?"

"I have an idea—"

"Forget it. You and Therese are finished with this case."

I envisioned Sergio setting his jaw. Again, mule met mule. "Hear me out. Whoever is targeting Therese thinks she is recuperating at a hotel where you've enabled surveillance. Most likely that person will send some lowlife perps to take her out. They'll either have no clue who paid them, or whoever is behind this will make sure they're dead once they've completed the job. He won't risk capture himself."

"I'm listening, but that's all."

"I admit my track record stinks, and I don't want to endanger Therese's or Alina's lives. Neither do I want anyone else killed. The FBI is pursuing the activation chip, so I can focus on finding Alina. What if I drove to see Rurik? Instructed him to contact Falin on the burner phone Falin provided. Tell Falin I'm willing to negotiate Alina's release, and I can meet him at a private location of his choosing, just the two of us. No mention of Edik Baranov, only money and Alina."

"Are you loco? Look where your attempts have gotten you? Why would he be interested?"

"Greed. He used Alina as a means of ensuring Rurik followed orders, especially after Daria's death. A media leak that Rurik is under investigation for his missing wife and daughter would help convince him he's not a suspect in Alina's kidnapping. Falin isn't about to cancel Baranov's assassination. He has an opportunity to win big with the Russian government. More likely he agreed to the deal and planned to leave the country before the assassination, which would exonerate him from directing the plot."

"He'll probably want more money." Sergio's tone indicated his sarcasm. "Too risky."

I inhaled deeply. "If Falin and I agreed to a public place like a bar, you have the resource to plant someone ahead of time. Wiring me is a mistake, but someone else makes sense."

Silence ensued as Sergio was processing.

"It might work," Sergio said. "Arresting Falin doesn't free Alina or stop the assassination attempt. He'd have his men watching every move inside and outside the meeting place. That means a solo effort on your part."

"Right. When should I talk to Rurik?"

"I'm regretting this already. When this is over, you will owe me big time. I need a few hours to work out details on my end. I'll send a Ranger to pick you up, and we'll discuss this more in detail. Rurik is to know nothing about our conversation."

"I'll make sure he understands that unless he helps me meet with Falin, Alina will never be free."

Late afternoon, while Therese dozed, I left the hotel for the Ranger office. Good thing she slept, or she'd have attempted to crawl out of bed and join me. I left her a note about meeting with Sergio, and I'd explain later. Probably deal with her aggravation and a taste of her fury. Those who knew me accepted my determination, like breaking in a horse and not giving up no matter how many times I got bucked off.

At the Ranger office, Sergio and I talked behind closed doors. I chose not to phone Rurik about a visit—preferred to catch him off guard. Then I readied myself to leave.

"You will either expose crimes or die trying." Sergio shook my hand and drew me into a hug. "I'm always afraid this will be our last time to meet, Bro."

I offered a smile. "Hey, the difference now is I'm sure where I'm spending eternity. I'll call later."

In the pitiful hobble to my car, I realized I'd soon find out the real Rurik Ivanov and hoped I lived to tell about it.

—

Inside Rurik's home, I knocked on his office door. He responded wearing the same jeans and wrinkled shirt from yesterday. Lines, like plow blades, dug into the edges of his eyes. Or he gave a good show.

"Blane, I'm surprised to see you." He peered around me. "Therese isn't with you?"

"She's recuperating from a car accident. I want Falin stopped."

"You're sure he's responsible?"

"Who else? Why is he after Therese?"

Rurik frowned. "I don't know. He hasn't said anything to me. Is she in the hospital?"

"No, a hotel room with a protection detail."

He gestured for me to sit. "Not sure I want to hear what happened, but you're here."

"We left here yesterday and . . ." I omitted the plan to scout out where Alina's necklace had been found and the ship channel area. "The vehicle and the driver are at large. Therese received a concussion and additional bruising."

"I'm devastated. Give her my best."

I inhaled, allowing him time to read me and me to read him. Most likely false from him, but I'd play along. "Falin and his thugs tailed us from the time we left your house."

He gripped the arms of his chair. "Surely you aren't thinking I am responsible."

"Of course not, Rurik. You've convinced me and Therese of your honesty. I have an idea, and I'm here to discuss it with you."

"To find Alina and make arrests?"

"That's the plan."

"What can I do?"

"The agents protecting you have your burner phone. Would you call Falin and ask if he and I can meet to negotiate Alina's release?" I filled him in on the plan.

"But what about Edik Baranov and his family?"

"Does Falin know what you've told us?"

"No. But the money isn't enough."

"What if I toss in a get-out-of-the-US-free card?"

Rurik stared beyond me. His features stoic. No twitches under his eyes or body movements to show deceit.

"I'm afraid for Alina . . . If he'd hurt her. Or take her with him." His impassive look remained in place. "I'll make the call. How do I introduce you?"

"He's aware I'm a Texas Ranger. Tell him I'm a negotiator and a friend."

"You're taking a massive risk."

"Is Alina's life worth it?" My concern for the child and Therese escalated with each passing moment.

Rurik swallowed hard. "Please ask the agents for my phone, and I'll make contact."

FIFTY-THREE

With the burner phone in his hand, Rurik paced the room, raising my doubts if he'd follow through with calling Falin.

"If you aren't sure about this, I'm leaving." I kept my voice low, soothing. All the while observing him.

"I'm afraid. No reason to deny it." He studied the phone.

"I'm right here supporting you."

One of the agents had installed an app on Rurik's phone to monitor his calls and texts. I'd hear the conversation, and if Rurik dragged out the call, the agents had a good chance of locating Falin—but he had the same technology, and he'd have his eyes trained on the clock.

Rurik pressed in a number, and a man responded. I moved to hear the conversation.

"Why are you calling? It's dangerous."

"I want to arrange Alina's release."

"Why? Who's with you?"

"A friend, a Texas Ranger, Blane Gardner—"

"I'm acquainted with him."

"He's willing to negotiate Alina's release, and I can supply more money. I've also arranged a private plane to fly you out of the country."

"Where did you get the plane?"

"A connection in St. Petersburg."

"Of course. My sister's money buys all you need. Why the Ranger? I'd rather talk to Therese Palmer."

"I sold my soul."

Falin chuckled. "Meaning what?"

"Giving up names and whereabouts of cartel members."

I only wish Rurik had that info.

"You're right. You sold your soul, and the cartel will dig out your heart and serve it to the buzzards at their next barbecue."

"Alina means everything to me, and I want her home. Blane requests a meeting with you, a public place but somewhere quiet. You name the location."

"And he brings backup to arrest me? I'm not a fool."

"Hold on while I step outside the room." Rurik opened and shut the door but stayed within his office. "Jurg, I've done my part and will follow through on our plans. Gardner knows nothing about other things, only that you abducted Alina for money."

"You expect me to believe that? How have you explained Daria?"

"Told the FBI we had an argument, and she left. A woman's burned body was found in her car. Only time stands between confirming the remains are Daria's."

"She's gone, Rurik. Nothing will bring her back."

"I'd like to give her a proper burial." Rurik drew in a breath. "Please, I'm under investigation for her and Alina's murders."

"I listen to the news." Falin swore. "About time they made an arrest."

"Look, you will be out of the country before the police file charges against me. I want Alina returned, and I have the money."

"Unless you're arrested, you and Alina will be on a flight to Russia."

"Right."

"A private plane and an extra three mil? . . . And the police suspect you killed Daria and Alina. I find that ironic, don't you? First, I need to validate a few things, then give you a time and location to meet up with Gardner."

"All right. Anything else you want me to do?"

"Go back on your word or set me up, and Alina is dead. We have a deal, and I expect you to keep your end."

"I understand."

What had Rurik agreed to do?

The call ended, and the agents indicated they had located the cell phone—a restaurant in the downtown area. The origination of the call did little good. Security cams might show Falin at the restaurant, except the video failed to show any signs of his men, Alina, or where he'd gone after leaving there.

Rurik handed an agent the burner. "I must be told if a call or text comes through."

I waited until the agent left the room. "What have you agreed to do?"

"To keep him informed. Nothing new."

I offered my best serious look. "Double-cross me, and you double-cross the US government."

"And if Jurg learns I've set a trap, I lose my daughter, my reason for living."

My core reaction slammed against my worst suspicions. Rurik had committed to helping the ROC pull off more crimes. But in what capacity?

FIFTY-FOUR

THERESE

Blane returned to the hotel, and I wanted a detailed update. I'd slept most of the day, eaten chicken noodle soup from a can, and I was ready to muscle up my return to life. Normally I'd be miffed that he moved ahead without me, but I was like the rental car—totaled and worthless. Doubtful the black market had any use for my body parts. I'd admit the truth to myself but not anyone else.

In the privacy of my room, Blane explained his findings. "Falin agreed to meet tomorrow night at ten. He'll text the address to Rurik sometime during the day."

With my head pounding like a bass drum in a marching band, I processed what Blane had told me. "Every day cuts into keeping Alina and the Baranovs alive."

"Unless Falin refuses to meet, it's the best option we've got. Doesn't mean the FBI and I are not thinking and looking at other angles."

I bit my tongue. "I'm sorry. You're doing everything possible to end the chaos. Wilderness survival is much easier than fighting bad guys. At least in nature I'm aware of the obstacles."

He moved a chair closer to my bedside. I worried Blane planned to unload devastating news.

"What started you on your career path?" he said.

I sighed. "I thought we were going to discuss any updates."

He shook his head. "Looking for ways to keep you from worrying about Alina."

My story lay locked in a vault, and trust shaped the key. We'd been through too many death encounters. Did this mean the time had come to talk about my family?

"Too uncomfortable a topic?"

"My background is on the website."

"If you're referring to the sixty acres your mother inherited outside of Austin, an area off-grid without municipal water, electricity, and modern conveniences, I read those things. What a learning experience. My incredible instincts believe there's more." He grinned. "Seriously, I see hurt in your eyes that tells me you've suffered from a tragedy. Possibly more than one."

I thanked God the drawn blinds and the faint lamplight shielded my facial expressions from his scrutiny.

"Have you ever shared your story with anyone?"

"No. Not ready now either."

"You have my attention. Your story goes no farther than the night sky."

Dare I dig deep within my soul? "Why? Because we've saved each other's lives?"

Compassion emitted from his eyes. "For some people, survival might be the reason. But not me. I want a relationship, beginning with a friendship. And that means to possibly help you work through a painful experience."

"I do trust you, Blane. You've shared your past with me, and I've thought about the same thing ever since." Although revealing my past scared me witless, I managed a smile. "I haven't taken a pain pill since early afternoon. Hoping I make sense."

"Take your time."

The pain in my head had diminished a bit, so I forged ahead. "My parents and I went through a terrible loss, but I doubt they understood how it affected me. You were right about having empathy for Rurik and warning me about not making a deadly mistake with misused sympathy."

I waited several seconds debating if I'd regret telling him about Kate. Would I feel better afterward? My life's backpack had been loaded with bricks. Heavy ones. "I was eight when we moved onto the property my mom inherited from her dad. My little sister, Kate, was three. She'd been diagnosed with leukemia, and my parents desperately wanted to believe nature and clean air would heal her. The doctors instructed my parents to keep her comfortable, which meant they'd given up."

I closed my eyes. Frail Kate danced in the tall grass. A gentle breeze tossed her white-blonde curls as her tiny body swayed . . . The same color hair that drew me to Alina.

"My parents acquired skills about living away from modern conveniences—raising food, drinking unpasteurized whole milk from our cows and goats, growing medicinal herbs and vegetables. I learned with them. We were committed to finding a cure for Kate. Dad made weekly trips to the library for research, everything from plants and medicinal herbs, to living off-grid, and lots of reading for me. Mom homeschooled me, which I guess was a good thing since I graduated from high school at the age of fifteen. We were closer than most families, loving and respecting each other the way God intended."

I drew in a ragged breath. "I trusted God for Kate's healing, but my parents trusted in nature. We didn't mingle with anyone for fear we might infect Kate with a deadly virus. When any of us left the farm or encountered anyone, the first thing we did was bathe in the barn and wash our clothes. For five years, Kate improved."

I forced myself to venture back to those days and dwelled on bittersweet remembrances of hope and heartache. "She died from complications with leukemia, but it took me several years to accept her death wasn't from my neglect. While she and I were on a picnic, she was bitten by an ant. My parents blamed me when she died, that I hadn't taken good care of her. Still hard at times not to think if I'd gotten her home sooner, she'd be alive today." I closed my eyes, and an image of my dear sister smiled at me. "There you have my story. You are the first to hear it."

"My honor." He paused. "You didn't tell your foster parents or any friends or family?"

I shook my head. "Too painful. You asked how and why I chose my career. The wilderness has much to offer. Incredible beauty, a kinship with the earth, and admiration for the plants, trees, and wildlife. The mountains are my favorite." I opened my eyes and met Blane's tender gaze from the chair beside me. Shadows danced on the walls and ceiling like friends, and I sensed his caring. "I've told you how I treasure the mountains, especially the ones where the peaks soar above the clouds. There is where I feel most alive—where purpose and worship join hands, where songs originate."

"In the Guadalupe Mountains, you explained your definition of respect, a blend of love and fear," Blane said. "Those words stayed with me during quiet moments there. Thank you for telling me your story."

"I appreciate your listening." I grasped his hand.

"The tone of your voice says how you miss her."

"A melancholy void. As the years passed, good memories have eased the sadness."

"How did your parents deal with Kate's passing?"

"Less than three weeks later, they both died within a few hours of each other. Dad had a stroke while milking the cows. Mom found him and collapsed beside him. I guess she couldn't live without Kate or my dad. I went into foster care until I was eighteen. The rest is history."

"Your family will always live in your memories," Blane said. "Kate suffered from leukemia, and there was nothing you could have done to save her. Sounds like your parents died of broken hearts."

"I blamed myself for years."

"Did Kate have a reaction?"

"No." Why had I caved to this horrid memory?

"You are a gifted woman with more skills in your little finger than most people will ever possess. You've risked your life and saved countless lives. Someday I want to hear you play and sing. Music is part of who you are."

"I broke my guitar the night Kate died. Nothing creative since. Seems wrong."

"I believe one day you'll pick up a guitar and sing again. Like not giving up on rescuing Alina, your secrets are safe with me."

God, have You placed this man in my life for something I'm not prepared for? "There is more to Blane Gardner than a handsome face and expert negotiation skills."

"Ah, the lady thinks I'm handsome. That's worth heading back to Dog Canyon and sleeping on the hard ground in the cold with a battered body."

"Watch out for the scorpions and centipedes."

He chuckled. "Anything crawls on me, and I'm screaming like a girl."

"The agents in the other room would be here with their guns drawn."

Please, Alina, fight for strength to live.

I never intended to tell anyone about my guilt over Kate's death. Had to be a God-thing that Blane allowed me to clear my conscience. Kate's death had no bearing on what I said and did during our last time together.

How comforting the spoken words freed me to attempt to forgive myself. How odd this man had approached me at just the right time to cleanse my soul. He nurtured my grieving heart in unexplainable ways. I sensed a kinship with Blane like no other man. *Please, God, don't take him from me too.*

FIFTY-FIVE

BLANE

Waiting on Rurik's call nearly made me crazy. Nearly. The only box I checked was Sergio had my truck delivered. I wanted my own vehicle and no one else in the line of fire. Therese perceived my angst, and we talked while I kept both ears and one eye on my phone.

"We need a diversion," she said. "Time is creeping by, and I see your impatience."

"Right. Tell me about your years in foster care," I said. "If it's hard, your story can wait until another time." I leaned across the small kitchen table where we shared coffee and grasped her scraped hand. "Negotiators are supposed to be patient."

"Depends on how you define patience. Waiting on a spark to burst into a flame takes patience unless you're about to die in an explosion. Waiting for a special occasion takes patience, and that's fine. Then we appreciate it more. Waiting for sunrise to hike takes patience, but I treasure the rhythm of a new day bursting across the sky." She gestured around us. "This is the pits. We both feel like caged animals, and we are action people."

"Injured action people."

"True. About my foster parents. They were amazing. Strong

Christians. They had grown children and grandchildren but weren't ready to relinquish parenting . . . and loving. They instilled strong values like my own mom and dad. Their counseling came at a desperate time in my life. They encouraged me to pursue a career that utilized my love of outdoors with helping others. I truly loved them when confusion and grief threatened to consume me."

"Are they living?"

She nodded. "They retired to Florida and work with shut-ins—ministering, transporting them, and delivering meals."

"How old are they?"

"Late eighties."

We laughed and the tension in my bones released.

An hour later, Rurik called from a number I recognized as belonging to one of the agents assigned to protect him.

Rurik greeted me. "Jurg will meet you at ten tonight at the DimLight Bar on the southeast side of town. Come alone. He'll have eyes on everyone who comes and goes. He has ways that are beyond your worst horrors so assume nothing. No wires. Trust me, he'll check. Falin has your phone number and your truck's license plates."

"You gave him my new cell number?" I gulped my irritation. "Of course you did."

"At the bar, tell the girl that 'vodka is best straight up.' You'll be shown to a table where Jurg will join you."

I ended the call and contacted Sergio. How the FBI would get a new bartender or server in place was beyond me. A slipup came with a high price. Sergio assured me the problem had a solution. "The FBI has an undercover agent who has worked at the DimLight in the past. She'll record what's said. You do your part, and we'll do ours."

I drove my Ford pickup to the DimLight, a sleazy bar in a sleazy part of town. I detected a car on my tail for the last twenty minutes. I expected it, and I'd have been shocked without one. Nothing on me or in my truck was wired. I was on my own. But I did have my SIG under my seat. Falin's men had plans to search my truck, and they'd find the firearm. Would they snatch it?

The DimLight lived up to my expectations. The first *i* in the name flashed on and off in neon red. Maneuvering my casted arm while exiting my truck made me feel like an old man. Then again, the bandage on my head gave the impression I was harmless. I scrutinized the other vehicles—most at least ten years older than mine—where and how they parked, and any new friends exploring easy prey. A parking area on the side of the bar held two vehicles worth three times mine.

By the time I reached the door, maneuvering over crushed gravel, the car following me had found its spot beside my truck. I smelled the liquor, unwashed bodies, and trouble on tap. A young woman wearing fewer clothes than a bikini model met me.

I eyed her like a man looking for action. "Vodka is best straight up."

"Yes, sir, we've been expecting you." She whirled around, and I followed her to a corner table lit by a battery-operated candle. The ambiance escaped me. She pointed to a chair not to my liking . . . It didn't face the door.

Three men sat at the bar and six together at small tables, nursing beer bottles and drinks. Staged and ready to open fire. One bartender and two waitresses clad in little more than the hostess. I looked pathetic, but their scrutiny almost made me laugh.

Within moments, I stared at my nemesis, more like an accountant than a killer, a man who preferred lifting numbers to weights.

Taking a chair that allowed him full view of the door, Falin pointed to my cast. "I assume this isn't your shooting arm." He nodded, and two men approached me from behind.

A man patted me down. Neither spoke a word to indicate their nationality. But they had features like chiseled rock and muscles bulged like CGI creatures. Did Falin think I was stupid enough to bring in a weapon or wear a wire? Tonight, observations trumped my chosen weapon, and I'd use it to my benefit.

The two men backed off, and I eased onto a chair. "Satisfied?"

"Temporarily." Falin turned to one of his men and ordered a vodka on the rocks.

"Not me. Taking some strong meds."

Falin laughed. "Nothing stands between me and a drink. Nothing but money."

One man headed to the bar, and I counted to ten, inhaling confidence. "I need proof of life, or this conversation is useless."

He reached inside his pants pocket and showed me his phone's screen. A live video with a time stamp indicated Alina asleep on a bed. A lamplight lit her face. Zooming in showed her steady breathing. Her cheeks were damp as though she'd been crying. Nothing in the room revealed the location.

"All right," I said. "Rurik's agreed to pay you three million more and supply a private plane to get you out of the country in exchange for Alina's safe return. All I need is a number to wire the money."

"Not that simple. Why stick your nose in this? First in Dog Canyon and here. Rurik's and my business have nothing to do with you."

"Three reasons—a child got tossed into the problem. The FBI wants to arrest him for murdering his wife and child, and I want my hands on the cartel."

"You'd rather he faced a judge on murder charges? Hmm. What's your view of the FBI?"

I huffed. "If I had respect for them, I'd be wearing their badge."

Falin tugged at his ear—indecisive about his next move or a gesture to throw me off. "Who's flying the plane?"

"A connection in St. Petersburg." I hid my tells.

A scantily clad waitress brought Falin's drink. He eyed her. "Haven't seen you lately."

I maintained a stoic facade.

"Filling in for a friend, the bartender." She bent to his level, and her cleavage plunged deep. "Do you need to see my résumé again?"

"Maybe later."

"I get off at 2:00 a.m." She lifted a shoulder with a seductive smile and made her way to another table.

"Check her out," Falin said to one of the men behind him.

I studied Jurg Falin seated across from me, a man who had the ability to get things done and put on a show. "Are you ready to seal this?"

He sipped on his vodka. "I name the day and time."

"Figured as much."

"I'll contact Rurik with the wire info and where I'll board the plane. Only he and the pilot at the site. At takeoff, I'll give him Alina's location."

"Doesn't cut it. He wants Alina *before* takeoff."

"I call the shots. His demands are meaningless."

"Timing is important. If Alina isn't at the meetup point, then no deal."

"And if he's been arrested?"

"I'll take Alina off your hands."

His eyes narrowed. "Monday, 6:00 p.m." He stood without finishing his drink. "Tell Rurik to expect my call with more details." He dipped his chin. "You can keep your SIG in the truck to show my generosity."

FIFTY-SIX

THERESE

I dozed on the hard hotel sofa until Blane returned from his meeting with Jurg Falin. If I went to bed, he wouldn't wake me with what happened tonight. At times my kidney made me nauseous or gave me muscle spasms. Nothing I needed right now.

The two agents watched a cop show, remarking how Hollywood never got it right. At least in movies, the good guys always won. I needed to shove aside the cynicism and remember God had this. Lately my display of faith needed reinforcement . . . I sounded like Blane.

A Ranger dropped Blane off after midnight. He'd left his truck in another part of town, not a secret to Falin since he had the license plate number. Blane asked to talk in my temporary bedroom, where he explained the negotiations with Falin and how the wired waitress had recorded the conversation.

"I phoned Sergio en route to meeting the FBI agent. I learned the DimLight has been under FBI surveillance for the past several months."

"Did they already have someone inside?"

"Yes, and Falin had talked to her in the past. FBI also confirmed listening devices as part of their surveillance."

"Why does Falin want the exchange on Monday?" I said. "He's a part of the Baranov assassination on Wednesday. Doesn't he want credit from Mother Russia? What am I missing?"

"His innocence in the event Rurik spills the truth. The second thing is the ROC is well informed about who put the plot together."

"And he gets the credit if they are successful." I pondered what I'd said. "But he'd also get the blame if his plans are foiled."

"True, but my guess is he has someone lined up to take the fall. I'd say Rurik or one of his henchmen."

"Poor Alina. Rurik's request to adopt her makes sense."

Blane hesitated, as though choosing his words with care. "Rurik's life is on the wrong end of a death sentence, and he knows it. He refused to cooperate with the ROC and has been blackmailed, and if the courts find him guilty, he'll pay the highest price."

"Makes me wish Texas permitted a polygraph test as valid evidence. Then I'd feel better about my allegiance. Or lack of."

"I trust Rurik's allegiance about as far as I can spit. But we'll find out. I received an update on the way here. Rurik's been in contact with someone associated with the Russian government long before Alina's abduction. Looks like constant communication until a month ago. How many burners has he stashed away, and why haven't they been located?"

"In the beginning I wanted the US to offer Alina and him a new beginning, but my only concern now is Alina."

"He's either working as a Russian spy and guilty of Daria's death and Alina's abduction or blackmailed into assisting the ROC. We're not going to find out tonight."

"Or something to do with Edik Baranov. Tomorrow?" I said.

He cupped my chin, a kind smile playing on his lips. "Wishful thinking, but I'll go with it." He stepped back. "We need sleep."

"Who told you about Rurik talking to someone associated with the Russian government?"

"Sergio, and his info came from someone high up at the FBI."

"Do they have evidence he's a spy?" I said, not really wanting to hear the answer when my concentration stayed fixed on Alina.

"Strong contender. I've read his tells and done my best to be objective." He exhaled. "Whatever the truth, Alina deserves a chance at life. I'm not giving up on negotiating for her freedom."

"This is bigger than both of us. Are you opening a can of worms with what you learned tonight? Think about all that has gone wrong."

"Do I detect a bit of concern?" He purposely widened his eyes, but I wasn't amused.

"And if I am?" I feigned irritation, but I did have a backpack full of worry and what he might do to compensate for his broken arm.

"There are trained people who thrive on responsibility, challenges, and danger. I'm one of them. If—"

A gunshot shattered the stillness.

"Stay back!" an agent shouted from the other room. "Active shooters."

Blane yanked his SIG from his back waistband. "Therese, call for help. Get flat on the floor. The walls are thin." The door slammed shut behind him.

I grabbed my phone with trembling fingers. Major Montoya had given me his number, and I did my best to sound calm amid the gunfire.

He answered before the first ring ended. "Don't leave your room. You'll make it harder for Blane and the agents to do their jobs. Those agents have backup on the way at the first sign of trouble. And I'll be there in a few."

I gripped my phone and wished it had a trigger. But this wasn't the first time I'd fought a battle on my knees or, in this case, on my stomach.

"We followed her here," a muffled male voice said. "Give us the Palmer woman, and we'll leave."

Gunfire erupted again. "That's your answer," Blane said.

What did Falin and the ROC want with me? Had Rurik led them to believe I knew their plans?

A cry rang out. *Please help the three people protecting me. No injuries. Or worse. I beg of You.*

Flashes of those who'd bled and died in Dog Canyon sickened me.

Wasted life. These were people with families, dreams, and hopes for the future. All the suffering. Why? Was it a stand for justice?

"Hear those sirens?" Blane said. "You're about to be dead men."

The sirens grew louder, reminding me of an orchestra reaching a crescendo.

"Like those agents, you're out of time, cowboy."

Gunfire cracked.

FIFTY-SEVEN

BLANE

I've always liked blue, and the police officers bursting through the hotel room door wore it well. Two shooters were sprawled out on the floor in their own blood. Neither one I recognized, and neither one breathed. One of the agents, a woman, struggled with a stomach wound. She was conscious, able to speak. The other agent might not make it. He had an upper chest wound on the left side. Blood trickled down his shirt to the floor. Paramedics streamed in—focused on the wounded.

I stood there without a scratch. Why? I should have been the easiest one to stop. My gaze swept around the small room where the stench of death stained the carpeted floor, walls, and sofa.

Therese lingered in the hallway with a female police officer. Her features paled with shock. I hated the devastation stalking her with what she'd experienced at Dog Canyon fresh and raw in her senses. I often had a rough time putting scenes like these behind me, and I'm sure the blood spatters were etched in her too.

"Are you okay?" I studied her haunted eyes.

"I want to be. You?"

"Not a scratch. Unfair with all that's going on."

Her attention darted around the room, resting on the paramedics working on the severely wounded agent.

"Don't look. There's nothing you can do."

"I can pray."

"Yes. We both can. Those agents have good people tending to them." I caught the attention of the female officer, a tall woman who spoke to a fellow officer. "Please, would you get Therese out of here?"

"Certainly. My car is right outside."

Therese moved to the wounded agent and knelt beside her. She whispered her thanks and prayed for her, but the other agent remained unconscious. The paramedics lifted him onto a gurney and carried him outside.

I bent to Therese and slipped her hand into mine. "I'll be with you as quickly as I can."

"Were the two men from your meeting with Falin?"

"No. The payroll must be huge. Whoever is responsible doesn't give up. But I'll get this handled and find another safe house."

She shook her head. "I'm done running. Home is calling me. No one else will be hurt or killed. This is my war."

"It's not your battle," I said. "There are those who want you dead."

"I'm still done." She arched her trembling shoulders.

I valued her convictions, but arguing with someone in shock only pushed them off the deep end.

Sergio arrived the same time as HPD and joined me in the hotel room with the FBI. Glad to see him. No point in repeating myself any more than necessary, especially when my concerns ranged from injured agents, Therese, Alina, stolen activation chips, and Edik Baranov. As I'd speculated, someone used local felons who had no association with the ROC. It all motivated me to end loss of life over greed and power—a reason to support all law enforcement and federal officers.

I argued with Therese to leave for another safe house, but she refused.

Around 3:00 a.m., I talked with Sergio privately about the next step. "It works in Falin's favor if Rurik is arrested and convicted of murdering his family."

"I'm not sure it's what Rurik might have told her but something she might have overheard or seen from Chandler and Falin," Sergio said. "Has she mentioned anything?"

"No. She's outside in a police car."

Sergio spoke to the FBI agent in charge of investigating the shooting. We made our way outside to Therese, where she'd fallen asleep in the rear of the cruiser. I regretted waking her for Sergio to ask questions, but she'd be the first one to insist on it. I opened the car door, and her eyes flew open.

"I have Sergio with me. He wants to talk to you."

She nodded sleepily and stepped out of the car. She wrapped her arms around her chest in the chilly early morning air. "I don't have anything to offer since I stayed away from the gunfire."

"My question concerns another matter," Sergio said. "It's late, and you've been through a tough ordeal. My apologies but this won't take long. During the time you were with Chandler and Falin in Dog Canyon, did you see or hear anything that Falin would view as dangerous?"

Therese inhaled deeply. "Nothing, and I've burned brain cells trying to figure it out. Tom Chandler had a cruel streak, threatening, abusive. Jurg Falin played the role of a more sensible man. He was subservient to Chandler and took orders." She moistened her lips. "At one point while Chandler was away from the cave, I got the best of Falin. Alina and I made our escape, but Chandler returned early and ended the plan. He called Falin a stupid Russian. Falin's temper erupted, and he shot Chandler. I saw a calculating, dangerous side of him and concluded Falin's cowardly behavior around Chandler had been a game. He'd planned to take the laser chips all along." She rubbed the back of her neck. "I'm repeating myself, but I thought going over them again might dredge up a detail. Guess not. Sorry, sir."

"You are doing fine, more than fine. Any indication where Falin planned to unload the chips?"

"Never discussed in my presence. The two sides I witnessed of him showed he's cunning and evil, like a cat stalking its prey. The only goodness was in protecting Alina. He spoke out against Chandler killing her and argued against selling her into human trafficking."

"She is his weak spot," Sergio said more to himself than us.

I spoke up. "The live video from tonight showed she's in a clean place."

"Would he take her back to Russia? He is her uncle," Therese said. "To continue blackmailing Rurik?"

Sergio leaned on one leg. "What value is he sitting behind bars?"

I broke into their conversation. "We're running in circles, like Falin is leading us by a leash. If he fails to show on Monday evening, we have only hours to renegotiate Alina's release and protect the Baranovs. Sergio, you've told me the Feds are working on Edik Baranov and his family's arrival. I don't have a good feeling about any of this."

FIFTY-EIGHT

THERESE

Against my better judgment, I slept in the third FBI-protected housing in three days. Musical beds. I'd argued, begged, and finally gave in to Blane and Major Montoya, who pointed out the danger of returning to my own home. We bartered, and I agreed to a two-bedroom apartment without protection, other than Blane in the next room and twenty-four-hour surveillance in the parking lot. The inappropriateness hit me hard, but Alina could be rescued today, and Blane and I weren't in any shape to give in to any romantic feelings we might have had for each other.

Someone once said, "Disagree with me, and I'll find a way to destroy you." That quote fit Falin's philosophy of life, but I strongly disagreed. I had more prayer power than he'd ever imagined.

Grabbing my phone on the nightstand, I read 11:35 a.m. The morning had slipped by—with no rattle of activity. My thoughts moved to the agents assigned to protect us and both hurt in the attack late last night. I prayed for their healing and no one else to look down the wrong end of a gun.

I rolled onto my back, inwardly groaning with every aching muscle and bruise. I should get up. Be productive. Check on Blane. Work on the next stage of rescuing Alina. I treasured my country and detested what the ROC planned, but I'd gotten into this mess to free the little girl. Let the big guns handle the big guns.

How did I stop the bloodshed and help an innocent little girl? Other than a few self-defense moves that were useless with the condition of my body, I had no skills to offer. Closing my eyes, I slipped into a dreamy state where Kate's image blended with Alina's. Yes, the similarity of their physical traits drew me to Alina, and like Kate, Alina had a fearless streak.

It hit me. Falin wanted me, and the shooters hadn't said *dead.* He hadn't killed me in the cave, so did that mean she'd be unharmed in his custody? If talking to me was so important, then I'd hear him out. Not necessarily smart. But desperation led to desperate measures. Kate might have lived if I'd done more, and I learned the hard way that others always came first. My life had never been about me. Pulling my charger from my backpack, I plugged in my phone near the nightstand. Later I'd need it.

I crept out of bed into a bathroom across the hall. I dressed in jeans and a sweatshirt and brushed my hair into a ponytail. I opened the door, smelled the heavenly aroma of coffee, and crept down the short hallway to the combo kitchen and living area.

Blane read something from his phone and smiled at me with those incredible eyes and tousled red hair. "Morning, sunshine."

"Morning. Today you are Rusty."

He ran his fingers through his hair. "That bad? I planned to shower when you crawled out of bed."

"You look fine, just bed hair. Nothing pressing on my end." I gave him my best smile. "Go ahead and shower." Guilt lingered for what I planned, and I opened a cabinet door. "Need coffee?"

"I'm good."

He asked the typical how-are-you questions, and I asked mine.

"Both of our agents underwent surgery to remove bullets and are in ICU holding their own. The prognosis is good."

"Glad I prayed for them."

"That makes two of us." He rose from the chair. "I'm going to jump into the shower. Will you be okay?"

"Yes. Later on, will you update me on anything according to protocol?"

"Yep, partner." He walked by and brushed his fingers across mine. Electricity fired through me. Not even my own father cared like Blane demonstrated. And I treasured every moment with him. How had I given my heart so easily in such a short time? Staying much longer in this apartment would have alarm bells ringing.

I sipped coffee until the shower water alerted me to the time. Snatching my backpack and stuffing in my phone and charger, I slipped out the front door onto an outdoor hallway. A hint of chilly air under a clear, blue sky refreshed me. I searched the parking area. Ah, the agents assigned to watch the apartment sat in a dark Chevy with tinted windows in the parking lot.

Back inside the apartment, I exited a rear glass door onto a balcony overlooking a narrow strip of weeds and a tire shop. We were on the second floor. What should I do? I didn't want to face Blane with my decision. I'd wiggled down steeper rocks than this. Swinging my leg over the wobbly metal fencing, I shimmied to the point where I jumped into the weeds. Oh, did my body complain.

Moments later, I hurried down the street. At an intersection, the street signs indicated the west side of Houston. I walked five more blocks and stopped in a coffee shop and plugged in my phone. I should be afraid of where my thoughts had led me, but fear and I courted a love-hate relationship.

Step one meant talking to Rurik, and all I had was his burner number from our original conversation. I risked the agents assigned to his home refusing to put me through without FBI approval. But the agents approved with no questions asked. They'd learn about the conversation later.

"Rurik, this is Therese. I need a favor. Can you call me on a separate phone?"

"Yes. But I doubt if it's possible." He ended the call and my phone rang within a minute.

"Rurik, I need you to call Jurg Falin. Tell him I'm ready to meet up. Alone. No one will be with me or know about the meeting."

"Terrible idea. He cannot be trusted."

"I'm willing to risk it."

"Why? You're asking for an early grave."

"To get your daughter back. Stop the bloodshed."

"The issue is a bigger problem between Jurg and me," Rurik said. "If possible, I'd have ended this long ago." He sighed heavily. "You'd be walking into a trap, and you've escaped death too many times."

"He wants to talk to me, and I have no clue why. But he knows I care about Alina while Blane and Major Montoya are determined to make arrests for all the crimes. I'm trusting my intuition on this. He's done well enough on his own building up criminal charges. Tell him I want a face-to-face. My choice of location. None of his bodyguard types."

"Blane and Major Montoya agreed to this?"

"That is my business."

"They have no idea?"

"Do you want Alina back or not?"

"You're on your own with this. I'll call, but I need to know where this will take place."

I checked the map on my phone. A McDonald's sat about a mile from my location. I gave the address to Rurik and suggested one hour. "I'm waiting here until you hear from Falin."

FIFTY-NINE

Seated in a corner booth at McDonald's, I waited for my meetup with Jurg Falin. My emotions caused me to shiver as though I'd stepped into a walk-in freezer and couldn't move. Thoughts of leaving tapped me on the shoulder, then Falin walked in alone at the precise time, dressed in jeans and a pullover. He slid into the booth across from me.

"Your face looks like you lost a fight," he said.

"But it's not over." I smiled and folded my hands on the table. Blane had instructed me to listen, to learn what motivated the other person.

"Your phone, please."

"It's in my backpack." He said nothing, and I reached inside and handed it to him.

He examined my phone and powered it off, then slipped it inside a sealed Faraday bag, preventing my phone from being traced.

"Satisfied?" I raised an eyebrow.

"Chandler said you were a worthy opponent, and while he didn't deserve to live, I respected his opinion about you. I figured sooner or later you'd discover the tracker. It's been a few places, but currently at a hotel with FBI agents who think they can trap me." Falin's narrow eyes, bald head, and rectangular face were by no means appealing, but he had a manner of confidence that some women admired. Me, I respected his intellect and took nothing for granted.

"I'm tired of this game and needless situation, and I've drawn one conclusion. I'll do anything to have Alina returned. How can I help you to make this happen?"

Falin regarded me as though I planned to trick him. "You care about her. I watched you with Alina in the cave."

"Yes." *I need help, Lord.* "She has a strong spirit, intelligence, and is very lovable."

He lifted a brow. "Like her mother, Alina has many of the same mannerisms."

"Her courage comes naturally."

He leaned back in the booth. "Rurik doesn't deserve her."

Odd response. "Why?"

"She's all I have left. He deliberately put her in danger and has kept her there."

I lowered my tone and filled my words with sincerity. "Why would he endanger the one person he loves?"

"Therese, is it okay if I call you by your first name?" I nodded, and he continued. "I'm Jurg. You think I'm the bad guy, but trust me, I'm not acting alone."

I bit my tongue to keep from asking him who wrote his playbook. *Patience.* He wasn't ready to give me answers.

"I'm patriotic and loyal to my country. I support Russia's policies and methods of keeping our country strong. Those are good qualities."

Until innocent lives were destroyed. "I'm listening, and yes, those are admirable traits. What has Rurik done or not done? I'll talk to him, get this resolved."

"There's nothing you can do. To Rurik, Alina is second to everything in his life."

"I'm sorry. I had no idea."

"My sister is dead. Instead of rushing her to the hospital when she suffered with unbearable pain, he asked me to check on her. Said he had an important meeting at the university and didn't want to leave her alone. He neglected to tell me he'd overdosed her with pain medication. He claimed she took them without his knowledge, but that's a lie. She lived for him and Alina."

Jurg pounded the table. "I'd nearly convinced her to try experimental treatment in Switzerland. The arrangements had been made. When I checked on her, she slipped into a coma and died before help arrived. Later I'd discovered he'd met with a university colleague . . . a female professor—Daria. I vowed to destroy them."

Heat rushed over me. Jurg's reasoning was a horrible vendetta. He justified murder and kidnapping in the name of his sister.

"He chose a pretty woman over his responsibilities, and now he has neither my sister, Alina, nor Daria. Since you support Rurik, you deserve the truth about him. The sniveling coward."

"He claims you tried to persuade him to join the ROC."

"A tidy way to eliminate him without blood on my hands. I will protect Alina from his influence."

The road some people traveled to ensure control sparked my anger. *Listen. Be his friend.* "I'm a wilderness-survival guide who attempted to help Rurik locate his daughter. Is that my crime and why I've been targeted? Accepting misinformation as truth?"

"I made a deal with Gardner for a Monday exchange. I assume you're aware?"

"I am. So why hire a couple of locals to come after me? You could have contacted me through Rurik."

"The agents overseeing Rurik's safety would have heard the conversation or he'd have told them." He tapped his thumb on the tabletop. "You have importance to him as the go-between in securing Alina. Gardner may be your sidekick, but Rurik trusts you more. You are valuable to me."

"How?"

"Two things—I want you to testify that Rurik told you he'd murdered Daria."

Destroy Rurik with a lie? "Why haven't you killed him?"

Jurg held up a finger, his features stoic. "Public humiliation for the death of my sister and Daria."

"All right. What else?"

"You observed things in the cave that could ruin me."

I was learning more. "What? I'm clueless."

A smirk played on his lips. "You saw where Chandler purchased the laser chips. Don't lie to me, Therese. One of my specialties is reading people."

I'd noted the manufacturer, but I hadn't spent brain cells on it. In the cave, I concentrated on keeping Alina and myself alive. But Falin had no reason to believe I had forgotten the name on the box of laser chips. "I understand." My executioner sat across the table from me. "Why order the hit here instead of the cave? Three locations?"

"Who said I did?"

I'd walked into a trap like Rurik had warned. "Then who?"

"Does it matter? I wanted you alive to find out who else knew about the chips. Someone higher up had a different idea. Back to my question. Where did the laser chips originate?"

"How does my answer equate to releasing Alina and stopping the bloodshed?"

"Answer my question first."

"A US source, and I assume the same seller supplies other things you need too. I assume the seller is open to anyone who has the cash. From your concern, my guess it's one of your major sources." I paused for him to contemplate my words. "If I reveal the seller, it's merely my word against a huge US company. They have attorneys on call to handle muddy issues like dealing with illegal weaponry. Or kill me and no one is the wiser." I shrugged while my instincts shouted at me to get out of the restaurant. "You haven't said how my awareness of your supplier affects Alina's release."

"You and I will make our own deal. She believes Rurik is dead, and if I take you to her, keep her pacified and your mouth shut."

SIXTY

BLANE

Why had Therese left the apartment? Put herself in danger? Not even a note. I should have done the math while she poured on the Ms. Congeniality charm. Panic burst inside me . . . Had she been abducted?

I phoned the apartment's business office and learned the building lacked a security cam. No surprise. The building teetered between condemned and strike a match. From the layout, she must have left through the front on foot. Unless someone picked her up.

What happened to the surveillance team assigned to keep an eye on us? Where were they at noon? Out to lunch? I stormed to the parking lot, recognized the car, and demanded the agents tell me where Therese had gone. No surprise they hadn't seen her. I phoned Sergio, not that he had an explanation. His instructions to stay put while he located her sailed through one ear and out the other.

Inside the apartment, I noted her backpack, phone, and charging cord were missing. Abductors didn't permit victims to gather their belongings. Where had she gone, and why?

If she showed up in a few minutes with the excuse of taking a walk . . . I might cuff her to the kitchen sink. Or kiss her, depending on my mood.

I grasped my phone and called one of the agents at Rurik's house. The Russian professor with the questionable motives might have heard from Therese. They confirmed she'd called for Rurik, but the conversation lasted less than ten seconds.

"She asked him to call her on another phone," an agent said. "We haven't found it."

The agent handed Rurik his phone, and I asked him my burning question.

"She doesn't want me telling her plans," Rurik said. "It is a private matter."

"Look at all she's sacrificed for you. Would you send her to her death?"

"Therese is a grown woman committed to rescuing my daughter."

The between-the-lines conversation hit me hard. "You helped her arrange a meeting with Falin. I already did that and look where it got us."

Rurik said something in Russian, which I assumed was cursing. "I arranged things at her request." He spouted his efforts to stop her, claiming to warn her of the danger. "She wore me down."

"Where's the meeting?"

"My betrayal would seal her death."

"Contact Falin on your burner and have him call me."

The seconds of hesitation ticked by. "All right."

I paced the small living area until my phone rang shrill.

"Gardner, this is Jurg Falin. What do you need this fine afternoon?"

"I believe you have a child and a woman with you. Both need to be released."

He laughed. "I have Therese as security for Monday's exchange. Then I'll tell you where you can find them in one piece and breathing."

"Bring her and Alina to the landing strip."

"My way or no deal." Falin's enunciation of each word showed his intent. "You want me to show you where to find their dead bodies today or where to find them alive on Monday?"

"You can guess the answer."

"Smart man. Are we finished?"

"I'd like to talk to Therese."

"I'll check on her availability."

Anger boiled in my veins with his sarcasm.

"I'm here, Blane," Therese said. "I'm sorry, but I needed to find out what Jurg wanted with me."

"Have you?"

"Yes, I'm aware of the stakes." She sounded in control.

"Where is he holding you?"

"I'm fine. It's better this way. No one else will be hurt."

Why hadn't I notified Sergio so he'd trace the call? "What will staying accomplish?"

"An end to the crimes. I'm not in immediate danger."

"You trust him?" While I kept my negotiator tone calm, my anger meter rose. No doubt Falin listened in.

"Doesn't matter. I'll see you on Monday evening."

"How is Alina?"

"I'm told she's fine."

The connection went dead, and my insides twisted like I'd inhaled poisonous gas. I'd see if Sergio could trace the call, but Falin seldom made a mistake.

I deliberated Rurik Ivanov and Jurg Falin, two men who valued power and control. Rurik's love for Alina overruled his emotions and resulting actions. He'd made repulsive illegal decisions, and I had no doubt he'd continue until his daughter was safe or he breathed his last. Neither did he care what happened to Therese. While the realizations made sense, Rurik's potential outcome laid out like a cemetery plot.

Falin, who had no regard for human life, viewed his enterprise worth murder and kidnapping. He applied psychological pressure on Rurik to comply to his demands, whatever they were. The Feds might hold back in rescuing a child caught in an international political feud, but an American woman increased the stakes. US policy traditionally stated we didn't negotiate with terrorists, but sometimes a crisis and public opinion influenced government action.

SIXTY-ONE

ALINA

One day rolled into the next, and I did my best to use the routine as a schedule and not worry so much. Daddy said schedules kept us organized and in a better mood.

But fear held me tight.

I cried for my daddy.

I feared a new life in Russia. My uncle who now treated me nice might be mean again. The faces of the men he'd killed kept me awake at night.

Red used to be my favorite color but no more. Daddy told me red meant life, and black meant death. He made a terrible mistake.

I kept my room neat, and the work pleased my uncle. I washed my clothes and hung them in the shower to dry, scrubbing the blood hard until the spots faded. I straightened the towels, washcloths, and wiped out the sink with extra napkins from the food he brought me. Then I completed the schoolwork my uncle downloaded on my iPad. He made sure every day I solved hard math problems, studied Russian history, politics, science, and read books in Russian he said were important. Daddy had encouraged me to work very hard on my studies, so this part of my day seemed a little normal. At school, my classes had been with bigger kids, and they weren't always friendly.

Late afternoon, my uncle's signal knock and voice startled me. I unlocked the door, surprised to see him with Therese. They came inside, and he locked the door behind them.

"Hi, Alina." Therese smiled. Her hands weren't tied, but her face had bruises.

"Has my uncle brought you to visit me?"

She bent to my level. "He has. I'm excited to see you again. Your uncle tells me the two of you are using different names. He's Isaak Mishin, and you're Larisa Mishin."

"Yes, ma'am. The names keep us safe from the bad people who killed Daddy." A flicker of something flashed in her eyes. Was she running from the people who wanted to hurt me?

"Sounds like your uncle is taking good care of you."

I glanced up at him, and he touched my cheek. "He is." Until I learned the truth, I must make him think I believed everything he said.

"You two can keep each other company while I'm gone," he said. "I'll bring your dinner back. Is a grilled chicken salad all right with you girls?"

"Perfect," Therese said. "Ali . . . Larisa and I will have a great time together."

Uncle Isaak kissed my forehead and left. The click sounded on the door, and I double locked it from my side.

Therese's visit confused me. My hands shook and I dug my fingers into my palms. "Thank you for coming."

She sat on the bed in front of me. "I am your friend. I asked to spend time with you." Therese put her finger to her lips to quiet me, and I nodded. She mouthed, *Your uncle is listening to us.*

I would not upset my uncle. "What sounds fun to you?"

"How do you spend your time alone?"

I explained all the things to keep me busy. ". . . and I finished my schoolwork. I can show you on my iPad."

"I'd love it." Therese looked at my math, and her eyes widened. "You're doing precalculus."

"I like numbers."

"I'd like to look at what you've done." She touched my arm and then her lips. She mouthed, *Have you been hurt?*

I shook my head. *My daddy is dead.*

Therese wrapped her arm around my shoulder. *Your uncle told you?*

I nodded. It must be true. I swiped at a tear, and she drew me into her arms. I tried to stop but still I sobbed. *Oh no!* My uncle would hear. Think fast. "I'm sorry to cry. But it is good to see you."

She bit her lip and hugged me tighter. "Friends cry when they haven't seen each other for a while." *You will be okay. I promise. God loves you.*

Therese said *God* again. She must believe He's real. Daria said there was no such thing as God. People who believed were weak and had forgotten how to use their heads. I hoped Daria had made a huge mistake.

Why would a God who loves you kill your daddy?

SIXTY-TWO

THERESE

Blane had spent his birthday alone with a broken arm and a concussion. He'd survived. My surviving to my birthday tomorrow was contingent on Jurg deciding if my life held any merit. I clung to my faith with both hands and the vision that God always had things under His control. But my insides cowered.

This hotel was a new property built near the ship channel, east of downtown Houston. A barge moved across the waters in the distance, and sailboats and yachts dotted the afternoon sun-kissed view.

Before we had left McDonald's earlier, he'd given me a baseball cap and adjusted it over my eyes to wear from the moment we exited the car and up four flights of stairs.

"One word to anyone, and I will pull the trigger on you and anyone else nearby," he'd said.

"Why would I want to spoil my end of the bargain to jeopardize Alina's release?"

"Your impulsive nature is not foreign to me."

I greeted a maid in the hall while Jurg swiped a room key over door 412. That's when I discovered Alina's prison was an adjoining room.

Now Alina and I ate our salad dinner and watched *Beauty and the Beast* in Russian. She crawled into bed and I took the sofa. Her soft, rhythmic breathing gave me peace. At times, barely audible moans interrupted her dream world.

Oh, God, please give me strength and wisdom.

Jurg told the child her father was dead? I found it easy to comprehend Jurg's greed for power within the Russian government, his patriotism, money, and desire to join the elite in Russia. What puzzled me lay with his obsessiveness toward Alina. He'd admitted she had a strong likeness to his sister and his animosity toward Rurik, but what else drove him to look like the caring uncle who wanted his niece safe and protected? I just didn't buy the whole brother-sister loyalty, not with Jurg. People had invoked honor for thousands of years and disguised their bravado with love. The nudge to my spirit said Jurg's crimes might have more to do with Rurik's relationship with Edik Baranov.

Jurg had offered me a deal that, in his words, "guaranteed my release." I no more believed him than Rurik. In Jurg's twisted logic, anyone associated with Rurik outside of Alina were viable threats. *"Make sure Alina is comfortable and believes everything I've told her is true. She's an incredibly bright child and may disbelieve my words."* Jurg had lifted his gaze to me. *"And I will release you unharmed when Alina and I board the plane."*

He had lied to Blane about releasing Alina before he left the country, and I had no way of informing Blane of the real plan. Why couldn't I recall the name of the company where the laser chips had originated?

Nothing. Absolutely nothing.

The night crept by until morning light trickled in through the window. I slept little between worry and incessant what-ifs, longing for faith to wrap me in its cocoon. An image of Blane never left me. Rusty, as Major Montoya called him. Regret looped through me. We had the start of something meaningful. I'd been attracted to him right from the first time I walked into the group of Texas Rangers, ready to teach survival skills. While the other Rangers complimented my every move, he kept his distance.

Our first date sparked a flame that had never been extinguished. Not long afterward, his lack of faith sent me running. Those days in Dog Canyon were horrific, except there Blane accepted Jesus. But unless a miracle happened, my days were numbered.

Alina curled beside me on the sofa. During the early hours of the morning, she had seen me sitting there and joined me. The fresh scent of her, like wildflowers, brought back memories of Kate and me on one of our picnics. I'd lost my sister, but I'd not give up on Alina. What kind of future lay ahead with an uncle who intended to rule over her like he controlled those around him?

Alina opened her sky-blue eyes. "It's not a dream. You're here with me."

I smiled at her. "I am. Did you sleep well?"

"Yes, ma'am. I dreamed you and I were at the beach. The sun was warm but not hot. You held my hand, and we walked in the sand searching for seashells."

"Such a beautiful dream. The beach always relaxes me, but I love the mountains more."

"Tell me about them." Alina's eyes held innocent curiosity. "The ones with my uncle and Mr. Chandler weren't fun."

"I'll tell you about mountains in a different place. They are the Rocky Mountains in Colorado. Close your eyes and breathe in a freshness like nowhere else on earth. Trees everywhere. Families gather near cold streams of water that gurgle like a song . . ." I let my memories take me to the place where bighorn sheep, deer, and elk grazed. I purposely shivered with my recollections of cold water and wintery hikes above the tree zone.

"I'd love to hike in nature," she said.

"We just walked a long way in our imagination. Aren't your legs tired? I grew up in the country and my little sister loved to walk with me."

Alina tilted her head . . . just like Kate used to do. "Does she live in Houston?"

"No, sweetie, she lives in heaven."

"Do you get to see her?"

"One day I will. I'm glad God gave us an imagination so we can enjoy anywhere in the world we want to be."

"God isn't real at my old house. Daria said God is pretend."

"God lives in your heart. All you need to do is invite Him in." I touched the left side of my chest. "He loves and wants the best for you." While I longed to say more, Jurg listened to everything we discussed.

"When my iPad has connectivity again, I'll look for stuff about Him. Does He have a website or e-mail?"

"No, but if you talk to Him in your mind, He hears."

Alina frowned. "How can He answer me?"

"Lots of ways, like a voice in your head or through something you read about Him."

"Sounds weird. I'll try talking to Him."

The last time I had sung "Kate's Song" was the day she had died, but a coaxing in my spirit told me I'd been silent too long. "Would you like to hear a song I wrote when my sister was your age?"

"Yes, please."

Years had passed since I'd allowed those words to flow through me, still every note and line were sealed to memory. Perhaps the music and lyrics were more for me than Alina.

I finished the song, and she hugged me. "Thank you. That was beautiful." Alina's tummy growled.

"You're welcome. And someone's hungry."

"My uncle will knock on the door, and we'll have breakfast soon."

"Great. Today is my birthday, and I'm excited to spend it with you."

Alina squealed. "Wish we could have a party."

My party would be to see her set free.

A knock on the door sounded, and Jurg's voice caused Alina to bound from the sofa to unlock the bolt from our side.

"Good morning." He held a tray of scrambled eggs, toast, juice, milk, coffee, bacon, and fruit. "Are you hungry, my sweet girl?"

The way he said *my* made my stomach curdle.

"Yes, thank you." Alina tossed a smile at me over her shoulder, her blue eyes sparkling. "Today is Therese's birthday."

He nodded at me. "Happy birthday. We'll need to have a special dinner tonight with cake and ice cream for dessert. I want to celebrate as soon as possible."

"Oh, me too," Alina said.

The man was a jerk. A narcissist and a killer.

SIXTY-THREE

BLANE

Only one person had insight into Jurg Falin's mode of operation—Rurik Ivanov. My drive to his home met with frustration woven with Houston bumper-to-bumper traffic, and road construction narrowed four lanes down to one. I sat in traffic and fretted, then prayed, palmed the steering wheel, and prayed again. Therese had recommended a radio station for a spiritual boost, and I tuned it in. I craved more of a high-voltage jolt. KSBJ lifted me with great music containing the faith-filled message I needed.

By the time I arrived at Rurik's, my pulse had slowed, and my blood pressure no longer tipped the charts. I'd been given the skills to persuade Rurik to open up and an awareness he'd probably been trained by experts to hide emotions and truth.

Inside Rurik's office, I closed the door, and we sat across from each other. Comfortable enough to relax but not so comfortable that I'd miss a cue. Nothing between us but a few feet of space to occupy our legs.

I carefully walked him through Therese's abduction. The security cams at McDonald's showed her entering the restaurant, Falin followed her inside, and the two left together about thirty minutes later—Therese wearing a baseball cap with the brim over her eyes. Nothing intimidating in his body language and no aversion in hers.

"I like you, Rurik, and I want to be on your side. But you've repeatedly omitted critical information costing the lives of others."

"Therese told you she wasn't in immediate danger, and she believed Alina to be all right." His chin quivered.

Real or an act?

I disguised my temper. My love for Therese superseded good sense. "I need the truth, or I'll have no choice but to request the FBI pull your protection detail."

Rurik moistened his lips. "My daughter's life is at stake."

"And a woman I care about is in danger, not to mention others who could be hurt." I kept my tone low and nonthreatening. "We both have emotions invested in a situation that to this point has been out of our control. To turn the tables, we need truth and logic."

Rurik blew out his exasperation. "The history is complicated."

"Life is complicated." I caught his attention and held it. "I'm tired of lies and games. Understand I have reliable intel from contacts in Russia and the US that I've not revealed to you. If I hear anything contrary from my confirmed sources, I'm recommending your arrest for Daria's murder and endangering a child. Your deceit has sent men to their deaths, possibly even your wife."

Rurik agreed, with the stoic expression I'd seen on more than one occasion. Was I fighting a losing battle? "I've asked this in a previous conversation, but I don't think you answered truthfully. Are you working undercover for the Russian government?"

"No, and I will be honest." He arched his back. "I received espionage training prior to accepting my position at Leonard University. Jurg planned to work undercover and direct the ROC here, claimed he needed my help. My refusal was hard since he and I had been friends a long time—"

"Before you married his sister?"

"He introduced me to Alina's mother."

"Why didn't you tell Alina that Jurg was her uncle?"

"Daria didn't trust him. She believed his thirst for power and greed might put us in danger."

"But he frequented your home?" I said.

Rurik set his jaw. "I'm the one in charge of my house. I made all final decisions. I told you Daria was often emotional. She responded to things said and done often illogically. I worked hard to keep my wife protected from her internal struggles but severing my friendship with Jurg wasn't one of them."

"How old was Alina when you and Daria married?"

"Two. We worked together at Lomonosov State University."

"How did Jurg react to the marriage?"

"Disapproved. He claimed she lacked maturity and compared her negatively to the strength and mothering of his sister. I loved Daria, and we dreamed of having children together. She never conceived, and it adversely affected our marriage."

"Is that why you took over parenting Alina?"

"I'd taken care of her since her mother died. Daria had never been around children, and claimed she couldn't mother a child who wasn't hers." Rurik picked up a photograph on his desk and handed it to me, obviously Rurik's first wife and Alina as a small baby. "Looking at my daughter is like staring into the face of her mother."

"I see the strong resemblance." I returned the photo. "Your first wife was diagnosed with cancer and according to the dates on my records, Alina must have been three months old."

"Yes, and she died of cancer when Alina was seven months old."

"Juggling grief with a baby is difficult. Who helped you?"

"I hired a woman who came to the home while I taught at the university. What does this have to do with rescuing Alina?"

"I need the full picture to find Jurg's weak areas. How did he handle his sister's death?"

"She suffered tremendously, and neither of us wanted her to continue living with the pain."

"Were Daria and your first wife friends?" I said.

"They'd never met."

"Has Jurg ever had a serious relationship or married?"

"No. He's married to the government. If they'd wanted him to have a wife, he'd have found one."

"Do you suspect Jurg killed Daria?"

"I'm having difficulty sorting out what to believe. But my instincts say he did." Rurik's gaze darted beyond me and back again. "She despised him and asked him not to come to the house. I relayed her feelings, and he suggested we meet for lunch or a drink outside the home, so we wouldn't upset her. We did that often."

"Was Daria aware?"

"No. She'd have been upset. I willingly took care of Alina and anything Daria asked. I loved her. I'd do anything for her except discard a man who'd been more than a friend to me, a brother to my dear deceased wife."

So far my findings weren't repudiated by any of Rurik's answers. Except his loyalty to a killer, a madman who lived to achieve his own agenda.

"What about Edik Baranov? How is he tossed into this mess?"

"Other than my cousin and what I've already told you?" He hesitated. "We . . . we talk frequently. I knew about his plans to defect Russia before the warrant for his arrest."

"Did you help him in any way?"

Rurik scrubbed his hand over his face. "Yes."

I lowered my voice. "How?"

He leaned back in his chair. "Upon his direction, I arranged for him to leave Russia under another name. Once here, we'd request Witness Protection to protect our families. I never anticipated Jurg would suspect me, demand I assist the ROC in the assassination with information, then kill my wife and kidnap Alina to ensure my cooperation."

Compassion pulsed into my tone. "Rurik, the information I'm about to tell you won't be easy to accept. Intel shows Jurg had an ongoing affair with Daria since the move to Houston and possibly while in Russia."

Rurik blanched, and his jaw dropped like a dead man giving in to death's call.

SIXTY-FOUR

THERESE

Late afternoon, a knock at the adjoining door interrupted the two of us coloring flowers in a coloring book. Alina listened to Jurg's voice and unbolted the door.

"It's party time." Jurg pushed a cart into the room, loaded with food under metal canopies, a birthday cake, an iced container that I assumed contained ice cream, and a dozen red roses. Even balloons decorated the cart.

"This is wonderful. Thank you." I wanted to gag on the words.

"Birthdays are special," he said. "Even in times of grave danger for my dear Alina, kindness must not pass our attention." He smiled at the little girl. "I will call you Larisa until we are home, then we can call each other our correct names."

Would his expression of kindness keep me alive? Doubtful.

"Can Therese come with us to Russia?" The innocence in her eyes reflected naivety.

"We'll see." He cupped her chin. "Thank you for thinking of our guest."

"I made Therese something for her birthday." Alina gathered up her handmade card from the desktop and handed it to him.

Jurg admired her colorful sketch of a mountain with lots of trees and flowers. She signed it, *Love, Larisa.*

How twisted were these people that their children easily accepted deceit?

SIXTY-FIVE

BLANE

Rurik needed over twenty minutes to recover from the blow of Daria and Falin's affair. His clenched fists and red face told me he'd been emotionally double punched.

"Daria's dislike for Jurg was a cover-up." Rurik ceased his pacing. "Why didn't I see the obvious? My wife and my best friend betrayed me." He said a phrase in Russian. I had no idea the meaning, but I made a good guess.

"Think back over a conversation with either Daria or Jurg. Anything could lead to Alina."

Rurik stiffened. "I'm so angry I can't think. All the times she ranted about him like he was a parasite. Jurg never said one thing derogatory about Daria . . . encouraged me to have patience, and he'd win her over. The few times before her ultimatum, he visited our home and complimented her cooking, how she dressed, the furnishings, everything in a respectful manner."

The range of passion, fury to grief, continued to wash over Rurik. I didn't blame him, but other urgent matters took precedence. "Take a deep breath. We will unravel Daria and Jurg's relationship later. Focus on Jurg and where he might have taken Alina and Therese. How was he with your daughter? How did he treat her?"

Rurik sunk onto a chair and placed his head in his hands. "Friendly. Gentle. He asked about school and appeared genuine in how she spent her days." He glanced up at me. "If he killed Daria, then he'll kill Alina."

"I understand. That's why I need you to think about your conversations with him. Where did he frequent in the ship channel area or any favorite spots?"

"Only the DimLight where you met with him. He conducted business there."

"Do you have connections with the owner or employees? Someone who might nail where he's at?"

Rurik shook his head. "He has informants working at the bar. Too dangerous."

"Why am I now finding out about his informants?" Was the FBI's informant aware of this or assumed someone watched her back?

"You are the one who requested a meeting." Rurik headed toward shutdown mode. "Jurg is capable of the worst of crimes."

I held up my hand. "You're right. My apologies."

He stared at the many books in his floor-to-ceiling bookcase, looking but not seeing while intensity flowed from his eyes. "Daria has a close friend. They spent a lot of time together. On the day of Alina's abduction, I called this woman. She said Daria hadn't talked to her in a couple of days. While I doubt Daria confided in anyone about her affair, she might have mentioned something."

I typed into my phone. Later I'd review the conversation. Why hadn't he told me or those investigating Daria's disappearance about this friend? The man poured acid on my ulcer. When the dust settled, Rurik and I would have a long talk. "Name and phone number? Address?"

"Zoya Basin." Rurik continued with her number and address. "They were friends back home. Did everything together—enjoyed weekend trips—" He stopped himself. "Those weekends might have been with Jurg. Daria always said how time with Zoya refreshed her, made her think of home in Russia."

I entered in Zoya's number, and she answered on the first ring.

I pressed speaker and introduced myself. "We're investigating Daria Ivanov's disappearance. We understand the two of you were good friends in Russia and here."

"Yes. She loved life. Everyone loved her. I have no idea who would want her dead."

Someone did. Violently. "Had she spoken to you about her marriage and Alina?"

"She and Rurik were very happy. She adored Alina and often wished the little girl would call her Mommy. But Rurik forbade it."

Rurik listened, not flinching or moving. Truth was a costly commodity. "What can you tell me about her affair with Jurg Falin?"

"Mr. Gardner, Daria ended the relationship before she and Rurik were married. Sir, I'll say this once, and I'll deny it later." She sighed. "Both men are capable of murder. It's second nature to them."

I thanked her and squeezed the phone in my hands. I hated the process of sorting out lies.

"She's a liar," Rurik said. "Daria kept her distance from Alina, just as I told you."

"You've lied to me in the past, and you're still withholding truth. Why? Isn't your daughter's life worth more than empty words?"

Rurik cocked his arm, fist clenched. I bolted from the chair and stopped his punch.

I gripped his fist. "Try to hit me again and I'm outta here. You'll be alone to deal with Daria's and Alina's murder charges. Is that your choice?"

"Jurg has vowed I will never see Alina again."

"Unless you comply with his demands. What are they, Rurik? Time is running out. The police will arrest you tomorrow morning, then how will you secure her release?"

SIXTY-SIX

THERESE

I woke to angry voices coming from Jurg's room. Two distinct male voices slashed through the darkness, at times low and other times the harsh tones increased. Alina stirred, and I lightly pressed my finger to her lips.

I crept from the sofa and pressed my ear to the adjoining door. The words spoken in Russian confused me. Alina joined me and wrapped her arm around my waist. She shook. Would she relay their words?

I listened to calculate the depth of anger, praying Jurg and the other man settled their heated differences. Alina released me and stepped backward while her attention stayed fixed on the door. She covered her mouth and yanked me back.

"On the floor. On the other side of the bed," she whispered.

I grabbed her hand, and we huddled together on the carpet farthest from the adjoining room.

"A man is very mad at my uncle," Alina whispered.

"What about?" I said in the same hushed tone.

"The other man ordered my uncle to kill me, you, and the Texas Ranger. My uncle told him he gave the orders."

A crack pierced the air, not loud, telling me the shooter had used a silencer. A door slammed.

Who stood alive on the other side?

Alina and I huddled together, her body quivering. We were not strangers to danger, and the ordeal in Dog Canyon had cemented us.

"Are you okay?" I whispered. "We must continue whispering in case someone with your uncle finds out about us."

"What if he's the one who's hurt? The door's locked."

"We'll wait a few minutes. I'm sure he's fine." But I had no guarantee, and if Jurg had been wounded or killed, the person responsible would waste no time coming back to eliminate us—if he knew where we hid. "Who was with your uncle?"

"I don't know. They said bad things to each other."

"I'm sorry. No one should ever experience the tragedies you've seen."

"My uncle—"

A knock at the inner door seized my attention.

"Alina, Therese. I must talk to you." Jurg's labored breathing alarmed me.

I rushed to unlock the door, and he pushed it open, falling into my arms. His weight knocked me onto my back with his body atop me.

"I'm shot," he said in a raspy voice. "My side."

"Alina, I need light," I said.

She scrambled to flip on the overhead switch. How could I move him off me without hurting him? But I must.

"Jurg, I'm going to roll you off me, but I need your help. Where are you shot?"

"Right . . . side."

"Then we'll move left."

He attempted to lift himself, and I hid the shock of his massive blood loss. *Don't panic.*

Alina knelt next to him, and her frightened gaze showed the seriousness of his injuries. She caressed his cheek, and his eyes met hers. For one this young, her courage during crisis spoke fathoms of the strong woman she'd one day become. Some might say Jurg didn't deserve a child's devotion, but Alina witnessed the evil behind his pain-filled eyes and demonstrated caring. I should too. Within the soul's portal of Jurg's eyes, love lingered for the little girl.

Wordlessly, Alina and I managed to roll him onto the carpet, while he endured the excruciating pain. When he lay on his back, Alina lifted his hand into hers.

Blood pooled around an open gap on his right side.

I hurried into the bathroom for a towel, then I applied pressure on the open wound. "See if you can find his phone," I said to Alina. "He needs an ambulance."

"No." Jurg moaned. "No hospitals."

"You will bleed out without emergency attention."

"I'm a dead man at the hospital."

No one should die like this. No matter what he'd done. "I'm not trained to remove a bullet. Is there someone you trust who would come here?"

"Yes." He closed his eyes. "In the nightstand nearest my window are three cell phones. Bring me the one in the middle."

Alina rushed into his room to retrieve the phone.

I stared into Jurg's face, holding the blood-soaked towel firmly. He drifted near unconsciousness, and I feared he'd lost too much blood to survive. "Stay with me, please."

He pressed his lips together while his eyes sealed shut. "I'm trying."

Alina handed me the phone. "What is the person's number?"

"Favorites . . ." His voice trailed off.

Under *Favorites*? "Jurg, stay with me. Who is he or she?"

"Vrach."

I scrolled but how he'd pronounced the name contrasted with the spelling, confusing me. Alina left his side to peer at the screen. She pointed to a name, and I pressed in the number.

"I'm calling from a number at which a man has been shot and needs emergency treatment."

"Where's the wound?" a male said in perfect English.

"On the right side."

"Bullet intact?"

"I guess. It didn't exit."

"I'll be there in fifteen minutes."

"Hurry. He's barely conscious. I'm trying to stop the blood flow."

The call dropped. Did the man have our location? "Fifteen minutes."

"Will he die?" Alina's voice rose above a whisper.

"I have no idea, but we can pray."

"Go ahead. Is God a superhero? Will he save my uncle and rescue us?"

"He can do anything."

"Then why are all these bad things happening?"

What could I say? All my life I'd prayed for healing—Kate, my parents, Blane, and other friends and loved ones stricken with illnesses and injuries. My prayers included enemies but never a man who'd planned to kill me and anyone else who got in his way. But God instructed believers to pray for all people, friends *and* enemies. As much as I wanted to grab Alina and leave him to die, my faith stopped me cold.

I grasped Alina's free hand, her other one grasping Jurg's. I held the towel in place in an attempt to plug the hole and clot the blood.

If he lived, he'd kill me . . .

"Heavenly Father, Alina and I are asking You to save Jurg's life. Touch him with Your healing power and restore his body. Stop the flow of blood and give him strength to fight the damage done to his side. Give the doctor wisdom and skill in treating him. In Jesus' name, Amen."

Alina sighed. "My uncle squeezed my fingers when you prayed."

I kept our hands entwined. "We gave him a reason to hold on to life. God knows our hearts, and He hears us."

Her eyes brightened. "He'll live?"

"God hears and responds, but His answer is not always what we want. That would make Him a wish-maker."

Alina's shoulders fell. "Like in a fairy tale?"

"Exactly. He's our Father and determines what's best even in those times we don't understand or agree."

She lingered over Jurg. "Like Daddy telling me not to eat ice cream before dinner. My body needs the good things first."

"Exactly."

She tilted her head. "I don't want my uncle to die like Daddy. Then I'll be all alone."

How would Alina feel about Jurg when she learned the truth?

SIXTY-SEVEN

Thirteen minutes after contacting the man for help, a call came in on Jurg's phone. With shaking fingers, I answered.

"I'm using the back steps to the fourth floor. I'll knock three times. Is he alive?"

"Yes. Barely—"

The call ended, and I leveled my gaze to Alina. "Please hold this towel in place with the palm of your hand while I unlock the door."

Silently she moved beside me and did as I instructed. "Thank you, sweet girl. You are an angel."

I made it to the door just as the knocks alerted me. My nerves hovered in panic mode, and I questioned my sanity in opening the door.

"Yes, who is there?" I said.

"A doctor looking for a friend in need."

I opened the door, and a man in his mid- to late thirties, wearing jeans, an Astros hat pulled over his eyes, and an Astros T-shirt pushed past me. He carried a backpack slung over his shoulder as though he'd checked into the hotel.

I gestured to where Jurg lay on the floor. Alina slid to her uncle's head and kept her vigil. Should I pull her away from all the blood and gore? Hadn't the child seen enough? She certainly had more grit than her father.

The doctor, at least I hope he'd taken the oath, knelt and opened his backpack. He lifted out a hard-cased kit about twenty-four by eighteen inches and a depth of about eight inches. With a deftness that I'd never witnessed by a paramedic, he squirted sanitizer on his hands, slipped on surgical gloves, checked vitals that displayed on a screen, and inserted an IV.

"Hold this up." He adjusted my arm height. "This will also put him to sleep. Alina, I need clean towels." He grabbed a chair from the desk and adjusted the IV.

Where had he learned her name? She disappeared to do his bidding.

"What is your name?" I said.

"It's better you don't know. I am a doctor and that's the important issue."

Alina brought a stack from our bathroom, then another from Jurg's—all sizes. The doctor picked through his case and laid instruments, bandages, gauze, and medicines on one of the towels in an orderly manner.

Watching him clean the wound amid blood once more convinced me I'd never work in the medical field. Alina observed with interest. She kept her distance from the doctor's work and wrapped her hand around Jurg's. The doctor inserted what looked like elongated tweezers into the wound. Jurg neither moved nor uttered a cry, which confirmed the anesthesia in his IV.

"Found it." He pulled out a bloody bullet and held it up to the light. "He will want this." He studied Alina. "Who shot your uncle?"

She shook her head. "We heard two men arguing. One left, then my uncle knocked on our room door for help."

"Good. Thanks."

"Do you make house calls on a regular basis?" I said.

"Whoever needs me and can pay the bill."

Alina and I watched him disinfect and stitch the wound. Normally I'd cringe, but I didn't want a child to outdo me. Strange thoughts darted in and out of a person in times of crisis. Why hadn't I found the courage to yank Alina out of there and leave the no-named doctor to Jurg?

When Jurg's life was no longer in danger, I'd get Alina to safety.

Such a rational decision . . . I wanted Jurg to live when he planned to kill me.

The doctor tore off his bloody gloves and again checked Jurg's vitals. He tugged his phone from his jeans pocket and pressed in a number. "I need a cleanup." He gave the hotel name, address, and room number. "Yes, I'm here for a while. Trying to stabilize him." He paused, his eyes on the screen with the vitals. "At least through tomorrow."

The doctor returned his phone and eyed Alina and me. "Both of you gather up any clean towels, clean clothes, and move into the bathroom. Take a shower and put your bloody clothes in a heap outside the door. I'll dispose of them. Wash the blood out of your hair and under your fingernails. Run the shower until there is no trace of blood. Do not open the door until I give permission."

"How long will the cleanup team take?" I said.

"Does it matter? You won't see anyone." His icy tone gave me chills.

"Just curious."

"Curiosity killed the cat."

"Will my uncle live?" Alina said.

"We will see." He infused a little more optimism in his voice when he spoke to Alina. "Now we wait. Do as I ask. It's all to keep you two alive."

I no more trusted his interest in our welfare than a wolf protecting its prey.

SIXTY-EIGHT

BLANE

I'd spent most of the night with Rurik talking, posing questions, and attempting to unlock the secrets he gripped with an iron fist. Each pause in his speech, hand movement, breathing, body language, and unconscious habit showed his concern for his daughter. The lies lingered below the surface, but they were there. As much as I debated his actions and motives, I wanted to build trust to find Alina and Therese.

"We've gone over the same things repeatedly, and your answers haven't changed," I said. "Why are you hiding the truth?"

"I've told you everything."

"Who heads up the ROC here in Houston?"

He inhaled and slowly exhaled.

"Jurg Falin? You claimed in the event of your death that all your assets were directed to the ROC under his management."

"No." He leaned back in his chair as though I'd taken the pressure off. "I've not been given a name, but I don't believe it's him."

"They killed Daria. Attacked Therese and me. And your daughter? What names are at the top of your list?"

"Possibly two. Only a handful of government officials are privy to the identity, and I'm not one of them."

Wariness crept up my spine and landed squarely in my words. "But you have a suspect."

"I might."

"Have you been in contact with that person?"

"Depends if I'm correct in my assessment."

I glanced at the time—4:10 a.m. "Excuse me while I step out to make a call." With the door behind me, I pressed in Sergio's number.

"Are you still at Rurik's?" His groggy voice said I'd wakened him.

"Yes. Gotten nowhere. Or maybe confirmation of a deeper web of Russian activity in Houston. Baranov is the key in all of this. If Rurik is telling the truth, he played a role in helping Baranov escape Russia. Once here, the two men would request Witness Protection for them and their families."

"Are you thinking the Feds have more info than what they've stated?"

"Why not? They want Baranov's intel. The Russians want him dead at any cost for stealing secured info from under their noses. Rurik is holding out, but what is the missing piece? His wife's dead and his daughter's been kidnapped. Then we have the laser-chip deal. Think about it, Serge. Baranov, Falin, and Ivanov—the three woven in crime. How does it all fit?"

"The link's probably so obvious we're fools for missing it."

I shared the conversation with Rurik from all angles. "Has the torched body been identified as Daria Ivanov?"

"Let me go to my study. A text flew into my phone around 2:30, but I've been battling a virus and ignored it."

We chatted while he made his way downstairs to his man cave—what his wife called his study, an eclectic mix of taxidermy trophies, books, fishing treasures, and a wall of family and Ranger portraits—including a brother in a mariachi band.

"I should have checked this instead of going back to sleep. Give me a moment to read this report from the medical examiner's office. I could kick myself for not checking my phone."

I yawned and braced my shoulders against a wall in Rurik's hallway.

"Rusty, the body of the woman isn't Daria Ivanov. The body has been identified as a woman from Dallas who was reported missing two days prior to Daria's disappearance."

The news tightened a bolt on who was behind the crimes. "What are we missing with Daria? Why stage her death except to incriminate Rurik . . . unless Rurik's behind the whole ordeal?"

"As in Houston's ROC leader?" His chair squeaked.

My instincts kicked in. "I bet Baranov is scheduled to arrive today, not Wednesday."

"I'm thinking the same thing."

"I'm calling the FBI and getting a heads-up on what's happening at the ship channel today. Looks to me like Ivanov and Falin are in this waist-deep."

"I'm leaving for your office in ten minutes. I want to make sure the agents keep Rurik in their sights."

In the kitchen, one of the agents scrolled through his phone, holding a mug of coffee. I asked him to wake his partner. Rurik could not leave the house or be out of their sight.

"Threats?" the agent said.

"Something along those lines. Your boss can fill you in."

"Sure." He set his mug on the counter and nodded at his partner. "I'll keep Rurik company until your shift kicks in."

I thanked them and headed back down the hall to tell Rurik I was leaving and to stay put. I knocked and got no response. Chill bumps spiked on my arms. I opened the door to his office.

Empty.

"Rurik? Where are you?"

Silence.

The agent checked the nearest bathroom. "He's not here."

"I'll check his bedroom," the other agent called from the kitchen.

An engine roared to life, sending me and the agents racing to the garage.

Rurik sped down the street in his SUV.

—

Sergio and the FBI issued a BOLO for Rurik's vehicle. The agents assigned to Rurik's protection were given permission to leave. We'd been played. Wringing his neck sounded as satisfying as a cold Dr Pepper on a hot August day.

I drove to the Ranger office, my course on autopilot while the neurons fired in my brain. Three scenarios emerged, all plausible and none had sufficient evidence.

One theory said Rurik and Daria faked her death and Alina's kidnapping to mask the ROC's assassination of Edik Baranov. Had everything Rurik claimed about his innocence and victim status been lies to lead law enforcement and media away from the intended crime?

A second theory said Rurik and Daria had been used as pawns in a vicious game of blackmail . . . to force Rurik and Daria to risk their lives and Alina's to ensure a smooth assassination. Which meant the Ivanovs were in danger and next in line for a death sentence once Baranov and his family were dead.

Another theory leaped into the center of the fire. What if Daria Ivanov and Jurg Falin masterminded the entire scheme?

I refused to discard any ideas until I had more facts. Confirmed reports neither proved nor disproved my suspicions.

The ROC had a vicious agenda.

The potential sale of laser chips from Tom Chandler to the ROC coincided with the kidnapping.

Edik and Rurik were cousins.

Daria and Jurg were involved in an affair while in Russia and in the US.

A woman's body had been found in Daria's car. Where was Daria?

A flight had been booked from Houston to Moscow on Tuesday for Isaak and Larisa Mishin. The scheduled flight left the day before the assassination. Jurg Falin had requested a private escort out of the country this evening. Unless the timeline was off on Baranov's arrival.

How would I ever sort out the truth? But God had the answer, and He'd help me find Alina and Therese.

Another text rolled in. HPD found Rurik's SUV abandoned on the west side of town. FBI just confirmed Edik Baranov and family arriving early afternoon. Has Falin contacted you where he plans to make the exchange and his destination? I have a plane on standby. Once you have confirmation, I'll have backup in place.

I replied, Haven't heard from Falin.

I'll meet you at the ship channel. Tell no one.

SIXTY-NINE

THERESE

Alina and I quickly showered, dressed, and tossed out our clothes at Dr. Zhivago's request, the name I'd given him for lack of another. I'd whispered to Alina if she recognized him, but she shook her head.

Male voices outside the bathroom door told me the cleanup crew had arrived. I didn't understand their conversation, but when Alina squeezed my hand, I mouthed my concern about what they were saying.

"My uncle is not doing well," she whispered. "The doctor can't stabilize him." She covered her mouth to avoid a gasp. "Running out of time."

I hugged her at the thought of Jurg's life draining from him. The child beside me was innocent of any crime, and I'd give my life for her . . . Just like my Kate. Memories of Kate's final hours trickled through me. Would Alina's fate be the same?

Your sister and parents' deaths were not your fault.

I blinked. The voice hadn't come from me.

Forgive yourself, Therese. I love you. The evil around you is not your fault.

A tear slipped down my cheek. *God, I'm sorry. I needed someone to blame. Please take this burden from me. The weight is too heavy.*

Alina studied me in childlike wonder. Should I tell her my spirit had been transformed?

"Our God has this," I whispered. "He loves us, and we will face what happens with courage."

She leaned into me and softly sobbed. "I'm afraid."

"That's fine. I am too."

Within an hour, the Russian crew left, leaving me with a morbid vision of what they used to clean up blood. Seconds ticked by.

"You can unlock the bathroom door and come out," the doctor said.

Alina and I left the bathroom. She gripped my hand harder, and her breathing came in short gasps. What should we expect now? Alina rushed to Jurg's side. Not a trace of blood anywhere but his clothes and skin. Not even an antiseptic smell remained.

I captured the doctor's gaze to discover our fate. Jurg was supposed to fly to Russia, but I doubted if he survived.

"I have a choice," the doctor said. "The ones who cleaned didn't mention you or Alina. How they avoided checking the bathroom is beyond me. No one gets in their way or they're eliminated."

Thank You, Lord.

"If you stay, you're both dead. Someone will return to check the room." He bent to Jurg and read his vitals. "He needs a hospital, but it's not permitted."

Silence dragged like a death sentence.

"I took an oath to save lives, not destroy them." He sighed. "Aren't you trained in martial arts?"

"Yes. Why?"

"Thinking through the best way to keep the four of us alive."

I joined him at Jurg's side. "What if I overpower you, and then Alina and I escape. Once we're safe, I'll call 911 for Jurg. That gives you time to get away."

"I have a better idea. You punch me in the eye and break a lamp. You and Alina leave—take the stairs. Five minutes after you leave, I'll call 911. I'll tell them Jurg phoned me and said he'd been shot and requested medical help. I got here. The door was open, and he lay unconscious. I treated him while they were en route. I'll leave the room when I hear the sirens."

"Perfect." I turned to my sweet Alina. "This is a lie, but it keeps all of us alive."

"And we all can get away from the bad men," she said.

"Right." Loved this little girl.

"I'm ready," the doctor said. "Be careful once you get outside. Something's going down."

I asked Alina to wait in the other room while I sent the desk lamp crashing to the floor and gave the doctor a black eye.

"You pack a powerful punch. I wouldn't want to be on the receiving end if you were angry." He offered a half smile.

"Thanks, I think. I pray this works."

In the hallway, I placed Alina's hand firmly in mine and inhaled freedom. We rushed to the exit and down four flights of stairs. We stopped at the registration desk. Two armed Customs and Border Patrol agents stood at the glass wall to my left. What kind of crime had happened? But first things first.

"I have an emergency," I said to the receptionist. "Please, can I use your phone?"

The young woman blanched. "We are locked down due to a dangerous situation."

"Please." Desperation laced my voice.

"I'll get an outside line." Her lips quivered. "The doors are all locked, and you can't leave. Neither can anyone get inside without security approving them."

I didn't have Blane's new number memorized, but I could call Major Montoya. I asked the receptionist to help me contact the Texas Rangers, and she agreed.

"Major Montoya, please," I said.

"He's out of the office. Can I help you?" a man said.

"Is Blane Gardner available, or can you give me his number? This is an emergency."

"Hold on while I get Major Montoya on the line."

"Tell him it's Therese Palmer."

Time moved slowly when lives were at stake.

"Therese?" His deep voice gave me a measure of comfort.

"Yes, I have Alina and we're safe."

"Where are you?"

"The Waterway Resort."

"What? I'm here with Blane. Stay inside where it's safe. Guards are posted at all exits. I'll send Blane to explain. The property is surrounded by FBI, Border Patrol, and Coast Guard. That hotel is nothing but window walls. Keep away from them." And he was gone.

I thanked the receptionist, but her attention veered to the vehicles surrounding the hotel.

I had questions, many of them. Major Montoya and Blane were here with the FBI, CBP, and Coast Guard? This had to do with Edik Baranov, but I didn't understand the day, location, and the confusion made me crazy. How long would it take for Blane to give me answers? This all had to be good news, right? Dare I believe the nightmare had ended?

I scanned the area. Earlier we had hidden in a bathroom, but now where? I recognized one of the FBI agents at the front door. He'd been helpful the night the ROC waited at my house to kill me, which had never made sense since they'd triggered bombs at my front and back doors. I told him about Blane's arrival and Major Montoya's instructions. He said hotel staff were in the kitchen, and we would be safe there. The agent escorted us to the area and instructed the staff not to leave the room. He closed the door behind him.

"What's going on?" Alina said. "Are bad people here?"

I drew her close to me. "No, honey. I think the cavalry has arrived."

SEVENTY

BLANE

Binoculars bounced around my neck while I ran to the Waterway Resort. I craved to see Therese and confirm she and Alina were unharmed. How had the scenario unfolding in the ship channel hit unexpectedly in a world of instant communication and technology? Maybe this wasn't a surprise, and the FBI covered the facts to keep Baranov and his family alive.

Sergio claimed a call to Quantico revealed a last-minute change in plans about the Baranovs' arrival. That meant following highly regulated protocol where at least two federal agencies assisted in an operation, and in this case three—the FBI, CBP, and Coast Guard. No Texas Rangers, but Sergio and I received permission to be on-site, spectators of sorts. Didn't suit me but at least we were here, and we were armed.

Intel had leaked to the ROC, but how wasn't clear. The FBI would tackle that later. No one on board the cargo ship would have knowledge about the Baranovs' escape to freedom, unless a crew member had identified them and told the Russians. Getting the Baranov family to safety where they could request asylum topped the priority list.

Two tugboats—both with armed men from the FBI, CBP, and

Coast Guard were to transport the Baranovs inland. The clock clicked down the remaining fifty minutes.

The ROC were here but where? No one on the guest list of the Waterway Resort caught my attention—but no reputable professional assassin used a real name. Since Therese and Alina had been held inside the hotel, it made sense the killers also occupied rooms. But I'd not check off an attack from the air or water.

At the hotel's front entrance, FBI Agent Blackburn talked with another agent. He and I had met the night Therese and I faced the ROC at her home. I shook his hand and his partner's. "We meet again," I said to Blackburn.

He introduced me to his partner. "The problems will end today."

I didn't share the same positive attitude. I explained to Blackburn why I was here, and he received permission to allow me inside the hotel. An ambulance arrived with its sirens blaring around us and flashing lights shoving traffic out of its way.

"Has someone already been injured?"

Blackburn shook his head and jogged to the ambulance. He spoke to the driver and made a call. One more time, I played the role of an outsider. The paramedics opened the ambulance's back door and rushed a gurney to the hotel door. Blackburn let them in.

"A man has been shot in a room on the fourth floor," he said to the other agent and me and hurried with them.

I waited until Blackburn and the paramedics reappeared with a man on the gurney. His eyes were sealed shut, and an oxygen tube had been inserted in his mouth. One paramedic held an IV. Blood was everywhere—Jurg Falin.

"Blackburn, he's one of the ROC involved," I said. "Who else was with him?"

"No one. I recognized him too. Not a speck of blood anywhere in the room."

"He's unconscious?"

"Yep. Vitals are not good." He gave me a chin dip, which told me he'd been updated about Falin and the security required to keep him alive.

The ambulance left and Blackburn escorted me to a kitchen door where he greeted the people inside.

"Ladies and gentlemen, the lockdown will continue about an hour or more. I understand this is an inconvenience, but your safety is our primary concern."

Therese rushed to me, her eyes wide and chin quivering. Alina trailed her. A lump formed in my throat. I was up to my eyeballs in love with this woman. She threw her arms around my neck and squeezed gently.

"I'm sorry for taking off," she said. "I tried to save the world by myself."

"We're good. You're safe and you have Alina." I released Therese and gazed at the blonde-haired angel. "You're one brave little girl."

Therese held out her hand, and the little girl grasped it. "Alina, I'd like you to meet Texas Ranger Blane Gardner. He is my hero."

"From the cavalry?" she said.

"Without a doubt." Therese gave me a light kiss. "What can you tell me?"

"Not much in the time left. Sergio requested I stay here. Rangers aren't involved in this mission." I shook my head. "What I can tell you is the expected arrival was moved up to today and this location. Please keep our conversation to yourself."

She mouthed, *Rurik*.

I whispered, "He left his house and can't be found."

"Escaped?" she whispered.

"Yes."

"Alina believes he's dead."

I frowned. "He might be or he's on the property."

A text from Sergio stopped me from saying more. **Cargo ship in sight. Confirmed passengers. Stay where you are. Situation not neutralized.**

"Stay here. I'll be back in a few." I closed the kitchen door behind me and made my way to the glass wall overlooking the cargo ship.

It moved unusually close to the hotel. I studied the area through my binoculars. Two tugboats bounced over waves toward it.

The possible use of the laser weaponry enabled by recovery of the activation chips from Dog Canyon pressed into my concern for innocent people becoming victims. Its use toward volatile cargo had the capacity to destroy the ship, everyone on it, and the two tugboats racing its way. Cameras were everywhere. How did the ROC think they'd get away with an attack?

I desperately wanted to be where the action brewed in the channel.

I refocused my binoculars and caught a flicker of movement on the cargo ship. A man, a small boy about four, and a slender woman gazed out over the railing. I recognized Edik Baranov from his pics. He lifted the boy into his arms, nodded at the woman, and they jumped.

I held my breath until Baranov surfaced with his son in his arms. His wife bobbed up, and together they swam toward an emerging tugboat filled with armed US Feds. Thank goodness they hadn't jumped into the brackish channel behind them. It had been deemed a sacrifice zone from the years of dumping petrochemical waste without heeding environmental regulations.

I lowered my binoculars and spotted an unmarked boat speeding toward the scene. Zooming back in, I counted at least eight armed men, and none were a part of the federal agencies involved with the transfer of the Baranov family.

Rifle fire broke out over the blue waters.

SEVENTY-ONE

The horror unfolded through my binoculars. Bullets spit at the water surrounding the Baranovs' swim to safety. One of the tugboats pressed in between the swimmers and the shooters while the second tugboat jumped the waves to retrieve them. The cargo ship slowly moved away from the firefight.

A federal agent defending the territory fell overboard from a rifle blast to his shoulder.

A shooter dropped to the deck of his boat.

A fourth boat skipped over water to the scene. US or ROC?

Hell had broken loose in front of me, and regret filled me for not being there. I'd been reduced to a storm chaser. I sucked in a breath and prayed for every man and woman risking their lives.

The fourth boat, filled with US Federal Law Enforcement, opened fire on the shooters, dropping two into the waves.

Feds pulled Edik Baranov and his family into a tugboat as an Airbus helicopter flew over the hotel and straight toward the firestorm. Bitterness rose up my throat at the memory of what had happened in Dog Canyon. I stared up at the attack helo, more like a flying tank with killer capacity.

The tugboat with the Baranovs sped toward the hotel's marina while the second tugboat and the shooters barraged the air with bullets.

The Airbus moved over the tugboat containing the Baranovs. US enforcers opened fire with AR-15s and blasted the aircraft. Nothing was foolproof, and enough bullets penetrating the metal would bring it down.

The Airbus exploded into a fiery inferno, flinging fire and metal in all directions. The aircraft whirled nose down toward the tugboat. I held my breath. The flaming helo zoomed to destroy the boat. Baranov and his family dived into the water. US personnel followed. Two helped the wounded swim to safety.

The fighting team and the shooters exchanged fire.

Would this ever end?

The firefight played out like watching a brutal action movie. Seconds poured into minutes.

A shooter held up his hands. Then another.

I watched the US take control. Breathing relief came easy. Breathing thanks to God followed. But the inability to assist slammed against my ego. Shooters were cuffed, the wounded treated and loaded into ambulances, and Edik Baranov and his family were again retrieved from the water along with others. In freeing Alina and with the Baranovs safe on US soil, the impossible had happened.

I pressed in Rurik's number, silently urging him to pick up.

"Blane, I'm sorry. I refused to stand by and do nothing while Jurg controlled my daughter's life. I've—"

"Rurik, Alina's safe. So are the Baranovs. The ROC failed in their operation."

He sobbed. "Thank you. Thank you for everything. Therese is unharmed?"

"Yes. Where are you?"

"Driving to talk to Jurg."

"He's been shot and is at a hospital. No idea who shot him or if he'll live."

"Where is Alina?"

"In the same building with me and Therese. I need your word

that you'll drive home and stay there. Providing the FBI gives me permission, I'll bring Alina to you."

"I can drive to the hospital."

"Not a good idea with what's happened."

"All right. I'm driving home. Since this is over, the FBI will reveal more of what is going on with Edik and his family. You'll get many answers to your questions. Tell Alina I love her and tell Therese thank you."

"Sure. It's over, Rurik."

"I'll believe it when Alina is in my arms."

—

I hurried back to the kitchen to find Therese and alert her that the US had retrieved the Baranovs. I'd let her tell Alina that her father lived, and he anxiously awaited his little girl. The moment I opened the door, the attention of seven hotel employees flew my way—and not in a good way. Three grabbed knives, and one picked up a skillet like a ball bat. All women.

A man shouted at one of the women, "He's a good guy."

"The situation is neutralized," I said. "I'm sure the FBI will give you the all-clear soon."

Gasps of relief swirled around the room along with questions of what had caused the problem. I assured them the FBI would provide an explanation.

Therese and Alina flanked me, and I grew seven feet tall. I whispered to Therese that I'd spoken with Rurik, and he assured me of heading home. She knelt and captured Alina's attention at eye level.

"Brave girl, you are safe. No one is out to hurt you. Your uncle is at the hospital, and I have great news. Wonderful news." She tilted her head with sweet curiosity, and Therese continued. "Mr. Blane just talked to your daddy. He's fine. Not hurt at all."

Alina wrapped her arms around Therese's neck and cried. "Daddy is alive? No bad people hurt him?"

"Right," Therese said. "And he's excited to see you."

Alina pulled back and frowned. "But Uncle Jurg said—"

Therese clasped Alina's shoulders. "Your uncle made a mistake. He feared something bad might happen to you."

"Alina, I told your dad I'd bring you home as soon as I learn we can leave here," I said. "Is that okay?"

"Yes, but I don't believe you. I have to see my daddy first. Is Daria there too?"

"No, just your dad." This child had already seen too much of the world's ugly reality to relay more. I'd brief Therese privately.

"Maybe she'll be home later. Can we go now?" Alina's tone lightened . . . Poor little girl, she'd been through one traumatic moment after another.

"Give me a moment to make a call." I yanked my phone from my jeans pocket, but Therese stopped me.

"Blane, before you talk to Major Montoya or anyone else, I must tell you what Alina and I experienced. I know the source of the laser-activation chips. That's a surprise, huh?"

I stared at Therese as though I'd discovered gold. "Incredible news."

She nodded. "The company's name is Hilltop Defense Distributors in Utah. The box Jurg took from the cave had the name stamped on the side."

I kissed her. Nothing else mattered. I pressed in Sergio's number. "Therese gave me a name for the source of the laser chips."

"I'll get men on it," he said. "Tell her thanks. And I owe her big-time. Might make her an honorary Texas Ranger. Give me a few minutes to check with the FBI to make sure they agree in returning Alina."

I explained the short delay to the girls, and with permission from Agent Blackburn, the room emptied into the dining area. We slid into a booth, and Alina curled up next to Therese. Wasn't five minutes until the little girl's eyes grew heavy and closed. Therese stroked her cheek, no doubt forming the right words to explain her ordeal.

"I never had any illusions about Jurg's plans for me, but he planned to take Alina to Russia." She paused and made sure Alina slept. "Vengeance for his sister led his motives with the kidnapping. Jurg had two objectives—take Alina and ensure the ROC succeed in their mission."

"Any mention about Daria?"

"No. Except he hated her."

I shared in quiet tones that the body burned in Daria's car was a woman from Dallas. "Did Jurg mention a boss, someone in control of the ROC?"

"I assumed he held that role. Then he was shot, but I have no idea who pulled the trigger."

She filled me in about the doctor and cleanup crew.

"A spiderweb of connections," I said. "To think, Houston is a large group, but it's one of many all over the world."

She stroked my hand. "Teaching wilderness-survival skills and tracking down those who are missing is a lot easier than what you and others do."

"I'm sure you've wondered if my faith is real," I whispered. "It is, and I will show you a changed man. Thank you for not giving up on me."

A text flew into my phone from Sergio. **You and Therese have permission to take Alina home. FBI is good. Keep Rurik there. I'll explain later. Let Therese drive and you keep watch, just as a precaution. I need to make a call, then I'll bring Rangers by the house to talk to Rurik. FBI will be en route then too.**

I replied, **Is Rurik under arrest?**

Not unless the FBI discovers crimes to charge him.

SEVENTY-TWO

THERESE

Major Montoya had requested I drive Alina home. Uneasiness crawled in and refused to leave. Maybe he'd hit the overreaction button with the awkwardness of Blane behind the wheel nursing a concussion and a broken arm. That must be it.

According to the major, Jurg was in surgery. It would be hours before the surgeon offered a report.

Alina had no words from the back seat. She distrusted us and believed her dad might truly be dead. Her emotionless face in the rearview mirror sickened me. Would she ever get past this?

"Are you frightened?" I said to her.

"A little. I want to believe Daddy is fine, but I don't want to be tricked."

No amount of persuading would convince Alina until she wrapped her arms around Rurik's neck. I'd feel the same.

Blane texted Rurik and gave him an approximate time of our arrival. This promised to be a tearful reunion. I touched Blane's hand. We had much to talk about, much to be thankful for, and I needed to tell him something special. Why wait? Recovering Alina and the Baranov family facing freedom were reasons to celebrate life.

"Blane, I need to say something."

He whirled my way. "I'm listening."

In less than a second, my bravado slipped away.

"What is it," he said. "Are you sick?"

"I'm fine. This sounds weird, like I'm in high school again. I . . . love you. Not sure how or why." I shrugged. "But is my confession okay?"

He laughed. "For those words, I'd break my other arm and crack my head again."

"Sometimes love is an uphill climb."

"Or a huge fall."

Alina giggled in the back seat. "She might marry you."

"I'm going to do my best." He faced me. "You've given me hope. We'll take it slow, like you said in the mountains."

His words held more meaning than Alina comprehended. Blane's past, my past, both scarred with tragedy, but we were survivors. We loved each other, and our ordeal together seemed stamped with God's blessings. Oh, how I loved happy endings.

We turned onto Alina's street and she gasped. "I want to believe my daddy is okay, but I'm afraid."

I parked in the driveway and unbuckled my seat belt. "He's here and he's excited to see you."

"Give this old man a moment to grab my bearings. I can manage. Just slow." He placed his gun in his jeans back waistband. The weapon reminded me of Major Montoya's warning for me to drive and Blane to keep watch.

Alina stood on the driveway bouncing on her toes. Why hadn't Rurik rushed out to meet her? Surely he'd been watching for us to pull into the driveway. Alina skipped, and I walked with Blane to the front door.

She turned the door handle. Locked. Alina sighed and rang the doorbell. No response. She knocked and rang the doorbell again.

"I'll text him." Blane slipped his phone from his jeans pocket.

I captured his gaze and saw the same concern. "Alina and I will wait in the car."

"Good idea. I'll text Sergio."

"No, Daddy will answer. He must be in his office."

Please, God, let this not be another tragedy.

The door slowly opened. Rurik attempted a smile at Alina through a bruised and bleeding face.

"Inside," a female voice said. "Or I open fire on Alina first."

Alina stiffened. "Daria?"

SEVENTY-THREE

BLANE

I suspected Daria played a role in the ROC, and she'd proved it. Not a good way to learn the truth.

"Wasting my time is a death sentence." Daria waved a Glock.

Therese held Alina's hand, and I followed them. Two men I recognized from the DimLight Bar held their weapons on us. One of the men yanked my SIG from my back waistband.

Rurik's lips trembled and he drew Alina into his arms.

"This is a tender reunion. Unfortunately, I'm in no mood." Daria ordered us into the living room where the three of us were told where to sit, except Alina. Daria seized her arm and kept the little girl beside her. The woman with shoulder-length sun-colored hair and stormy blue eyes looked more like a model than a killer.

"What is this about?" I took in the two armed men and their weapons.

"I need your help," Daria said. "Rurik's already refused as his face clearly shows."

"Which is?"

"Jurg asked him to comply with one simple request, and like the pitiful coward they both are, I had to take over." Her face hardened, and her eyes resembled granite. She sneered at Therese. "I figured Jurg would botch up eliminating you." She huffed. "I set the explosives at Therese's house, then to be sure, I had you tailed and run off the road. But you survived. Now, you've used up all your chances."

"You faked your murder and initiated Alina's kidnapping?" I said in my negotiator voice.

She smirked. "Smart man. This coward still failed." She waved her gun in Rurik's face. "Tell the good Texas Ranger what you refused to do."

Rurik swallowed hard. "Kill Edik Baranov and his family. I . . . I didn't believe Jurg would harm Alina."

Daria cursed. "Jurg doesn't give orders. I do."

Daria led the ROC in Houston? The unanswered questions made sense. All of it. Sergio and the FBI needed to hurry. "You ordered the hit on Therese and me?"

"Smart man. Now I can take care of you myself."

Rurik attempted to stand, but one of the men shoved him back down. "Please do not hurt Alina. She's innocent."

"Spare me. She's a nuisance." Daria placed her Glock to Alina's temple. "Where did Jurg hide the laser chips?"

"Why would he tell me? The man despised me."

"So do I. Living with you was like a death sentence. Hated the pretending." She smirked. "I held you in the palm of my hand as soon as I knew your wife was dying. I told Jurg I'd made a mistake in marrying you and convinced him to have an affair. Got him to join the ROC. My game. My benefit."

"You're an animal." Rurik spat out the words.

"It's over. Jurg told my man you knew the chips' location. Here's the deal. Tell me where to pick them up or I blow a hole through Alina's head."

"Rurik, if you have the info, tell her," I said.

"He didn't tell me. Daria, please. Jurg lied. I have no idea where he's hidden them."

"Jurg got greedy and wanted my job." She laughed. "He had no clue I was calling the shots. Being with him was as nauseating as being with you. He thought if he kept the chips, he'd secure Russian accolades. His life is a weak thread." She pulled Alina closer and wrapped an arm around the little girl's neck. "One more time, where are my laser chips?"

Alina bit down on Daria's arm. She jerked back, but Alina held on. The gun fired, narrowly missing one of Daria's men. Using my casted arm, I knocked the gun out of her hand, sending her backward against a rock fireplace. Alina broke from her grip and scurried to Rurik, and he placed her behind the sofa.

Rurik bolted and grabbed the wrist of the man closest to him, bending his hand back until it snapped and forcing the man to drop his gun. Rurik snatched the man's gun and pulled the trigger into the man's right shoulder.

Therese struggled with the second man while I ensured Daria lay still. Rurik ordered him to put down the gun, but he fired into Rurik's chest.

Alina screamed.

Rurik fell onto the sofa and sent a bullet into the man.

I took Daria's Glock and pointed it at the wounded men. "Therese, call Sergio. He's on his way."

Alina hurried to her dad. She kissed his cheek. "Daddy, don't die. I need you. We need each other."

SEVENTY-FOUR

THERESE

In the early hours of the morning, Blane and I sat at Rurik's hospital bedside with Alina asleep in my lap. Rurik had undergone extensive surgery to remove the bullet in his chest and now recovered in ICU. Hospital regulations stated only two people in ICU, then Blane put on his hero cape and secured permission for us to stay together. I fought sleep with less and less willpower. Blane and I had fallen into a comfortable silence, as he jerked and nodded off too.

The truth had surfaced, and as I attempted to rise from a dream state, I put the facts in somewhat of a chronological order.

Daria Ivanov led the Houston ROC. From what she'd said at Rurik's home, she must have targeted Jurg and Rurik while in Russia. She'd used both men to advance her agenda. Rurik had been easy prey while Jurg believed the ROC boss was in Russia. But he double-crossed that person by holding on to the laser chips. Jurg was expected to make a full recovery. Maybe then he'd provide the chips' whereabouts. Seeing Daria arrested and escorted from Rurik's home gave me satisfaction . . . Whether that was right or wrong.

Jurg had a ruthless streak except his mannerisms softened with Alina, proving that even killers had a tender spot deep inside. He faced serious charges, which might persuade him to give up enough intel for a lesser charge. The way I viewed his circumstances, he had a death sentence either way.

Major Montoya slipped into the room. I shouldn't be surprised.

"The FBI told me the whole story after interviewing Edik Baranov. Rurik had been in contact with him since before the defection, like he'd confessed to Blane. Rurik had been helping Edik by meeting with Jurg to find out more about the assassination attempt. The calls Rurik made to Moscow were to Edik, a plan to help him and his family escape. Looks like Rurik had no idea about Daria's involvement or Jurg's vengeance for Alina's mother. At this point, the Baranovs have been whisked away to an FBI safe house. He told the FBI that Daria Ivanov controlled the Houston ROC, and he was prepared to reveal intel from the Russians, including a government military operation to use AI robotics and chemical warfare on its own people. The Baranovs would be granted asylum in Witness Protection."

Rurik had been innocent of many wrongdoings, but he had concealed ROC details to save his daughter and told Jurg about the Rangers heading into Dog Canyon. Blane and Major Montoya doubted he'd be charged with criminal activity upon the testimony of Edik Baranov.

I jumped from one part of the last few weeks to another. Danger. Fear. Awareness. Thankfulness. Love for Blane, a gift I never expected to receive.

I jarred awake to the sound of Alina excitedly calling out to her daddy. I held her firmly, not really understanding if her voice meant good or otherwise. Sunlight filtered in through the window to spotlight Rurik's face and opened eyes.

"Be careful, sweetie," I said. "Your daddy is very sick, and you don't want to hurt him."

"Can I hold his hand?"

Rurik slowly lifted his hand and she feather-touched it. "I've never . . . seen anything more beautiful than my Alina."

She leaned in closer. "I love you, Daddy."

His face contorted in obvious pain.

"I'll get the nurse," Blane said. "She can give you something for the pain."

Rurik swallowed hard and gave a slight nod. "The button."

Blane pressed it. "You had us scared."

Good opener to ease the tension between them.

"Scared all of us," I said.

Alina kissed his hand. "Uncle Jurg said you and Daria were dead, but I believed you wouldn't leave me. Are you feeling better?"

"Better having you with me."

"Does your chest hurt?"

"A little. I'm sorry you saw all that violence."

She tilted her head. "I've seen lots of bad things. Mr. Blane thinks I might need to talk to a special doctor who will help me put the stuff in the right place."

Rurik closed his eyes. "Yes. He's right."

The nurse entered the room and added meds to his IV. "This will make you sleep."

Rurik turned to Blane and me. "Thank you isn't enough. You saved my daughter, my cousin and his family, and you stopped Daria. I want to talk to the FBI, to show I'm loyal to the US."

"Major Montoya told us how you've been helping your cousin," Blane said.

"Good. Very good. Therese, I'm drifting to sleep, but first, can you care for Alina until I'm out of here and figure out what your government intends to do with us?"

An image of us laughing and picking wildflowers seemed like a forgotten dream, just like in days gone by with Kate. "I'd be honored. She and I have become good friends."

SEVENTY-FIVE

ONE YEAR LATER

THERESE

Blane had often talked about returning to the Guadalupe Mountains and Dog Canyon to take photographs. He wanted to capture the light to reflect in his landscape painting.

"Aren't you concerned you might fall again?" I'd said repeatedly.

"Nope. I don't intend to go anywhere except on a trail. Well, maybe a little off-trail but not like we did last October."

Receiving closure for Kate, searching for Alina, facing the ROC, the lies, betrayal, and outcome bothered me still. But I agreed to come, and I'd be watching him every step of the way. His arm had healed nicely, and through PT, he'd received full mobility.

Rurik interviewed with the FBI and gave them critical details. Like the Baranovs, Rurik and Alina were given new identities and placed in Witness Protection. Blane and I had talked to them about God, and they promised to seek Him. I'd never see sweet Alina again, but she lived on in my heart . . . like Kate. And my heart was a safe place.

Jurg Falin recovered. Bitterness kept him closemouthed, and he refused to relay where the chips were stored or his intentions in using them. He faced a lengthy prison term. No doubt he'd assist the ROC behind bars.

Daria had been sentenced to life at a maximum-security federal prison in Beaumont, Texas—United States Penitentiary. So many charges against her that she'd never see daylight. But she'd chosen her priorities.

The FBI filed charges against Hilltop Defense Distributors in Utah. They ceased operations, and those involved faced federal charges including negligence, conspiracy, and aiding and abetting criminal activities, and those initial charges were before other federal agencies like the ATF joined in the prosecution. During the investigation, the FBI uncovered laser-weaponry components and other arms sales with the cartels in Mexico and overseas.

Blane searched for the two teen boy angels—Gabriel and Michael. Never found them, even though the police had their last names and addresses. No such persons or addresses existed. We often laughed about it.

"You're quiet," Blane said as he drove along U.S. Highway 62 from Hobbs, New Mexico, to the Guadalupe Mountains.

"The last time we drove this road, I was at the steering wheel of a Jeep, and it was pitch black."

"I remember, and you were adorable."

I swung to him. "We were both scared and too full of ourselves to admit it."

"We did take on the impossible." He kissed my hand. "Look what we gained. Eternity and more."

I grinned. "That was poetic, Agent Gardner."

"Thank you. I do have my finer moments."

Over the past year, he'd joined my church, a men's Bible study, and applied for training to minister to prison inmates. "You have many fine moments."

"Whoa. Can I hear those words again?"

"No way. Wouldn't want you to get a swelled head. We're spending the day in the mountains for you to take pics?"

He nodded. "I might let you see the paintings when they are done. True originals."

I'd seen his paintings, and they were outstanding. "Honestly, they are gallery worthy."

He lifted his chin. "I hit the jackpot."

"We both did."

"Okay, pretty lady, why is a guitar riding with us?"

"I bought one a couple of months ago." I sensed myself grow warm. "I wrote you a song." I was about to lose what courage I had. What if he didn't like it?

We drove into the park with memories flowing through me, and from Blane's silence, he experienced the same. He drove along a familiar path and parked where we'd parked months ago. We gathered our things, including my guitar, and hiked the path that held beginnings and endings, a bittersweet trail.

Blane snapped pics and adjusted his camera lenses to take near and far shots. One hour into the hike, he stopped and studied the magnificent high desert scenery surrounding us. Turning to me, he grinned. "Stunning, right?"

"Perfect," I said.

He took my guitar case and set it beside me. "Do me a favor and close your eyes."

I shut them tight. "What's next?"

"Give me a moment." A little later, he said, "You can open your eyes now."

Blane knelt on one knee in front of me.

I gasped. Was this the real thing? Was I ready? Was I prepared to make a commitment? Did Blane love me enough for a lifetime? Thrilling excitement left me hot and cold.

"Therese Olivia Palmer, I've loved you since I first saw you. You showed me the real meaning of love. You helped me find Jesus. You risked your life for others and demonstrated courage all the way. Would you do me the honor of becoming my wife?" He held out a small silver box with a ring designed for a queen.

I touched my mouth and stared into his warm eyes. "Oh, Blane, I love you so much." I bent on one knee and faced him. "Yes, a million times yes."

He kissed me like he'd never done before, a dizzyingly delicious kiss. When his lips left mine, he pointed to my guitar. "Are you ready to play for me?"

Shaking, I nodded. We eased onto the ground. "It's a simple song. Nothing fancy."

He kissed my cheek. "I'm waiting."

I studied the ring on my left hand. Perfect. Absolutely perfect.

I tuned my guitar and strummed the strings. Blane gave me a kiss—for courage.

"I call this 'Blane's Song.'"

If you are a dream, keep me dreaming,
If you are a breath, keep me breathing,
If you are a gift, keep me giving,
If you are life, keep me living,
If you are love, keep me loving,
If you are a song, keep me singing,
If you are my heart's journey, keep me walking.

How do I write the words rich and true?
How do I write a timeless melody?
Of how you mended my pain-filled life
And sealed my love for you.

If you are a dream, keep me dreaming,
If you are love, keep me loving,
If you are my heart's journey, keep me walking.

Blane leaned over and kissed me. "I think it is *our* song and not just mine. I can't wait to begin walking our life's journey together. Dreaming dreams and growing our love."

"I'm ready for *us* together, a lifetime of incredible love, purpose, and building a home together that honors God."

A NOTE FROM THE AUTHOR

Dear Reader,

Life's journey is a series of unexpected twists and turns, bringing us challenges and success, light and darkness. With faith in God as our guide, each experience shapes us into better people.

Therese and Blane's story weaves the power of forgiveness to show God's boundless and unconditional love. His presence rose in their lives like sunshine in an eastern sky, guiding them to trust Him and each other for the sake of a child. Alina stood as a symbol to every child's right to a bright future, who deserves the opportunity to make a positive impact on our world.

I hope you enjoyed the story. As I write this, my heart goes out to those who feel lost, abandoned, or forsaken with a prayer that they find the eternal rewards of faith in God.

Expect an Adventure.

DiAnn

ACKNOWLEDGMENTS

Many thanks to all those who helped make this book possible. You are incredible, and I value your time, support, encouragement, and expertise. Thank you for believing in me and my love of story.

In alphabetical order: Joyce Boudreaux, Dream Team (the best book launch team ever), Ruby Egert, James R. Hannibal, Karl Harroff, Heather Kreke, Steve Laube (Steve Laube Agency), Dr. Deborah Maxey, Dean Mills (my best cheerleader), Michael Sauter, Julee Schwarzburg, Sara Turnquist, Leah Vranken, and Kathi Wilson.

DON'T MISS THE NEXT THRILLING READ FROM DIANN MILLS!

WATCH FOR IT IN STORES AND ONLINE IN 2026

DISCUSSION QUESTIONS

1. Therese and Blane are willing to risk their lives for people they don't really know. Why do you think they were willing to do that? Would you do the same?
2. What are some similarities between Therese's job as a wilderness survival expert and Blane's job as a negotiator with the Texas Rangers? How do you think these common points helped their relationship progress?
3. Did you think that Rurik was being honest or deceptive about his innocence? Did your feelings about him change as the story progressed?
4. Therese, Blane, and Rurik all deal with the loss of people they love. How do they process these losses differently? Which character are you most like in dealing with your own losses?
5. Major Sergio Montoya and Blane were close friends. Have you ever had a friend who felt like family? What drew you to that person?
6. Blane hears God speak to him, telling him he needs to forgive himself for his girlfriend's death years ago. Have you ever felt strongly that God was speaking to you? What did you sense Him saying?

7. Therese felt a great weight lifted when she heard God's voice telling her that Kate's and her parents' deaths were not her fault. Have you ever felt a weight lifted like that?

8. Alina wonders, if God can do anything, then why are all these bad things happening? How would you respond to someone who asks why so many bad things happen if God is so good?

ABOUT THE AUTHOR

DiAnn Mills is a bestselling author who believes her readers should expect an adventure. She weaves memorable characters with unpredictable plots to create action-packed, suspense-filled novels with threads of romance. DiAnn believes every breath of life is someone's story, so why not capture those moments and create a thrilling adventure?

Her titles have appeared on the CBA and ECPA bestseller lists; won two Christy Awards, the Selah Award, and the Golden Scroll; and been finalists for the Inspirational Reader's Choice Award and the Carol Award.

DiAnn is a founding board member of the American Christian Fiction Writers and an active member of the Blue Ridge Mountains Christian Writers, the Advanced Writers and Speakers Association, Mystery Writers of America, the Jerry Jenkins Writers Guild, and International Thriller Writers. DiAnn continues her passion of helping other writers be successful. She speaks to various groups and teaches writing workshops around the country.

DiAnn has been termed a coffee snob and roasts her own coffee beans. She's an avid reader, loves to cook, and believes her grandchildren are the smartest kids in the universe. She and her husband live in sunny Houston, Texas.

DiAnn is very active online and would love to connect with readers on social media or her website, diannmills.com.

CONNECT WITH DIANN ONLINE AT

diannmills.com

OR FOLLOW HER ON

f DiAnnMills

 diannmillsauthor

 @diannmills

 DiAnn Mills

BB diann-mills

CP1720